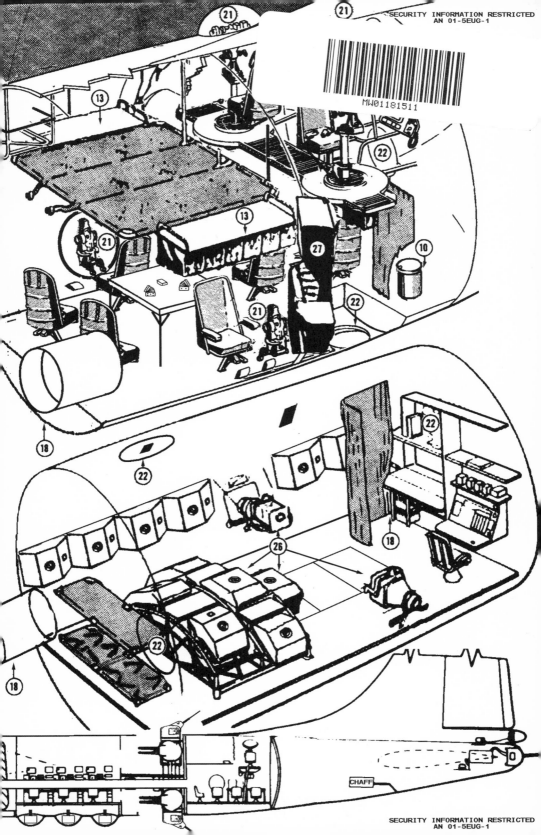

MW01181511

To Magne,

alliance Anshaw WTS-02

Pictures

from

Baikonur

by
William B. Trescott

Pictures from Baikonur
Isbn: 1-888748-11-7
©2002 by William B. Trescott
and Trucking Video Books
Sargent Texas

Original artwork and compositions
©2002 by William B. Trescott
William Trescott Productions

Cataloging in Publication (CIP) Data:
Library of Congress Control Number: 2002092593

The Library of Congress refused this book's application for CIP for the following reason:

Ever since the advent of desktop publishing, like the wealthy middlemen who raise the cost of milk and eggs, large publishing houses have used political influence to help them remain in business. A self-published author can earn many times what a published author gets from the sale of a book. By denying CIP to self-published authors, the Congress discriminates against writers who take risks to expose scandal and government wrongdoing. Books on certain subjects are considered too risky to be published at the large houses. Yet it is these orphans which are most likely to printed domestically rather than imported from overseas. Discrimination against self-published authors costs America jobs. In order to abide by the Constitutional principle of equal treatment under the law, Congress should offer CIP to every book, not just those published by large publishing houses.

Printed with pride in the United States of America
by Sheridan Books of Ann Arbor Michigan

The type is set in Berling, a 1950's era Roman font.

DISCLAIMER

Names of public figures
which appear in Pictures from Baikonur

Dwight David Eisenhower (Dave)	President of the United States
Richard M. Nixon (Dick)	Vice President of the United States
John Foster Dulles (Foster)	Secretary of State
Charles E. Wilson (Chuck)	Secretary of Defense
Senator Stuart Symington	Chairman of the Senate Defense Appropriations Committee
Senator Joseph McCarthy	Chairman of the Senate Government Operations and Investigations Committee
Admiral Arthur Radford (Art)	Chairman of the Joint Chiefs of Staff
General Curtis LeMay (Curt)	Chief of the Strategic Air Command
Governor Adlai Stevenson	Democratic Presidential Candidate
Sir Anthony Eden	Prime Minister of Great Britain & Ireland
Sir Winston Churchill	Former Prime Minister of Great Britain
Nikolai Bulganin	President of the Union of Soviet Socialistic Republics
Nikita Sergeievich Khrushchev	First Secretary of the Supreme Soviet
Marshal Georgi Zhukov (Georg)	Soviet Defense Minister
Andrei Gromyko	Soviet Deputy Foreign Minister
Joseph Stalin Dzukashvili	Former Dictator of the Soviet Union
Georgi Malenkov	Former President of the Soviet Union
Lavrenty Beria (Lev)	Former Head of the NKVD Secret Police
Vyacheslav Molotov	Former Soviet Foreign Minister
Wladyslaw Gomulka	Secretary General of the Polish Communist Party

Crew of RB-36H-40-51-13753 by order of command rank:
Officers:

Colonel Michael Peterson — AC (Aircraft Commander) "Skipper" and his wife Phyllis

Major Henry Johns — Pilot "Hank" and his wife Linda

Major Merril Hughs — First Raven (ARR-8, APR-4,APR-9, & APA-17 "Ferret" Electronic Intelligence Radio Operator) and his wife Loretta

Major John Kewscinski — PN (Photo-Navigator, K-17C,22A,38, & 40 Camera Operator) and his wife Mary

Major James Newcomb — VO (Video Observer, APQ-24 Radar Bombing System, Western Electric APS-23 Radar, & Sperry A-1A Bombing-Navigation Computer Operator) and his wife Shirley

Major Scott Holbrook — WO (Weather Observer, Meteorologist, General Electric 2CFR87 Electrical Periscopic Nose Gunner) and his wife Alice

Captain Gerald Whitefeather — Second Raven (ARR-8, APR-4, & APA-17 "Ferret" Electronic Intelligence Radio Operator) "Jerry" and his wife Margaret

Captain Harold Wong — Third Raven (ARR-8, APR-9, & APA-17 "Ferret" Electronic Intelligence Radio Operator) "Harry" and his wife Eunice

Lieutenant Duane Nawrocki — AN (Astronavigator, AN/APN-5,6,9A, & 14 Long Range Navigation "LORAN" Radio Operator)

Lieutenant Robert Beaumont — First RO (AN/ALA2, ARR-8, AN/APA-38, AN/APT-1,4,5A,6, AN/APR-4,9, ARQ-8, & APA-17 "Ferret" Electronic Countermeasures Radio Operator)

Lieutenant Gordon Grant — Co-pilot, General Electric 2CFR87 Electrical Gunner

Crew of RB-36H #51-13753 by order of command rank:

Enlisted men:

Master Sergeant Marvin Murphy — First APE (Aircraft Performance Engineer)

Master Sergeant. Lorenzo Washington — Second APE and his wife Polly

Technical Sergeant Victor Hernandez — Second RO (BC-348, ARC-3,21X,27, AN/APX-6 IFF, & ARC-8 Radio Operator, General Electric 2CFR87 Electrical Gunner)

Technical Sergeant Peter Sandringham — General Electric APG-41 Tail Radar Gunlaying systems Gunner

Staff Sergeant William Trescott — PT (Photographic Technician, photographer)

Staff Sergeant Howard Shultz — General Electric 2CFR87 Electrical gunner

Staff Sergeant James O'Connor — General Electric 2CFR87 Electrical Gunner

Airman Patrick Nakamura — General Electric 2CFR87 Electrical Gunner

Airman Frank Calabrese — General Electric 2CFR87 Electrical Gunner

CONTENTS:

DEDICATION:

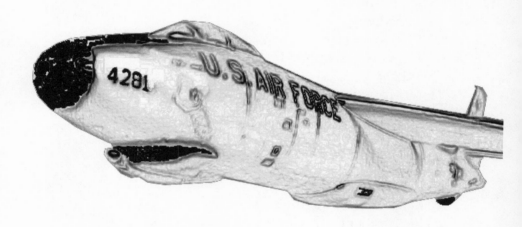

**This book is dedicated to
the more than two hundred officers and men aboard the
more than thirty aircraft that disappeared under
mysterious circumstances
during the Cold War and . . .**

The crew of the "Ruptured Duck"

who patriotically risked their lives to prove that thermonuclear weapons were survivable and upon who's true life adventures the events in the first chapter are largely based

THE CREW OF THE RUPTURED DUCK
B-36D tail number 49-2653
during Operation Castle at Kwajalein Atoll, May 1954

George Savage collection

Left to Right Back Row:

Bob Lemay	Earl Wilder	George Brinker	Bill Tosh	Ed Anderson	Charley Stiff
Pilot	Engineer	Scanner	Radar	Navigator	Scanner

Front Row:

John Wallace	George Savage	Mill McKane	Neal Kaufman	Juan Terry	Denzel Clark
Navigator	Commander	Engineer	Radio	Radio	Gunner

. . . and

Colonel George J. Savage (USAF retired),

Aircraft Commander of

"The Ruptured Duck"

(who provided much needed technical advice)

George Savage by Don Pyeatt

There is a saying in the aviation industry that "there are old pilots and there are bold pilots, but there are no old bold pilots." George Savage is an old bold pilot.

The Man Who Tried to End War

At the tender age of sixteen, the son of a successful car dealer received a wonderful present from his father—not a car (he had dozens), but what every little boy dreams of having when he grows up—his very own airplane. It was a tiny Aeronca C-3 "flying bathtub." Dad must have thought that if young George discovered flying before he discovered girls, he would stay out of trouble. How wrong could a father be?

When the Japanese bombed Pearl Harbor, George joined the Army. Just five days after graduating from Aviation Cadet training, this fortunate teen-ager became a full blown flight instructor. Girl trouble soon followed. Another instructor begged him to go on a blind date. George asked Betty to marry him on the second date. Dad would have approved because married men were less likely to be given dangerous combat assignments; but Betty said no. She didn't want to marry a smart alec instructor when other young men were fighting for their country.

Month after month, George volunteered for combat until he was given command of the most formidable weapon in the world—his very own B-29 Superfortress. This magnificent huge shiny airplane had a good effect and a bad effect on George's love life. Betty agreed to accept his ring, but now she refused to walk down the aisle with him until she graduated from college—just in case something happened to her mighty young hot shot bomber pilot. They would not see each other again until the war was over.

George was awarded the Distinguished Flying Cross and promoted to Captain after safely crash landing and saving his crew when two of his four engines were shot out over Tokyo. There should have been a ticker-tape parade for such a hero, but the Army would not let George go home to marry Betty unless he agreed to end the war first. George was awarded his second Distinguished Flying Cross for personally ending the war by himself when he personally destroyed Japan's last remaining oil refinery (even though stuck bomb doors caused him to run out of fuel at the same time as Japan did and crash his second B-29)!

After a four year engagement, Betty finally married George in 1947. She wanted to be sure she had that college degree in writing before she married a man who still enjoyed flying after two plane crashes. Young people really waited in those days, but the Air Force made George and Betty wait even longer. Just months after the wedding, the Russians closed the land route to Berlin and George was volunteered to fly hundreds of plane loads of food (and coal) to the two and a half million people starving (and freezing) to death there.

In 1954, a weapon was built that promised to end war forever—the hydrogen bomb. But, the most awesome power ever devised by man could not be viewed as a credible deterrent to aggression unless the Air Force could prove that a man could survive dropping it. Was married life not all that George expected? Was Dad right about women after all? Was marriage not bliss? Whatever the reason, Major George Savage volunteered to be the first pilot to survive the H-bomb.

Flying the largest military aircraft ever built, a ten engined B-36 Peacemaker bomber with only curtains over the windows for protection, a fifteen megaton bomb was exploded behind and beneath this brave test pilot as he flew over Bikini Atoll in the Pacific. Night turned to day. Inspection panels blew off as parts of the plane's belly caved in. Smoke filled the aft cabin. Physicists didn't know then that lithium 7 changes to lithium 6 in a thermonuclear explosion and makes the blast three times more powerful. They were expecting only five megatons. George was offered his third Distinguished Flying Cross, but amazingly, he turned it down because eleven other members of his crew who had taken the same risks were only awarded the Air Medal.

Could it be that George was hen pecked? Was he trying to become a "G.I. Joe" action figure? When the first H-bomb failed to kill him, the world's most invincible man volunteered to survive five more hydrogen bombs! After each earth shaking blast, just to prove he had the "right stuff," George kissed his hundred ton flying naval vessel onto the pavement with such tenderness, that a jay alighting on a leaf would have trembled the world worse. It was a good thing he did! After a year, when the radioactivity cooled off enough to do a proper survey, his ship was scrapped in place because massive structural damage made it "too dangerous to tow across the runway." Savage logged "a little sloppiness in the controls," but refused to report "The Ruptured Duck" unfit for duty because the loss of three American bombers would have made him a "Japanese ace!"

His bomb tests failed to forever end war, so the Chuck Yeager of bomber pilots was ordered to finish his career flying C-141 jet transports full of wounded home from Vietnam. Not a single disabled soldier ever complained about a rough landing. Ending up like many a war hero, held hostage behind a big mahogany bomber at the Pentagon by huge stacks of paper, George retired from thirty two years in the Army and the Air Force in 1974. All that worry about George's and Betty's love life proved to be untrue. They celebrated their 50th anniversary way back in 1997. Betty gave George five children (two of which were found to glow in the dark), fifteen grandkids, and an increasing number of great grandchildren. With rewards like that, who needs three Distinguished Flying Crosses anyway? Having survived thirty combat missions, two crashes, six hydrogen bombs, and ten thousand hours flying aircraft with up to ten engines on countless missions of mercy through three wars, George Savage, Great Grandpa of the Air Force, is surely one of the most accomplished pilots in history.

INTRODUCTION

Imagine flying a plane as big as a jumbo jet filled with 33,000 gallons of gasoline and remaining in the air for two days without landing or refueling! The RB-36 carried 600 gallons of oil, 50 gallons of drinking water, 100 frozen dinners for its 20 man crew, 6 beds for off duty officers, a fully equipped galley, 2 toilets, 3 radar antennas, 22 radios, 4 parabolic spy antennas, 17 giant aerial cameras, an on board film developing lab, 1,200 pounds of finely shredded aluminum to fool Russian radar, 9600 rounds of six inch long 20mm ammunition for 16 six foot long cannons, and sometimes the most powerful weapon ever created by man—a 15 megaton hydrogen bomb. Some RB-36's even carried jet fighters in their bomb bays to defend themselves. Who needs "Star Trek?" This thing was real!

The Convair B-36 bomber was the largest plane in the world from August 1946 to November 1947 when Howard Hughes' Spruce Goose flying boat rose barely fifty feet into the air. By that time, the XB-36 had flown to almost *fifty thousand* feet and set an unofficial world altitude record for large multiengined aircraft. Just a year later, a B-36A set a world distance record of 9,600 miles unrefueled. In January 1951, a B-36D set a world endurance record for large multi-engined aircraft by remaining in the air for more than 51 hours without refueling. With two 43,000 pound grand slam bombs on board (the largest conventional bombs ever built), a B-36 set the world's payload record as well. For twenty three years, the B-36 and its identical twin, the RB-36 reconnaissance bomber, remained the largest *successful* aircraft ever built until the Boeing 747 Jumbo Jet eclipsed them in 1969, but they remain, to this day, the largest combat aircraft ever built and the only aircraft ever mass produced to be powered by ten engines.

The B-36's awesome weapons, the thirty one thousand pound, seven megaton TX-14 "Alarm Clock," and the forty three thousand pound, fifteen megaton TX-17 "Runt," were the largest, heaviest, and most powerful portable explosive devices ever devised by man. Each B-36 and RB-36 had the power to destroy whole cities, even small countries, with more destructive power than all of the weapons used in all the wars in history put together. Without modern nuclear safeguards such as presidential command codes, each B-36 aircraft commander became the most powerful man on earth whenever he departed on a two day mission.

Though, for many years, the Air Force officially denied that reconnaissance missions were flown over Russia before the Francis Gary Powers U-2 incident in 1960, some RB-36 veterans have privately claimed to have survived such missions. Soviet Premiere Nikita Khrushchev wrote in his memoirs, "I would even say that America was invincible, and the Americans flaunted this fact by sending their planes all over Europe, violating borders and even flying over the territory of the Soviet Union itself."(Khrushchev Remembers, Little Brown, p.362) Aviation historian Dennis R. Jenkins writes in his book "Convair B-36 Peacemaker" (Specialty Press, p.86), "Increasing Soviet air defenses were making it more difficult for the large strategic reconnaissance aircraft to penetrate Soviet airspace . . . "No details have been released concerning the missions flown by the FICONs, but stories have circulated that the RF-84K's (parasite fighters carried in the bomb bays of RB-36's) made several overflights of the Soviet Union on reconnaissance missions prior to the U-2 becoming available." Historian Richard Rhodes writes, "SAC had reconaissance aircraft flying secret missions over the Soviet Union twenty four hours a day," a statement attributed to the Chief of the Strategic Air Command, General Curtis LeMay himself (Dark Sun—The Making of the Hydrogen Bomb, Simon & Schuster 1995, p.568).

Historians say that the Cold War was not a real war because no one was killed. Those who flew the missions know better. Navigating by the stars like the mariners of old, out of the range of normal radio communications, aircraft sometimes went missing and were never seen again. A Navy PB4-Y2 and an Air Force RB-47H are known to have been shot down over the Barents Sea with the loss of sixteen men. Colonel Harold "Hal" Austin's RB-47E was shot in the wing and fuselage by a MiG-17 while flying an armed photographic reconnaissance mission over Murmansk, a city that welcomed Americans in World War Two†.

Believing the USSR was still a friendly wartime ally, crews were not always fully informed about the risks they were taking. Austin's co-pilot, Carl Holt, wrote, "I thought we were in a Cold War with Russia, not a hot one, since all the reconnaissance plane 'shoot downs' had been kept very secret. "During our de-briefing with General LeMay, I said to him, very innocently, 'Sir, they were trying to shoot us down!' Smoking his usual long cigar, he paused, leaned back, and said, 'What did you think they would do, give you an Ice Cream Cone?'"† Holt returned fire with his tailguns over Soviet territory—an act of war—but the Soviets had their own reasons for keeping the incursions secret, such as not having to explain to the Russian people why a dozen of their most advanced fighters could not shoot down a single American bomber skywriting over four hundred miles of twisting contrails in clear weather.

These missions were rarely offically authorized. According to Colonel Austin, LeMay apologized for not awarding him the Silver Star saying, "I'd have to explain this mission to too damn many people who don't need to know."† Korean Airlines 007 was only the last of many victims. More than thirty Air Force and Navy aircraft of various types disappeared under mysterious circumstances, along with more than two hundred aircrew during the Cold War. "Pictures from Baikonur" dramatizes one such incident.

Historical fiction fills the gulf between what is proven and what cannot be disproven. In any history of war or espionage there is bound to be gaps. By its nature, historical fiction distorts history. "Pictures from Baikonur" is intended to be an entertaining dramatization of what *might* have happened in the first half of 1956 to cause the rapid capitulation of western forces during the Hungarian and Suez crises later that year. Historians have had nothing but rumors and allegations to write about, because the men who flew these missions have been threatened with imprisonment if they divulge national secrets. Colonel Austin writes, "If General Curtis E. LeMay was still alive, I might have second thoughts on telling about this mission even though it's been over 40 years."† By casting a sharp light on secret activities about which no official information has been released, it is hoped that "Pictures from Baikonur" will pressure Air Force officials to be more forthcoming with the truth.

Historical fiction may take a back seat to non-fiction in standards of accuracy, but there are important benefits: First, a fiction writer can create characters who will make a story interesting to readers who would not otherwise be curious about obscure footnotes of history. It may be a fact that no woman ever flew aboard a B-36 or RB-36 reconnaissance bomber; but it would be unpardonable for a twenty first century author to write a book without female characters. Why would women want to read it? For this reason, strong female characters are included in "Pictures from Baikonur." The Second benefit of historical fiction is that events occurring over several years can be combined to make the story shorter and more exciting. The bomb test portrayed in the first chapter is a combination of three nuclear test programs: Operation Castle, Operation Bootstrap, and Operation Red Wing; which were completed between 1954 and 1957. The conversation with Marshal Zhukov in "Conversation with the Enemy" actually occurred during a private lunch with President Eisenhower at the Geneva Summit in 1955. Most historical events in "Pictures from Baikonur," such as Khruschev's secret speech, the spy incident which ended the 1956 London Summit, the ASTR airborne nuclear reactor tests, the President's heart attack, and the Labor Day tornado of '52, are historically accurate both in time and place.

If an RB-36 veteran were to write this book instead of a fiction writer, he would probably insist that the two day long picket flights

†"A Cold War Overflight of the USSR" Daedalus Flyer, Vol. 35, Spring 1995, www.b-47.com/Stories/austin

along the Soviet border consisted mainly of numbing cold, achy joints, itchy clothes, and endless hours of boredom. A long sauna or whirlpool bath after a mission was a mandatory treatment for the lingering effects of high altitude on the body. Blood clots and a condition similar to the bends, suffered by deep sea divers, were some of the risks of sustained high altitude flight. To increase alertness and reduce the amount of nitrogen in their blood, crews were required to use oxygen even though their cabins were pressurized. Idle chit-chat, such as the dialogue in this story, would normally have been impossible, but like many Air Force crews, the characters in this book violate procedure by opening their masks to talk to one another, even though they risk narcosis should there be a decompression accident. Few actual crews ever saw a MiG fighter. Those who did were terrified, even though the MiG's were rarely able to climb to the altitudes at which the RB-36 flew. The Soviets really could not do anything about the high flying RB-36, so they did not try to. "Fighters were something you hoped you never see," commented one veteran.

Because of the dread seriousness of their work and the perfection of their weapon, B-36 and RB-36 crews did not paint scantily clad women on their ships like those that graced the noses of W.W.II bombers. Those planes flew together in large formations. A plane with a pretty girl painted on it would be defended by others flying along with it. A call for help over the radio was more likely to be answered if an airplane had a feminine name. By the 1950's, bomber crews had become single combat warriors who went into battle alone. Calling for help was impossible, except by Morse code signals reflected off of the ionosphere by atmospheric skip. Like Goliath beating his shield, atomic warriors were expected to deter aggression by stepping across national borders and daring little Davids in tiny single engine jets to come up and fight. After thermonuclear combat, crews were expected to bail out, or abandon their ships on the salt deserts of Iran if not too badly damaged by their own bombs to land safely. Ships were rarely given names. Most were known only by their tail numbers. There was no point in naming something that was intended to be destroyed. To better survive thermonuclear blasts, aircraft were left unpainted, except for anti-radiation white on the underside and a coat of reflective clear lacquer with no attempt at camouflage.

Like noble knights of old dressed in shining aluminum instead of armor, and dark green T-1 pressure suits instead of medieval tights, Cold Warriors decorated their ships with the crests and badges of heraldry. Some B-36's and RB-36's wore shields with a Latin inscription: "Mors ab Alto"—"Death from Above;" or a Hawaiian inscription: "Kiai o ka Lewa"—"Guardian of the Upper Regions." Later, they all wore the badge of the Strategic Air Command—a plate mail gauntlet clutching lightning bolts. Crews sometimes called their flying naval vessels "starships" because of the Milky Way band of stars painted around their noses, and because, near 50,000 feet, stars could sometimes be seen in the daytime. On the landing gear doors, painted even larger than the crests and mottoes, were giant "NO SMOKING" signs. With huge quantities of bottled oxygen, electrically primed ammunition, and highly flammable aviation gas seeping though thousands of rivet holes in the huge "wet" wing spar, the main danger from cigarettes was not cancer. Ground crews called these ten engined wonders "Magnesium Monsters" because of the special lightweight metal they were made of that allowed them to fly higher than any other combat aircraft, and because of the thermonuclear dragon's breath that could descend from their bellies.

If you are curious about the true life events upon which this story is based, I recommend: Meyers K. Jacobsen's "Convair B-36—A Comprehensive History of America's Big Stick" (Shiffer 1997), which tells the personal stories of many B-36 and RB-36 crews; Dennis R. Jenkins' "Magnesium Overcast" (Specialty Press, 2001), from which I obtained a great amount of technical information; Wayne Wachsmuth's "B-36 Peacemaker, SAC's 'Long Rifle' of the 1950's," (Squadron/Signal, 1997); and the feature film "Strategic Air Command" starring Jimmy Stewart (Paramount 1955) which includes beautiful aerial photography of B-36 and B-47 bombers. "B-36: Saving the Last Peacemaker," by Ed Calvert, Don Pyeatt, and Richard Marmo, is a photo essay on disc documenting the Herculean efforts to save the last B-36 ever built, "The City of Fort Worth," tail number #52-2827, from destruction. The photo of myself on the inside back jacket was taken on the flight deck of #2827.

I would like to thank Don Pyeatt of the Aviation Heritage Museum of Fort Worth Texas, who helped provide many B-36 photos upon which much of the artwork is based; David Menard of the United States Air Force Museum Archives in Dayton Ohio, for providing detailed interior drawings from B-36 flight manuals upon which the art on the endsheets is based; and Thomas Dwyer for his detailed description of an interception he made on a B-36 as part of an F-86 training mission, upon which the realistic combat is based. I would like to extend special thanks to B-36 Aircraft Commanders Colonel Glenn Loveall, Colonel Dick George, Colonel George Savage, Colonel Les Lennox, and Aviation Mechanic Laurie Bavetz for reading and correcting the many technical inaccuracies in my original manuscript. Most of all, I would like to thank all the veterans of the Air Force and the other armed services for the sacrifices they made to keep our country safe. Even if the actual missions fictionalized in this novel are never declassified, the terminology, jargon, and procedures of the men who flew them will be preserved.

A glossary is provided

AMERICAN HERITAGE ASSOCIATION
B-36J RESTORATION TEAM

Aviation Heritage Association

The Aviation Heritage Association has put more than 115,000 man hours into restoring the last B-36. Another 50,000 hours will be needed when a museum facility is finally opened.
The Aviation Heritage Association is seeking financial help in restoring and preserving this and other historic aircraft.

financial contributions can be sent to:
**AVIATION HERITAGE MUSEUM & EDUCATION CENTER
CONTRIBUTION & SPONSORSHIP DIRECTOR
P.O. BOX 821
FORT WORTH, TX 76101**

See
www.aviationheritagemuseum.com
or
www.b-36.net
for more information

Pictures from Baikonur

BIKINI BOMB
January, 1956

"There it is! "I see it," Grant shouted through the bubble shaped visor of his space suit, pointing his inflated glove at the blackened ocean ten miles below.

"Where," asked Major Johns, sitting beside him in the armored commander's chair, his voice barely audible over the drone of the engines? Their enormous round white helmets banged against the green painted frames of their multi-windowed greenhouse canopy as they craned their necks to see.

"Its just ahead of that contrail, doing six hundred knots!"

Turning his wheel as far as it would go, Johns rolled the huge ten engined RB-36 to the right. Giant sea swells, shrunk to the size of pond ripples, sparkled under the moonlight like brilliant sapphires spread on black jewelers' velvet. Looking beyond some tiny white rings made by foamy cascades crashing against tiny pink pearly coral reefs, he spotted a straight white line slowly streaking across the glinting black ocean. "That's no contrail," he said. "That's sea foam kicked up by jetwash."

Rocketing fifty feet above the black moonlit waters of the tropical Pacific, the six engined shark shaped B-47 thundered toward its target. Looking straight up through their long narrow Plexiglas canopy, two helmeted pilots, wearing green elephant masks, watched Johns' and Grant's own fluffy ten engine wide contrail carve a big white "S" into the black sky above them.

Above the "S," faint globs of Milky Way spilled like a river across the darkness. The crescent Moon fought Mars, Jupiter, Saturn, Venus, Sirius, Rigel, Canopus, Capella, and Aldeberan, to dominate the cold empty sky. The creamy, bluish white, cloud dotted horizon appeared flat and straight to the men below in the jet, but to Johns and Grant, it visibly curved beyond the nose of their giant sky scraping ship. Guided by an arrow of swept back moonwashed silver wings, the B-47's straight white streak approached ten dark brown teak decks belonging to ten gray-black Japanese warships. Grant closed his curtains to shut out the stars.

"ALERT FIVE, ALERT FIVE," a voice crackled over the radio, "THIS IS NEPTUNE, THIS IS NEPTUNE, ALL IS GO, ALL IS GO, COMMENCE BOMB RUN, COMMENCE BOMB RUN, OVER!"

"ROGER NEPTUNE, BEGINNING BOMB RUN," Major Gregory Simmons, the B-47's pilot, replied. "I-P IN THIRTY SECONDS, SIGHTING—RADAR, TYPE OF RELEASE—AUTOMATIC, OVER." There was static. Major Johns closed his curtains.

Flying "point" in the violently shaking shark shaped nose of the jet, Captain Robert Beauchamp, Simmons' bombardier, was aiming through his telescopic bombsight.

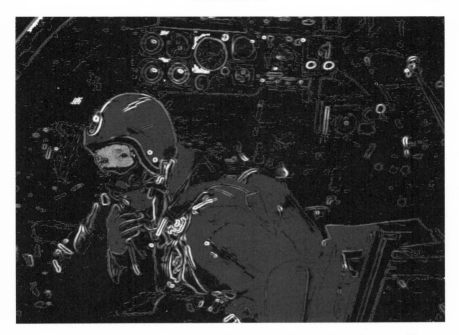

He looked up momentarily at the control panel in front of him, then down into the radar camera beside his left knee. Pressing his brow against the soft padded hood and flexing a small joystick on his desk with his right hand, he maneuvered the aircraft until a dot of bright green light was positioned in the center of a group of fainter green blips he saw on his screen.

   With an elephant trunk mask covering his face, a yellow life jacket covering his chest, a green parachute, white helmet, and black gloves covering every patch of skin, Beauchamp appeared to be part of the machine. He looked up again and turned a switch on his control panel from "DOORS SAFE" to "DOORS OPERABLE," then lifted a small red cover. He clicked the tiny switch underneath to on. A whirring, clicking, tumbling sound of cogs and gears churned from the mechanical computer behind his seat like an old fashioned cash register. On the walls of the ship, vacuum tubes under silver covers flickered on and off like Christmas lights. "READY," he announced on his open mike. "I-P IN TEN SECONDS."

"BOMBING SOLUTION COMPUTED AND LAID IN," announced Simmons.   "INITIAL POINT IN FIVE SECONDS. "STANDBY."   A tone was heard in everyone's headsets.

"WE HAVE TONE," a ground controller responded.

Simmons let go of his wheel as Beauchamp's bombing-navigation computer automatically pulled the big jet into a climb. "BOMB DOORS OPEN," said Beauchamp, his

eyes concentrating on the white bomb rack light above the radar camera as he was pressed firmly into his seat. The B-47 pointed straight up, then began to fall on it's back. The six screaming engines under its thin wings belched clouds of gray smoke. Its wings flexed upward with aerobatic stress until the wingtips were bent as high as the tail fin. The humid, sea level air condensed in low pressure waves above the the jet's wing, forming large white epaulets that made the wings seem on fire. Beauchamp heard a clunk and watched the white light on his panel go out. The tone in everyone's headsets stopped. "BOMB'S AWAY," he said calmly.

For a moment, the "Cherokee II" hovered dangerously loose inside the B-47's bomb bay. The computer flew the plane away from the bomb, looping the big jet onto its back until it was completely inverted. The Cherokee II continued almost straight up. The Indian war chief painted on its side began to rotate around and around as the bomb started to spin through the blackness like an expertly thrown football. Simmons switched off the autopilot and grabbed his wheel, turning it sharply to the left as he would turn the steering wheel of a car. The big jet stood on it's wing, then rolled upright. Pushing the wheel forward into a dive, Simmons abruptly pulled it back just before hitting the water. The B-47's wings, relieved of their stress, flapped like those of a bird.

The sound of oxygen regulator valves opening and closing in time with heavy breathing drowned out the engine noise on both aircraft, as everyone concentrated on their instruments. Pilots scanned their altimeters, airspeed, and attitude indicators. Engineers scanned their manifold pressure gauges and warning lights—then everything went white!

Night turned to day. The light was so blinding, that high above the blast in the stratosphere, Grant and Johns marveled that they could see their hand and arm bones through their space suits as though on an X-ray machine. The floor of their giant ship glowed with earie blue light. The white curtains covering the windows glowed red and smoldered. The sky outside was blue. Four of the ten engine fire warning buzzers blasted a deafening roar. All four turbojet temperature gauges were pegged. The two flight engineers sitting back to back behind Johns and Grant jumped in their seats. Smoke filled the cockpit, turning everything gray.

"Fire, fire," shouted Johns!

"Where is it," Grant yelled as Washington, the Second Engineer in the seat behind him groped for switches on his left panel to activate the engine fire extinguishers?

Below, in the B-47, Major Simmons, looking in his rear view mirror, watched the red fireball approach. It swelled larger and larger until it filled half of the sky. His six throttles were pushed as far forward as they would go. His gloved right hand unconsciously pushed them harder and harder until he felt them bend from side to side. He removed his hand from them momentarily, then without thinking, began pushing on them again. The big jet trailed brown smoke as more fuel was injected into the engines than could be burned. The daylight blue sky in front faded to mauve, then violet and purple as the artificial sun filling the rear view mirror grew larger and then dimmed.

Sitting behind Simmons, Jennings, the B-47's Co-pilot, swiveled his seat around to face the rear. He watched the dark blue sea behind the tail fin turn to a frothy white meringue under the fading fireball as it grew closer. A wall of spray that seemed to stretch from horizon to horizon advanced toward him faster than the speed of sound. The B-47 shook violently as the shockwave rippled through the tail and body of the plane. Simmons frantically steered left and right and left like a car spinning on ice, as the fifty foot tall, churning white wall of water passed underneath the big jet. They flew over a snow white sea under a dark crimson sky. "WHAT HAVE WE DONE," asked Simmons though his open mike, as he flew back to Hawaii as fast as his six engines would take him?

The shock wave took more than a minute to reach Johns and Grant high above. When it did, engine inspection panels blasted off in a shower of debris. The radomes were crushed in instantly and the bomb bay and lower turret doors stove in, opening a great wide wound in the belly of the ship. The engine nacelles were dented as the percussive pressure wave struck like a thunderclap. Johns struggled to maintain control as large chunks of the horizontal stabilizer caught fire and blew off where engine oil trailing from the inboard engines had blackened them.

"MAYDAY, MAYDAY," yelled Johns, pushing his radio button! In the ship's photo lab, a space suited photographer, looking like the Pillsbury Dough Boy, was shooting at the glowing fireball with the huge port lateral camera. Electric motors whirred as the expensive, twenty foot long, foot wide roll of Kodachrome flew across the giant camera back with every click of the shutter. The heavy camera had two cables connecting it to the ceiling with counterweights, so it could be lifted to aim. As he ran out of film, he frantically struggled to change film backs and photograph the glowing mushroom cloud. His pressure suit made every movement difficult. With his eyes dazed by the glowing fireball, he never noticed the cabin filling with smoke.

In the aft cabin, Gunner Shultz marveled at what seemed to be a giant eye staring back at him. The cabin was so full of smoke, all he could see was his own reflection in his visor. Ignoring the eye, which seemed to fade as he turned away from the artificial sun outside, he unclipped his safety strap and crawled in his space suit over to a fire extinguisher, feeling for it with the tips of his inflated gloves. As the fireball outside dimmed, he could see a dimmer light on the other side of the compartment and moved toward it, blasting burning insulation near Gunner O'Connor's blackened gunsight blister. As their two space suits rubbed against each other like balloons, Shultz could feel that O'Connor was shaking. After several squirts of methyl bromide, he could no longer see any light, so he yelled, "fire's out. "The fire is out," he repeated, pressing the interphone button on his chest.

"This is AC, is everything all right back there," asked Johns, his thumb on the interphone button on the top right horn of his wheel?

"Scanner to AC, yes sir," answered Shultz!

"It is now," seconded O'Connor, ashamed that he had

not grabbed the fire extinguisher first. Shultz could not see the look on his face.

"Is there any reason why this mission cannot be continued," asked Johns?

There was silence. The aft cabin was black with smoke, but the hoses blowing into the suits kept everyone supplied with fresh air. They could not see out of their Plexiglas blisters.

"Continuing the mission," Johns announced, unaware of the damage to the ship. He courageously turned toward the towering dark red mushroom cloud to collect dust samples in two large scoops, shaped like donkey's ears, attached behind the cockpit.

The ship shuddered and fell suddenly as it entered the cloud. High altitude winds had only just begun to dissipate the upward thrust of superheated air. Grant yelled. It was not possible to hear what everyone was saying, due to the muffling effect of the helmets. Sound bounced around inside the metal spheres to deafen anyone who talked too loud.

Inside, the cloud glowed dark brown. Radioactive fallout obscured the rapidly dimming superheated gasses. Lightning flashes became the only illumination. Downdrafts and wind sheers flung the ship up and down more violently than any nimbus. The ship dropped a thousand feet in just two seconds as pencils, note pads, flight computers, and coffee mugs slammed up against the ceiling. Then it lunged two thousand feet upward, shoving everyone into their seats, as they crossed the middle stem of the mushroom. They were bathed in a lingering red glow. Except for Shultz and O'Connor, every man sat alone, tormented by his own fears, wanting to scream for help or for mother, or to beg the Lord's mercy. They were too afraid of being labeled cowards to seek one another's compassion. Johns and Grant gripped their wheels with all their might, wrestling with the controls until their arms hurt. Feeling with his fingertips, Shultz nervously inserted five weather sonds into their ejection tube, one at a time, while holding on for dear life in the bouncing smoky aft cabin.

The red light abruptly dimmed as the ship fell a thousand feet from the updrafts in the center of the cloud, back into the dark brown, downward moving gas of the mushroom dome —sending objects again flying to the ceiling. Each man felt sure the wings had just been torn off and that he was about to die. Some lost control of their bladders and bowels, messing their pants and urinating in their suits. Kewscinski, the Photo-navigator, bent over and vomited inside his clear helmet visor so he could not see out. With grit teeth, everyone yelled, but the helmets muffled the sounds while pride, fear of reproach, and perhaps courage, kept them from deserting their posts. Johns decided that he had had enough. He began to turn back when the ship abruptly popped out of the cloud into the clear black sky. Sirius, Rigel, Canopus, Capella, and Aldeberan twinkled wildly in protest of their new man made rival. Finally able to let go of his wheel, with hands shaking, Johns reached up to shut down the four turbojets and reduce power on the six piston engines to descend, his lips silently praising God that he had not finished turning around.

THE WOMEN
February 1956

One month later, on a bright sunny morning in a woody, hilly subdivision on the North shore of Lake Worth, opposite Carswell Air Force Base near Fort Worth Texas, Major Henry Johns let his wife Linda out of their beige and white '53 Ford. Playing the gentleman, he walked around the front so she would not have to open her door by herself. Wearing curlers hidden by a green scarf over a plain brown dress, she kissed him goodbye, scanning the horizon for any bystanders who might gossip. After a passionate embrace, she pushed him away and walked briskly down a dirt driveway to the flat roofed, white asbestos shingled bungalow of Phyllis Peterson, wife of the Squadron Commander, Colonel Mike Peterson.

Wearing a sea foam green house dress, partly hidden by a frilly red polka dotted white apron that did not quite cover her modern synthetic fuzzy pink slippers, Phyllis was a bit embarrassed to come to the door. She did not expect to see Johns waiting by his car. The Johns's lived just up the hill from the lake. Linda could have walked. Phyllis watched the Major sheepishly wave at his wife as she went in.

Shirley Newcomb, the Bombardier's wife, and Mary Kewscinski, who's husband was Photonavigator, were seated in the dining room beside someone Linda had never met. "This is Loretta Hughs," introduced Phyllis, "she just moved in from

Washington DC. "Her husband Merril is taking over as Raven." None of the women really knew what that meant, but they all pretended that they did. Loretta shook hands. She was a big girl, with black hair tied in a bun behind bangs and thick black Bakelite horned rim glasses with tiny slanty lenses. She was not pretty, but she wore purple pumps under an aquamarine dress adorned with plastic beads to make up for her shortcomings.

From the dining room, Linda looked out the window at her husband. Johns nervously paced back and forth in front of his Ford, starring down at the dirt. Sensing something was wrong, she went back to the door and stepped onto the porch just in time to watch him speed away. Puzzled, Linda went back in.

The formality of the occasion seemed odd for breakfast. The table was set with silver and fine Japanese porcelain on a white table cloth. Normally they would have eaten in the tiny kitchen nook. The silver tea service looked out of place next to the toaster and the chrome coffee percolator. A shiny chrome electric can opener and waffle iron were prominently displayed on the whitewashed kitchen counter where they could be seen from the dining room. No doubt about it, Phyllis had an all-electric kitchen and the other girls were meant to notice. On the china hutch, the fine porcelain normally displayed had been replaced with cheap Fiestaware. A seventeen inch Stromberg Carlsen Television sat on a table in the parlor, bathing the room with an icy blue glow. A test pattern occupied the screen since there was no program to watch at that time of the morning.

Normally, the girls would have met at Linda's, but Colonel Peterson was taking over Johns' new ship, so it was Phyllis' duty to provide breakfast. Perhaps she was just trying to make a good impression, or maybe she was trying to show off since she was the wife of a Colonel, but the tight lipped seriousness with which she buttered the toast suggested something was wrong and this made the other ladies nervous. Her blond but whitening hair was styled as if for church. The table was spread with a variety of jams and marmalades including some expensive and hard to find ginger marmalade the Colonel had brought back from TDY in England.

"You didn't need to spread your good tablecloth," said Linda, ashamed to be the only one in curlers as she looked at the others around the dark green dining room, one wall of which was spangled with walnut framed black and white photos of the Colonel, his old planes, and war buddies.

"I know," replied Phyllis, "but it will just get eaten by moths if it is never used."

"Yes but you should save it for special occasions," added Linda. "The men aren't even here."

"Why should the men always have to be here to have a special occasion," asked Mary? "Aren't we special too?" Mary, a Catholic girl, had a brown blouse the same color as her hair with a gray skirt. She wore a small crucifix around her neck and a pink sweater with a dark blue cursive letter "*M*" on the left shoulder.

"Mike didn't come home last night," said Phyllis.

"Merril didn't either," seconded Loretta. "He said they were doing something secret and they weren't going to be allowed off the base after they received their classified information."

"John didn't come home either," said Mary.

"I was just a girl when Mike left for the war," said Phyllis, rubbing the back of her middle finger against the corner of her right eye, which seemed glassy as though she had dropped an eyelash. "We were married, and then he went away for two years. "When he came back he was never the same . . . so serious!" The girls looked at her silently. She continued, "I've never seen him more nervous before a mission . . . not even then. "When they sent him to England, it was still being bombed."

"Hank wasn't himself either this morning," said Linda. "He wouldn't say where he was going. "He said something was discovered that they had to photograph."

"He shouldn't have told you that," said Phyllis. "He could get in trouble."

Linda continued, "The last time Hank acted so strange before a TDY was four months ago when they sent him to an island in the Pacific. "I read in the paper that a bomb was exploded there called 'Operation Red Wing.' "I asked him when he got home if he had dropped the bomb and he said no, but I told him he would have to sleep on the sofa if he didn't tell me, so he finally admitted he was there, but he said he didn't drop the . . ."

"No, they didn't drop it," interrupted Shirley. Shirley had bleached blond hair piled into a bee-hive and was wearing saddle shoes and white bobby socks under a flattering pink dress. She plucked her eyebrows and had penciled faux brows higher up. "Jim would have been bragging for weeks if he had dropped a hydrogen bomb. "He would be bragging to everyone that he had the world's most powerful thumb or something." The other women laughed. Shirley continued, "He never talked about the TDY. "He was angry about what happened there. "I thought that a trip to the Pacific would be wonderful, and I told him that I wished I could go with him, but he said nothing happened and he didn't want to talk about it."

"What do you mean nothing happened," asked Mary? They dropped an A-bomb and John Photographed it."

"Jim never mentioned it," said Shirley.

"Merril won't tell me anything," complained Loretta.

"Hank wouldn't tell me about it," continued Linda, "but I know one thing, there was some kind of accident and his ship was lost. "That's why we got transferred to Texas."

"Yes, they got a new ship," added Shirley, "but Jim never said anything about an explosion."

"I love Hank," Linda continued, "but I hate the way he keeps everything to himself. "When he was imprisoned in Korea, I used to write every day even though the letters were never delivered except once a month. "He would write back once a month, and only talk about the temperature or the stewed cabbage the Koreans made him eat that gave him gas and how it was always snowing or raining. "The way he described it, Korea is the coldest, wettest place on earth. "I did nothing but worry."

"Did they torture him," asked Loretta?

"No, but the Commies didn't take care of the men the way they should."

"That must have been rough," said Shirley. "Jim usually seems excited when he gets back from a TDY, but last time he was so upset he didn't want to talk."

"Jim wasn't there," said Linda.

"Why wasn't he there." asked Shirley? "Did he do something wrong?"

"No, they decided another plane would drop the bomb so they didn't need a video observer," explained Linda.

Shirley gasped! "That explains why Jim was so angry when he got home. "He likes to do everything himself. "It must have been agony for him to remain at the base while everyone else flew off on a mission."

"Its no different than for us women," reminded Linda.

"Yes, but he's a man," exclaimed Shirley!

"A woman can't even leave the house without permission," said Mary, "but men can fly halfway around the world for a month, drop an atom bomb, and not even say where they've been."

"They never do," chimed Loretta! "How would you like to be married to an intelligence officer? "I can't even tell people what Merril does for a living."

"What does he do," asked Shirley?

"I'm not sure I really know," answered Loretta! The other women chuckled.

"Men and their damn secrets," exclaimed Shirley!

"Shirley, I'll have no swearing in my house," Phyllis raised her voice. "I'll have no swearing at my table!" Her hands were shaking. She started to cry.

"I'm sorry, Phyl, it just kinda slipped out," answered Shirley. "Forgive?"

"Did Jim meet you in a brothel," snapped Phyllis, obviously distraught?

"Phyllis," shouted Linda!

"Don't you two start again," warned Mary, "or I'm going home."

"Phyl, I'm really sorry," answered Shirley. "It won't happen again." Linda put her arm around Phyllis and rubbed her shoulder. Phyllis closed her eyes so tightly, tears flowed out of the slits. The others could see that she knew something that they didn't and it was wearing on her mind.

There were several seconds of silence until Loretta asked, "Who's this," pointing at a portrait of a soldier on the wall to change the subject?

Phyllis looked up. "That's Bill McAtee, Mike's nose gunner," she answered. "He stayed in the Air Force. "I met him once."

"Who's that," asked Mary, pointing at a different portrait?

"That's Jim Anderson, Mike's buddy during the war. "His ship was shot down and they never saw him again. "They used to go everywhere together," continued Phyllis. "He used to mention him in his letters, but I never met him. "We went to see his family once. "That's something I'll never forget. "They cried and cried . . . Mike too! "He bawled like a baby. "I've never seen him get so upset. "I didn't know what to do or what to say. "I just sat there feeling uncomfortable since I never met the man. "I always made him tell me where we were going after that."

"I wish Hank would tell me where he was going," said Linda.

"Sometimes I wish I'd never asked," Shirley replied.

"Such an ugly plane," commented Loretta.

"Mike used to say the B-24 was more like driving a truck than flying," Phyllis explained.

"Such a beautiful girl painted on the side," said Linda!

"Is that you painted on the nose of the plane, 'Phabulous Phyl,'" asked Loretta?

"Yes, that was Mike's plane."

"Did you always dress topless in front of his men like that," asked Mary?

"Not once in a million years," the older matron answered!

"Who met who in a brothel," asked Mary?

"I'm sorry Shirl," said Phyllis, now dry eyed, looking at

the prettiest woman there. "I was up all night worried about Mike. "I'm probably not going to get much sleep this week either."

"Apologies accepted," said Shirley. "I'm worried about Jim too . . . except, he was excited when he left this morning."

"Excited," asked Phyllis?

"Yes, he seemed thrilled about the mission."

"Well, look at the bright side," Linda quipped, "he left you the car."

"No he didn't. "Jim drove to the base," said Shirley. "He said he needed to pick up Bob and Victor. "I told him I wanted to get a driver's license, but he said that there were enough women drivers and he would be d, a, m, n, e, d, if he was going to let *his* wife drive a car. "He says women don't have what it takes to drive."

"I have a license," said Mary.

"Good," answered Shirley! "Then you can take me shopping."

"Where do you want to go?"

"To Dallas," Answered Shirley!

"Oh, that's too far," said Mary. "I'd be afraid I'd hit something."

"Its only thirty miles."

"But I didn't ask John for permission. "He'd be furious if I dented his Pontiac Star Chief. "You should hear the noises he makes when he drives it. "Sometimes he yells, 'hundred sixty horsepower vee-eight, ahoowa, ahoowa'—just yells for no reason at all, just like a little kid!" The other women laughed.

"Men," exclaimed Loretta!

"Phyllis, you're a good driver," said Linda. "Why don't you take us to Dallas? "C'mon, it'll be fun. "Why sit at home worrying about Mike when you can be shopping?"

"Yeah, Phabulous Phyl, please," asked Shirley? "I want to teach Jim a lesson for not telling me where he's going. "I'm going to say that I was so worried about him that I bought all sorts of things and if he wants to take anything back, he'll have to take me to Dallas again!"

The other women laughed and repeated "Please, please, please, pretty please," all in a chorus.

"Well Mike will be upset if the gas tank is empty when he gets back," answered the Colonel's wife.

"I'll chip in to buy gas," offered Linda.

"When do you want to leave," asked Phyllis?

"Tuesday, as soon as the kids leave for school."

"No, Jimmy might see and tell his father," said Shirley.

"Well, he'll certainly find out if you buy a lot of new things in Dallas," Linda replied. "Besides, what are you worried about? "The wife of a Colonel ranks the same as a Major. "Just tell him that Phyl ordered you to go!" The women laughed.

"Okay as soon as the school bus comes, I'm coming," said Phyllis.

"Hurrah," said the girls!

"Fall in for pre-flight inspection!"

HUMANITY OF THE MONSTER

February 1956

Shrouded under a black cape, a portrait photographer bent down and aimed a varnished wooden box at twenty men standing in front of their ship, each wearing an identical dark green flight suit, a red leather helmet with black rubber ear-phones, black flight boots with thick rubber soles, an olive drab parachute looking like a backpack, and a yellow "Mae West" life jacket. A sign warning "Hot Guns" dangled from the nose of the ship. Bomber jackets and quilted pants liners under their flight suits made their arms and legs look as thick as tree trunks. Most had kneeboards attached to their right thighs, except for Grant who was left handed and wore his on the left. Dangling from clips in front of the kneeboards were white computers—circular slide rules with one logarithmic ring inside the other and a sliding vector card inserted through the middle. A pair of black goggles, headphones, a small duffle, and an oxygen mask lay on the ground in front of each man.

Johns' new ship, 753, was covered with antennas like cat's whiskers. Booms stuck out holding long wires that ran along the sides. Some of the wires were a hundred feet long. Other wires stretched from the cockpit to the top of the tail fin. Some were only twenty feet long. Strange black blisters protruded from its chin and belly. There were antennas hidden in the tailfin and in small white plastic bumps along the sides and top. The photographer held up two fingers, then one. Emerging from under his cape, he saluted. Eleven officers and nine enlisted men saluted back. A Brigadier, standing beside the photographer in winter blues, returned their salutes and nodded permission to board the ship. Though they were dressed identically, it was possible to tell the officers from the enlisted men because the enlisted men boarded quickly, bounding up the ladders leading up into the nose wheel well and tail hatch, while the officers, who knew where they were going, climbed slowly and reluctantly, like old men, as though they might never touch the red Texas clay again.

Taking a photo before a mission was bad luck. It was generally only done with green crews. It jinxed an experienced crew, as though they were not coming back or something. There was so much brass along for the flight, most of the groundcrew saw nothing unusual about taking a photo. Pentagon seat-farters needed flight time to qualify for fifty percent hazardous duty pay, so the ship's normal "Crows," as the enlisted Electronic Intelligence Team was called, were being replaced with three "Ravens" from the Pentagon. Colonel Peterson, the Squadron Commander, was taking over from Johns as Aircraft Commander because the First Raven and mission leader, Major Merril Hughs, outranked Johns. Johns was only a Brevet Major—a Captain with a spot promotion. Now considered a "sharp tool," as members of select crews were called, Major Hughs became a "light" Colonel for the duration of the mission, so a "full bird" Colonel had to be in charge. Johns didn't care much about losing command. He and Colonel Peterson were friends. They played Bridge with Phyllis and Linda on Thursday nights and often flew together, since Peterson lost his own ship when he was promoted to command the entire squadron.

After two hours of checklists, the hard part began—waiting for the order to start the engines. The clocks on the various instrument panels seemed to tick loudly, as did everyone's wristwatches. Second hands swept by hypnotically. The Magnesium hull of the ship was heating up under the hot Texas sun. Once on board, everyone removed their parachutes, leather helmets, life jackets, and pants liners. The ground crew stood around the ship in army green coveralls murmuring to each other. The three regular "Crows" grumbled about not being able to go with their buddies as they wandered around the hard stand with nothing to do.

At exactly 9:53, General Allen returned in his blue staff car and saluted. Colonel Peterson, sitting in the left pilot seat, the armored commander's throne, returned the salute and announced, "Set ignition and breakers, start engines."

"Roger start engines," replied First Engineer Murphy, who sat back to back with the pilots facing a large panel with more than a hundred gauges. Pressing his interphone button on the ceiling above his head, he commanded, "Ground this is panel, clear three two one four five six." A Chevy V-8 engine, without a muffler, started and roared at full throttle inside a yellow, box shaped ground power unit fitted with tiny little wheels.

Sergeant Hawley, the crew chief, pressed a button on another power unit and a second Chevy V-8 started with an un-muffled ear splitting roar. "This is Ground, three clear," he replied through a headset connected to the left landing gear leg, "fire guard standing by." Next to him was an airman with a giant red, spoke wheeled fire extinguisher.

Murphy pushed in the ignition breaker switches on his right panel. The ground crew listened to a mournful whirring sound as Murphy pushed the number three starter button. The whir changed to explosions and then a clattery roar, as clouds of smoke chugged from the foot diameter exhaust stacks under the wing. The huge three blade, black painted, yellow tipped propeller turned in front of their faces. "One, two, three," Hawley counted as each propeller blade went by. The engine sputtered, then backfired, belching flame out of its exhaust stacks as it broke wind with more smoke. "Three started, two clear," shouted Hawley into his headset. The other five piston engines repeated the smoky, noisy performance as they growled to life.

The engines always ran rough at first and it was a matter of pride that they were not turned over to the flight crew until they purred smoothly. This gave the flightcrew time to complete their preflight checks with someone else watching for fires. Everything inside the ship vibrated visibly. It was impossible to place a pencil or coffee mug on a table without it shaking onto the floor.

"Power stabilizing," said Murphy as he and Second Engineer Washington, sitting beside him in the corner, behind Johns' right pilot seat, watched their gauges. "Okay to taxi."

"This is seven five three calling for taxi instructions," announced Colonel Peterson as he pressed the radio button on the left horn of his control wheel.

"ROGER 753, CLEARED TO TAXI TO RUNWAY THREE FIVE," a voice replied in the pilots' headsets.

"Remove chocks," commanded Peterson, this time pressing the interphone button on the right horn of his wheel. Hawley unplugged his headphone jack from the landing gear leg and ran to join three other groundcrewmen standing to the side with large wooden wheel chocks hanging over their shoulders. "Release brakes," ordered Peterson, "Power!" Murphy pushed the throttles and the two hundred ton ship began to creep forward over the buckling, two foot thick concrete.

When they arrived at the runup pad at the end of the runway, Peterson turned the giant ship using a small steering wheel beside his left knee. "Full power reverse safety check," he commanded. Shoving the throttles on his desk forward individually, Murphy momentarily revved up each engine to full power while the gunners watched to see which direction the dust was blowing behind the ship. If a wire got crossed, the propellers could reverse on takeoff with fatal results, so each propeller had to be checked individually.

At Phyllis Peterson's house, Loretta questioned her host, "It sounds like they're taking off!" The noise of a hundred lawnmowers roared across the lake.

"Don't worry, we've got time," said Linda. "Hank always revs up the engines to warn me before he comes."

"Mike does too," added Phyllis.

"Seven five three ready for takeoff," announced Peterson, pushing his radio button.

"SEVEN FIVE THREE CLEARED ONTO THE ACTIVE," answered Bob Morrison in the tower, "HAVE A SAFE TRIP!"

The giant ship made a slow turn to line up with the end of the runway, its nose bobbing up and down as the brakes howled to a stop.

"Start jets," commanded Peterson!

Johns reached up to the overhead panel and flicked four starter switches to spin up the jets. First there was a whirring sound rather like four vacuum cleaners, then percussive thunder followed by clouds of brown smoke as Peterson advanced the throttles to idle. The combustion chambers thundered, one by one, as flames propagated through the cross-fire tubes. When the four tachometer gauges on the top center of the pilots' instrument panel pointed straight up, Johns reached up and switched the starters to off.

"Take off power," ordered the Colonel! The six piston engines began to roar like a thousand lawn mowers as Murphy pushed the six throttles on the engineer's panel. The grass and mesquite trees at the end of the runway swayed and bent with the turbulence from the huge pusher propellers as Washington adjusted the mixture levers for takeoff. The front landing gear leg was thrust instantly downward by the force, giving the ship a sinister, nose down appearance, like a giant scorpion with its tail raised in the air. The two whining jet pods, equipped with two engines each, jerked at the wing tips like the paws of a cat ready to pounce.

Washington stared intently at the waveform on his three inch engine analyzer screen as he completed pre-flight diagnostics to synchronize the six reciprocating engines. It was this engine synchronization that made the RB-36 so loud. Six pistons in six engines always fired at once, sounding something like a single engine plane amplified through six giant stereo speakers. Grant, who was sitting on the floor of the cockpit, back to back with Peterson, flicked a switch on the aft bulkhead.

A hatch opened behind the greenhouse cockpit canopy, out of which emerged two gun turrets with two 20mm cannons each, looking like the weapons of a navy destroyer. This gave the men in the photo lab an avenue of escape in case there was a crash. He then buckled his safety strap. Everything inside the ship vibrated.

"Activate water injection," ordered Peterson. "Turbojets full power," he added, as he moved the overhead jet throttle levers forward. Two shimmering clouds of brown smoke appeared behind each jet pod as the noise inside the ship rose to banshee levels. Alcohol flames danced from the dozen foot diameter exhaust stacks under the wing, like a top fuel dragster, as the menthol water mixture temporarily increased horse-power. The grove of mesquite beyond the end of the runway bent and swayed as if in a tornado. The wing tips and tail visibly twisted and shook up and down and side to side in the turbulence. The huge ship seemed alive.

Peterson called out the last nineteen numbers of the checklist and the engineers or scanners answered, "Hatches closed, "thirty degrees," or "three diamonds," to tell the positions of the six flaps or engine cooling nozzles from the markings painted on the cowlings.

"Release Brakes," Peterson commanded. Johns flicked a tiny silver switch beside his left knee on the center console. Those facing forward were pressed back into their seats as the nose jumped up to its normal height. Papers slid off desks as those facing aft felt their safety straps digging into their shoulders.

Propeller tips tore at the air with miniature sonic booms as the giant ship accelerated. Every piece of tin within a half mile rattled from the sonic vibrations. Turbojet thunder throbbed like a waterfall. It was said that on a still morning, one could hear an RB-36 taking off all the way to Fort Worth. Twenty two thousand eight hundred horsepower was generated by six fuel injected Pratt & Whitney R4360-53 Wasp Majors. One hundred sixty-eight throbbing five and one half inch wide pistons were fed by twelve turbochargers, six superchargers, and three hundred thirty six platinum tipped spark plugs. They turned eighteen of the largest propeller blades ever fitted on an aircraft faster than the speed of sound. Four General Electric J-47-GE-19 turbojets generating 5,200 pounds of thrust each, thundering louder than Niagara Falls, increased the total horse-power on the ground to more than forty thousand. Just because it weighed two hundred tons, didn't mean a fully loaded RB-36 couldn't out-accelerate a car. It may have been as big as a Navy submarine and its two forward upper gun turrets may have made it look like a Navy destroyer given wings as its ten engines hurled it down the runway, but it was still faster than anything on wheels.

Traction bars thumped against the floor of Sergeant Hawley's personal flame-painted red Plymouth convertible as he let out the clutch to follow the big ship down the runway. He had a large orange and white checkered flag attached to his rear bumper and a hemi-head V-8 with dual quad and tunnel ram sticking out of the hood. But it was not his car he was most proud of. The ship's engines were "his" engines. Why would he care about a silly street rod when he had twin-turbo-supercharged, fuel injected, twenty eight cylinder corncob radials to work on? To Hawley, fixing up cars was just a hobby. The two hundred ton monster out-accelerating him down the runway was the real hot rod, and he was intensely proud to be the one who souped it up. He was going to make sure everything was right—right down to the last moment before takeoff. The flying naval vessel cracked and buckled the runway with ten, five foot diameter, one inch thick tires squashed flat with twenty tons each. Without removing his right thumb from the steering wheel, Hawley expertly moved his column mounted gearshift forward and up into second gear, then depressing his clutch for a split second, down into third gear. For a few moments, he seemed to be gaining, but his flame sided street rod could not keep up with Johns' and Peterson's two hundred thirty foot wide RB-36.

"Look at the Chief go," exalted Gunner Shultz as he watched the red hooded convertible fall behind. The hundred mile per hour wind from the six churning propellers lashing at his orange checkered flag held Hawley back. Oily brown smoke poured out of the turbojets in front of his car. In order to get maximum power, more fuel was injected into their engines than they could burn. The brown smoke settled onto the grass on either side of the runway, polluting the lawn with an oily tan color.

Once the ship reached its one hundred twenty knot take-off speed, the jets put out more power than the propellers, so it was really more jet than propeller plane, but propellers allowed the RB-36 to do what no other plane in the world could do—remain in the air for two days without landing and still fly to the edge of the Earth to drop the world's most awesome weapon.

On the floor of the radio room, below and behind the cockpit, six men sat facing aft, but some were able to look over their shoulders to see through the glass nose of the ship and watch the fence blocking the end of the runway grow slightly taller each time the nose wheels thumped over a joint in the concrete. The vibrations were violent enough to make their teeth chatter. Just as it appeared that the soft Plexiglas nose would pound into the fence, the bumping and thumping stopped. The fence dropped down out of sight, passing silently underneath.

"Gear coming up," announced Gunner Nakamura, echoed by Gunner O'Connor from the Plexiglas gun blisters in the rear of the ship, as they watched the canoe doors drop open from the wing roots to make room for the giant, four wheel silver columns folding inwards and up into the wing. With a bump and a thump, the nose gear was up with the doors closed under it. Everyone was able to breathe a sigh of relief. The men stood up and gazed down on the green waters of Lake Worth passing under the window. Grant flicked a switch, and the four battleship guns disappeared into their sliding panel behind the cockpit. Aerodynamic forces on the wings dampened the engine vibrations and the flight became smooth.

Hawley slammed on his brakes just before hitting the

fence. He got out of his car and pressed his hands and face against the fence like a convict behind bars. He watched the smoke from his ten thundering engines rise over the lake. The oily smoke settled on his clothes and hair and covered the leather seats of his convertible, eliminating any trace of new car smell. Hawley didn't care. He had joined the Air Force because he wanted to fly. How he longed to go along!

The two-mile long runway lined up perfectly with the subdivision on the other side of the lake. It was mainly rich executives who had cottages there, but there were a few shabby asbestos shingled bungalows directly under the traffic pattern where nobody but Air Force officers wanted to live. A land developer owned them and rented them to Peterson and a few of the others, like Hughs, who didn't think they would live there long. Only Generals and Colonels could afford to live there long term, but the others rented homes just up the hill from the lake so their kids could bother Phyllis and the Colonel to go swimming. The Petersons didn't mind, because their only daughter, Denise, was almost grown. The fact that the traffic pattern passed directly over their homes greatly motivated everyone to get things right. A ship once had to ditch in the lake to avoid killing wives and children when two propellers reversed on take-off. Five men were killed.

Happy it was Saturday, the children ran toward the lake when they heard the ship coming, then pointed at the number "753" stenciled boldly on the side as it penetrated the sunny blue sky. "That's my daddy's plane," little Jimmy Newcomb yelled, before the sound of a thousand lawnmowers combined with four whistling howling jets drowned out his voice. His shrill childish shrieks seemed to be replaced with almost silent fish-like mouth movements. "Mine too," little Bobby Johns added with a barely perceptible squeal. The Kewscinski boys added to the cacophony.

Phyllis, Linda, Mary, Shirley, and Loretta emerged onto Phyllis' tiny back porch, just fifty feet from the lake, to watch their husbands leave for work, waving wildly as the ship smoked and thundered toward them. The thousand lawnmowers changed to a chorus of bass fiddles and tubas mixed with Thor hammering valkirie voices, dropping abruptly in pitch as the ten engines roared overhead. Oily brown smoke descended on the neighborhood. No man could see his wife because of the trees, nor could wives see their husbands because of the Plexiglas, but each knew that the other was waving until the ladies were forced to cup their hands over their ears. Vortexes from the wingtips swirled the trails of brown jet exhaust into devil's horns as the ship thundered up into the white puffy clouds.

"One can hardly expect a two hundred ton object as big and heavy as a Navy minesweeper to pass over one's house without rattling a few dishes," shouted Linda at Loretta proudly. The other ladies rushed back inside to watch the television test pattern. If it turned to static momentarily, then they knew the plane's electronic countermeasures were working properly. Few in Fort Worth knew what caused their televisions and radios to occasionally go haywire.

Aboard the ship, the noise was a combination high and low pitched hum coupled with the hissing of air moving past the many antennas. It was easy to ignore. Everyone was used to hearing it. Before long, they would all swear that the engines made no sound at all. The gunners waved from their Plexiglas blisters as they flew low over the heads of the children. The children could easily see the men's waving hands and smiling faces in the bubbles just a hundred feet above them and waved frantically in reply before the jet blast forced them to cover their ears.

"Lake Worth is the best place to live in the entire world," shouted Jimmy Newcomb when the noise abated a little. "Where else do such big planes fly so low?" Canadians would soon look up and see nothing but vapor trails.

"Your turn to drive Gordon, three three five mark two," the skipper said to the young co-pilot as Johns reached up to shut down the four jet engines and close their nose doors to save fuel. Murphy and Washington adjusted their throttles and mixture levers to achieve the best possible fuel economy.

Peterson unbuckled his harness to get up. Grant climbed up from his takeoff position on the floor and turned around to take the skipper's place in the armored command chair. Gordon was anxious to move into the left seat since the right seat, though identical in every respect except for the armored steel back, did not count as flying time. Normally Johns would take the left seat, but he had plenty of hours and didn't mind giving his co-pilot some much needed flight time to help pad the young man's pay envelope. After all, Gordon needed the money to help feed his many girlfriends. Peterson descended down the stairs into the radio room.

The RB-36 was such a huge plane, it had two decks. Crews often used naval terms to describe it. It didn't have a cockpit. It had a "bridge" just like a ship, which was also called the "flight deck." Two pilots and a flight engineer manned it most of the time, with one pilot and one engineer off duty. The pilots faced forward and the engineers faced aft, completely surrounded by instrument panels. Not only were there two of every possible flight instrument, but there were eighty four engine instruments including oil and cylinder head temperature gauges, manifold pressure, oil, menthol-water, and fuel pressure gauges, tachometers, and ten fuel gauges for the nine fuel tanks. Even the overhead panel was filled with lights, circuit breakers, and jet throttle controls under the greenhouse canopy. All of this complex instrumentation prevented Peterson from knowing what was really important—what the rest of the crew was doing, so he had to adopt a "walking around" type of management style to properly control his flying twenty man organization.

Below in the Radio room, Beaumont and Hernandez sat in two swivel chairs which could be turned forward or aft to monitor the many radios and black boxes crammed against the bulkheads. A large Plexiglas bubble on each side of the cabin, not unlike the ones on Captain Nemo's Nautilus, lit the small cylindrical room extremely well. Each bubble contained a gunsight and camera that cast a shadow shaped strangely like a crucifix. The floor and walls of the ship were covered with drab army-green canvas decorated with long white candy-cane twirls of one and two inch thick wire bundles connecting more than fifty dimly glowing metal covered vacuum tubes to their associated instruments. Wire bundles running along the floor were enclosed in thick white vacuum cleaner hoses for protection. The ceiling was covered with gray canvas which was illuminated by more silver covered vacuum tubes emitting a dim orange glow. On the starboard side of the radio room, opposite the stairs that led to the bridge, there was a flexible urine tube that looked like a tin funnel with a long flexible spout connected to the wall. A valve allowed it to be drained overboard onto unsuspecting civilians. A green curtain hung from the ceiling forward of it which concealed a small nook equipped with a bucket and a toilet seat. It was the only place on board that offered any privacy. A small airline type window allowed the man doing his business there to look out over the clouds as he relieved himself, but there was no way to empty it overboard, so everyone avoided using it as long as possible.

"How'd the radios check out," Peterson asked?

"Everything's fine, sir," answered Beaumont, "it looks like we're good to go."

"Great! "Good job on those pre-flight checks," commended Peterson as he patted Hernandez on the shoulder. He ducked under the cockpit stairs into the forward cabin, which was lit even better than the radio room by a giant multi-paned curved window that covered the entire front of the ship. "How is the radar and loran working?"

"Fine sir," said Holbrook, the Weather Observer."

"Loran is working fine, sir," said Nawrocki, the Navigator.

"Good! "Thanks for your hard work," said Peterson. "There's nothing I like better than a routine flight." Nawrocki and Holbrook looked at each other with puzzlement over the boss's unusual friendliness.

The twelve and one half foot diameter fuselage was tall enough to have two full decks with private cabins for every crewman. Instead, long narrow communication tubes, about as wide as a man's shoulders, passed through the many equipment and weapons bays to connect the ship's three small pressurized crew compartments together.   These tunnels were like the intestines of a monster. Since 753 was a reconnaissance bomber, it had a pressurized darkroom and photo lab embedded in its neck, between the forward weapons bay and the bomb bay, in about the same place where the crop or gizzard on a dinosaur would be. An eight foot long tunnel, about two feet in diameter, led like an esophagus through the radar compartment. Peterson inserted his head and arms into the hole. A small window on the side of the tube allowed him to see the big radar antenna rotating down inside a blister that hung below the neck of the ship like a giant Adam's apple.

Hernandez watched the Colonel's feet disappear, then pressed his interphone button and said, "Skipper on his way aft."

Kewscinski, the Photonavigator, who was laying in his bunk in the back of the lab, watched the skipper emerge from a giant mouse hole under his desk on the opposite bulkhead and turned away so he would not have to get up and salute. If he got up, Peterson might take his berth and Kewscinski liked sleeping where he was just fine. Peterson walked between the two giant green baked-enamel lateral cameras and the many large white plastic film magazines strapped to the curved green canvas covered walls, and stepped around the telescopic camera sprouting like a huge white mushroom through the green canvas covered floor. He had to climb over the five, even taller, white topped multi-cameras that covered almost half of the floor, to get to the other end of the lab. Newcomb, the Video Observer, was already asleep in the bunk below Kewscinski, so the skipper had to climb over his feet to continue aft through the sixty foot tunnel that lead to the bowels of the ship.

A mechanic's creeper called the "tube trolley" took men through the long intestine which passed through the bomb bays. A rope hanging from the ceiling allowed a man to pull himself along while laying on his parachute. This was easy when going aft. The RB-36's nose high flying attitude created a downhill slide to the rear of the ship.   The tube was extremely claustrophobic. Peterson's shoulders and belly had only an inch to spare on all sides. The dark, unpainted aluminum ceiling was only three inches away from his face and chin. The cable above him rubbed his nose and cheeks if he did not keep pulling. Though it was a short fast trip lasting only a few seconds, it was always a relief to arrive in the monster's bowel.

Gunner Nakamura stood up, snapped to attention, and saluted as Peterson emerged from a big mouse hole near his gunsight. 753's back office was lit by four large Plexiglas bubbles equipped with gunsights and cameras similar to those in the radio room. One was on each side of the ten foot gray canvas ceiling, near the aft end, and one was on each curved dark green canvas wall of the cabin near the front. As in the nose of the ship, the walls were decorated with twisted white candy-cane bundles of wires inside white vacuum cleaner hoses connecting various silver covered vacuum tubes and black boxes. Other hoses, painted green, led to the oxygen manifolds where coils of green vacuum cleaner hoses dangled from the men's black oxygen masks.

Nakamura and Sergeant O'Connor, sitting on comfortably padded swivel chairs, gazed out of the two lower bubbles as clouds passed beneath them. The upper bubbles were connected by a walkway upon which Sergeant Shultz and Airman Calebrese were sitting in similar swivel-chairs. These chairs revolved around their gunsights like an amusement park ride, allowing them to aim their guns in any direction. In front of the walkway on the left side of the cabin, was a shiny aluminum galley cabinet with a two burner stove and coffee pot. The other gunners saluted Colonel Peterson without getting up from their seats. Safety straps, designed to keep them from being ejected from the ship in the event of a decompression accident, held them firmly in place. The skipper returned the salute, and closed a curtain behind the galley cabinet which hid another bucket and toilet seat.

When Peterson emerged, Sandringham, who was sitting at his tail gunlaying system console on the starboard side opposite the toilet saluted. "How'd the guns check out,

Sergeant," asked the skipper," as he returned the salute?

"Oiled and broiled Sir," Sandringham replied, "I even hot dipped all the ammo feeds. "We're not going to have any hang fires on this flight. "We're going to have one hundred percent fire off this mission, Sir! "Can I get you some coffee, sir?" Sandringham got up and lifted the brushed aluminum coffee pot from the galley stove.

"Thank you Sergeant," commended Peterson, slapping the man's shoulder. "I appreciate all the hard work you've done, but it might keep me up and I need some sleep." He removed his parachute and climbed up the ladder to the walkway where Shultz and Calabrese were sitting. They saluted again. Calabrese took the skipper's parachute and placed it in a rack behind his seat. "How are your guns?"

"Oiled and broiled, Sir," answered Calabrese!

"Yessir, oiled and broiled," agreed Shultz. "We left them in the sun a whole two hours so the oil would soak in before we wiped them clean."

"Thank you Airman, Sergeant," commended Peterson as he shook their hands. "I appreciate all the hard work you've done to prepare for this mission." Calabrese beamed. The skipper spread open a green curtain, which hid three pipe berths hanging from the ceiling across the width of the cabin like an attic loft. Inside, three Ravens were roosting.

Ravens Wong and Whitefeather had taken barbiturates to adjust their sleeping schedule for the coming mission, so they were fast asleep. Hughs, their commander, had been up all night with Peterson doing the mission planning, so he did not think he needed a sleeping pill. When he saw the skipper wanted his berth, he had no choice but to vacate. Hughs climbed down and sat in a swivel chair against the front bulkhead and tried to sleep sitting up. Eventually he had to take a pill. Along the peak of the gray canvas attic loft, ran a large gray canvas covered tube which carried de-icing heat to the tailplane and fin. The warmest place on the ship to sleep was underneath this. Peterson was soon in dreamland, lulled to sleep by the constant drone of the engines.

It did not quite have all the comforts of home, but a plane that stays in the air for two days without landing must have enough provisions for twenty men to live comfortably, or they will end up smelling like a hobo jungle by the time it lands. As the lowest ranking man on board, it was Nakamura's job to empty the chamber pot. On the floor, between the galley cabinet and the toilet, was a circular entrance hatch about the size of a manhole cover exactly where the monster's anus should be. It was through this anus that the men in the aft cabin climbed in and out. Some thought it strange that the only entrance into the back of the ship should be through the bathroom. It seemed equally strange that the only entrance to the front of the ship was through the forward landing gear doors, which opened like the mouth parts of a giant insect and prevented the officers' head from being emptied during flight when they were closed. Unless the flight was nearly over, officers were obliged to travel aft to use the enlisted men's latrine, or endure the smell of their own bodily emanations for days until the ship landed.

The Air Force is the most civilized of the armed services, so to "dig the latrine," Nakamura merely clipped his safety strap to a frame partition, unlatched three dogs, and lifted the hatch. A two hundred mile per hour wind swirled through the cabin causing the green canvas privacy curtain to fly up like a demon flapping its wings. Rows of little homes near a muddy Pony Express station called Colorado Springs, just South of Denver, could be seen through the hole in the floor.

Dumping the bucket had to be done with great skill, or the two hundred mile per hour wind would fling excrement all over the canvas insulation covering the aft bulkhead and soak in. The last time that happened, the smell drove the gunnery sergeants mad, trapped as they were for two days in the tiny cylindrical twelve by fifteen foot cabin with him, so Nakamura was made to spend the next three days scrubbing it clean with his toothbrush. By the time they let him disembark from the flight, he had been aboard for nearly a week! The trick was to barely dip the edge of the bucket into the tornadic slipstream so the wind would blast it clean.

Sergeants Sandringham and O'Connor stood at the entrance to the tiny bathroom holding the curtain open as Shultz gazed down from above, all screaming instructions at the top of their lungs. Nakamura could not hear them because of the wind. After carefully tipping the bucket, the lowest ranking airman replaced the hatch and calmly stated when the deafening noise stopped, "That'll teach'em for not raising our pay."

"How is dumping the Colonel's feces supposed to get us a raise in pay," asked Sergeant Sandringham, his ears still ringing from the noise?

"Oh no," said Shultz!

"It's where they're building that new officer's college, *isn't it*," asked O'Connor?

Nakamura stood, then snapped to attention and shouted at the top of his lungs, "YES, SERGEANT!"

Colonel Peterson, unable to sleep because of the noise and shouting, was furious, but he remained in his bunk.

"Permission to come aboard, Sir?"

THE
RENDEZVOUS
February 1956

Near Calgary Alberta, a small jet intercepted the giant reconnaissance bomber. Out of the top of its nose, an unusual fin emerged with a hook on top, which loomed in front of the cockpit. Four huge drop tanks hung from its wings. The pilot was Lieutenant Anthony Avery, a 25 year old jet jockey who thought he was immortal. He formed up beside the flying battleship. Recognizing Lieutenant Grant in the left seat, he saluted. Grant was happy to oblige. For all Avery knew, Grant was the Aircraft Commander. Gordon was intensely proud of flying the largest plane in the world, though both knew that flying a fighter was better. Tony had graduated from West Point with honors. Gordon's marks were mediocre.

Because of jealousy, bomber pilots refused to salute fighter pilots unless they were higher in rank. Pilots of little planes had to salute the pilots of big planes—that is how it worked. The least maneuverable aircraft is always the lead plane in a formation and the pilot of the second plane has to salute. The RB-36 was the most masculine plane in the Air Force. Without power assisted controls, no woman could fly it. In the air, RB-36 pilots did not have to salute anybody.

For years, Navy aviators refused to salute, claiming that, because they could take off and land on aircraft carriers, aviators were better than pilots. If they only knew the truth! Grant soon formed up with another giant ten-engined flying naval vessel he had spotted in the distance. The other ship was GRB-36-D-44-92099, a FICON featherweight III Fighter-Conveyer. Tony's plane was a Republic RF-84K "Thunderflash." After Tony formed up below and behind 099, a hydraulic trapeze lowered twenty feet below its bomb bay. Tony approached the belly of the other ship with the most delicate of pitch and throttle adjustments. Everyone except the sleeping officers stopped what they were doing to watch, leaving Johns to fly the ship by himself. Every window had a face in it and every gunsight blister held two or three heads with others straining to look.

"Co-pilot to Radio," asked Grant over the interphone, "can you pipe in what they are saying?" Sergeant Hernandez clicked a couple of switches and turned a knob to tune one of his radios to the fighter's frequency.

Martin Jenkins, 099's trapeze operator, was immediately overheard saying, "OKAY TONY, WHENEVER YOU'RE READY! "READY TO LATCH ON."

"ROGER, I'M BEGINNING MY APPROACH," the fighter pilot replied. The little plane slowly flew under the larger one.

Joining two planes together in flight was a very difficult and dangerous thing to do—way beyond the ability of naval aviators. It was even more difficult than it looked. If Tony pulled back on his stick to gain altitude, his plane would slow down. If he dropped the nose to speed up, he would fall. Tony had to carefully adjust his throttle by rolling his left wrist—not by shoving the throttle with his left arm as he might do to suddenly increase power. There was always a delay of several seconds before a throttle adjustment would result in an increase in thrust, so docking required huge patience as hearts pounded faster and faster.

The danger was, if Tony got too close to the mother ship before hooking up, the slipstream between the two aircraft would cause them to slam together. It is a scientific fact, called Bernoulli's principle, that fast moving air flows at a lower pressure. There is normally slower moving air and thus higher pressure under the wing than there is above it. If Tony's plane got too close to the mother ship, his jetwash would suck air from under the larger aircraft and cause the big plane to drop, while at the same time, low pressure between the two aircraft caused by the faster moving air would cause Tony's plane leap upward as if drawn by a magnet until his fragile canopy smashed against the massive trapeze. He would be killed instantly, if he got too close.

"C'mon Tony, first try," shouted Gordon, as everyone held their breath. They watched the little jet slowly approach the trapeze until the hook on the strange fin in front of the cockpit slammed into the trapeze. The hydraulics in the trapeze absorbed the impact and slowed the smaller plane by abruptly lifting its nose and stalling its wings. 099 seemed to shudder after the impact.

"CONTACT," said Jenkins, as Tony's plane bounced up and down a few times.

"ROGER CONTACT," said Avery.

"HOLD STILL, I'M LATCHING ON," warned Jenkins as he lowered the rear of the trapeze to the second position, engaging Tony's jet securely by two pins behind the cockpit. "GOTCHA," said Jenkins!

"POWERING DOWN. "ENGINE OFF," said Tony.

"ALL GREEN," said Jenkins.

"All right Tony," shouted Gordon, oblivious to the fact that the crew of the other two planes could not possibly hear him!

"LIFTING YOU UP," said Jenkins as he flicked a tiny switch to retract the little jet into the bomb bay of the flying aircraft carrier. The little jet dangled half inside and half out of 099's bomb bay with only its wings and belly protruding as specially shaped bomb bay doors closed tightly around its cockpit.

"Can a Navy swabo do that," Gordon asked over the interphone? He did not expect or receive a reply since every Air Force man knew the answer. Tony left little doubt about the superiority of Air Force pilots over Naval aviators.

"JENKIN'S FILLIN' STATION, PLEASE WAIT FOR ATTENDANT," Tony asked? Johns and Grant looked at each other with puzzled expressions as Avery read a message painted on the front bulkhead of the mother ship's bomb bay that only he could see.

"THAT'S SO YOU FIGHTER JOCKEYS DON'T TRY TO PUT THE GAS IN YOURSELF AND PUT ME OUT OF A JOB," they overheard Jenkins reply!

"WELL THAT'S GOOD," said Tony, "I BROUGHT FOUR BIG EMPTY GAS CANS I WANT FILLED!"

"RIGHT AWAY SUH. "WILL THAT BE CASH OR CHARGE?"

"CHARGE! "MAY I USE YOUR BATHROOM?"

"OF COURSE SUH! "YOU MAY EVEN RENT A ROOM AT MY MOTEL. "I'VE GOT A GENUINE FROZEN TV DINNER WAITING FOR YOU IN MY RESTAURANT AND ALL THE COLD BROWN COFFEE YOU WANT TO DRINK."

"IS THE MAID SEXY?"

"MY WIFE THINKS I AM."

"TOO BAD."

"WHY?"

"IF YOU HAD A SEXY MAID, I THINK I'D LIKE YOUR FLYING CITY. "I MIGHT EVEN RECOMMEND IT TO MY FRIENDS. "DOES THE ROOM COME WITH A TELEVISION?"

"WE HAVE RADAR. "THAT'S BETTER THAN TELEVISION . . . AND YOUR ROOM IS EQUIPPED WITH CAMERAS TO TAKE PICTURES OF NAKED RUSSIAN WOMEN TAKING THEIR SUN BATH. "WHAT MORE COULD YOU WANT?"

"I WANNA SEE YOUR PHOTO ALBUM."

"SORRY, DON'T HAVE IT WITH ME, PRESIDENT EISENHOWER BORROWED IT AND NEVER GAVE IT BACK. "YOU'LL HAVE TO GO TO RUSSIA AND TAKE YOUR OWN PICTURES."

"AW SHOOT! "I KNEW THERE WAS A HITCH"

Although half of Canada could tune into the uncoded transmissions, few would have suspected they came from the United States Air Force. The flying aircraft carrier would replace all other weapons. It made every ship and gun in the Navy's arsenal obsolete. A Navy aircraft carrier took six days to bring sixty slow straight winged planes across the Atlantic. A fleet of sixty Air Force FICON's could bring sixty fast swept wing jets half-way around the world in just a day—and each jet launched from the air could carry twice the payload of a land or sea based plane. Men would never again have to fight hand to hand in trenches. A fleet of bombers protected by their own fighters could go anywhere in the world, unopposed, and devastate any country on Earth with nuclear fireballs.

LIVING THE NIGHTMARE

February 1956

"Bandit three o'clock low," a voice yelled over the interphone, "coming in fast with no wingman!"

"Test your weapons," shouted Peterson!

"It's coming up fast, almost straight up," added another voice! "How can it do that?" There was a clattering sound behind his head, like someone kick starting a big two-cylinder Harley-Davidson motorcycle backfiring with no muffler. "Vroom, pop, pop, pop!" The plane was filled with the gunpowder smell of spent brass coming from a bag under the dorsal turret. There was a dull thud, as two B-24's above and in front exploded in a ball of flame. Wings and chunks of fuselage fluttered wildly around like cardboard blown by a strong wind.

"Twenty three is hit," a voice shouted! A green and gray German plane marked with black crosses flashed silently upward, followed by a trail of smoke and thunder. It was just a wing with no tail. "What kind of plane is that," the voice asked?

"I dunno," the skipper replied, "I never seen anything like it!"

"Watch out, it's looping back down for another pass!"

The skipper watched the strange Nazi lunge straight toward him from above and in front. It seemed to grow larger and larger while remaining still in the same position in the sky. "Vroom pop pop pop pop pop, vroom vroom pop pop pop pop

pop pop," came from behind his head as loud as before, and also from the turret in the nose. The strange plane became decorated with bright lights, which seemed to swarm around it like fireflies. Bill MacAtee's head spun around in the Plexiglas turret as his guns fired an arc of tracers. The fireflies got closer. The skipper felt his bladder draining into the seat of his pants as the hairs on the back of his neck stood on end.

There were some loud bangs and thuds and a bright flash of light. Peterson was tumbling. The sky was green, then white, then blue, green, white, blue, green, white, blue. "Everybody out, we're hit, we're hit, everybody out," Peterson shouted as his controls suddenly went limp! "Get out Jim! "Jim, get out!"

A bomb broke loose from the bomb bay. A message was written on it: "Hey Hitler, take this!" The front of the bomb had a button much like a electric door bell ringer. It came forward and pressed into the co-pilot's seat. Peterson grabbed the front of the bomb and tried to push it back into the bomb bay. As the button depressed, the bomb began to make a ringing sound like an alarm clock. The message scrolled on the bomb suddenly changed and said, "time's up!" The alarm clock stopped ringing, then there was a loud explosion and a flash. He watched his arms and legs fly separately away from him. Peterson screamed! It was light and then dark, and then red, and then orange and an ugly Black man said, "wake up!"

"Wake up, Skipper," the Black man said, silhouetted by the dim orange glow of the vacuum tubes on the aft bulkhead, "it's only a dream, wake up!" Peterson's hands were shaking and he was sweating profusely. He rolled out of bed the wrong way onto the man beside him.

"SON OF A BITCH," shouted Captain Wong, one of the Ravens!

"Be careful how you address those birds," Captain Whitefeather exclaimed from the bunk on the other side of Peterson, referring to the eagle shaped pins worn by a full-chicken Colonel.

"He's not my commander," Wong retorted!

"TEN HUT," shouted Major Hughs, Wong's commanding officer, who was trying to sleep in one of the swivel chairs below!

"YES SIR, replied Wong, laying on his back saluting! Peterson, on top of him, returned the salute and scrambled out of bed, jumping from the attic loft down to the floor. He stripped off his wool lined leather bomber jacket. The jacket had his W.W.II unit insignia painted on the back—a blue devil throwing a yellow bomb. He very nearly stepped on Gunner O'Connor who was trying to sleep on the floor.

"Can I get you some coffee Sir," asked the Black man, whom Peterson now recognized as Washington, the Second Engineer?

"Sure," the skipper replied. "Sorry Harry," he said to Wong, who did not reply.

"You've had that dream before," asked Washington?

"I used to have it for a while after the war. "This is the first time in years."

"Who's Jim," Washington asked? "You were yelling 'get out Jim!' "Do you mean the VO?"

"No, a buddy I used to fly with in B-24's."

"He make it?"

"No."

"But you weren't shot down."

"He was."

"So he wasn't a member of your crew?"

"In the dream he was my nose gunner."

"So who was your real nose gunner."

"At the time, it was a guy from Boston named Bill MacAtee."

"Did he survive the war?"

"Yes, we completed our twenty five together."

"Well, if I get shot down only in my dreams, I'll say luck is on my side," Washington added.

"You'll need it where we're going," the skipper replied.

"Over Russia?"

"Someplace like that."

Just then, the engines were throttled back. Everyone got a sinking feeling in the pit of their stomachs as the ship started to descend. The skipper quickly gulped down his coffee, strapped on his parachute and helmet, then disappeared head first into the communication tunnel. All of the enlisted men jumped up to pump Washington for information on where they were going. None had ever seen the Squadron Commander so agitated.

The dim orange light from the Radio room's vacuum tubes greeted the Skipper as he emerged from the tunnels. The dim light from the tubes was augmented by the green glow of Beaumont's radar detection scopes, which illuminated his face, giving him a fiendish look. None of the "weathermen," as the crew in the forward compartment were called, had been privy to the skipper's vibrato performance in the aft cabin, so none of them were aware of the conversation the intelligence officers were having over their doubts about his fitness to continue the mission.

As the skipper climbed up to the bridge to see if all was in order, Grant began to get up to vacate the left seat. "Stay put number three," said Peterson, "I've got some business to take care of down here first."

"It will be 20 minutes to final approach," Johns informed his superior. The skipper headed for the urine tube.

A little postage stamp of light became visible in the distance through the big front window. Seeing it, Peterson climbed up to the bridge. Grant made another attempt to get up.

"Stay there son," uttered the skipper. . . "Have you ever landed a B-36 on ice before?"

"No Sir, I have not Sir," the young pilot answered. Thule† was almost at the North Pole on the Northwestern corner of Greenland. It had been night for three months.

"There is always a first time," said Peterson, as he motioned for Murphy to move over. "Land the ship!"

"Prepare for final approach," announced Grant over the interphone." Murphy slid into Washington's seat behind Johns.

†Thule — pronounced Too'lee

Peterson turned Murphy's seat around to face forward so he could watch the young man's performance. A flat topped mountain called "Old Dundas" or "Umanaq" by the Eskimos reached up out of the black to grab planes that went off course.

"Okay, here it goes," said Grant. He turned off the autopilot. Johns instinctively made a grab for the controls, then stopped himself, smiling broadly. Grant gently rocked the wings until they were on track, then reached over and cracked the throttles open for a few seconds while he maneuvered into position for descent. He could have ordered Murphy to do it, but he liked the feeling of twenty two thousand horsepower in his hand. Realizing he was coming in a little high, he said, "Gear down, flaps down," and then, "Attention all hands, landing positions!" Johns obliged, and after a whir and a few clunks, there was considerably more rushing noise outside the ship. Everyone scrambled to get their helmets and face masks on when they heard Grant announcing the landing. There was a sudden feeling of lift as well as mechanical noises and an even louder rushing sound as the flaps went down.

Grant moved the throttles forward and back a couple of times to adjust the glidepath as he wrestled the unpowered controls of the giant. Washington climbed up from the radio room, but Murphy was in his seat, so he strapped himself to the back of the left seat, which was Grant's usual takeoff and landing position. From Murphy's seat, turned around to face forward, Peterson could watch all of the instrument panels.

Grant pressed his interphone button and began to call out the landing checklist: "Pilot to crew, gear down?"

"Check," answered Johns beside him.

"Left gear?"

"This is Scanner, left down and locked," replied Nakamura from the lower left aft gunsight blister.

"Right Gear?"

"This is Scanner, right down and locked," said O'Connor from the lower right gunsight blister.

"Flaps thirty degrees?"

"Check," said Johns.

Grant continued, "Cowl vents closed?"

"Three diamonds," answered Nakamura.

"Three diamonds," echoed O'Connor.

Normally, Washington handled the six mixture levers and the turbo boost wastegate controls, while Murphy controlled the throttles and prop speed lever. There were two sets of throttles and speed levers, one set for the pilots, on the console between their seats, and one for the engineers on their desk. Grant struggled with his throttles as he adjusted the ship's heading a little to the right to compensate for a sudden crosswind. Murphy did Washington's job.

"Nervous," asked the skipper? Grant fought the controls.

"Don't worry," said Johns, "its only a four million dollar ship. "The Air Force has two hundred fifty of them."

"Only twenty lives are depending on you," reminded Peterson. There are thousands of ground crew and desk warmers who would love to have your job if you don't make it.

As the first of the runway lights began to pass underneath, Grant pulled back on the wheel and the nose shot skyward. He then gently relaxed back pressure and lowered the nose. There were a couple of squeals and vibrations as the main landing gear touched down. "Reverse thrust," the young man commanded! The skipper looked down and clicked the three electric propeller reverse selector switches and pitch control switch on the left rear of the center console to slow down the ship.

"Reverse," commanded Peterson! The engines growled as Grant pushed the six throttle levers forward to full reverse power. Johns then reached for the left front of the console to turn on the landing and navigation lights. A Russian trawler was frozen into the ice just offshore, so the landing had to be done without lights. Unlike a normal fishing trawler, this one had radar and sophisticated listening equipment. They no doubt knew that a plane had landed, but unless they had men on the ice, they did not know what kind of plane. For all they knew, it could have been a B-50 or a KC-97.

The crew in the tower watched the one hundred foot high cloud of snow kicked up by the reversing engines envelop the huge ship as it slowed. It was so cold, more than forty below zero, that a contrail of blowing snow followed the giant down the runway. When the engines started blowing the air forward, the cloud swallowed up the nose of the ship. The pilots could not see anything. "Forward thrust," Grant requested.

The skipper clicked the propeller reverse switch to the normal position, then patted Grant on the shoulder and said, "Nice job Gordon."

"I'll take it from here," insisted Johns.

Because of the ice, the ship had to be steered with the throttles. The brakes and nosewheel steering were almost useless. When on the ground, stepping on the left pedal slowed the left landing gear and made the ship turn left. At least that was the way it was supposed to work in theory. On ice it was a different matter. The skipper clicked the outer two engines into forward thrust and the inner four into reverse. That way Johns could steer the ship with the throttles. He opened the throttle on the rightmost engine and also the throttle on the second engine on the left which was in reverse to make the left turn off the runway and then opened up the leftmost engine to turn right to avoid hitting the hangar. Grant removed his hands from the controls once they became unresponsive, and grasped the nose steering wheel beside his left arm with both hands. The steering wheel was a little smaller than a car steering wheel and the steering column was almost vertical like that of a truck. It had a mushy hydraulic feel. Still, the hundred ton, two hundred thirty foot wide starship could be driven just like a car when it was on the ground. With piles of snow and ice at the edge of the pavement, there was fear of burying the gear if Grant slid off the runway. Johns worked with him to park near the hangar.

MARY
BJORGGESSEN
February 1956

"RISE AND SHINE PUMPJOCKIES," bellowed Davis, the Sergeant in charge of the multi-engine ground crew! The blasting polar winds piled snow drifts against the sides of the barracks, which were converted from walk-in freezers, so deep that even an RB-36's ten engines could not be heard inside. Instead, the foot thick metal covered foam walls reflected and amplified every sound the occupants might make giving Davis the voice of a god as he interrupted the silence: "GET THOSE WHORES OUT OF HERE! . . . "INCOMING PLANE! "There's a big plane out there that needs gas," his voice boomed! "Get your sorry butts out there!"

Four of the men who jumped out of their bunks were naked. They were followed by four chubby Eskimo girls. The men struggled to don their insulated coveralls and inflatable "Mickey Mouse" boots, then flung on their thick parkas. The girl's boots were of hand sinewed sealskin and their parkas were polar bear skin lined with glistening white fur that framed their round faces and button noses beautifully. Some of the girl's parkas were decorated with blue quillwork.

Everyone knew the drill. The girls had to leave for inspections or if the base had visitors. But, it would be wrong for the men to leave their girlfriends out in the cold when it was forty below if they truly loved them, so the girls followed them into the garage where the giant yellow fuel trucks sneezed to life.

"Aaaaaaaaaaaaatchoo," the air starters went, snorting one at a time until all six of the huge engines were started. A smokestack on the six foot long hood of each truck was connected to a long black hose that led the exhaust outside the building. The trucks were much too big to fit on a normal road. Their drivers were proud of their ability to operate the huge vehicles in such a severe climate. Yet, any of the men would leave the base immediately if they were allowed to.

One did not get transferred to Thule by being good at one's job. It was a punishment. One month at Thule counted as two on any other deployment. These guys were the "bad boys" of the Air force. Allowances had to be made for the sake of morale. Their commander, Colonel Cox, who was accused, but not convicted, of being found in bed with an enlisted man's wife, would be surprised if they didn't have their girlfriends with them, so he always gave plenty of warning before inspections.

The six giant fuel trucks moved out of the garage, followed by two fire trucks, an ambulance, a tractor pulling a cargo pallet, a covered command car, two de-icing trucks, four covered Jeeps pulling portable heating units, and two jeeps pulling Auxiliary Power Units. One of the four girls hid in the cargo pallet so Colonel Cox would not see her.

Carefully, the big reconnaissance bomber and the convoy approached each other, sliding as they tried to slow down. As the ship slid to a stop, men got out of the trucks and chocked the wheels. Then, with large hammers, they nailed railroad spikes through the chocks into the ice to prevent the ship from moving. Kewscinski opened the bomb doors and the guy driving the tractor positioned the cargo pallet underneath.

Normally, the engines would be shut down, but such cold weather might damage them, so they were left running, except for the jets. This meant that if the fuel trucks slipped on the ice, they might slide into the whirling propellers—so might a man! Fortunately, the ship was equipped with central point fueling, so all of the hoses could be led over the ground into a receptacle in the bomb bay. Long thick flexible tubes were draped from the heating units into the jet engine intakes to help warm them so they would start when it was time to take off. Murphy and Washington monitored the fuel gauges, tank selector valves and transfer pumps to insure that the fuel ended up in the right place. The de-icing trucks began to spray the tail surfaces and wings with alcohol as men with large wheeled fire extinguishers stood under the wing.

O'Connor and Shultz were in the bomb bay climbing into the wings with Aldis lamps to look for leaks. There was just enough room in the wings behind the fuel tanks and in front of the flaps for a man to crawl. The engines fit close inside their cowlings, but there was enough room for a man to knock ice off of fuel lines and inspect the electrical panels and alternators.

As soon as the skipper climbed down the ladder from the front landing gear well, the forty below zero wind found its way into every zipper, crack, and crevice of his flight suit. He waddled over to the command car where Colonel Cox was waiting with the rest of the men from the ground crew.

"Lets see," Cox began, wearing an identical parka, indistinguishable from his men, "a hundred twenty thousand pounds of 115/145 ethyl octane . . . . that's twenty thousand gallons at thirty cents a gallon, so you owe me six thousand dollars!"

"Sorry friend," the skipper replied, "that's more than I make in a war! "How about we swap the gas for some fresh veggies?"

Cox replied, "I thought you must be one of those ten thousand dollar a year men with five telephones, two secretaries, and a dictograph machine sitting on your desk to be flying around in a four million dollar flying battleship and buying so much gas at once! "But, that's okay, your credit is good at my fillin' station, just pay me back when you get rich. "Sign here, c'mon? "I'll take the veggies in hock, but I can't guarantee they'll be here when you come back for them with so many hungry men freezing in perpetual darkness."

A crew of men began to unload boxes from a cargo pallet hanging in the bomb bay. In wartime, bombers mainly carry bombs, but in peacetime, they mostly carry cargo. There is a tremendous need for supplies at any far-away base, so every available aircraft is pressed into service—even one on a secret mission. Indeed, if 753 showed up without a pallet of fresh bananas, that would actually raise suspicions. A load of supplies easily explained what they were doing there.

When the pallet on board was empty, the man on the tractor pulled the full pallet underneath out from under it. Kewscinski salvoed the racks holding the pallet and it fell onto the packed snow and ice with a crash. That was easier than climbing on top of the ship with winches to lower it down gently in forty below zero weather. Once both pallets were on the ground, the man on the tractor joined them into a train and towed them away.

The skipper signed the requisition forms, thanked Colonel Cox, then got out for his walk around inspection. When he got to the tail of the ship, he wished he had skipped it. Every piece of exposed skin ached from frostbite. Brilliant ethyl alcohol flames dancing out of the dozen turbo exhausts under the wing swirled tauntingly around the propellers, creating an artificial illusion of warmth in the cold black air. Washington had set the mixtures to auto-lean while they were on the ground to try to keep the manifolds at their proper temperatures and the spark plugs from fouling up while the heating units were disconnected.

As the Colonel climbed the ladder in front of the nose wheel, Major Holbrook, the Weather Observer, offered some coffee. "Didn't the forecast call for sun today," Peterson asked as Newcomb secured the boarding ladder and closed the hatch?

"That was Texas," Holbrook answered, "not Alaska!"

"Greenland is supposed to be green," said Newcomb.

"Only in your dreams," assured the meteorologist!

The skipper climbed up to the bridge in time to see the fuel and de-icing trucks pulling away. He tapped Grant on the shoulder, who got up from the left seat and headed for the aft cabin to get some sleep. Peterson sat down. Colonel Cox's command car pulled in front. A man in the back emerged from under the tarp with two orange flashlights signaling to apply brakes. Three men, holding huge wheel chocks high over their heads, began to climb in the back of the little truck. The man with the flashlights waved the ship forward. Major Johns flicked the switch to release the brakes as the skipper was donning his oxygen mask and strapping himself in. They followed the car to the end of the runway, where it turned in a wide arc. Johns held down the right brake and applied power to the left engine while the skipper turned the steering wheel beside his left knee clockwise and then counterclockwise, to line up with the runway, as the command car veered to the opposite side of the runway to head back to the garage.

As the ship slid to a halt, the girl hiding in the bomb bay was having second thoughts about her decision to visit America. As she lay on top of the long communication tunnel, Mary could hear the tube trolley passing through underneath. This caused her some alarm, so she climbed down as the command car was leaving. The turbojets thundered and belched flame as the skipper and Johns started them. As soon as her feet touched the ground, the bomb doors snapped shut, nearly decapitating her. It would be a long walk back to the barracks. She was frightened.

"Full power reverse safety check," ordered the skipper. He reached down to turn off all of the navigation lights except for a taxi light on the nosewheel. The girl had noticed men climbing in and out of the nose wheel well before, so she ran forward and tried to sneak aboard through the nose wheel doors. The boarding ladder was folded against the ceiling in the raised position. She pulled herself up by grabbing the nose doors' pickup arm, which dangled inside the maw of the landing gear well like the uvula of a giant bottom dwelling fish. On the ground, the RB-36 had the appearance of an animal feeding because its nose gear was so much shorter than the main landing struts—low enough for her to pull herself up. Splaying her legs wide apart with a foot on each two inch thick gear door hinge, Mary pushed against the upper entrance door to try to sneak aboard. It was locked. The only latch handle was on the inside. The ship started to move.

"Here we go," said Johns, who had been holding the brakes with both feet. "Release brakes," the skipper commanded . . . "Turbojets full power!" The girl was surprised that the ship accelerated so quickly. She wanted to jump down, but it was moving too fast. She banged on the entrance door to get someone's attention. The men were used to hearing chunks of ice hitting the inside of the wheel well during snowy takeoffs and landings, so no one paid attention to her tapping.

The men in the garage looked out the windows, watching the big silver ship roar by with flaming exhaust and an orange blue glow coming from the turbojets. One of the enlisted men asked Davis, "where's Mary?"

Mary began to regret her decision to visit America. She looked down between her legs at the heavily loaded tires bumping and thumping over the snowy ice. She never thought the ground could move so fast. She banged on the upper entrance door harder, hoping someone would hear her. The men were all sitting in their takeoff positions on the floor of the radio room. The wind was terrible! If she jumped now, she would be squashed flat by the tires. If she waited too long, she would be crushed when the wheels retracted up into the well. Like rock salt out of a shotgun, packed snow flew up and hit her every time the tires slammed through a drift. Her only chance was to jump into the soft snowdrifts at the end of the runway, once the ship was airborne.

Abruptly, the bumping and thumping stopped. She watched in amazement as the end of the runway rapidly fell away under her. She could barely see. The wind turbulence inside the wheel well made her eyes smart. There was nothing below but hard packed ice. Spinning at over one hundred and twenty miles an hour, the giant landing wheels suddenly came toward her. The big taxi light blinded her. The landing leg struck the gear door pickup arm and mashed it against her crotch. The huge spinning tires dug into her thighs, one on each side, chewing into her like the rasping tongues of a giant lamprey licking her flesh off her bones. She screamed as the landing gear doors slammed shut under her feet like the jaws of a monstrous insect. Her pelvis was crushed and pinned between the pickup arm and a structural beam that ran lengthwise along the ceiling. The tires cut like buzz saws into her buttocks and elbows. The light abruptly went out, leaving her in pitch dark. Screaming and crying and screaming again, she banged on the hatch above her. The thought had never occurred to her that airplanes ate people. She had thought the giant ships were only infested with people.

"VO to AC, Skipper, there's something wrong with the nose gear," warned Newcomb, sitting on the floor of the radio room with his back directly against the landing gear bay. "It's making some real strange squealing noises."

"Oh shit," answered Peterson! Because of the trawler just offshore, a dangerous chandelle maneuver had to be performed just after takeoff to fly past Old Dundas. Major Johns and the skipper flew the ship together as a team. Both of them struggled to keep the giant exactly 100 feet off the ice. Peterson was looking over his shoulder and leveling out whenever the wingtip kicked up snow. The Russians would cheer at the size of the fireball a fully loaded RB-36 with two days worth of gas on board would make if it splattered into the side of the invisible flat topped mountain.

"Okay, were on one ten, level out," Johns said. The skipper leveled out and stopped turning.

"There's still some strange noises coming from the nose gear," reminded Newcomb.

"What kind of noises," asked Peterson?

"Squealing and banging noises!"

"Better check it out then!"

Newcomb and Kewscinski, the Photonavigator, got up

from the floor and scrambled back to their seats in the forward cabin. Because the belly of the ship was curved, the forward cabin had a rather small floor—the whole fuselage being a giant tube twelve and a half feet in diameter. Newcomb opened the hatch to the landing gear well. A dour, teary eyed, round faced Eskimo girl starred up at them, bawling bitterly. "Yelber my," she screamed! "Hender en laiger. "Tilkahl straks en laigert! Newcomb and Kewscinski looked at each other in dismay. The boarding ladder, which was folded up against the hatch, trapped her in the well like prison bars. She cried.

"Skipper, you're not going to believe this," Newcomb exclaimed over the interphone after he plugged in his jack!

"Did we roll a bearing?"

"No sir."

"Leak in the oleo strut?"

"No sir."

"Well, what is it," Peterson demanded?

"We have a stowaway, sir!"

"A what?"

"A stowaway, sir . . . a little Eskimo boy!"

The rear compartment exploded in laughter as they could hear what was said over the interphone. "Well, they got to cancel the mission now," exclaimed Wong, looking under his bunk at Hughs, who was trying to sleep in the swivel chair immediately below. Major Hughs jumped out of his seat, snorted, and disappeared head first into the sixty foot tunnel, laying down on the tube trolley to begin the laborious process of pulling himself hand over hand to the photo lab, which was steeply uphill since the ship was climbing. He violated regulations by not first donning his air bottle and parachute which were required in the tunnel in case of a decompression accident.

"An Eskimo," Peterson asked again, not quite believing his ears?

"Yessir," Newcomb repeated.

---

† Hjælpe mig! Hente en læge! Tilkald straks en læge! — Help me! Bring a doctor. Call quickly a doctor!

"Wait a minute; how long before the turn Duane?"

"I don't know, sir," answered the Navigator. "Just a minute, sir." Nawrocki struggled past them to get from his takeoff position on the floor of the radio room to the front desk to look at his chart. Nawrocki's desk curved around in front of the left side of the giant observation window so that he could record what he saw on a map. Since it was dark, the giant front window of the ship just let in the bitter cold. He had to turn on his desk lamp to read his chart. "Coming up in six minutes," he replied over the girl's tearful wailing!

By then, Hughs had made it up past the obstacle course in the photo lab and past the men in the radio room who had risen from their posts to get a look at the little black head sticking out of the landing gear well. "I think we should end this," he said to Kewscinski.

Mary continued to cry, scream, and yell, "Yelber my! "Hender en laiger."

"End the mission, why? "Because of a little Eskimo boy? "Ship ain't go'in down; not low on fuel," Kewscinski protested?

"You didn't see the performance Mike gave in the aft cabin just before we landed," explained Hughs. "Besides, how are we going to get him out of there without lowering the gear? "We cant just leave him in there. "It looks like he's smashed up pretty good. "He seems to be in pain. "Maybe his back is broke."

Mary tearfully repeated, "Yelber my! "Tilkahl straks en laiger." She continued to cry.

"What do you mean Mike's performance," asked the Photonavigator?"

"He had a bad dream and jumped on Harry's chest."

"So?"

"Then he lets Grant make the final approach."

"Everybody has a first time," Kewscinski answered. "I was kinda hoping he'd bust the gear or something, considering where we are going."

"There are too many things going wrong," protested Hughs. "I'm surprised that Eskimo is still breathing the way he's smashed in there." Mary continued to sob and cry.

"Mike got his bad dreams flying those iron coffin B-24's," explained Kewscinski. "There never was such a clap trap piece of junk that tried to pull itself skyward. "He survived 26 missions when a lot of his buddies didn't make it. "As for Grant, he'll probably have bad dreams about this mission."

"I know I'll have bad dreams about it," Hughs finished. "As for Grant, he looked pretty pleased with himself when he climbed into bed."

"Okay skipper, turn left to zero zero five mark seven," Nawrocki said over the interphone, "continue climb at five hundred feet per minute."

"Roger, zero zero five mark seven," repeated Johns.

"I'm coming down," said Peterson.

"Well, how are we going to get him out of there," asked Hughs? "As soon as we lower the gear, he'll fall to his death."

"So what," exclaimed Newcomb! "Its what he deserves." Mary sobbed.

"Haven't you ever dreamed of stowing away on a plane when you were a kid," asked Holbrook, as he made his way to his gunner's seat in the nose beside Nawrocki?

"Maybe we can attach a safety strap to him so he can dangle when we lower the gear," suggested Kewscinski.

"What are you going to attach a safety strap to? "He's not wearing a parachute harness," replied Newcomb!

The skipper descended down the steps and glared at Mary silently. "What is your name," he said to the girl?

She was frightened and didn't answer, then shreiked, "Yelber my! "Hender en laiger!"

"What language is that," asked Peterson?

"Probably Eskimo, sir," suggested Hughs.

"Maybe he's mentally retarded," accused Kewscinski.

"Most of them are," stated Newcomb, "that's why they're so primitive. "It's in their genes."

"Mary sobbed and screamed, "Yelber my. "Versa venlee, kurr my til en laiger†!"

† Hjælpe mig! Vær så venlig, kør mig til en læge! — Help me! Please, take me to a doctor!

"Maybe you can disconnect the boarding ladder from the bulkhead," suggested Hughs.

"Hernandez," shouted Newcomb, "bring me your tool kit!" Hernandez passed a crescent wrench through the toilet compartment. Newcomb began unbolting the ladder from the forward bulkhead inches from the girl's face. "Dammit, I dropped a nut," he cursed!

"Well, we won't need to use the landing gear again for a couple of days," said Kewscinski, "but you better have it fixed by tomorrow night, 'cause I really would like to be able to land when this is all over."

"We'll be landing sooner than that if we can't get this cabin pressurized," warned Peterson. "He'll freeze to death if we just leave him there."

"Help me," said Newcomb, as he disconnected the remaining bolts and shoved the ladder to the side. Mary was finally quiet. There was just enough room for her head and arms to squeeze through. Newcomb and Kewscinski pulled her out of the narrow hole like taffy. She screamed from her bleeding wounds.

"What is your name," the skipper repeated toward the sobbing girl as they set her down on the floor?

She replied tearfully, rubbing bloody sores on her back and legs, "Mahnger tak†!"

"Okay, Mahngertak, what are you doing here?"

Mary frowned and said, "Aw yay bear‡!"

"You saw a bear," Kewscinski asked? Mary didn't understand. "He can't be more than ten," the Photonavigator continued.

"Dammit," exclaimed the skipper! Mary wept.

"Are you going to turn back, sir," asked Hughes?

"Turn back? "Is there any reason why we shouldn't continue the mission?"

"You can't take a child into Russia," Hughs asserted! Hernandez, poking his head in from the radio room

† Mange tak — Thank you very much
‡ Å, jeg be'r — That's all right

immediately recoiled with alarm because the enlisted men had not been briefed as to where the ship was heading.

"Aren't there children in Russia," answered Peterson?

"Are you sure you want to continue," asked Kewscinski?

"I'll have egg all over my face if I don't," the skipper retorted. "I gave my word I would do it. "Are there any obstacles to completing the mission?"

"It would help, sir, if I knew what the mission was," interrupted Lieutenant Beaumont, who was poking his head in beside Hernandez. Just then, Hernandez, heard a "beep bah beep beep beep bah beep" in his headset, which he was always required to wear, even if he sometimes left one ear uncovered. "Sir, we have an incoming coded message."

"Is it for us," the skipper asked?

"I believe so, sir."

"Put it on the interphone." Hernandez sat back at his desk and flicked a switch. Soon the entire crew was practicing their Morse. The skipper was given four versions in his hands. Mary sat cross legged on the floor and rubbed her sores. The message was short: "J6LXM7XOXOXOXO."

"Well that's it, they gave us the go," the skipper said to Kewscinski. He pulled on the small beaded silver chain that held his dog tag around his neck until a small manila envelope appeared from under the chest of his flight suit. Hughs did the same. They opened their pouches and pulled out pages labeled J6LXM7. Peterson read aloud what was written on the paper folded inside: "Duane," he said to the Navigator, "our orders are as follows: one, proceed to staging area grid coordinates one zero one point two two four and orbit; two, intercept civilian Aeroflot aircraft bound from Khantayka and follow in formation with said aircraft to Omsk; three, perform low level triangular stereoscopic photography over town in Kazakhstan called Tyura-tam; four, overfly secondary targets Ur-rum-chi, An-si, Chi-chuan, Lin-fen, Kat-feng, Nan-ching, Hsu-chow, and Shanghai. "I don't think I need to tell you what country that's in . . . "And five: Land in Okinawa to await further orders." He handed him the paper.

Nawrocki looked at him with a look of utter horror as he took the letter and squeaked a feeble "Yes sir."

"I knew it," exclaimed Beaumont! "Once they started strapping those cameras to the gunsights, I knew we were going to Russia. "Why this little village in Kazakstan? "There's nothing there! "They're just trying to get us shot at."

"Sorry Bob," Peterson replied, "I can't say anything more. "Does anyone know of any reasons these orders cannot be carried out?"

"I'll have the boarding ladder reattached in a few minutes," said Newcomb, "but we won't be able to use it with this nut missing. "As soon as the doors open, it will fall to the ground and be lost forever. "We'll never get it back." Everyone stared at the girl then back at Peterson silently. Mary looked down at the floor as she rubbed her wounds with a sad expression.

"Very well, you have your orders," said the Aircraft Commander! He looked at the girl. "Send the boy aft . . . I'll be at my post." He ascended the steps and sat down in the commander's chair. Hughs followed him to the bridge to have a private conversation.

Talk immediately erupted in the radio room below: "What does the 'XOXOXOXO' mean," asked Holbrook?

"Kisses for good luck," answered Beaumont.

"General Allen has a sense of humor that way," added Kewscinski.

"That's only because he doesn't have to come with us, sir," quipped Hernandez.

"John, would you mind telling me what all these cameras on the gunsights are about," asked the Weather Observer, pointing at his periscopic gunsight in the nose?

"Well, you'll probably find out anyway," Kewscinski answered, "the Rooskies've got a new plane called the MiG-19 that they think can shoot down a B-36. "They want us to find out if it can shoot down the B-52."

"So this Kazakstan business is just a ruse . . . to get us shot at?"

"No, there really is something there in Kazakstan that they want us to photograph."

"Something worth putting twenty lives at risk, now twenty one," he asked, pointing at the girl?

"If what they think is there . . . yes," answered the Photonavigator.

"We had better get him aft," suggested Newcomb.

"Agreed," answered Kewscinski. "Come here," he said to the girl. Mary stared up at him sheepishly.

Kewscinski and Newcomb reached down and lifted her off the floor by her armpits. Mary screamed and fought to free herself, but the two of them were too strong for her. They manhandled her into the radio room. Forcing her down, they inserted her head into the tunnel to the photo lab. Mary blocked her arms against the sides of the tunnel and screamed, "Nay, stop!" For all she knew, the icy cold passageway led outside the ship.

"Dammit," yelled Newcomb, "go!"

"Move," hollered Kewscinski, "or I'll whip your ass!" He violently shoved her into the photo lab and followed her through the tunnel, poking her injured buttocks. Once in the lab, despite her screams, the two of them again grabbed her by the armpits and manhandled her onto the tube trolley, violently dragging her over the multicameras.

"Ow," cried Mary, as she bumped her knee on the camera chassis. She sobbed as the corners of the film backs dug into her sores. When she tried to fight back, the two of them just lifted her off the floor and shoved her into the tunnel head first.

"That'll do it," said Kewscinski as he gave her a push.

"Problem solved," said Newcomb! He slapped his hands together with a glancing blow.

"He's Merril's problem now," seconded the Photonavigator.

Mary did not know that she was supposed to use her feet to slow down. The ship had not finished climbing, so it was downhill to the aft cabin. She got moving so fast, that when she got to the other end, she flew out of the tunnel head first, like Supergirl, and landed in the arms of Airman Nakamura, who was attempting to sleep near his gunsight. Both of them screamed. Wong, who was still in his bunk, was awakened by the commotion. He laughed when he saw someone else had become the victim.

It was warmer in the aft cabin than it was in the front of the ship and Mary's sores were hurt again in the fall, so she took off her parka and dropped down her chaps to rub the places where the tires had abraided her skin. She did not really have pants. Each leg was a separate piece of polar bear fleece with a long slit in the middle so she could go to the bathroom outdoors without removing them. Like most Inuit, she did not wear conventional clothing underneath.

All the men starred at her in amazement and some of them whistled. The fact that her bare legs were covered with sores and blood drips did nothing to discourage them. Sandringham and O'Connor both yelled, "Oh Nellie," in a chorus. Immediately recognizing the unusual attention from the men as being the same as she usually received at the base in Thule, she instinctively raised her arms behind her head and arched her back, pointing her young breasts at them with a goofy smile on her face. The men at Thule always liked that. Calabrese and O'Connor, both devout Catholics, began crossing themselves. She might have been a frowney, round-faced Eskimo girl, but her figure showed not a little Danish heritage. The men forgot all about having to go to Russia.

"What's the matter O'Connor," asked Sandringham, "never seen a naked woman before?"

"NO," answered the waist gunner! "Is she an angel from God?" The men burst out laughing.

"Don't have any sisters then I take it," continued the tail gunner?

"I have one, but I'd kill her if she took off her clothes in front of men like that, and I certainly ain't no peeping tom," answered the Irishman.

"Go on Sandy, toss her a quarter; see if she'll bend over backwards for you," suggested Shultz!

"No Howie, just put the coin in the slot," Sandringham answered! "Maybe she'll sing and dance."

"You guys are sick," said Nakamura, who discovered he was soiled by some specks of Mary's blood.

"Do you suppose a silver dollar would fit," Shultz egged Nakamura on?

"Bigger than what you got to put in there," answered Sandringham!

"Save that talk for the barracks," thundered the Second Raven, Captain Whitefeather, from his bunk, "she's from a different culture. "She doesn't know any better."

When Mary saw the Captain was a Native American, she immediately assumed he was an Eskimo and tried to talk to him in her own language. She was confused that he didn't understand so she said, "Day gladder my ad treffer dem†."

Then Captain Wong interrupted, asking, "Tal nee Svensk‡," leaning over the edge of his bunk to look at her below?

"Dansk," she answered.

"Vad hayterr day name*?"

Mary could barely understand him, but she answered "Mary."

"I didn't know you spoke Eskimo," remarked Whitefeather as he climbed down from the bunk?

"It's not Eskimo," Wong answered, "it's Danish."

"How do you know its Danish?"

"She said so."

"I didn't know you knew Danish!"

"Not Danish, Swedish!"

"But you just said she spoke Danish."

"Yes, but I know Swedish."

"How can you understand her then?"

"The Swedes have a saying that Danish is the easiest

---

† Det glæder mig at træffe Dem — A pleasure to meet you
‡ Talar Ni svensk? — Do you speak Swedish?
* Vad heter det namn? — What is your name?

language in the world," answered the Chinese man; "no matter how badly you speak it, you will always speak better than a Dane." The big Indian frowned. "Mary vad," Wong continued?

"Mary Beorjessen," she answered.

"Obviously, she is only half Eskimo," said Wong. "Her father must have been Danish. "The Danes colonized Greenland, you know. She must have learned Danish from them."

"All right Mary," said Grant. Asleep, he had missed the episode in the front of the ship. When he looked over the edge of his bunk and saw a naked girl on board, he assumed he was dreaming. Grant continued, "Now we've got our own red light district," half wondering if he was still asleep. "I think I've been without a woman for too long!"

"Well sir," replied Shultz, "we've got exactly what you need. "You won't mind then if we all take advantage of the situation?"

"Not at all, Sergeant," exclaimed the young officer! Wong and Whitefeather looked at each other disdainfully.

"All right," cheered Sandringham! He and Shultz clapped and rubbed their hands together.

"Lieutenant, control your men," ordered Whitefeather, looking up at Grant! "So where did you learn Danish," he asked Wong, who was still in bed, laying beside the young co-pilot?

"I told you, not Danish," answered Wong, his head bent over the edge of his bunk, "Swedish, I mean she talks Danish and I can speak some Swedish and they are similar enough that she can understand me."

"Well," the big Indian insisted, "I think you should start by making her understand that on nuclear bombers of the United States Strategic Air command, Eighth Air Force, Seventh Bomb Wing, Four Hundred Ninety Second Reconnaissance Squadron, we do not walk around in the buff!"

There was an explosion of laughter. "Ask her why she stowed away," suggested O'Connor.

Wong translated, then after hearing her answer, he said, "She wants to visit America."

"Tell her she is a foolish, stupid girl," insisted Whitefeather, "this ship is going to Russia, not America. "America is in the opposite direction!" The enlisted men on the floor rolled and squirmed, slapping their knees with laughter, then abruptly stopped laughing as they realized what the Second Raven had said.

Wong refused. "Her mother was probably a whore, just like her, and gave her her daddy's name," he said, "I can't imagine a Roald Amundsen type would marry a dumpy Eskimo woman."

"Roald Amundsen was Norwegian," corrected the big Indian. "They'll marry their own daughters if their sweat lodge is dark enough!"

"What's the difference," Wong quipped, "she'd only be able to find an Eskimo husband there. "In the States, she'll have better prospects. "By the way, a Norwegian sweat lodge is called a sauna."

"Well you marry her then."

"Sorry, ain't got no use for fallen women. "My Eunice is woman enough for me," the Third Raven answered.

It had taken Hughs a bit of time to crank the tube trolley back to the photo lab with its little wire and pulley system. The trolley ran on rails and was connected to a thin, one hundred twenty foot cable that looped around a pulley at each end of the tunnel. The front pulley had a crank, so it could be used to transfer food and coffee from one cabin to the other. The ship had leveled off; so Hughs had to pull himself through with the rope on the ceiling. He heard the laughter even above the drone of the engines, which everyone on board had become used to, but he did not know what it was about.

Even while still in the tube, he could see Mary's buttocks, so he yelled, "get him covered up . . . what are you all a bunch of perverts?" Startled, Mary turned around. Hughs' jaw fell open as he emerged upside down from the tunnel. Craning his neck until the top of his head rested on the floor, he gasped when he saw Mary's upside down pubis and said, "That eunuch Kewscinski said that . . . that . . . was a boy!" There was another explosion of laughter. Angered, Hughs commanded, "cover her up!" Upside down, his frown was mistaken for a smile and that made the men laugh even more.

"Aw shoot," protested Grant, looking at him from over the edge of his bunk!

"Have a heart, Major," pleaded Sandringham.

"Throw me a blanket," Whitefeather commanded Wong. He held the blanket open in front of him and moved toward Mary. She jumped out of her furry chaps and sealskin boots, climbing over Nakamura. Shultz, Sandringham, and Grant hollered and yelled as though a girl had fallen off the stage at a strip club. The Indian started chasing the naked girl with the blanket. Mary wasn't sure of his intentions. She screamed as her sores were groped painfully by the men on the floor.

"OLE, El Toro," Grant urged from the bunk as he threw his blanket down to Gunner O'Connor! O'Connor began chasing her behind the Indian.

Whitefeather finally had her cornered back where she started, between the tunnel and the port gunsight. When she lunged right at him, he caught her in the blanket. "Anybody have any way to secure this piece of gear," he hollered, as she frantically struggled to free herself, screaming?

"Ow," shouted O'Connor, as he blanketed her from the other side!

"What's the matter," asked Hughs, still trapped in the tunnel?

"The little minx," answered the gunner, "She bit me!"

"Human bites are the worst," advised Nakamura.

"How about a paper tack," offered Wong?

"If it's a big one it might work. "I'll hold it, you push it through," advised Whitefeather. Wong twisted the ends like a wire so it would be secure. As soon as they let her go, she tried to pull the blanket off over her head, shamelessly exposing her entire figure except for her head and arms.

As she fell over backward, Sandringham and Shultz hooted and hollered and whistled, slapping their knees. "Baby,

baby, baby," added O'Connor has he applied pressure to his bleeding thumb. Mary arched her back so that her firm young breasts pointed straight into the air—inches from Hughs' face. Her loins were visible to all.

"I guess we don't need to worry about morale on this trip," quipped Whitefeather.

"Didn't your intelligence training prepare you for this eventuality," mocked Wong?

"I hereby nominate her as Morale Officer," quipped O'Connor!

"I thought you said she was a minx," accused Shultz!

"I don't mind being bitten by a creature with skin as smooth as that," the Irishman answered.

"You'll have to take that up with the skipper, Sergeant," Wong smiled. "I'm not sure he will want a morale officer who bites."

When she realized she could not remove the blanket, Mary covered herself and picked up her parka, instantly bursting into tears. She saw the bloody black marks on the parka's elbows and buttocks left by the spinning tires, but she had not had an opportunity to examine the back where it had been ripped to shreds. There were several holes where it had been worn right through. Virtually half of it was blackened by carbon from the tires. She pulled a large bone needle and some sinew out of her right boot and sat down on the floor. She cried as she sewed the holes closed. No amount of spitting and rubbing or wetting the black area would remove the stain.

"In her culture, industriousness and craftsmanship are more valuable than beauty," commented Whitefeather. "A torn parka suggests carelessness and stupidity."

"Oh no, she wet her pants," shouted O'Connor with a look of disgust!

"Oh god, it stinks," exclaimed Shultz!

"Give her some soap," suggested Calabrese, his face contorted in horror.

"You had better show her how to use the toilet," Hughs commanded angrily, still trapped inside the tunnel. "I don't want her defecating on the floor."

"Yessir," answered Wong. "Den hair vaigernt," he said as he grabbed Mary by the arm and somberly pulled her behind the curtain.

† Den här vägen — This way

"Navigator to AC,

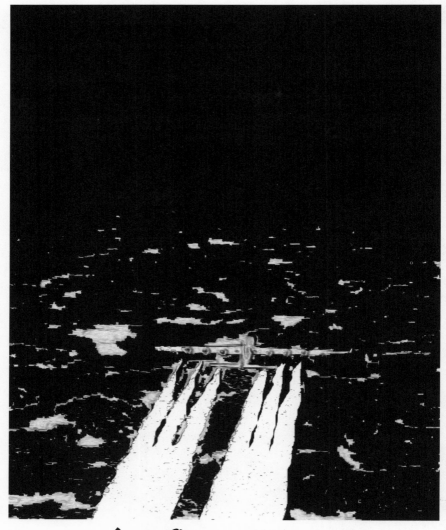

we're flying over the North Pole!"

THE NORTH POLE
February 1956

"Attention all hands, this is AC," announced the skipper over the interphone. "For those who are interested, we're overflying the North Pole right now. "Its about 80 miles on the left. "Now you can say you have seen it and brag about it."

"But it's dark, sir," exclaimed Nawrocki, as he got his bubble sextant out of its case and climbed up into the Plexiglas astrodome on top of the cockpit. He shot a fix to prove he was there. Off in the distance, a white light flashed randomly from 099's forward gunsight bubble as Hernandez carried on a conversation in Morse code with the other radio man using his Aldis lamp.

"Hank," asked Peterson, looking across the center cockpit console, "why is it you never put up for transfer into B-47's? "Why stay with the RB-36? "They're due to be scrapped you know. "They'll assign you to a desk if you stay here too long. "Why not switch to jets?"

"I just don't like the tactics, that's all."

"You mean you don't like bombing people?"

"I've bombed enough people. "The H-bomb is different. "It's not just an A-bomb. "It works on the same power as the sun, the greatest power in the universe. "I'm not sure I want so much power."

"You mean the power to play god," Peterson laughed?

"I mean the power of the stars," answered Johns. "An H-bomb is an artificial man-made star on the surface of the Earth as powerful as the sun."

"So your main objection is religious. "Man is now equal with his maker?"

"Yes, I am a religious man and the H-bomb is not something I want to mess around with. "The purpose of war is to win victory. "What is the point of utterly destroying whatever it is you are fighting for?"

"The Communists know that in an atomic war every civilian is going to be killed," Peterson explained. "They want to skulk below the ground in bunkers a mile deep and come out like rats when it is over. "The H-bomb is the ultimate bunker buster, using the power of God against buried Communists. "If we target plane after plane on the same spot until there's a hole a mile wide and a mile deep, the Commies will know that they personally will be held accountable and they won't even think about trying to conquer Europe. "The Commies need to know that there is no hole deep enough for them to hide in that will protect them from the power Our Lord has trusted upon us."

"So you think flying nuclear bombers is a noble profession," asked the second in command?

"Better to deter aggression than to have to fight."

"Just one question," Johns asked, "there will be multiple H-bombs on each target; so what happens when a guy is on his way to his Emergency War Plan site and one of these artificial suns goes off in front of him?"

"We give them eye patches," answered the Colonel. "If a bomb goes off, you say to yourself, 'okay, now I'm blind in one eye,' so you move the eyepatch to the other eye and keep on flying until you're blind in both eyes."

"Then what?"

"Geez," interrupted Murphy, who was sitting back to back with him, "when the 153rd started wearing eye patches and calling themselves the 'pirate squadron' after they got their '47's; I thought that was just a gag."

"Its no gag," answered Peterson! . . . "Then your co-pilot takes over."

"Do you remember reading in the Bible," asked Johns, "how God warned Moses not to look him in the face?"

"I believe he wore a veil after that," answered Peterson.

"Is that what happens when you're blind in both eyes," asked Murphy, "you wear a veil? "What about when both pilots are blind in both eyes?"

"By that time, you'll be close enough to the target for your navigator to get you there with radar," explained the skipper.

"Is that why they removed all the windows from the nose of the 'E' model," asked Johns, "so the navigator will always be able to see his radar camera?"

"Yes."

"Then what," inquired the First Engineer, "how do you land?"

"Convair is working on a new type of B-36 called the Crusader with a radiation proof cockpit," answered Peterson. "You may have seen it take off. "It will solve most of the problems of thermonuclear combat."

"This is Navigator, its about time to start our descent," Nawrocki announced over the interphone. The constant din of the engines became suddenly noticeable in its absence. Hughs, Wong, and Whitefeather took that as their cue to start monitoring Communist radio transmissions, so they got out of bed to get ready for work. Mary climbed up into the vacant bunk beside Grant, who was asleep. Hernandez got up and flashed the message to 099 with his Aldis lamp so as not to break radio silence. A light flashed from 099's right forward gun bubble with the Morse for "message received."

"AC to crew," announced the skipper over the interphone, "just so you know what's going on, we've been ordered to intercept a Russian civilian airliner and follow it through the Soviet radar perimeter, so gunners man your posts, but don't shoot at anything unless you are ordered to do so. "There are some things there that Fort Fumble wants some pictures of. "It has been sixteen hours since we left Texas. "Back home, its morning," Peterson continued. "When it is day in the United States, it is night in Russia. "The Russians are on their night shift and they are drowsy. "We are on our day shift, so there is no excuse for everybody not performing at our best. "Bob, do you have anything yet?"

"Radio to AC, I'm getting reflected signals from ground clutter," answered Beaumont, as the glowing green screen of the panoramic pulse analyzer he was watching gave his face a fiendish look. "I don't see anything that looks like our airliner yet."

Beaumont's screen was a little more than three inches across. It would violate radio silence for Newcomb to send out radar pulses, so the head radio operator tuned his two APR-4 radar search receivers to the frequency of the Russian search radar and, by remote control, rotated the parabolic dish antenna in the chin blister under the nose of the ship to look for planes.

The problem with this method was, depending on where the pulses were coming from, they always gave a false reading. The direction to the target was correct, but the range was always wrong. The signals were so faint, that spikes on his screen were often lost in static. He set the screen to display a green glowing horizontal line. Planes showed up as little glowing peaks or spikes sticking up from the line. He adjusted the amplitude on the screen so that the original pulse from the radar went beyond the top of the screen. Secondary pulses reflected from planes made smaller spikes in the line to the right of the main pulse. The trick was to compare the distance of the spike from the main pulse of the Russian radar station to the smaller one reflected from the plane. Once he found a target by rotating the parabolic antenna, he could measure the amount of time in milliseconds it took for the secondary pulse reflected from the other plane to be detected after the main pulse from the ground radar had been received. He counted the number grid lines etched on the glass face of the screen between the two spikes. for any given direction, the longer the time delay, the farther away the target was.

"Radio to AC, target one five seven," hollered Beaumont in his sing-song Louisiana Cajun accent.

"What course," asked the skipper?

"It looks like two-twenty," he answered.

"It must be our plane. "Everybody! "Helmets on, chutes on! "Prepare for collision. "Steering to intercept . . . call out if you see anything." Everyone donned parachutes, helmets, and face masks, except for Grant, who was asleep. The communication tube was sealed shut during formation flying to reduce the risk of a decompression accident. Flying formation in an aircraft as large as an RB-36, without power assisted controls, was hardly more sophisticated than two ships managing to travel in the same direction at the same time without hitting each other. The trouble was, the pilot of the Russian airliner did not know he was supposed to be the leader in a giant game of tag.

Holbrook kneeled down at his periscopic sight to man the nose guns. If Peterson was wrong and the target was military, he might have to defend the ship. "White and green navigation lights ahead," Holbrook announced. He could see farther through the sight. The two ten-engined flying naval vessels were lit only by their cockpit instrument lights and a dim orange glow from the vacuum tubes.

"I see them," the skipper said. "Activate secret weapon!"

Beaumont watched the waveform on his pulse analyser screen change from jagged spikes to a crisp green sine wave as his jamming transmitter synched to the incoming radar beam. "Secret weapon activated," Beaumont answered. The civilian airliner disappeared momentarily from Russian radar.

The skipper adjusted the throttles to match speed with the airliner. It was a Russian copy of a lend-lease C-47 that had been converted for civilian use. The C-47 was the military version of the twin engine DC-3, the most popular civilian airliner in the United States. The flying battleship loomed up behind the little airliner. Except for not having any five inch guns, the RB-36 was larger and more heavily armed than a Navy destroyer.

Behind the flying battleship, approached the flying

aircraft carrier. When both ships were in position, the skipper ordered, "Deactivate secret weapon." Beaumont clicked the jammer switch off. "You can turn on the formation lights now." Johns flicked a switch and three blue lights lit up on the top of each wing tip and the tail, along with a white light on the top and bottom of the fuselage and two dim amber tail lights for 099 to follow.

753 was flying behind and below the airliner in the same position a B-47 would if it was taking on fuel from a KC-97 tanker. As the airliner's tail wheel loomed dangerously close to the canopy, Johns asked, "Aren't we supposed to protect civilians?"

"Its no different than taking on fuel," said the skipper. The GRB-36, with the RF-84 Thunderflash slung underneath, took a similar position behind and beneath 753, wearing no lights at all. The two 20mm cannon in the nose came up in front of the windscreen and pointed at the airliner. "Nosegunner," yelled Peterson! "Put those guns away!"

"Yes Sir," answered Holbrook.

"What are you trying to do, shoot them down," hollered Kewscinski, the Photo Navigator, from his seat behind and to the left of Holbrook at the navigation desk?

"What did you say," asked Holbrook as he turned around and released the action switch on the side of his hand grip? The guns immediately drooped to their parked position, pointing downward in front of the huge front window. "I thought I'd brag when we get back that I actually aimed my guns at a Russian plane."

"That'll be worth a few drinks," quipped Newcomb.

"I just hope we don't have to shoot them for real by the time we get to Okinawa," said Kewscinski, sitting beside him.

Washington looked out the window from his rearward facing seat behind Johns and said, "Marv, look at that green glow on the wings."

"It must be the tail light of the airliner," the Chief Engineer replied.

"No, that's not bright enough," said the Second Engineer. "We must be in the aurora borealis." The two engineers stared upward in amazement as a green curtain descended over all three ships. It seemed to extend to the East and West as far as their eyes could see. Sparks ran along the wires that led up to the tailfin and the wires that ran between the masts alongside the fuselage as Saint Elmo's fire descended on the ship. Two vacuum tubes blew out in Beaumont's radio set.

"Dammit," Hernandez cursed as he removed the blackened glass with a pair of insulated pliers and replaced the tubes with spares. Excited by the aurora, Nawrocki ascended up to the astrodome with his sextant to shoot a fix. The view of the airliner flying through the aurora was spectacular. His fix took longer than usual. He ended up taking two sights as an excuse to stay longer on the bridge.

Cupping his eyes against the tiny airplane window, a boy named Sasha, the son of the Political Commissar of the Lower Tunguska region asked, "Dada, kak da†?" The commissar, who could not see out because of the bright interior lighting, gave him a pencil and paper and invited him to draw a picture of what he saw.

† Дада, как да? — Uncle, what's that?

THE AIRLINER

February 1956

"This is Raven, I'm picking up some civilian radio transmissions," announced Whitefeather over the interphone from the mission control room. The mission control room was the most secret part of the ship. The sixty foot long communication tube passed right through this room so that crewmen could travel from one end of the ship to the other without being able to see inside. Converted from the aft bomb bay, the mission control room had a green painted cantilever truss along the sides to support the weight of the bombs that normally hung there. Unlike other parts of the ship, which had to be kept dark to preserve the gunner's vision, two bright lights lit the windowless room and a large wall map of every known radar installation in Russia and China covered the truss on the port side, hiding the tube. To save weight, the converted cabin was not pressurized, so three space suits were hung on a rack at the front bulkhead for the intelligence officers to wear at high altitude.

The right side of the cabin was covered with sophisticated black boxes covered with dials and switches connected by white bundles of wire cables to three rotating parabolic Ferret antennas that hung down in blisters under the ship. Each antenna had four radio tuners and two receivers as well as green panoramic pulse analyzer screens like Beaumont had.

Normally this equipment would fit in the aft cabin, but on a full blown radio intelligence mission, two of everything was carried. Two large gray Norelco magnetic tape recorders were mounted on the trusses above each man's console. These were far superior to the primitive magnetic wire recorders most RB-36's had, but they had to be kept warm or the celluloid tapes would break. Magnetic tape crumbles to confetti at seventy below zero. A dozen eight inch clear plastic tape reels rotated in a row, recording various civilian and military broadcasts. As with the electronics in the front of the ship, the covers of some black boxes had been removed to save weight, exposing the many silver covered vacuum tubes.

Although the bomb racks made the room seem smaller than the other cabins, the overall rectangular shape of the room made it seem more like an ordinary room on the ground, not unlike one of the portable communications trailers that are used to set up an emergency airfield. A insulated cabinet on the aft bulkhead held additional magnetic tape reels.

"AC to Ravens, what's on the radio," asked Peterson, busy at having to hand fly the giant ship so close to the airliner.

"Tommy Dorsey," Whitefeather replied, as he fine tuned the dials on one of his four sophisticated receivers.

"Well, put it on the interphone so everyone can hear!" After hearing the "Moonlight Serenade," which seemed very appropriate even though there was no moon, they heard "Old Man River" sung by Paul Robeson, before a voice started announcing in Russian.

"What is he saying," asked the skipper?

"He's saying what a good thing it is that he is not a slave like Paul Robeson," answered Whitefeather. "He says he is grateful that he lives in a country where there is no slavery or capitalist exploitation."

"That's stupid! "Doesn't he know Paul Robeson is a millionaire?"

"I guess not," answered Whitefeather. "He says that Paul Robeson is not allowed to sing or he will be beaten!" Chuckles could be heard through the ship from the other crewmen overhearing the conversation on their headsets. "Now he says Paul Robeson is a prisoner and he is not allowed to leave the country," Whitefeather continued.

"Well, that's just a lot of Commie nonsense," answered the skipper. "Isn't there anything else on? "An American can leave the country whenever he wants. "Besides, Paul Robeson is a Commie himself. "He was named before the House Committee on un-American Activities. "He told a reporter that when America has a Communist Revolution there will be equality for Negroes!" Washington turned around and looked at Colonel Peterson with surprise.

"He says Paul Robeson's passport was taken so he can't leave the country," continued Whitefeather over the interphone.

"Now that's a Commie crock of bull! The government can't take away anyone's passport."

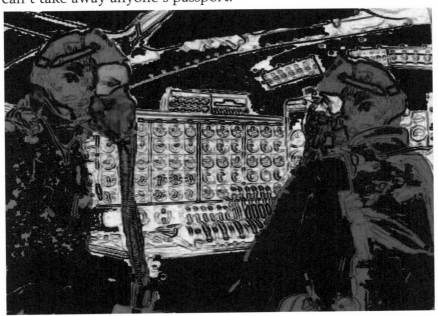

"Excuse me, Sir," interrupted Washington, "you're wrong. "Paul Robeson's passport has been taken."

"And what would you know about that, Sergeant," asked the Skipper?

"Permission to speak freely, sir?"

"Yes Sergeant."

"We Colored people know. "We read real careful when

the best Colored singer of all time can't even leave the country to sing for the new English Queen."

"He's a Communist sympathizer. "Why would the Queen of England want to listen to him?"

"Because he is a good singer," Washington blurted, forgetting to add sir!

"What if he wants to go and sing in Russia then," asked Peterson?

"They should let him," Washington answered. "Maybe the Russians will listen to what he has to say."

"Are you a Communist, Lorenzo." asked the skipper?

"No Sir. "I am a Master Sergeant in the United States Strategic air Command Eighth Air Force Seventh Bomb Wing, and a proud member of the Four Hundred Ninety Second Reconnaissance Squadron, Sir," Washington answered . . . "but I am also a Negro, and I think Paul Robeson deserves to be treated like every other American with equality and freedom."

"And what would you do if we gave you equality," Colonel Peterson replied snidely, "turn our neighborhood streets into jungles full of dope and hemp smokers, with fatherless children running lose, barefoot, and unsupervised, our daughters afraid to go to school because of who or what they might meet on the way?"

"A Colored man can do any job a White man can do," Washington argued. "The only reason so many use dope is that no one will give them a chance. "How is a man supposed to support a family if he can't get a job? "I want my son to grow up to be a doctor. "Why can't you White folks understand, we ain't got no use for your knobby kneed, boney, flat ass daughters?"

"You won't find a better mechanic than Lorenzo," Johns interrupted without taking his eyes off the civilian plane in front that he was struggling desperately not to hit. At times, the tailwheel of the airliner loomed ominously close the fragile greenhouse cockpit.

"I'll tell you one job your son will never do," the skipper continued, ignoring him, "that is examine my wife and daughter!"

"Well Sir, that's fine," answered Washington. "I'll just

tell my son if your wife gets in a car crash and needs doctoring, to just let'em bleed that blue blood all over the ground."

"Lorenzo, you don't mean that," Murphy interjected!

"Yes I do," the Second Engineer continued. "I've been in the Army Air Force since the war and where has it got me? "White men ten years my junior already command their own units."

"A Colored in command," said Peterson? "That will be the day!"

"Yes, but you've got a flight assignment," reminded Murphy. "Most other Negroes are in charge of kitchen patrol. "General LeMay ordered that all engineers on newer crews be officers."

Murphy is right," agreed Johns, "you are doing the job of an officer so I don't see what you are complaining about."

"Him," shouted Washington!

"I just don't think that Coloreds are equal with Whites," the skipper explained.

"We don't want to be equal, Colonel, we just want equal rights under the law so we can be the best we can be."

"And what would you do if you had equal rights?"

"Vote, Sir! "It's preposterous that White Women can vote when Colored Men can't."

"I'll agree with you there," quipped Peterson. The others laughed. "Who would you vote for if you had the right to vote," he asked?

"Any White guy who would give a Colored Man a chance! "Why shouldn't Paul Robeson be allowed to sing for the Queen in England?"

"Because he's a Commie, "the Colonel insisted! "It has nothing to do with his Color. "Paul Robeson is an excellent singer. "I'd even say he's the best since Caruso, but if he's against freedom and democracy, then his activities have to be controlled."

"But Sir, isn't preventing a person from doing what he wants also against freedom and democracy?"

"Yes Sergeant, it is," answered Peterson, "but these are dangerous times."

Sasha, on the Russian airliner, was a very bright boy. It was said he would grow up to be a political officer like his father. In only a half hour, he drew a pretty good likeness of a B-36 jet pod illuminated by green boreal light. When the commissar saw it, he went forward to the cockpit to ask his pilot if there was any military activity in the area. Fighters escorted bombers on training missions every day, but he didn't want them to be

taking such a risk of collision with his son on board. The
commissar ordered the pilot to contact air traffic control and ask
if there were other aircraft in the area.

The Russian radar men had been noticing the unusually
large radar blip for some time, but thought nothing of it until
the pilot said he saw another aircraft. The blip was as big as an
entire fighter squadron. Two MiG's were scrambled.

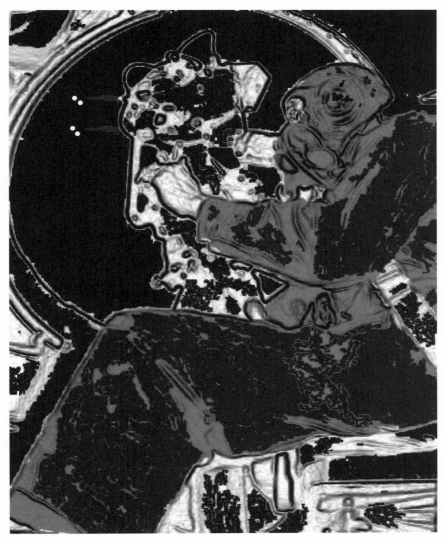

"This is Dorsal Gunner, Bandits three o'clock high,

intercept course," Shultz shouted into the interphone!

"Dive, dive," shouted Johns! The skipper pushed forward so hard and fast on his wheel, everything in the cabin that wasn't tied down, including papers, pencils, coffee mugs, half eaten tunafish sandwiches, and even Mary Bjorggessen, flew up toward the ceiling.

"Drop chaff," ordered the skipper!

"This is Gunner, what size," asked Sandringham, who had been relaxing at his post with nothing to do since his radar was turned off.

"This is Radio, half inch," said Beaumont. Sandringham shoved the rectangular packet into the tube beside his desk, replaced the cover, and pulled the lever. A rush of air was heard as the packet burst open below and behind the ship, spreading a confetti of aluminum foil to blind the Russian radar like ink from an octopus.

Mary, who had crawled into a bunk beside Grant after the three Ravens left for work, woke to find herself pressed against the ceiling. She crawled upside down, straddling the ceiling de-icing duct like the rider of a giant worm, and discovered a topsy-turvy world where everyone else was upside down. Eskimos don't swim, so she found the sensation of floating to be quite frightening. She screamed.

Gordon, who had not realized she was sharing his blanket, did not have his headset on and did not know about the incoming planes. He grabbed her and yanked her back into bed just in the knick of time. She giggled gleefully. She thought this meant he liked her.

When Johns pulled out of the dive, just moments before pounding the ship into the invisible black ground, everything slammed downward with three times the force of gravity, smashing many of the flying coffee mugs. Mary was pressed into the green canvas so hard, it felt like her flesh was being pulled off her bones. The tube of the pipe berth dug into her face and she could not move her arms or legs. She thought she was still in a dream, but the pain from her sores and bruises convinced her otherwise. Certain she was the victim of some kind of witchcraft, she started screaming in Inuit. Gordon stared at her half naked form in amazement, not knowing quite what to make of her strange incomprehensible cries.

Tony Avery had been able to get out of his plane and sleep on a bunk in his mother ship's photo lab while crossing the pole, but he had been ordered to sit in his little jet in the bomb bay since entering Russian airspace. When the skipper and Johns dived, Major Howard, commander of the flying aircraft carrier, was taken by surprise as giant four foot tail gun barrels missed his canopy by only a few feet. Propwash disrupted his airflow violently, shaking Tony to attention. "Lieutenant Avery, get ready to launch," ordered the Major!

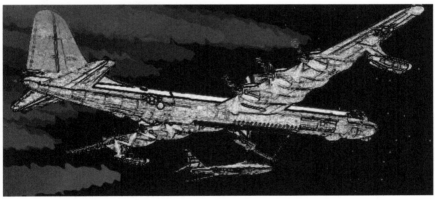

Before he knew it, Tony was being lowered out of the bomb bay on the trapeze. The wind noise startled him. He could see the C-47 below and in front of him. 753 was gone—its blue formation lights barely visible several thousand feet below. He heard the thunder from the four turbojet engines being lit, and reached down to the throttle panel to air start his own little engine. As he watched the tach pass nine hundred, his engine making a sound not unlike a vacuum cleaner, he advanced his throtte and the jet thundered to life.

"Ready Tony," asked Jenkins, the trapeze operator?

"I'm not up to temperature yet!"

"There's no time for that," interrupted Major Howard! "Launch! "THAT'S AN ORDER!"

"Sorry Tony," insisted Jenkins.   Tony heard a loud metallic clunk, like a bomb being released—only he was the bomb.   He pulled the handle to unlatch his nose hook, and dived down.   753 was disappearing fast in the mists near the ground. The dozen formation lights, three blue in a row on each wingtip, three blue and one white on the top rear of the fuselage, and two amber in the tail made cone shaped patterns in the ground fog that resembled the multicolored body of a deep sea jellyfish.   Tony began to fear a flameout, since his engine temperature was not right.   Percussive thunder was still coming from his cross fire tubes.

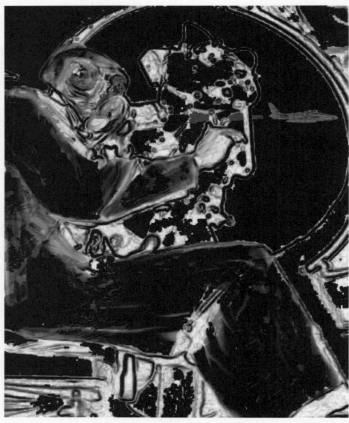

"This is Dorsal Gunner, incoming plane, eight O'clock high," yelled Calabreze into the interphone from the top left rear gunsight blister!

"What type," asked the skipper?

"F-84, Sir!

"Jeeze, you gave us quite a scare," answered Peterson!

Relieved of its payload, the GRB-36 FICON shot upward at a thirty degree angle with six propellers turning and four jets burning, shoving the one hundred ton ship ever higher with better than forty thousand horsepower. 099 had been through the Featherweight III program. All excess weight was removed except for the tail guns, allowing its huge magnesium wings to climb to over 50,000 feet, well above where Russian planes could fly. If the Russians suspected that an American plane had penetrated their airspace, they would certainly find one—and they would not be able to do anything about it. That was part of General Allen's plan. Russian P-8 radar could easily locate a high flying aircraft, but could it track one near the ground, hidden by chaff?

Major Howard ordered his chaff dispenser activated. His electronic countermeasures team began jamming every Russian signal so Tony and 753 could escape undetected. The flying battleship was too heavy with fuel, bombs, and ammo, to fly above the fighters. Tony's little fighter had four enormous drop tanks, which when full of fuel, were much too heavy for it to lift off the ground. Launched from the air, the little fighter could carry twice the normal amount, but the extra appendages ruined the plane's handling and destroyed any chance of outmaneuvering the MiG's. His only hope, if attacked, was to drop the tanks and dock with the mother ship. He didn't have enough internal fuel to make it to a friendly base.

Major Howard made a bee line for Thule. He had not stopped to take on fuel as Peterson did, so his ship was light enough to make an escape. His job done, he knew his engines would be running on vapors by the time he landed. He had no intention of going back for Tony if something happened. Luckily, the Russians had no way of knowing that there was more than one American aircraft.

"This is Scanner, incoming planes, two O'clock high," yelled Shultz!

"What type," asked the skipper?

"MiG's, Sir!"

"Oh shit! "Turn off the formation lights." Tony watched the blue lights go out and strained his eyes to follow the huge shiny black shape in front of him. Without any navigation equipment, he would be completely lost if he removed his eyes from it. He had enough fuel to make it to Iran and bail out, but he had no hope of completing his mission without the big ship's navigation equipment to lead him to the target. Without jamming equipment, Russian radar would quickly find him and fighters would be scrambled to shoot him down.

Peterson gambled that if he stayed directly underneath the airliner, the radar operators on the ground would not notice the decrease in altitude. Russian radar could only determine range and direction. The gunners watched the lights of the MiG fighters approach. Wong, in the mission control room, recorded their transmissions. They flew above the airliner just under the wavy green auroral curtain in hot pursuit of the flying aircraft carrier. Peterson decided that it was time to make an escape, so he turned at right angles to the airliner and awaited word from the gunners on whether the tactic had worked.

Tony was late making his turn and got lost. His heavily laden fighter did not handle well with such huge tanks under the wings. Both wings stalled when he tried to turn. He almost fell into the black earth. After brushing a few tree tops, he began a slow climb to search for 753. With so much fuel on board, his abused little engine strained at full military thrust just to keep the wings level. He dared not use his afterburner to climb, or he would not have enough fuel to reach safety in Iran. His stall warning horn startled him several more times as he inched his way up foot by foot away from the ground.

The commissar pointed out the window at the MiG's as they flashed by and asked his son, "Raz-vye tam?"

"Noo, poh-jaloot," answered Sasha. Everyone on the plane remarked what a good picture the lad had drawn and how

† Разве там? — Is that it? ... Ну пожалу — Well, possibly.

closely it resembled the fighter planes.

"They're breaking away," said Shultz.

"They're trying to attack the FICON," agreed Wong, who was recording their broadcasts. Nawrocki, Holbrook, and Kewscinski visibly prayed that 099's engines would not malfunction. The flying aircraft carrier was in great danger if anything went wrong that would prevent its climb to 53,000 feet. Designed for lift rather than speed, the RB-36 flew at a ten degree up angle in level flight with the propellers aimed downward at a twenty degree angle. It could out-turn any fighter or air to air missile at high altitude.

"Good idea Hank, it worked," praised Peterson. Johns was too busy wrestling with his wheel to answer as he concentrated on the lights speeding silently under the ship which marked the edge of the hard black invisible nothingness.

In a cold sweat, Tony was so nervous, he almost cried as he changed course for Iran. Feeling truly alone and afraid, he cursed. Five thousand miles from home, he was lost over a country that would torture him and probably hold him hostage for the rest of his life if his engine so much as hiccuped. At twenty one, Tony felt he was too young to spend the rest of his life in prison. He began to regret volunteering for such a dangerous mission. His only hope was to pick up the AN/APX-29 homing beacon of the other GRB-36 that was supposed to be flying out of Morocco to snatch him out of the sky and carry him home. If unknown winds blew his tiny plane off course, Tony might end up too far from the rendezvous point to find it. 'Why doesn't 753 have one,' he thought to himself? "They have to maintain radio silence," he said out loud into his mask even though there was no one to hear his complaints.

Tony looked at the picture of his young wife taped to the dash and pondered what he should do. At seventeen, Jo-Ann was too young to be a widow. Would she divorce him if he was listed as missing? What if she was pregnant and didn't know it?

It had not occured to him when he volunteered that he might lose his life. He had to fly low to avoid Soviet radar, but with all the chaff in the air, he thought he might have one last chance to look for 753. After regaining some airspeed, he decided to climb. He concentrated on the lights on the ground, hoping the giant reconnaissance bomber would occult one of them as it flew over.

"This is AC, I'm going to need a new course to target Duane," the skipper said to the Navigator.

"Coming up, sir," answered Nawrocki. "Turn right to two-two-five, sir."

In the United States, a giant flying battleship blasting over rooftops at more than two hundred miles per hour with engines roaring only a few feet above bedrooms and church steeples would elicit thousands of complaints. In Russia, where there are no telephones, there is no way to complain. To be sure, every person in every house heard the giant ship and the little Thunderjet fly over to wake them. But in Russia, it is unpatriotic to criticize the military. "Aren't they all heroes," people would say? The thought that it might be an American plane waking them out of winter hibernation would never have occurred to them. They would have been angry if they knew, but they were told that the Red Air force would never allow such a thing. They believed it was impossible for a foreign plane to fly over their country. Did they not defeat the Nazis? How could the soft, backward, artless Americans do what the fierce and sophisticated Germans could not? What poor excuses for planes the Americans had sent during the lend lease—planes like the P-39 which had the engine installed behind the pilot and car doors on the side which trapped him inside if he needed to bail out. The Russian people cheered when the two American planes flew over. Not a single person complained about the rumbling thunder that nearly blew their roofs off.

"Pilot to Gunners, where is the F-84," asked Johns over the interphone?

"This is Scanner, we lost sight of it sir," answered Shultz.

The skipper gulped and turned around with alarm to look behind him, but calmly said over the interphone, "This is AC, will someone bring some sandwiches up here?" Shultz ordered Nakamura to take some boxed dinners forward. Peterson nervously turned the formation lights back on, not quite sure if the MiG's would be able to see them and added, ... and bring a fresh pot of coffee!" Nakamura went over to the galley unit and poured coffee into a Thermos. The formation lights could be seen by Avery if he was directly above them, but only a single white light on the belly and the dim amber tail lights were visible from any distance.

THE RUSSIAN FOG
February 1956

Tony thanked God and let go of his stick momentarily to clasp his hands in prayer when he again saw the blue formation lights bouncing up through the fog below him like a bioluminescent jellyfish bobbing in the depths of a black ocean. He gleefully turned and dove toward them. "Russian planes have red lights," he convinced himself, not quite sure if he was about to intercept a Russian bomber armed with a dozen 23mm cannons.

Colonel Peterson had not eaten since Texas. The entire mission had given him a queasy stomach from planning to execution. Flying at low altitude at night was violent enough to upset anyone's stomach as the ship pitched up and down to follow the terrain. Hank Johns was an excellent pilot—the best! He flew B-26's during the war in Korea at low altitude and at night, but he had his hands full keeping the big RB-36 off the ground.

Big as it was, the two hundred thirty foot wide, hundred sixty two foot long ship did not have power assisted controls. Rather than being connected to the control surfaces directly, the cables from the control wheel were attached to little servo-trim tabs on the control surfaces that worked opposite to the way the surfaces worked. Thus, to bank to the left, the control wheel was steered to the left and that yanked a cable that pulled the right aileron servo tab up. The wind hitting that pushed the right aileron down, and the wind hitting that caused the wing tip to generate more lift and roll toward the left.

The rudder and elevators were even more complicated because they had additional trim tabs controlled by large trim wheels that looked like car steering wheels hung vertically on either side of the center pilot's console, in addition to the servo tabs connected to the control column and rudder pedals. When Johns pulled back on his wheel to climb, the servo-trim tabs on the elevators went down. This caused the elevators to move up, pushing the tail down to make the nose of the plane go up.

The disadvantage of such a complicated arrangement was that the control surfaces could not easily be moved or completely tested while on the ground, and there was absolutely no feel for what the ship was doing while in the air. It was not much fun to fly—sort of like sitting on the porch and flying your house, according to one General. The sluggish controls made altitude keeping difficult. The ship assumed a ballistic path through the air, sometimes making Nakamura feel weightless and sometimes making his limbs feel like lead, as he shoved the skipper's dinner ahead of him through the narrow intestine and danced over and around the cameras in the photo lab like a waiter in a crowded restaurant.

"What I would give to trade this for a B-26 right now," Johns exclaimed, as Nakamura stumbled up the stairs from the radio room onto the bridge!

"Which one," asked the skipper, "the Douglas or the Martin?"

"Either one!"

"How about a B-24?

"You can keep your B-24! "All I want is a real plane, not a flying truck!"

"Or a flying naval vessel, sir," commented Murphy.

"Someday they're going to figure out a way to put power assisted controls on this thing," Johns complained.

Nakamura saluted as he passed the boxed lunch over the throttles. "Thank you Airman," said the skipper, returning the salute. Nakamura wanted to stay since he didn't get up to the bridge very often, but Murphy nodded that he should leave. The ship approached an illuminated onion dome church steeple directly ahead with a crooked cross on top.

"We're going to hit it, sir," yelled Nakamura! Johns pulled back on his wheel to fly over it. Thinking there would be a collision, Nakamura yelled and dove down into the radio room only to find himself floating weightless over Hernandez, who was trying to sleep on the floor, as Johns bunted the ship back toward the invisible ground.

Shaken, after hitting the floor and waking Hernandez, Nakamura apologetically returned to the aft cabin and shouted at Shultz as soon as he emerged from the tunnel, "Why the hell did they have to build this thing so dangerous? "This isn't what I signed up for. "We're all going to be killed!"

Shultz had brought aboard a small folding card table which he erected in the middle of the cabin. Normally, the Crows would sit facing the front bulkhead, but because they had been replaced by Ravens, their secret radio equipment had been moved to the aft bomb bay. The two seats that normally faced the forward bulkhead could be turned around to face the table. This is where Shultz liked to sit. He and O'Connor would play for pennies during the two day long picket missions along the Russian border while Sandringham and Calabrese kept watch. They were not enjoying their game.

Nakamura's outburst made Shultz jump in his seat. Everyone was edgy. Both he and O'Connor knew they should have been asleep, since they were off watch, but something about being deep inside Russia on a mission they had not exactly volunteered for wore on their minds. O'Connor and Calabrese kept looking out of their bubbles to reassure themselves that there were no Russian fighters. They all stared at Nakamura except Sandringham, who was in Shultz's usual seat on the ceiling, beside Calabrese, scanning the foggy horizon with binoculars.

"There are peacetime airplanes and there are wartime airplanes," answered Shultz, as he motioned for Nakamura to sit. He cut the younger man into the game. Mary, who was awakened when Nakamura shouted directly underneath her, climbed down from the loft and plopped into Nakamura's lap as he swiveled his gunner's chair to face the table. His look of surprise elicited a humorous response from Sandringham and Calabreze, high above in the dorsal gunners' seats. Nakamura's own chair, shaped like a bucket seat, was not large enough for two.

Shultz continued, "The B-17 was liked by its crews because it was designed in peacetime. "It would be un-acceptable to the public, if large numbers of planes crashed on people's houses in takeoff and landing accidents. "During the depression, when money was scarce, Congress was not willing to replace a plane that crashed. The B-17 had to be as safe and easy to fly as a civilian airliner."

Mary suddenly put her arm around Nakamura's neck and kissed him on the forehead. He tried to push her away—trying to look serious as he received another kiss, not knowing quite what to do. "Once the war started," Shultz continued, "combat performance became the only important design consideration. "It was felt that if a pilot did not have the right stuff to survive takeoffs and landings, it was better for him to crash and kill himself flying solo than to take a lot of men and ammunition with him. "The B-24, B-26, and the B-36 were wartime aircraft. "Their designers were radical free-thinkers given license to violate every rule of aviation safety in search of better performance."

"So the RB-36 is designed unsafe," asked Nakamura?

"Nonsense," Shultz exclaimed, "solid as the earth!" He stomped his foot on the thinly carpeted floor, then added, "Wouldn't you two rather make use of a bunk?" Mary grinned at him.

"No, I want to know the truth," answered Nakamura with a shaky voice. Mary frowned and pouted.

"Alright." Shultz continued. "The B-36 was designed at a time when Hitler was winning the war. "They decided to build the largest plane the world had ever seen, to fly higher, faster, and farther than any plane in history; then bomb Germany and Japan from the United States." The Gunnery Sergeants studied how Mary's kisses kept migrating closer and closer to the younger man's mouth. Nakamura just stared intently. Shultz continued, "It was to fly so fast and so high, that defensive armament was unnecessary because no enemy fighter would be able to reach it."

Mary squirmed in Nakamura's lap. "So that makes the RB-36 dangerous," he asked?

"Flying close to the ground to get under Soviet radar makes it dangerous," explained Shultz. "It was not made to do that but, in terms of size and performance, there is not a plane in the world that can touch it."

"That's right," agreed O'Connor, still hypnotized by the black bubble on the other side of his gunsight! "RB-36 crews aren't like other aviators. "Most planes take off and land, '36's land and take off. "We're sky people! "We eat, sleep, and live in the sky. "We only land when we want to."

" . . . And we always want to," interjected Shultz.

O'Connor chuckled and glanced away from his gunsight bubble at Nakamura, then resumed staring out the window with a serious expression visible in his reflection, made smaller by the curved Plexiglas, and added, ". . . And when they get the bugs out of that new atomic engine, we'll be able to fly like Peter Pan to Neverland and never land!" He opened his eyes wide as though they would pop, then smiled as he glanced at the girl. Mary smiled back as though she understood the conversation. He returned his gaze to the window. "Why do you think there are so many bumps and bulges in the landing gear doors," he asked without looking away from his bubble? Before anyone could reply, he answered his own question: "It's 'cause the designers thought landing gear was unnecessary and General LeMay poked them in the shoulder when they were doing their drawings and said, 'aren't you guys forgetting something?'" The others laughed. "Someday we'll even be able to swap out engines in mid air," he added, "and if we drop a wrench, some Russian Commissar will get a knot on his head."

Shultz chuckled, "And if you don't get the engine mounts tightened right, you'll drop an engine on some Commie's house."

"Shucks, we can do that now," said O'Connor, without disturbing his gaze out the window. Both sergeants chuckled. Mary continued with her kisses. "That's why they're putting the atomic engine in the bomb bay . . . so you can drop it like a bomb, and glide to safety if you think it's going to explode."

"I thought you said it wasn't going to have landing gear," reminded Shultz?

"Like I said," repeated O'Connor, "we're sky people! "We don't need landing gear. "We all got parachutes on our backs. "We'll just jump out and flap like birds until the ground gets too close, and then float down gently under our silk umbrellas."

"I take it you've never *floted down gently* ' that way," corrected Shultz. "It's more like jumping off a house onto a child's swing with a several minute delay until the swing breaks, and then the ground comes up and slams you silly. "If the wind is blowing, it's like being dragged behind a car, provided a tree doesn't reach up and grab you with a dozen swatting baseball bats."

"You mean I might be plucked out of Neverland by the Haunted Forest," asked O'Connor, with only the slightest glance away from his bubble.

"I mean I wouldn't jump out of a plane unless the wings came off and it was on fire, and even then I would think twice about it," insisted Shultz.

"Why, if the war was over, did the Air force decide to build the RB-36," asked Nakamura, trying to look serious and not quite knowing how to get the bare bottomed girl off his lap? "Weren't the Ruskies fighting on the same side as us?"

"During the war," Shultz answered, suddenly looking serious, "bad weather forced a B-29 crew to land in Russia. "Rather than refuel the plane so it could continue to kill Japs, the men were taken prisoner and never seen again, even though Russia and the United States were both Allies at the time. "No one knew what happened to the men and they were listed as missing in action. "When the war ended, rumors began to circulate among freed Nazi prisoners that there were Americans in their Gulag and even referred to them by name." Nakamura continued to ignore Mary's advances. She whimpered and pouted to get his attention.

"When the American Consul General asked about the fate of the men," Shultz continued, "he was given letters they had written to their wives explaining that they felt dissatisfied with the capitalist system, and that they were so convinced of the superiority of the Communist way of life that they had remarried and had no desire to return home. "One of the men wrote to his wife using a nickname which was actually the name of her cat. "She had little difficulty convincing Army Intelligence that no one would write a 'Dear John' letter to a cat."

O'Connor laughed and said, "Only a big mouth, hairy hat Russian would believe that a red blooded American aviator would leave his voluptuous American wife for a moley, blue skinned Russian woman."

"Or that spotty, flat-chested Russian women are better looking," added Shultz! Nakamura sat pensively. He was frightened about being in Russia and there was nothing that Mary could do to calm his nerves. She was enjoying the greatest adventure of her life.

"American women are pure, clean, virtuous, and submissive to their husbands," volunteered Calabreze from his dorsal gun bubble.

"Hit me," shouted O'Connor, asking for another card! Shultz dealt another hand to continue the card game.

"Russian women have hairy underarms and smell like men," added Calabreze. They ignored him.

"Our Ambassador, Bernard Mumley," Shultz continued, "demanded that the ship and its crew be returned. "It came back in a hundred crates . . . every rivet had been removed and the men were never seen again. "On the first of May, nineteen fifty, just after the Commies blew up their first A-bomb, the T-4 was seen flying over Red Square in Moscow to show they had a plane that could drop the Commie A-bomb on our heads. "The T-4 is so identical to a B-29, that B-29 parts can be used to repair a T-4 and T-4 parts can be used to repair a B-29, and that's why all the officers have poison needles . . . 'cause if a '36 ever went down . . . " He didn't finish.

Nakamura turned white when he heard that. He was already losing the card game. It was hard for him to pay attention to a hand of cards when all he could think about was that his life was in danger, and that a half naked girl, wearing nothing but a blanket slit up the back, was sitting on his lap wearing no underwear.

The constant pitching of the ship kept spreading the deck of cards over the table. Every time Major Johns, a hundred feet away on the bridge, pushed on his wheel to fly down a hill, the cards flew off the table. Sometimes the table even lifted off the floor. Frustrated, O'Connor suddenly blurted out, "This ain't no card game, it's a séance! "Did you see how the table flew up in the air when you mentioned those dead men?"

"We're flying mightily low over the graves of our fallen comrades," observed Shultz.

"How can you know where their graves are," asked Nakamura? "Russia is the largest country in the world." Mary frowned when she realized her advances were being rejected.

"What else goes on hilltops," asked O'Connor in reply? O'Connor looked over at Shultz. Shultz looked back at him with a sly look and a crooked smile, then looked down at his hands. His thumbs were on the table, but his fingers were under the edge. O'Connor smiled back and put his fingers under the edge in the same way.

As the ship flew into a fog shrouded valley between hills, Calabreze and Sandringham could see the fog rise up behind like devil's horns tinted green with auroral glow. Vortexes of fog, spawned from the wingtips, swirled the cloudy air like an unrolling Torah scroll—which was immediately torn in two by Tony Avery's little RF-84 flying close escort.

The next time Johns flew over a hill, the table again flew up off the floor, only this time Shultz and O'Connor helped it to fly all the way to Grant's bunk, causing the deck of cards to fly all around the cabin. Nakamura yelled, "ARRUCH," and propelled Mary onto the floor where the table had been. She screamed! The table fell on top of her bare bottom, which caused her to try to stand up, overturning the table onto Shultz and Nakamura.

All of the gunners burst out in laughter, except for Nakamura. When the table struck the lump he made under his thin canvas bunk, Grant sat up and hit his forehead on the large de-icing duct above him. "COOL IT DOWN THERE," he yelled!

"YES SIR," replied Shultz, saluting the lump in the canvas above him. The table was again levitating off the floor thanks to Mary being underneath. Grant crawled to the edge of the bunk and looked down.

"Sorry sir," said O'Connor, "we were discussing the men from that B-29 that went down in the war and was never heard from again and the table flew up by itself."

Just then, Johns flew over another hill, causing the table and Mary once again to jump. "See," said Shultz, "it did it again!" Grant recoiled in surprise. He wasn't aware that Mary was under the table. He thought for a moment that the table was, in fact, demon possessed.

"'Guess American ghosts can haunt an American plane from a thousand miles away," remarked O'Connor.

"We were conducting an experiment to see how far away ghosts could haunt and at what speed they could haunt at," explained Shultz.

"Well, next time you hold a séance, Sergeant, tell the ghosts to be more quiet," commanded the young Lieutenant. The drone of the engines became more noticeable. Mary emerged from under the table and looked up at the sleepy co-pilot, who's head seemed to be hanging upside down from the ceiling as he craned his neck to see under the bunk.

"Lieutenant Grant," called Nakamura?

"What?"

"Is it true that all officers carry poison needles?"

"No, it is not true," answered Grant, "only those with top-secret clearances."

Just then, the ship entered some heavy turbulence. "What the hell is going on," asked Grant as he grabbed his parachute from the rack behind Calabrese! He jumped down and strapped it on, before disappearing head first into the tunnel. Rain streaks appeared on the gunsight bubbles. The card game in the aft cabin was over as everyone grabbed their seats to avoid being thrown up off the floor. Shultz folded his card table and strapped it in the latrine, behind the galley unit.

On the bridge, Johns flicked a switch on the bottom right of the instrument panel to activate the wipers.

"You didn't warn us we'd be going through a thunder storm Scott," chided Peterson over the interphone as he reached for the left front of the center console to turn on the navigation lights.

In the little jet, Tony breathed a sigh of relief as the huge reconnaissance bomber lit up with red, white, and green navigation lights to add to the dozen blue, white, and amber formation lights. "Red, white, and blue," Tony cheered! He was surfing in the ship's left wingtip vortex to save fuel, so he could not see the green light. "How patriotic," he yelled to himself! "What will the damn Rooskies think when they see that?" He was no longer afraid of getting lost in the clouds.

"That was my plan," answered Holbrook, the Meteor-ologist, "to hide in the cold front, I mean. "What do you expect me to do, predict the weather?"

Johns wrestled like a bullfighter, grabbing his wheel by the horns, to keep the ship level and prevent it from being dashed into the ground by wind sheer. "Someday they're going to figure out a way to put power assist on these things," complained Johns, panting.

"Nonsense," retorted the skipper, "then women would be able to do our jobs. "You have to be a real man to fly the B-36." Johns grunted agreement as he struggled with his wheel, stomping on the giant rudder pedals, right and left, as though he were exercising on a giant weight machine. "No woman has ever flown a B-36," added Peterson in a sly effort to avoid having to do it himself. "WASP's flew every type of aircraft flown during the war, even the B-29, but no woman has ever been born who can handle an RB-36."

"Should we be running the navigation lights," asked Grant, who had moved to his battle station in the forward left gunsight blister behind and below the skipper's seat? "Won't the Russians see us?"

"So what if they do," answered Peterson, turning around to look at him? I just want to make sure that Avery out there can see us. "We sure as hell don't need a mid-air collision over Russia."

"What if a Russian plane sees us," asked the young co-pilot?

"We don't want a Russian plane to hit us either," explained Johns.

"Look son," continued the skipper, "this cloak and dagger stuff is fine for good weather, but one in three ships lost in the war was destroyed in collisions with other aircraft. "Flying safety is more important than anything else, even in combat, even in Russia. "If you're going to get into a dogfight with somebody, you had better hope they know how to handle their ship, or they might fly right into you."

"But if he is a good pilot," asked Grant, "wouldn't you be afraid he'd shoot you down?"

"I'd rather fight a good pilot who was a lousy shot than a lousy pilot who was a good shot." The four men on the bridge chuckled, though this had to be considered gallows humor coming from a B-24 pilot.

"Yeah, but those guys with the rocket planes weren't very good shots, were they," asked Johns?

"The rocket planes couldn't hit a barrage balloon with their slow firing guns, but their exhaust would disrupt the formation as bad as any flak burst," answered the Colonel. "They didn't have to hit us. "They just scared the hell out of us, and the younger boys flew into each other."

"Navigator to AC, sir, approaching target," a voice said over the interphone, as the ship pounded up and down in the turbulence like a six by six army truck driving through bomb craters.

"AC to John and Jim, time to do your thing," Peterson responded.

"Roger AC," replied Newcomb, tapping Kewscinski on the shoulder as he got up from his seat in the observation cabin. The Colonel watched both men disappear into the tunnel on the left side of the radio room.

THE TOURIST SNAPPING PICTURES

February 1956

Whenever Major Kewscinski was asked what he did in the Air Force, he always said he was a photographer. He was a hard man to figure out. He was conceited, while most photographers are outgoing. Why, people asked, would a man who did nothing but click officer's portraits and battlefield photos be so intensely self assured and proud of himself? Kewscinski would admit to shooting battlefield photos occasionally, but always refused to say how, or when, or where. He often bragged that he was the greatest photographer in the world! Everyone knew he had fancy cameras. If the size of one's camera, like the size of one's ego, determined one's rank or status in the profession; Kewscinski was, without doubt, the world's greatest photographer. His seventeen cameras were certainly the biggest in the world.

After climbing out of the eight foot tube into the photo lab, Kewscinski adjusted the focus of each of his five multi-cameras and three vertical cameras to compensate for temperature and altitude. He then tested the film advance drives as he clicked the shutters to manual control and advanced the first frame of the hypersensitive fifty foot rolls of foot and a half wide black and white film into position. This mundane but necessary task being done, Kewscinski had the right to be proud of himself.

In daylight, Kewscinski's cameras were capable of a 1/400th of a second shutter speed. At night, as with all cameras, flash had to be used. This was made significantly more difficult by the fact that the seventeen cameras were located in a reconnaissance bomber moving at better than three hundred miles per hour. Professional photographers employ best boy grips to set up their lighting. Kewscinski was no exception. Major Newcomb, the bombardier, was Kewscinski's assistant.

As Kewscinski was getting his cameras ready, Newcomb slipped through the right side access door into the bomb bay to arm his bombs. The ship was armed with forty 80 pound flash bombs. The bombs contained flash powder, the same stuff movie directors and fireworks pyrotechnicians use. The plan was to drop the bombs on the Russians and photograph them as they came running out of their houses in various states of undress to avoid being killed. There is nothing like a bomb going off a few feet above one's roof, to get a person out of bed quickly. Americans would be furious if bombs were to go off over their homes. Not so the Russians. They were often photographed cheering and waving at the big silver ship overhead. Are not all aviators heroes? Who does not enjoy fireworks? The thought that an American plane might be dropping the bombs would never have occurred to them. They were told that the Red Air Force would never allow a foreign plane to fly over their country. Aerial photography was illegal.

Not all Russians were convinced. The Red Air Force began getting telegraph messages about unidentified flying objects. Some messages reported zebra patterns of blue lights dancing on the horizon, or underneath low lying clouds. Others reported a sound like a motorcycle regiment, which was loud enough to rattle trash containers, while watching a single bright white light and two dim amber lights passing overhead followed by thunder.

Marshal Zhukov, the Soviet Defense Minister, did not believe in UFO's. The old bear was angry to be awakened out of his winter sleep. He put his pants and his shoes on, then ordered his forces on alert, before sending a cable to Doctor Professor Uri Klimanov, the world's leading expert on extraterrestrials. The esteemed doctor professor had a theory that an alien spaceship had landed in the Lower Tunguska region in 1908 and leveled trees for miles—close to where the majority of the UFO reports were coming from. Now that it was 1956, Zhukov feared such a thing was probably an American aircraft, but without an accurate fix on its location, there was no way of intercepting it. He thought it would be best to explain it to the Politburo as a UFO, rather than admit that his men failed to prevent an American bomber, possibly armed with a nuclear weapon, from entering Soviet territory.

Arming bombs is a technically simple procedure. Newcomb only had to screw the fuse in the back of the bomb until the blasting cap pressed against the main explosive charge. The time delay fuse would start to burn when the bomb was released. That gave it time to clear the belly of the ship before the bomb exploded bright enough to light up the whole sky. The constant pitching was not felt as strongly in the bomb bay as it was in the tail, where the bunks and card table were, but it made it hard for Newcomb to climb up to arm the top two bombs on each of the four racks.

Once he was done, Newcomb joined Kewscinski, who was getting the trimetrigon cameras ready. These smaller cameras, buried under the floor of the lab, had grid lines etched into a film screen that could later be used to determine the ship's position and altitude relative to known landmarks on the horizon. Once the altitude was known, the size of objects on the ground could be determined to within a foot of accuracy.

Before they left the camera bay, there was just one more thing to do: That was to open the camera bay doors. This was done by remote control. A light on the photo lab instrument panel indicated if the doors were open, but it was no substitute for checking with an Aldis lamp and seeing with one's own eyes. If the bomb bay doors did not open, the gunners would know it immediately. They could see them open. If the camera doors did not open, there would be no way of knowing. It wasn't possible to look through any of the cameras to aim them. Forgetting to open the lens covers could end a recon man's career.

"Over target in five minutes," warned Nawrocki. Newcomb returned to his post in the nose of the ship. Kewscinski followed him through the eight foot tunnel and took his position at the Norden bombsight, taking Nawrocki's seat, but kneeling on a special knee rest under the navigation desk which curved around the front window. He removed the desk and passed it back to Nawrocki, who strapped it to the front of the landing gear bay.

Four swivel chairs faced two desks on either side of the cabin. The front two seats gave Kewscinski and Holbrook, the Weather Observer, an illusion of flight as they had a 180 degree view through the giant front window. Holbrook's view was obstructed by his periscopic gunsight, which had two handgrips looking like the handlebars of a racing motorcycle. Unlike a submarine periscope, Holbrook's stuck forward through the front of the ship rather than up through the top. His somewhat smaller meteorological desk was covered with tubes leading to the outside, which fed a humidograph and filters to sample the air if the ship happened to fly through a cloud of nuclear fallout.

Dangling over the right hand chart table with a black, baked enamel finish, like a dentist's x-ray machine, was Newcomb's radar camera. It was mounted on a fork hung from the ceiling, so that it could be swiveled up and down and left and right. That way, Newcomb could swivel it to a comfortable position during long hours of observation, or it could be swung out of the way when it was not needed. The display itself consisted of a ten inch plan-position indicator behind a forty five degree angled glass that allowed the film camera on top to photograph the display even while the Major was viewing it. A long black rubber hood was curved to fit his eyes and face, so no stray light could distract him from the faintest blip on the screen.

Kewscinski and Newcomb did not take long to check out their equipment. Most of their testing had been done on the ground. The rain stopped.

"AC to Jim and John," said the skipper over the interphone, "we're probably only going to get one shot at this before the rain gets to the target.

"VO ready, sir," said Newcomb.

"Photonavigator ready, sir," seconded Kewscinski.

"Activate radar," ordered Peterson. "Autopilot on. "She's all yours."

"Roger," said Newcomb, as he clicked a switch in the APS-23 control panel from standby to transmit. The six foot wide rotating bomb-aiming radar came to life, filling his black ten inch display screen inside the camera with a pie shaped pattern of yellow-green blips. He manipulated a joystick sticking up through the left side of his desk to position a bright dot of light on the screen to correspond to targeting information on his map.

Kewscinski then flicked the door selector switch for bomb bays two and three on his bombing control panel, which was hung on the wall near his sight, and turned the bomb door safety switch from safe to operable. Nawrocki and Holbrook watched the bomb station indicator lights for all the racks in bomb bay two light up on the "christmas tree," as Kewscinski's bombing control panel was called, as he checked the rack selector and interval release settings one last time.

"This is PN, bombs armed and ready," announced Kewscinski into the interphone. Newcomb twirled knobs to enter offsets from the coast of the Aral Sea, which showed as a sharp black line on his otherwise green, blip-speckled screen. He kept his forehead pressed against the camera hood. His hands knew where all the switches were, without having to look. It was easier for him to track the edge of the sea, than the lumpy target blip itself. When he finished, the computer began calculating.

Lights atop vacuum tubes flashed a psychedelic pattern as the wheels and gears inside the computer made a tumbling sound. The computer could not actually see the radar display. It was the corrections Newcomb input with his joystick that told the computer how to steer the ship to compensate for crosswinds. All he had to do was to keep the bright dot positioned on the coast of the Aral sea and the computer would automatically lay the bombs over the target. Once it started tracking, the computer was quieter as the wheels and gears turned more slowly. The patterns of the lights on the adjoining vacuum tube chassis also changed more slowly. Newcomb snapped pictures of the radar display with the built in film camera so that the radar image of the ground clutter could be compared to the aerial photographs later.

"PN to AC, I see the visual target," announced Kewscinski as he began looking into the eyepiece of the Norden bombsight.

"Lighting the turbojets," said the skipper. "Everyone at your stations!" He flicked the switches to open the pod nose doors, which blocked the intakes, when the jets were not being used, to prevent windmilling. Johns reached up and clicked the four starter switches to "ALTITUDE," while Peterson advanced the throttles. There was no reason to start the jet engines one at a time, because the wind blowing though them got them spinning faster than the electric starters would.

"Military power," ordered the skipper! Murphy shoved the throttles to maximum for the high speed pass over the target. Johns grabbed his bouncing control column by the top so he could pull up if the computer flew too low. Washington adjusted the mixture levers to compensate for the additional power. After about a minute to give the jets time to warm up, Peterson reached up to the ceiling and shoved the jet throttles to military power. The ship shook and shuddered as never before, clattering like a freight train beneath the turbulent downdrafts in front of the storm, doing better than three hundred knots a hundred feet from the ground. Lights illuminating farm buildings streaked by under Kewscinski's bombsight. Everyone had to be strapped in or be tossed out of their seats.

In the aft cabin, Nakamura strapped Mary into Shultz's favorite seat against the front bulkhead, as Shultz and Sandringham assumed their normal battle stations—Shultz in the dorsal bubble and Sandringham at the tail radar console.

In the forward cabin, Kewscinski crouched down and rested his forehead against the top of the bombsight. A dim red light illuminated the track lines, which he could adjust for the crosswind. Holbrook saw the lights of the city coming up in the distance through the glass nose of the ship. Altitude and airspeed were automatically fed into the Sperry A-1A bombing navigation computer under the navigation desk. The rotating cogs, gears, and vacuum tubes inside the computer controlled the autopilot and kept the ship on target. All Newcomb had to do was keep the electronically painted dot over the coast and snap pictures with the camera attached on top of the hood. For all of Kewscinski's conceit about the number and size of his cameras, it was this little camera on Newcomb's radar scope that was the most important to the success of the mission. It would photograph the radar approaches so that when they returned with a TX-14 Alarm Clock to nuke the place, the entire target would be completely obliterated in one blast.

The thought had occurred to Newcomb that the Russians might have put up a lot of lights in a field to deceive Kewscinski, but when he adjusted the gain on his radar, the town seemed to be right where it should have been according to Nawrocki's plot and the radar signature of the sea and surrounding hills.

"This is VO . . . one minute," Newcomb announced with his face pressing against the radar camera. He could see blips from large buildings, off to one side, that were not lit very well, so he twirled the knobs to adjust the offset to zero and positioned the bright aiming dot in the middle of the blips from the buildings. The computer slowly turned the ship to alter course. This always made the pilots on the bridge feel queasy as their wheels gyrated by themselves, in front of them, when the computer was in control. Bombing accuracy was more important than comfortable flying. Newcomb's ship came in third at the Fifth Annual Bombing-navigation Competition at Walker Air Force base in '54. He was one of the best.

If Newcomb was wrong about the target location, Tony Avery would still be overflying the optical target. That's what he was there for. He didn't have radar in his little plane. If the Russians did try to hide the site by lighting up a field, or planting radar reflectors in a pattern to look like buildings on the radar screen, one plane or the other would be flying over the real target. No one knew where the map of the target had come from. That was classified. Was it accurate? Only the photos they were about to take would tell.

"Thirty seconds," announced Kewscinski, his eye still pressing against the optical bombsight. The computer abruptly pulled up on the controls to climb to the proper altitude for photography. Everyone was pushed into their seats with twice the force of gravity as the ride abruptly smoothed out and the speed was reduced during the abrupt climb. The ceiling was low, causing Johns to bunt in order to stay under the cloud deck. Everything loose flew up as he shoved his wheel forward to get back below the clouds.

"Right bomb door open," announced O'Connor over the interphone.

"Left bomb door open," seconded Nakamura. A loud turbulent rush came from the belly of the ship as though the landing gear was down.

"Activate chaff dispenser," commanded Peterson. Sandringham flicked a switch on his console in the tail and the automatic dispenser just behind the aft bulkhead came to life, spraying little strips of foil out the back, like the tinkles of a frightened cow. Sandringham also turned on his tail radar set just in case the Russians had fighters in the area.

"Green light," announced Kewscinski. "nineteen, eighteen, seventeen, sixteen, fifteen, fourteen . . . "

An explosion lit up the sky in front of the ship. "Holy moley, what's that," exclaimed Holbrook, looking into the light amplifying forward gunsight? The explosion turned into a flare and ascended into the sky with a trail of fire, lighting the ground for miles in every direction. Kewscinski was blinded. Holbrook grabbed Kewscinski's big hand held box camera and began taking pictures, frantically cranking the film between each click of the shutter.

"Try to get film of it through the sight," suggested Nawrocki! A thunderous roar was suddenly heard.

"Here," said Holbrook. He gave the big camera to the Navigator. Nawrocki jumped out of his seat to aim. He pressed the camera against the optically clear bombsight glass beside Kewscinski's knees to get a better view, as the trail of fire ascended. The two of them seemed stacked on top of each other like mating birds as the ship jumped up and down. When Nawrocki got into position, the flare exploded into a brilliant fireball that lit up the sky like daylight. Holbrook switched on his guns but did not arm them. He turned the gunsight like a submarine periscope, but his eyepiece didn't move, only the guns in the nose turret outside the ship did.

"Nosegunner, I thought I told you to put those guns down," hollered Peterson! The two one-inch cannon loomed up in front of the cockpit. "What are you trying to do, shoot it down," he added as the flare exploded? To Beaumont and Hernandez in the radio room, it almost seemed as though he had shot it down. A "boom" shook the ship.

Holbrook squeezed the trigger. "I got the gun camera rolling," he explained.

"I guess we'll have to buy him two drinks now . . . one for aiming at a Russian plane and another for shooting down a Russian rocket," commended Kewscinski with a strain, as Nawrocki shoved his shoulders into Kewscinski's knees trying to aim the camera.

"You will if my pictures are better than yours," teased Holbrook, as they stared in awe at the sheer size of the explosion which was still lighting up the sky. Nawrocki scrambled over to Grant's gun bubble to continue with the pictures, but Grant had already activated his gun camera just as Holbrook had done, so Nawrocki climbed up into his astrodome in the middle of the flight deck.

"Not now Lieutenant, we're overcast," said the skipper. "We have a radar fix." The darkening explosion went silent and only the roar of the engines were heard.

"I'm just trying to get pictures of the explosion, sir," answered the Navigator. He began frantically snapping and cranking the film.

"AC to Raven, Merril, there was some kind of huge explosion directly in front of us," Peterson said while pressing his interphone button. Abruptly, the delayed thunder of the explosion deafened them, drowning out the engines.

"I know," answered Hughs, needlessly shouting loud enough to cause distortion, "I've been expecting it. "That's what we're here for. "I'm just a little surprised that they decided to launch today. "I guess they wanted to get it off early before the bad weather got here. "We're just a little late getting over the target."

"Should I abort?"

"No sir! "Make sure Jim overflys the launch pad. "The telemetry we got is a whole lot more valuable than a picture of it sitting on the ground!"

"Telemetry?"

"Sir, would you mind not talking for a while," asked Hughs? "We're busy back here. "I'll explain later. "Just make sure you get a picture of the launch pad . . . it's very important. "Over and out!" He unplugged his interphone jack.

"Bombs away," announced Kewscinski, as the computer released the first of twenty flashbombs. His countdown was replaced by two minutes of earsplitting explosions, six seconds apart, just under the rear of the ship. Everyone cupped their hands over their helmets to give extra hearing protection. Mary, who didn't have a helmet, covered her ears and cried. She had never heard explosions so loud. She had never heard ringing in her ears before and she looked around to try to see where it might be coming from. A clockwork mechanism in the bombing navigation computer released the ten bombs on each rack, one at a time, independently—one every six seconds.

Kewscinski was crouched over his sight. In his right hand, was a little button on the end of a cord. When he pushed it, nine camera shutters would open. He released it after each flash explosion so lights on the ground would not streak the films. He did not have to advance the film. The film advanced automatically whenever a flash of light was detected by a photocell. A whirring was heard in both the flying battleship and the little fighter as powerful motors wound the huge films across their detachable camera backs. The camera in Avery's plane also worked automatically with a photocell, but he had no way to stop the lights on the ground from ruining his films. All Avery could do was to turn on the power to the cameras and fly straight.

Lights on the ground left permanent streaks on Avery's films, due to the motion of his plane while the shutters were open. So did the light from the rocket. Kewscinski pushed the button to open his nine shutters just before each flash, that way they would remain open as little as possible and not ruin the film. This was the skill that Kewscinski was so proud of, though most of the crew thought absolutely anyone could do it. Newcomb had the much more difficult job of actually aiming the cameras, which he did by using his radar and the bombing-navigation computer to steer the ship.

"This is PN, I hate to tell everybody this," Kewscinski hollered over the interphone to the skipper, "but smoke from that rocket probably ruined my pictures. "I think we are going to have to do it again."

"The Rooskies are going to be stirred up like a hornet's nest when they figure out we photographed their rocket launch," warned Grant exuberantly. He seemed to be enjoying himself, despite the danger, as he stood at his gun bubble at the foot of the stairs looking for fighters.

A light on Kewscinski's Christmas tree went out when the first rack emptied. Then another minute of earsplitting explosions ticked off every six seconds. The bomb doors snapped closed automatically, with a thump.

"Right bomb door closed," said O'Connor over the interphone.

"Left bomb door closed," seconded Nakamura.

"Well, let's get it right," exclaimed Johns!

"Okay Skipper, make your turn," Kewscinski yelled into the interphone. He turned the "doors operable" switch to "safe." "Lets do it again . . . and have Merril radio those Rooskies to stop launching rockets and ruining my pictures." There was no answer from the mission control room. Hughs had unplug- ged his interphone cord.

The ship rolled on its side. The city lights which had been below, were now pasted on the top left of the observation window as the skipper and Johns made a chandelle maneuver. Everyone was pressed into their seats. Newcomb's and Kewscinski's faces were pressed into their hoods. To fly a cross shaped course over the target, they had to turn two hundred seventy degrees to line up on the next leg of the bomb run so the photos would overlap properly and an accurate general map of the town could be drawn from them. Newcomb had noted the position of the blips on his chart. The radar camera had a freeze frame ability that he could use to see how the display changed over time. Blips that did not change, he circled on his map and then drew a line to make sure nothing would be missed on the second pass. If the Russians had planted radar reflectors in a field, he would waste film, but nothing would be missed. Blips from reflectors get larger and smaller on the screen as one orbits them, but buildings reflect constantly or change only slowly.

"This is Scanner, searchlights up," shouted O'Connor over the interphone from his post at the right lower gunsight blister! The other lights on the ground went out all at once. Except for a dozen searchlights, there was nothing but blackness all the way to the horizon.

After a second chandelle maneuver, the ship leveled out. "All yours Jim," said the skipper. Avery's little jet could no longer be seen. Several Russian planes were orbiting the launch sight with their bright takeoff and landing lights turned on. It could only be hoped that the wind would blow the smoke away and the next photo run would be successful. There would not be another chance. Peterson flicked switches on the center console to turn 753's navigation and formation lights off. Not able to see anything, Kewscinski looked up from his sight and threw up his hands in a shrug. It was up to Newcomb to aim the bombs using his radar.

Newcomb continued to photograph his radar display as Kewscinski selected "RACK 2" on his auxiliary control panel and set the "doors operable" switch for another run on the target.

"Looks like someone down there doesn't like all the noise you're making, John," commented Holbrook. In the time it had taken to complete the second turn, four more searchlights had turned on, which were wildly sweeping the sky to find the big silver ship. Luckily, they were aiming their lights straight up from the blackness as though they were searching for a plane flying at high altitude. Large discs of light could be seen streaking across the clouds overhead. Kewscinski became worried that a light might hit the ship while the shutter was open, and ruin all the film. Peterson was worried that a light might hit the ship and radar guided artillery would blow 753 out of the sky. He had not expected that such a small target would be so well defended. The only thing that stopped the anti-aircraft gunners from firing, was that there were Soviet planes in the area.

"Right bomb door open," announced O'Connor.

"Left bomb door open," seconded Nakamura. A loud turbulent rush came from the belly of the ship as though the landing gear was down.

"Bombs away, bombs away," Kewscinski repeated. There was another minute of deafening explosions, six seconds apart, before another light on the christmas tree went out to warn that the auditory discomfort would be extended to two full minutes. Kewscinski photographed two criss-crossing swaths ten miles long and three miles wide, forming a giant "X" on the black ground below. It didn't take the searchlights long to find the huge American, once it was illuminated by its own flash bombs from underneath. Nakamura and O'Connor watched with alarm as tracer bullets came swarming up like fireflies. The altitude was carefully chosen by Hughs, Peterson, and the other mission planners to be just high enough to evade small arms fire, but low enough to provide good photography under a cloud deck. It was Holbrook who forcast the weather.

Loud flak explosions went off above the ship, illuminating the clouds above and startling Kewscinski, who wasted a shot by releasing the shutter at the wrong time. Then he missed the next shot because the shutter was closed when the flash bomb went off. The bombs were considerably brighter than the flak. "Dammit," he cursed! Kewscinski forced himself to concentrate on what he saw, rather than on what he heard, as he stared into the bombsight. Fortunately, the flak gunners did not have time to get their altitude adjustments right. The shells were exploding too far above to do any damage. The pictures were designed to overlap, in order to provide a stereo view, so the missed film did not create a large gap in the pictures. Kewscinski was a perfectionist, however, so the missed film made him very angry.

"Right bomb door closed," said O'Connor.

"Left bomb door closed," seconded Nakamura.

"Lets get out of here," cried Johns as he turned the autopilot off and dived to increase speed away from the target. A loud "whump, whump" was heard somewhere in the ship, but with what and where, who could tell in the dark? Murphy and Washington scanned their instruments for the slightest fluctuation in engine performance as the gunners looked over the surfaces of the wings.

"Okay, we're away, lets get some altitude before the fighters find us," commanded the skipper!

"This is Tailgunner, we have trouble," exclaimed Sandringham, watching his two four inch radar screens! "Bandits coming up seven O'clock."

"How many," asked Peterson?

"Two, sir . . . I mean four . . . I mean two groups of four! "Eight!" The other gunners could not see the approaching fighters because they had no navigation lights.

The skipper threw the ship into another wingstanding turn and asked after leveling out, "Did they alter course to follow? "Are the chaff dispensers still working?"

"Wait! "They're out of view, sir," replied Sandringham. "Yes they are, Sir." Newcomb began adjusting his radar's gain to detect and track aircraft. A moment later, Sandringham could see them again and added, "They're following their original course, Sir!"

A cheer went up through the ship. "Good," remarked Peterson, enthusiastically.

"They're heading away from us," observed Sandringham.

"Okay, we need a new course to get out of Russia."

"AN to AC, coming right up, sir . . . It'll be one zero one mark forty five, sir," announced Nawrocki.

"One o'one mark forty five," repeated Johns. "Maximum climb?"

"I want you to put as much distance between my ass and Russia as you can . . . as fast as you can," commanded Peterson, "before we run out of chaff!

"Yes Sir," answered Johns, "Will forty seven thousand feet be enough?" The searchlights suddenly dimmed and went black as the ship ascended into cloud.

"Unless The Lord calls us to heaven," Peterson exclaimed exuberantly! "You've been at it a long time, Hank. "Why don't you relieve Gordon in his nice warm bunk? "They'll never find us in this cloud."

"I'm right here," advised Grant.

"I'm okay, I can dose if I have to," answered Johns.

"That's what I'm afraid of," replied Peterson. "Lieutenant Grant, report to the bridge," he shouted. Grant unplugged his interphone jack from the left forward gunsight and climbed up to the flight deck. "Enjoy that nice warm bed Hank. "If they told me right, there's a pretty young girl back there keeping it warm for you!"

"I don't think Linda would like that."

"Take my bunk in the radio room then," replied the skipper. "Enjoy!"

Except for a break in Thule, Johns had been in the right seat since Texas—more than 24 hours. Colonel Peterson detected a possible character flaw in his loyal friend. He did not know how to let go. Letting someone else do the driving made him nervous. New pilots like Grant were assigned to Johns because he was a good instructor. Johns was sore from sitting in one position for too long. He immediately needed to relieve himself once he got up. The body loses water at altitude, so one need not go to the bathroom quite as often, but sooner or later nature calls. He needed a rest whether he liked it or not.

"Take a sleeping pill . . . that's an order," Peterson commanded! The bunk in the radio room, hung over Beaumont and Hernandez, made the little cabin seem much smaller, but Johns was close to the cockpit if he was needed. Besides, the skipper's bunk was really his bunk anyway. 753 was his ship.

Johns did not obey the order to take a pill. He no sooner climbed into the bunk, than he was fast asleep. As far as he was concerned, it had been more than twenty hours of continuous black uninterrupted night. Johns' night would last a few hours more. For Grant and the rest of the crew, there seemed to be some zodiacal light on the deeply curved horizon. Morning in Soviet Khazakstan was evening in Texas. It was time for bed. Nawrocki climbed up to the astrodome again. He wanted to shoot another sight before the stars began to disappear. The most dangerous part of the mission was now over, and now all they had to do was scrape the roof of the sky all the way to Japan.

From the tired eyes on the observation deck, the curved horizon seemed to be decorated with a thin blue line. Where the Earth's atmosphere touched the ground, there seemed to grow a rainbow of colors. There was a violet flash almost dead ahead, then a green one, and finally, a red one. But, the red one didn't go away. It rose and turned into a big red ball, over-whelming the dim golden light from the vacuum tubes with a solid orange glow that made the men up front squint their eyes. The ship was moving at more than two hundred fifty miles an hour, so the Sun seemed to rise faster than normal. The ship's speed combined with the rotation of the Earth. It had been twenty two hours since the sun had last been seen. All were glad to finally view the sunrise.

"We're at angels forty five," Grant called out over the interphone! Everyone felt safe and tired.

"Alright, we did it," shouted Newcomb! "We got away!"

"We survived, sir," corrected Beaumont.

"Time for me to go to work," announced Holbrook, the meteorologist, who up to then had been little more than a passenger. At night, there was little for him to do but change fallout filters, since he could not see the clouds. It had been night for almost a day. The rear gunners could see the billowy white contrails streaming behind the hot engines scarring the super cold stratosphere as far as their eyes could see. Their bodies told them it was time to sleep because it was bed time in Texas, but all they could do was shiver from the cold. They were clean on the other side of the world.

Ну,

полный
ход!

SVETLANA
February 1956

Two soldiers came banging on the bedroom door of a Russian woman. Forcing it open, they barged in to the private quarters of Svetlana Periskova and yelled, "Von wlye-tit camawl-yet Amerikan-ski†," telling her that there was an American plane!

"Eya yes-shech-yeh vinaw-vat‡," she replied sleepily, as though she was being accused of something? The men grabbed her from her bed by the armpits and dragged her down a hallway to a locker room. A third man grabbed her long blond hair from behind, and stuffed it into a white cotton skull cap. Lifting her arms up by the elbows, they pulled her nightshirt over her head, stripping her naked except for the skullcap and exposing a slim athletic figure with strong arms and a firm flat tummy hardened by years of military calisthenics. Her nipples stood erect as freezing air swirled around pale white goose-bumps. Sitting her down on an icy wooden bench, the men pulled drab green coveralls onto her legs, then stood her up again to insert her arms into the sleeves and pull the zippers closed over her shivering nude body. Sitting her back down on a parachute harness, one man laced thick soled boots onto thick wool socks as the other buckled the harness around her loins and

† **Вон летит самолет Амерйкански — There's an airplane, its American**
‡ **И я еще виноват? — And I am to blame?**

shoulders. They then pushed her out the door to a truck that was waiting. A parachute dangled loosely from her rump.

Three similarly dressed men were already in the truck, along with their six handlers. As Svetlana sat on one of the cold benches in the cargo bed, the two men who had awakened her pressed a leather helmet with earphones and goggles onto the skullcap. She rubbed her sleepy blue eyes.

The truck stopped in front of an open end Quonset type shelter, underneath of which was hidden a tiny silver plane with sharply swept back wings and a swept back tail decorated with red stars. The entire nose of the plane seemed to be missing. In its place, was a gaping jet intake hole with a septum in the middle, looking something like the face of a coward who's nose had been cut off for fighting unfairly. The plane's crew chief fired up the engine. It made a sound like a vacuum cleaner until he gave it spark and advanced the throttle. It thundered to life with a belch of fire and smoke out of the afterburner. Two crewmen knelt on the ground, waving their arms from side to side to prevent passers-by from being sucked into the ugly, hog-like snout. The men in the truck helped Svetlana climb onto the left wing. The crew chief jumped out of the cockpit and knelt on the right wing to help strap her in. As she slid onto her ejection seat, which was really just a metal bin to hold the parachute under an ice cold armored steel seat back, another man knelt on the left wing. They inserted the pin in her single point ejection harness. She clipped her face mask onto her helmet, its hose dangling like an elephant trunk, then pushed the transmit button on the side of the throttle and called, "Radio check," which means the same in Russian as in English.

"Sergei zd-yes†," a man answered!

"Pasha zd-yes," another answered!

"Mikhael zd-yes," she heard her third man answer!

Commander Leonov, below in the bunker, abruptly hollered, "Chtah-sss-vami? "Bistrah‡, bistrah!"

"Yest tovarich†," answered Lana!

† Сергеи здесь — Sergei here
‡ Что с вамй? Быстро! — What's the matter? Hurry!

The two groundcrewmen jumped from the wings and moved to the side of the plane, holding wheelchocks over their heads.

Svetlana pressed her radio button again and said to her men in English, "All right boys, follow your mother," a line she had heard in an American western movie about the Hatfields and McCoys, as she flicked a little silver switch to release her brakes. It was a short jolty ride to the end of the runway. Her three other tiny silver planes, which were also spangled with red stars, followed like a group of bobbing chickens over the rough potholed apron. The runway had been rolled flat and was frozen like an ice rink.

"Noo, polnoi hod‡," she commanded, and slowly advanced her throttle to full forward! Flames shot from the tails of the four tiny jets as they plowed through newfallen snow, leaving a powdery contrail behind them. There was plenty of room on the runway for them to take off together in finger-four formation, just a few feet apart. Sergei was on her left and Pasha and Mikhael were on her right. The four little planes, side by side, needed only half as much room as an RB-36. She pulled back on her stick after only a few seconds of acceleration. Her "boys" followed. The four of them stood on their tailflames and shot almost straight up as their landing gear clunked up into their noses and wings.

"Vector dvah dyeh-vyah-nostah, altitude chyeh-tirnaht-saht kilometra, range dvah-sto kilometra," Commander Leonov commanded over the radio. "Presledova!"

"Yah nyeh pah-nyee-mah-yoo, tovarich," answered Lana. "Gahvahreet myeh-dlyeen-yeh-yee! "Vector dvah dyeh-vyah-nostah*," she asked, not quite sure if she heard the intruder's bearing correctly?

"Da prava, vector dvah dyeh-vyah-nostah§," Commander Leonov repeated. "Polnie hod!"

"Yest tovarich," Lana repeated! She could hardly believe

† Ест Товаричь — Yes, (I have it) comrade!
‡ Ну, полный ход! — Well, full speed!
* Я не понимаю . . . Говорит медленнее! Вектор два девяносто? — I didn't understand . . . Speak slower! Vector two ninety?
§ Да права, вектор два девяносто! — Yes, right, vector two ninety!

her ears.   Her commander was sending her in the wrong direction! If there was an American plane trying to enter Soviet airspace, it would approach from the south or east, not from west by northwest.   It must be just a training exercise, she thought.   But if it was, why would she be told to intercept the intruder at fourteen kilometers?   No Russian plane could fly eight miles high.   It couldn't be a Russian plane trying to defect. An airliner would be easy meat.

"Stranno," commented Sergei! "Zapoot-annoy delo. "Ya prostaw nyeh maw-goo pon-yat†."

"Ya krichat vaw vs-yeh gor-wloh," shouted Leonov, seemingly at the top of his lungs, "vector dvah dyeh-vyah-nostah! "Von! "Marsh! "Ne-med-lennaw‡!" Svetlana did not question her orders again.   She could detect the edge in Comrade Leonov's voice.   He only got that way during inspection when he might be criticized.   Clearly there really was an American plane, or at least Leonov thought there was.   But if there was an American plane approaching from the west by northwest, then it had to have entered the motherland somewhere else and it was trying to leave the Soviet Union. If it were trying to leave, and had only now been detected, then had it already done what it had come to do?   No wonder Marshal Zhukov wanted it shot down! A disturbing thought entered her mind: 'Kiev is on vector 290!' Her mother lived in a little village just north of Kiev. If the plane had bombed Kiev, would her family be safe? The thought made the cold hairs on her icy neck stand on end.

As Lana and her men passed through the final layer of icy cirrus clouds into the bluish black morning sky, she could see a huge white vapor trail about ten miles in front of her.   The clouds and the ground seemed to merge into a furry blanket of white wool beneath her.   Fifteen seconds later, she could see a fiery glint of silver in front of the contrail.   The Sun was beginning to rise over her shoulder, bathing her cockpit in a

---

† **Странно! . . . Запутанное дело. Я просто не могу понять.**
— **Strange! A confused deal. I simply don't understand.**
‡ **Вон! Марш! Немедленно! — Out! March! Immediately!**

warm glow. The wind made a soothing rushing sound on the sides of her little plane. There was no other noise beside the whine of the engine. As the big ship grew larger and larger in her gunsight, she squinted to see if it really was American. "Chtaw etaw za ludy†," she asked her wingmen?

"Amerikanski," replied Sergei, authoritatively. His eyes were better than hers. After a few moments, she too identified it as an RB-36. There was now no doubt that it was American. No Russian plane shared this configuration. She nervously dialed sixty meters into her gunsight reticule, its maximum setting, so she would be able to tell when it was time to open fire.

"Arm cannon," commanded Svetlana, which means the same thing in Russian as it does in English. "Pasha, ya poidu nalevo, a tooee ee-di napravo‡." She heard a loud sound in her headset. It was unpleasant, so she took her thumb off the talk button and turned the volume down. She heard some garbled sounds. It was a bad time to have radio problems.

Sergei flew up beside her and made a gesture pressing his index finger against the side of his helmet while rotating his wrist. She replied with the same gesture. Pasha and Mikhail also gestured that they also had radio problems. Strange, that everyone's radio would fail at the same time! She remembered reading a report from another pilot that also had radio problems when intercepting an RB-36. It occurred to her, that they had not received any flight direction since they approached within ten miles of the American plane. Leonov was constantly shouting instructions during training maneuvers. He would talk even more, if it were actual combat. She should have heard something. She could hear only the sound of her engine, which hummed a continuous mechanical flute like tone, and the rushing of wind past her clear plastic cockpit canopy.

She made a gesture similar to cocking a bolt action rifle. Sergei and Pasha understood immediately and waved an a-okay. Pasha repeated the gesture to Mikhail, who's plane was far to

---

† **Что это за люди? — Who are these people?**
‡ **Паша, я пойду налево, а ты иди направо. — Pasha, I'll go left and you go right.**

the right and behind her in the finger four.

She switched her guns to armed and three electric bolts rammed three shells into the breeches of her three cannon with three loud clunks. Under her right foot, was a 37 millimeter anti-tank gun. Shooting down big planes requires big ordinance. Each projectile was a steel jacket fragmentation grenade, six inches long, and an inch and a half in diameter. With its brass cartridge case, it was more than a foot long. Under her left foot, were two 23 millimeter cannons. Each steel jacket projectile was four inches long and nearly an inch in diameter, with a lead core for penetrating through engine cylinders and cockpit armor. The cartridges for these guns were almost a foot long. She touched the trigger on her joystick to test her guns. "THUMP, thump thump," they answered!" She could hear the reports of her other planes' guns as she glanced between her panel and kneeboard, reading through her pre-combat checklist.

Her closing speed with the bomber was nearly a thousand miles an hour. She didn't think she could get a good shot at this speed. She wanted to see the giant American first. If it slowed down and lowered its landing gear to surrender, she would not shoot. Perhaps it was trying to defect in order to escape the exploitation of the capitalist system, she thought to herself? What a big trophy it would make! She briefly reminisced about the ceremony when she was awarded her first Hero of the Soviet Union Medal for bombing a German gun emplacement at night with an old PO-2 biplane. That was the most important day in her life. The little gold star with the little red ribbon said more about her character than a chest full of lesser medals. 'It is not easy for a woman to lead a fighter squadron,' she thought to herself. 'Women do not receive such opportunities without being better qualified than the men—especially a squadron with the newest jets.'

Что это за люди?
Who are these people?

Быстро,
быстро!

INTERCEPTION
February 1956

"Scanner to AC, incoming planes, two o'clock low," yelled Shultz into the interphone! "Four Migs!"

"AC to crew, battlestations," commanded the skipper as he flicked the dozen nose shutoff door, pod preheat, and nose de-ice switches to spin up the turbojets. He altered course, turning toward the fighters to make it harder for them to aim, and ordered, "Masks on, chutes on, activate radar, gunners test your weapons!"

Beaumont poked Johns out of bed. The sleepy pilot jumped down onto the radio console, surprising Hernandez with his feet on the man's desk as he scrambled up to the bridge to relieve Grant. Beaumont folded the pipe berth up to get it out of the way.

Peterson clicked the four spark switches and advanced the throttles in the overhead panel to air-start the jets, but only three of them lit. The right inboard turbine apparently had frozen up with ice in the fuel lines. He pulled the throttle back and turned off the spark to avoid a hot start and closed its nose door. Grant clumsily vacated the right seat and virtually fell onto the lower deck, as the skipper turned the ship violently with only one hand on the wheel. Gordon's hands were shaking. He strapped himself into the left forward gunsight sling, fighting twice the force of gravity as the ship turned. He reached over to the gunner's control panel and switched the guns from "off" to "ready." Washington and Murphy watched the upper forward gun bay covers rise up and slide to the sides. The turrets, looking like those of a Navy destroyer, rose up into position side by side. Hernandez got up from his desk and strapped himself into the sling at the right forward gunsight. Loud clicks were heard as electric bolts rammed shells into the breaches. Ear splitting bangs followed, as each gunner squeezed off a few rounds to heat up their gun barrels.

"Gosh, they're coming up fast," remarked O'Connor as he flicked the switch on his panel to open the lower turret door and deploy his guns, "over five hundred knots closure!" Sandringham activated his fire control screens for the tailguns. Shultz deployed the aft dorsal guns. They too added to the din as they tested their weapons.

"AC to crew, everybody look alive," ordered the skipper! "This is what you trained for, lets not have any surprises."

"Permission to fire," asked O'Connor from the lower right bubble that controlled the belly guns?

"Do not fire until fired upon," replied Peterson.

'The B-36 is a pretty plane,' Lana thought to herself, as she stared at it through her goggles with equally beautiful blue eyes. The rising sun reflected rainbows of color from the silver under surface of it's mighty wings. She watched the intruder peel off and stand on its right wingtip, turning aggressively toward her to cut off her advantage of a side shot. A lump rose in her throat. She wondered what kind of men would fly in a plane like that. Were they like Russian men? Had they bombed Kiev? Too bad she would have to shoot them down in order to meet them. Perhaps a few would survive bailing out and be taken before Leonov in chains. She strained her eyes to see signs of landing gear. Instead, she saw a hatch open on the belly of the plane. Four guns came out, two rotated and fired at the ground.

Her ice blue eyes narrowed in anger. She noticed the American symbol with its white star in a blue circle and red, white, and blue epaulets, as she sped past the guns. She rolled to turn and get back into attack position, but her wings began to stall because of the altitude. She was violently shaken as her four planes passed though the ship's fluffy white contrail. The turbulence caused Pasha and Mikhael to break formation. 'What right do you have to fly over our country and drop your atomic bombs on our children,' she thought to herself, her stiff upper lip hidden by her mask?

Lana looked over her shoulder to see the giant climbing at an unbelievable angle with black smoke pouring out of its jets. 'Who gave you permission to come here and fire your guns over my country,' her quick intelligent mind rambled on inside her pretty blonde head as she tried to think what the proper words in English would be to say to her prisoners after she forced them to bail out. 'Do you think you have the right to fly and drop your atomic bombs wherever you choose,' her mind raced, rationalizing what she was about to do? Her wingmen were thinking the same thoughts. She furrowed her brow.

Looking at her reflection in the Plexiglas canopy, she saw only a fighter pilot. There was nothing in her helmet, mask, or goggles to suggest she was merely a woman, except for the big blue eyes, now narrow with anger. She let go of her stick and pressed the backs of her gloves against the sides of her canopy, then crossed her forearms like an "X" in front of her breasts several times—the signal for high and low scissors. Sergei waved an "a-okay" that he understood the signal. Pasha repeated the gesture to Mikhail, who waved recognition, then the two of them rolled to the right and shrank from view until Lana could see only their contrails curving away in the distance.

Grant, Hernandez, Shultz, and Calabrese in the upper gun positions could all see the four little planes flying away from each other, their white cloudy contrails streaking wide circles in the dark blue, high altitude morning sky. The zoom climb had taken them to almost fifty thousand feet, but they could not stay there for long. It took Lana and the others a long time to turn around at such a high altitude. The Sun momentarily blinded her as it bathed her windscreen in light that seemed to highlight every scratch and smudge in the clear plastic.

If she went too fast, Lana could exceed the speed of sound and her planes could become unstable, even dangerous, in such close proximity. If she went too slow, or tried to turn too sharp, she could stall and slide into a potentially lethal flat spin in the thin air of the stratosphere. Lana took her time. There was no hurry. The RB-36 was not very fast. She knew the huge ship was going ballistic and it would soon have to start back down. Any turn results in a loss of altitude. Halfway through the turn, she shoved her throttle fully forward and fired her afterburner momentarily to climb.   Sergei followed, mirroring her every move, although this meant there would be little fuel left for landing.

The chief failing of the MiG-15, which her MiG-17 had been designed to replace, was instability at high altitude that made accurate gunnery impossible. The MiG-17 had a thinner, more swept back wing, with extra fences on the upper surface to help prevent stalls and a much more powerful engine to climb to altitude quickly. Her plan was to use this advantage to attack out of the sun, where the American gunners would have a hard time seeing her. She approached from below and on the right of the huge invader as a reckless motorist might blind side a semi-truck while entering the freeway. She dropped her underwing fuel tanks and Sergei did as well.

"This is scanner, the ones at four o'clock low just dropped their tanks, Colonel," yelled Calabrese! Everyone in the crew began to feel tense. Dropping tanks was an extremely provocative act that could not be misinterpreted.

"This is AC, permission to fire live rounds," granted the skipper, as he kept his eyes on two other jets approaching from the opposite direction! Every heart started pounding. Breathing became heavy. Adam's apples rose in every throat making it impossible to swallow. Bowels and bladders loosened so that every man who needed to go to the bathroom immediately did. Some drooled into their masks—a dangerous thing to do since it could cause the joker valve to freeze.

"Break left," commanded Peterson! Both he and Johns steered hard to the left then pulled back on their wheels while standing on their left rudder pedals. The Colonel kept his eyes on the planes in front as Johns watched his instruments as a good co-pilot is trained to do. The bright blue and purple stratospheric horizon rose like a vertical line in front of them with outer space behind them to their right and the mountains and morning clouds in front of them on their left. Peterson stared down the oncoming jets.

One would think that Svetlana's little fighters would be able to fly circles around the giant and fire at will. Certainly, down near the ground they could. But in the stratosphere, things were different. In thinner air, it was the big reconnaissance bomber that had the advantage in maneuverability. To fly high, the little planes had to travel at very near the speed of sound, which was also very near their stall speed. They could not climb or descend or throttle back, if they wanted to maintain altitude. They were essentially ballistic. If the fighters turned too sharply, their wings would stall, and they would fall out of the sky. If Lana dove directly at the intruder to aim her guns, there was a chance that her controls would lock because of an atmospheric phenomenon when approaching the sound barrier called compressibility—a shock wave can develop on the top of the wing, rendering the control surfaces useless. She would not be able to turn away in time, and fly directly into the American ship. If the RB-36 had forward firing machine guns like a fighter, it would have a better chance of hitting her than she had of hitting the big reconnaissance bomber. It was not a fair contest. All Peterson had to do to spoil their aim was turn. The ship's sixteen guns were mounted in turrets. The bomber could aim at the fighters, but the fighters could not aim back. The only advantage Svetlana had was numbers. Her men could attack from several directions at once. For this reason, she divided her flight into two, so that whichever way her prey turned to avoid her, either she and Sergei, or Pasha and Mikhail would have a clean shot with three cannon each, before being shot down themselves. Twelve cannon against sixteen is not a fair contest, but it evened the odds. The fighters' guns were larger.

There are rules in aerial combat, just as there are rules for safe driving. While the goal of combat is to maim or kill one's adversary, both the aggressor and the defender must be careful to avoid a collision. If a car on the highway is out of control, it is sometimes necessary for a safe motorist to make an evasive maneuver to avoid crashing, even though the other motorist may be at fault. In the First World War, air combat had been referred to as a gentleman's game. Colonel Peterson might very well have avoided the gunfire if he had simply flown straight and not turned. But then, Svetlana would have had no choice but to risk ramming his ship, which would be deadly for everyone. The skipper and Johns both knew she would make this sacrifice to protect her country from a nuclear holocaust. Of course she would! They would. She had no way of knowing that the giant bomber was only a tourist snapping pictures. Russians are not known for warmly welcoming uninvited guests, especially Russian women when they are out in the country by themselves. Russian men are known for fighting to the death to defend Russian women. If a defender in aerial combat is not a gentleman, or if he is a coward who panics and freezes and fails to make an evasive maneuver, both the aggressor and the defender may die. The outcome of the battle should be determined by skill and marksmanship, not by stupidity. Before one can win in combat, one must first survive the combat. Thus, it is only the gentlemen who live to tell about it. Just as in chess one is sometimes obliged to sacrifice a pawn, by the unwritten rules of war, the larger plane was obliged to turn directly in front of the guns of the smaller planes in the hopes of completing the turn and spoiling their aim before they flew close enough to score. There was a chance of being shot, but there was a certainty of being rammed if Peterson did nothing.

Lana watched in amazement as the giant ten engined ship diving in front of her stood on its left wing, its right wing absolutely vertical—a perfect shot, if only she was closer. It began to roll back upright as soon as Pasha and Mikhail zoomed past, their aim ruined. Lana gently moved her stick back and to the left to roll inverted into a high yo-yo and follow the big American down. She had been listening to the "chirp, chirp, chirp, chirp" the giant plane's tail radar made in her radar detection set. When the chirps changed into a constant tone, she knew the bomber had locked radar on her. She nearly lost control of her bowels, she was so afraid. Why hadn't they fired? Perhaps, she was still too far away.

The bright sky blue horizon formed a diagonal line across her gunsight from top right to bottom left, with the dark blue sky below on the right and the purple mountains and shiny silver target streaming long contrails above her on the left. The ship became a black silhouette. A bright glint of silver on the upper surface passed in front of the sun into perfect firing position. If only she was closer! She was blinded.

The contrails from the five planes twisted into a streaming white knot in the sky. Leonov watched helplessly from the ground with binoculars, unable to communicate with his subordinates. He hoped that Lana would maintain a cool enough head to make the same decisions that he would, if he were up there with her.

It was now a tailchase. She had them. If the ship continued its descent, she would have the advantage in the thicker air below. As expected, the ship made an aggressive vertical maneuver as soon as it leveled out. Lana rolled upright to follow it up. She could not climb in the thin air, so she again shoved her throttle fully forward, even though this meant breaking off the attack after her first pass and diving for the ground if she and Sergei were to have any fuel left for landing. Her totalizer gauge showed she had only three hundred kilograms of fuel left. She could not match the bomber's rate of climb.

'They must be ballistic,' Lana thought to herself. If she did not panic, or try to follow too aggressively and stall, maybe the American would come back down before she passed underneath. She chopped her throttle and leveled out. Sure enough, the huge bomber, now above her, started down. 'Which way will he break,' she wondered? If it broke to the North, the American would be flying into reinforcements that were surely on their way. To the South was China, where the obsolete propeller planes were no threat to the giant bomber. Lana rolled right. So did Peterson. She shoved her throttle fully forward and wrapped both hands around her joystick. "Trusosti oomreetah," she shouted, as she squeezed both triggers! "Ouideetee otsuda†!"

† Трусости умрите! . . . Уйдите отсюда! — Coward, die! . . . Get out of here!

"Scanner to AC, they're opening fire," yelled O'Connor, observing muzzle flash and fireflies emerging from under the noses of the little silver planes.

"This is AC, return fire," yelled Peterson!

Sandringham had already grabbed the little gearshift-like control handle under his desk with his left hand to lock radar on his target. With his right hand, he pressed the fire button on his console to fire the tailguns at fighters he could not directly see. A sound like a large motorcycle being kick started, only ear-splittingly loud, came from the back of the ship as he fired two short bursts, giving his guns ten seconds to cool off between each three second burst.

O'Connor, leaning off his bucket seat to push his head inside his Plexiglas blister, his knees resting on pads on either side of the gunsight, flicked his attack factor switch from "pursuit" to "straight on" and turned his pedestal sight, twisting the hand grips on the sides until the glowing target circle exactly enveloped the approaching planes. Depressing the action switch under his right palm, he squeezed the trigger to unleash two of the four cannon in the ship's belly. His little GSAP movie camera, attached to the sight, started whirring and clicking, though he could barely hear it beside the deafening muzzle blasts of his two cannon exploding beneath him.

Lana's instruments were a blur of vibration. The American ship seemed to be dancing in time with the crack of her guns. Her ears rang from the splitting thunder. "POP pop pop POP pop pop POP pop pop." Each time the big anti-tank gun under her right foot fired, it seemed to stop her little jet in mid-air. The tracers seemed to wobble like fireflies in front of her, due to the vibration. It wasn't possible to tell which glowing dots were hers and which had come from the American. The left wing of the giant exploded into a fireball. Smoky debris flew close to her engine intake as she climbed through the black contrail behind it. Her little plane was badly shaken by turbulence.

The air in the aft cabin instantly turned cloudy, due to sudden decompression, as the men heard an ear splitting "WHUMP, whump whump!" O'Connor's Plexiglas blister exploded. Playing cards that had flown off the table and garbage left from sandwiches and TV dinners swirled about in the cabin toward the hole in the side of the ship. Even the card table flew from behind the galley unit toward the hole as if levitated by magic. Blood spattered the walls and floor.

Grant, who's butt was in a sling to prevent him from falling to the floor while the ship turned with twice the force of gravity, was taking aim with the left-forward gunsight. His sight was shaped something like the handlebar of a motorcycle, but instead of a speedometer and gauges, there were black boxes containing gyroscopes, with a gun camera mounted on top that nearly obstructed his view. The sight itself was a slanted piece of glass angled at forty five degrees toward him. It reflected a yellow dot of light, projected from beneath, that seemed to hover in mid air wherever the sight was aimed.

He did not aim the guns directly. Instead, Grant fed information into a computer that calculated a firing solution based on the movements of the sight. While B-17 gunners during World War II could only lob bullets in the general direction that enemy planes were heading and hope that they would fly into them, like geese into a shotgun blast, the computers in Grant's gunlaying system had the ability to fire a 20 mm shell exactly to the location that the enemy would be when the projectile got there. All Gordon had to do was keep the bright yellow dot centered on Lana's plane and selsyn motors built into the gyro's on the sight would tell the computer how fast he was turning it. There was a circle of smaller yellow dots that could be expanded or contracted by twisting his left hand grip to communicate the adversary's range to the computer. Grant first had to turn the target size setting knob to the size of the enemy plane that was being fired on. For the MiG-17, this was thirty three feet, equal to the wingspan and the length of the fuselage. Then the circle of bright yellow dots was made larger or smaller by twisting the grip, much like revving up a motorcycle, until

the circle exactly surrounded the enemy. The computer could then calculate the change in range as well as direction. There were also knobs to set the temperature, altitude, and airspeed on the gunner's control panel, as well as an attack factor switch at the base of the sight, which had to be set to "pursuit" when the adversary was trying to get away. He had done that before the battle began. As long as Grant kept the yellow dot and range circle exactly on the target, his computer could not miss. He squeezed the trigger.

Every bullet Grant fired pounded into the closest of the two MiG's unerringly. Belts of seven inch long, electrically primed ammunition shot out of his guns like jackhammers, at twenty rounds per second. When the closest plane exploded and broke up, he released his trigger and trained his guns on the leader. He was only able to fire off fifty rounds before both of his guns jammed. Grant struck the base of the sight with his fist and yelled, "Dammit," as he watched his stream of fireflies arc out above the mountains on the horizon and ahead of Lana's little silver plane, then miraculously seem to turn in mid air to meet her as chunks of aluminum, fire, smoke, and other debris burst from her glistening red starred shiny aluminum skin!

Lana was puzzled when the loud bangs did not stop, the moment she released her triggers. They seemed to be coming from the back of her little plane as she climbed away. She was thrown forward against her shoulder straps. Her engine started making squealing vacuum cleaner noises. Her controls became unresponsive as her wings stalled. The plane sounded frighteningly silent, except for the ringing in her ears and the startling, "whump, whump, whump," of metallic pounding which seemed to come from her armored seat back as the last few of Grant's explosive shells hit like boilermaker's hammers.

Little triangular pieces of metal, arranged in a circular pattern like little king's crowns, started poking up from the surface of her wings, forming jagged dotted lines as Grant's armor piercing tracer rounds passed through the silver skin. Rectangular chunks of control surfaces flew off behind her into a trail of brown smoke, blown loose by the explosive shells. She moved her left hand over to the throttle to try to restart her engine, but it was no use. The big blue eyes of an extremely frightened woman stared back at her from her Plexiglas canopy. She repeatedly crossed herself in Eastern Orthodox fashion: forehead, heart, right breast, left breast; forehead, heart, right breast, left breast; forehead, heart, right breast, left breast, thinking that might help the engine to restart. "Ah tepyer voi bawitessț," she shrieked, speaking to herself!"

Her little plane needed to travel at five hundred miles an hour to continue to fly eight miles up. Without its engine, in the thin air at the edge of space, her little plane began to tumble and fall. With all her might, Lana pressed her feet into the rudder pedals to keep her helmet from coming off her headrest and banging from side to side against the Plexiglas canopy. She removed her hand from the throttle and tried to feel for the ejection trigger, a loop of yellow cable between her legs. She struck herself in the facemask twice due to the plane's violent convolutions before she got both hands on the grip. Her tumbling plane fell like a rock. She would have to fall five miles before the air would be thick enough to fly without an

---

† **А, теперь вы боитесь!** — **Now you are afraid!**

engine—or support a parachute. She could not make sense of what she saw: blue, white, green, brown; blue, white, green, brown! Land and sky blended into a blurry milkshake as the nose of her plane tumbled up and down and down and up.

Washington noticed two red lights on the left engineer's panel, but he could not hear the fire warning buzzer above the ringing in his ears. "Fire on one and two," Murphy shouted at him! Washington was watching the fireball on the wing instead of the lights on his panel as he should. Murphy yelled even louder, "Extinguishers one and two!" Murphy cut fuel to the two left engines. The ship lurched to the left. This made it harder to pull out of the dive.

"Break right," commanded the Colonel! Johns instantly applied right aileron and rudder to compensate. They had to level out before they could pull up.

"Feathering one and two," Murphy yelled, as he flicked switches on his desk to feather the props.

Johns grabbed the throttle for the remaining turbojet under the right wing and looked at the skipper. Peterson nodded his approval. Johns cut power to prevent a flat spin. The ship fell out of the sky.

Washington clicked up two switches on his left panel, then lifted the fire extinguisher discharge switch up until the smoke and flames on the burning wing were replaced by a white trail of methyl bromide. "Loosing fuel in tank two," he shouted. "Tank one gone!"

"Opening tank two transfer valve and turning on booster pump," Murphy replied, flicking switches on his right panel. "Opening crossfeed. "Turning all the other tank valves off! "Lets use as much fuel out of there as we can."

"Okay," replied Washington as he watched the fuel flow gauges!"

"We're hit, we're hit," yelled Wong in the mission control room. "Help!" Johns got up from his seat and strapped on an emergency oxygen bottle, and went below. Only command officers were allowed to enter the mission control room—that meant only the skipper or Johns could render aid. The air in the radio room became cloudy due to sudden decompression. Johns tapped Grant on the shoulder and pointed at his seat beside the commander's chair, before disappearing into the communication tube to find out what damage the Soviets had done to his four million dollar ship. Grant ascended onto the bridge, taking his place at the controls.

The battle was over in less than thirty seconds, but it seemed like thirty minutes due to the speed at which everyone's hearts were pounding. Combat is not like a car crash where a stupid idiot overestimates his ability to control his car and the next thing he knows he is in the hospital. When danger can be seen approaching, the heart pounds and the pulse quickens. Adrenaline causes nerves to frazzle. Bowels and sphincters relax. Knees and elbows weaken. Thoughts race by at ten times normal speed, as memories of evil acts done in childhood resurrect themselves to crucify the mind. Mothers' and fathers' voices shout that it is time to die. Each heartbeat thumps like an Indian war drum. Lungs burst from the chest in an effort to breathe ever harder. Fifteen seconds after the battle, after friends are dead and the enemy has escaped, fear turns to rage and the mind is filled with kill, kill, kill! As cowardly enemies retreat, hatred makes the heart beat stronger.

Lana struggled in vain to regain control of her tumbling silver plane. She wept out of desperation and cried, "Oh kakoi oo-jass! "Ya prismert†," she added, feeling certain she was about to die. She could not safely eject while her plane was tumbling. That made her cry. She thought of a verse from Pushkin:

I fight for peace,
but die for the fatherland.

Then as if to bargain with her maker, she said it out loud,

† О какы ужась! Я при смерть! — All is lost! I'm about to be killed!

"Ya bawrots-ya za mir,

ja vyed oom-yer-yet za rad-yi-noo†!"

Even if she survived the ejection and her parachute opened, she would freeze to death before she reached the ground. If she did reach the ground alive, she would still freeze to death, exposed, without shelter from the Russian winter wind blowing across the steppes. If she somehow managed to keep warm, the wolves and bears would eat her smooth white loins during the hard winter night. She began to remember another verse from Pushkin:

Canon thunder,

trampling horses,

neighing moans,

and death and hell from all sides,

so she said it aloud,

"Grom pooshek,

taw pot, rjan-ye, ston

ee smyert ee ad saw v-sekh stawrawn‡!"

She gave up trying to control her plane and removed her hands from the joystick. Then, pushing the talk button on her throttle, she placed her cold right glove over her chest and said, "Kraseevah Seryozha, ya zah-bloo-deel-sah! "Dah svedanya maya drooga*." She didn't know if he could hear her, but perhaps someone would tell him that his name was among the last words from her lips.

Lana began to worry that there might be a God. She had been baptized and raised a Christian until she was fifteen, when the local party member came and closed the church. She signed a paper renouncing her beliefs as a condition of entering pilot

† **Я бороться за мир, ж вед умереть за родину!**
‡ **Гром пушек, топот, ржанье, стон, И смерть и ад со всех сторон (Пушкн)**
* **Красива Серюза, я заблудился! До свидания моя друга. —**
Beautiful Sergei(affectionate nickname), I'm lost! Goodbye my good friend (or lover).

training. She remembered staring at the clouds and wondering what it was like to fly like a bird. Who would think, that after surviving so many missions in a rickety biplane in wartime, she would lose her life in a modern jet in peacetime?

Lana could see only a bright flickering light through her tears, so she began to apologize to God for having fallen short of being a good Christian. "Ya kayatsya vee gryehhah†," she shouted! She opened her eyes. The bright flickering light was gone. It seemed she was inside a tornado. The world spun around her gunsight. She recognized, at once, that she was in a spin. Not a tumble or a flat spin, but a normal spin from which every recruit in pilot training is taught to recover. She grabbed the joystick and stomped on her right pedal. The agile little fighter instantly responded by aiming straight at the ground. Lana pulled back on the stick and confidently felt her buttocks pushed hard into her parachute seat cushion as the horizon leveled out in front of her.

"Kak zdess krassivaw," Lana shouted joyfully! "Spah-seebah Sanct Peter! "Bahl'shoyee spahseebah‡! She repeatedly crossed herself three times: forehead, heart, right shoulder, left shoulder; forehead, heart, right shoulder, left shoulder; fore-head, heart, right shoulder, left shoulder, in Eastern Orthodox fashion.

Lana aimed her nose downward to prevent a stall. Without its engine, her MiG-17 was more sled than glider. Its blunt, cut off nose caused handling problems. If she was to survive winter at the foot of the Tien Shan Mountains, she would have to land in one piece. She recognized the road between Ayaguz and Alma Ata. Perhaps she could land there if the telegraph poles were not too close. At least near a road, someone would find her charred bones for a proper funeral. In the newfallen snow, the road was nothing but a pair of wagon tracks with hoof prints between.

† Я каяться в грехах! — I repent of my sins!
‡ Как здесь красиво! Спасибо Санкт Петр! Большое спасибо! — What a beautiful day! Thank you(God save you) Saint Peter! Big thank you!

Lana remembered that the wind was from the west when she took off, so she turned west and looked for a reasonably straight stretch of road ahead. How strangely quiet her plane was without an engine, she thought to herself. Air whistling though the many gunshot holes made a rushing sound. She clicked the landing gear switch to down and there was no sound. The hydraulics were out. She repeatedly jerked the handle of her manual hydraulic pump to extend the gear, but she had no way of knowing if it was down or shot away. The indicator light would not light up.

Lana violently shoved her stick from one knee to the other to try to rock down the gear. Her head and shoulders banged against the canopy—still no indicator light. She flicked her flaps switch, but there was no electrical power to lower them. She pulled back on her stick to see what her new stall speed was, then lined up with the road for her approach. This was not the first time she had to crash-land in combat. The last time she did it, was at night behind enemy lines. Flash backs of the previous crash dogged her mind and interfered with her concentration. Belly landing a supersonic jet having a stall speed, without flaps, of 150 mph on an icy road was a more delicate matter than landing a 40 mph biplane in an open field. She kept both hands on the joystick.

Suddenly, Lana heard a loud boom. Over her right shoulder, a small mushroom cloud of black smoke could be seen behind her in the distance, growing out of the white snow. When she saw it, a shiver went up her spine so strong it made her hands shake. "Etaw Mother, radio check," she demanded!

"Pasha zd-yes," a voice answered!

"Mikhael zd-yes," she heard her third man answer!

"Sergei, radio check," Lana repeated! There was silence.

"Sergei, radio check," she repeated again! The silence continued.

"Dvaht-sat ahdyeen, raadeeoh check," she heard Commander Leonov demand. "Dvaht-sat ahdyeen, raadeeoh check," he repeated!

"Seryozha, raadeeoh check," she shreiked, bursting into tears as she looked back again at the column of smoke!

"Sergei Andreiovich, aht-fehteet srah-zoo," commanded Leonov! The silence continued. "Sergei Andreiovich Rostov, dvaht-sat ahdyeen, Ya spra-seet," the commander begged! The silence continued.

"Seryozha, raadeeoh check," Lana cried, looking over her shoulder again at the column of smoke. "Ya ouveryat ve lyoubve. "Ya lyoubeet bez pamyateet, she sobbed!"

Telegraph poles on the side of the road were rapidly reaching up to grab her. It was too late to change her mind about landing. She would have only one chance. 'They are no closer than my wingman,' Lana reminded herself. This made her think more of Sergei, who used to be there. She wondered, for a moment, if it would be best to push her stick all the way forward and end it all, but professionalism took over. 'The wreckage must be recovered for spare parts,' she thought to herself.

Lana flared and stalled it in with a thud. She pulled the throttle all the way back to deploy her drag brakes as soon as her wheels touched. There was no hydraulic pressure to apply the brakes. The landing gear seemed to make unusually loud thumps because of the silence of the engine being off. The belly of her plane immediately skidded when the gear collapsed. The snowy surface was glazed over with ice. There was a headwind, but it took a long time for the little jet to slow down, gobbling snow into its large intake hole as it went.

Lana was belly landing at over one hundred seventy miles per hour. It seemed as though she was driving on that road for miles. When she was moving slow enough, her right wheel, which was partly extended, sank into the snow and jerked the plane completely around until it was going backwards. The nose rose into the air, then thumped down onto the ice. She screamed as it stopped. Her hands shook. She was a nervous wreck.

† **Я уверять в любви. Я любить без памяти! — I proclaim my love. I love you madly!**

Ripping off her goggles and face mask, Lana dropped her pretty face into her shaky hands and sobbed. She had failed. Her plan had failed. Her squadron had failed. The entire Red Air Force had failed to stop the intruder. Her country had failed to protect its borders. Was her family still alive? She had failed as a leader. Whatever the giant American had come to do, it had gotten away with it. She let it get away. She let her country down and now there would be questions about her competence. There would be questions about the competence of any woman to lead a fighter squadron. There would be questions about the competence of women to fly airplanes. She let her wingmen down and now one of them was dead. What was Leonov going to say? Her years of training had been wasted. She let Sergei down, and now her lover was dead. What was she going to tell his parents?

Lana banged her pretty forehead repeatedly on her gunsight until she became sick to her stomach, then she vomited on the floor, bawling like an infant. She did not want to climb out of her plane unwounded. If only she had augured in, she thought, death would be easier. She could not stop her hands from shaking. There was silence under a beautiful sunny sky, still scarred by the twisted white contrails of stratospheric combat. How was she going to live without Sergei? All of her plans for the wedding were ruined. She wished her broken little plane would burst into flame so she could die with dignity.

Lana crouched quietly, waiting for something to happen. Purple, snow capped mountains glistened in the distance. Newfallen snowflakes sparkled on the surface of the ice like diamonds. Bells jingled. With teary eyes, she looked up. A black figure approached along the road, shimmering as if in a mirage in the blowing snow. She could tell from his narrow worsted wool coat and large furry hat that he was a Cossack.

Weeping, Lana bent down, hoping he wouldn't notice her—but how could anyone miss a supersonic jet crashed in the middle of the road? The jingle bells got louder and stopped beside her little plane. She looked up.

The Cossack's wagon was a flat wooden board with a bulbous axle from an old military vehicle bolted underneath. Shotgun ammunition stuck out of small pouches on the front of his black worsted wool coat. His hands were stuffed into a fox fur muff. His mule was decorated with red yarn and round silver bells. Leather reigns connected the animal's halter with the muff. Out of military habit, Lana snapped to attention as she always did when civilians were around. He looked at her and then drove on, as though he saw jets in the ditch every day.

Lana cranked her canopy back. With a gruff voice to distract him from noticing her teary eyes, she commanded, "Prahsteetyeh, pah-mahghee-tyeh mnyeh†? The man looked at her with surprise, then clicked his tongue and drove on. Lana pulled the pin on her ejection harness and climbed out onto the wing. Because the landing gear had collapsed, she fell only three feet into the snow. A cutting wind reminded her that she should have worn something under her flight suit. Teary eyed, she chased after him with quivering knees, her parachute flopping behind. When she caught up, she repeated, asking for help, "Prahsteetyee, pah-zhah-loostah, pah-mahghee-tyee mnyeh? "Ya idoo-wle prye shkom‡?"

He could not understand her. The only Russian the Cossack knew was how to make small talk with pestering government bureaucrats, so he said, "Strannaya paw-gawda; toh jarko, toh hawladno*," remarking about the weather.

"Nyeh toh ch-tah hawlawdah, no vs-ye je praw-hlwlad-nah," she replied, insinuating that the weather was the same as always. She repeated that she needed help, "Pah-mahghee-tyee mnyeh?"

He pulled on the reigns inside his muff and stopped, looking at her from head to toe. How strange she looked in her green flight suit and leather helmet. He had never seen a woman dressed that way before. Lana stood at attention. Her cold

† **Простите помогите мне? — Excuse me, can you help me?**
‡ **пожалуйста ... Я йду ле пре шкомь? — please ... must I go on foot?**
* **Странная погода, то жарко, то холодно — Strange weather, first hot, then cold**

breasts seemed to almost poke through her uniform. The idea that a woman would be flying a jet airplane seemed ridiculous. Yet, her pink bloodshot eyes indicated that she had been crying. Her shaking knees revealed she was in trouble and needed help. "You Russians think you are very important," the Cossack mumbled in barely intelligible Russian.

"With Communism, everyone is important," Lana replied slowly, trying to help him understand. Noticing some large milk cans on the back of the wagon, she continued tearfully, "Without milk, we pilots would not be able to fly!"

In somewhat better Russian, the man replied, "Now I can see that you are a hero." He patted the seat on the front of the wagon. She climbed up. He covered her shaking knees with his blanket. She burst into tears on his shoulder.

"Navigator to crew,

those mountains down there are the Chinese border . . .
"We're out of Russia!"

ESCAPE
THROUGH
CHINA
February 1956

The crew was strangely silent. From his curved desk against the huge front window, Nawrocki the Navigator watched the beautiful snow caps of the Tien Shan Mountains divide decks of low cloud, revealing pale green valleys between them under the dark blue star-spangled sky. With the cabin depressurized, everyone had to wear masks.

After passing through the photo lab on his way to the back of the ship, Johns opened the hatch to the communication tube. There was a large window in the left side that wasn't there before. Every time an anti-tank round had hit, it blew away several square feet of metal. Fortunately, they were designed to explode only if they hit something solid like a wing spar. Russian planes were made of heavy aluminum riveted together. Their ballistics experts never considered that Consolidated Vultee would build a ship out of paper thin magnesium. Many of Svetlana and Sergei's projectiles had passed right through without exploding.

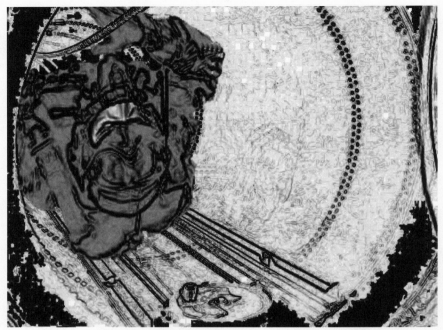

Johns entered the sixty foot long tube, which now had jagged holes in it, feet first, so he could bend the metal down with his boots as the tube trolley passed. When he arrived, the aft cabin was a mess of debris. There was a banging sound coming from outside the ship. Johns rolled Nakamura over, being careful not to step on his intestine, which was draped all over the floor like a coiled snake. He removed Nakamura's mask. Nakamura began panting heavily. Shultz shouted from high up in the top right gunner's chair with hands still shaking, "What are you doing? "If you take his mask off, you'll kill him!"

Johns looked up at Shultz with a piercing gaze, then removed Nakamura's helmet. Nakamura's eyes were wide open with a look of utter horror as he gasped for breath. Blood came out of his mouth as he tried to speak. Two seconds later, his eyes glazed. Johns took the bloody mask and helmet, and put them on Mary, who had passed out on one of the bunks. Blood dripped from the ceiling and spattered on the floor like a roof leak. "Help me get Calabrese down," ordered Johns! Shultz got up from his seat shaking, feeling wet underwear sliding against his legs. He bent over, moving across the catwalk to Calabrese's chair.   They unbuckled the corpse and shoved the Italian's remains over the galley unit into a bunk beside Mary.

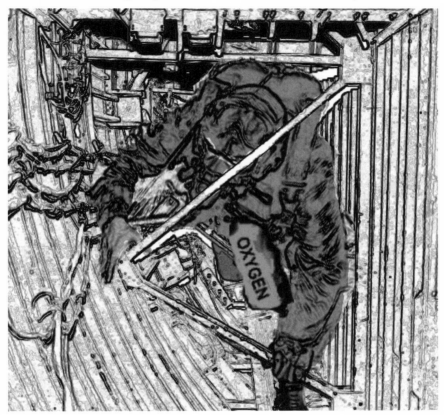

Johns then crawled through the structural triangles beside the gun bay to get into the mission control room. Whitefeather and Wong were wearing their space suits and had removed a blood spattered tape from Hughs' tape recorder, breaking the tape between the reels where it went through the machine. Whitefeather gently wiped the blood off the reel with a piece of paper. Johns tried to get their attention by waving his arms, but they didn't notice him enter the room, so he plugged in his headset and asked, "What are you doing that for? "Aren't you going to help him?"

The two space men jumped with surprise, when they heard someone on their private channel. "This is all he has," replied Whitefeather, swivelling his chair and turning his whole body to look at Johns. "If this tape is ruined, he died for nothing."

"Died," exclaimed Johns, as he pulled back the body which was hunched over their desk? The back of Major Hughs' space helmet had a neat round, one inch hole. As Johns lifted it up and looked into the front of it, all he could see was the inside of Hughs' skull, which was whitish pink in color with drops of blood dripping down the inside of it. A Russian expert, Hughs had been listening in on and recording the Soviet fighter pilots' conversations. Johns jumped back and began frantically wiping his flight suit with his bloody gloves until it was smeared red. He had not realized that the fluffy pink stuff all over the desk and floor was formerly the contents of Hughs' head. Major Hughs was a very intelligent man who knew several languages. Whitefeather took the other tape reel and put it in a can covered with blood. He wrote "Mrs. Hughs" on the label. "Why 'Mrs. Hughs,'" asked Johns?

"This end was never recorded," replied Whitefeather, "its not classified. "I intend to give it to Loretta when we get back." He silently placed it with the other tapes.

"AC to crew, how bad were we hit," inquired the skipper as he reached up to shut down the jet engines? Johns and Wong gazed at each other across the bloody mayhem in the mission control room. The bomb bay interphone was on a private channel so they could only talk to the skipper. "THIS IS AC, DAMAGE REPORT," demanded Peterson! Wong swivelled and nodded for Johns to answer.

"Mike, we lost Merril," answered Johns, "Nakamura and Calabrese are gone too. "I'm going back to the aft cabin." He unplugged his jacks and crawled back through the triangular stringers beside the gun bay. When he returned to the aft cabin, he asked Shultz, who was still sitting in his gunner's chair looking at the motionless bodies in the bunk, "Where's O'Connor?"

"He certainly didn't run away," Shultz snapped!

"Oh no," Johns exclaimed as he noticed an air hose and safety strap disappearing under the card table and through the hole where the lower right Plexiglas blister used to be. The banging sound was coming from there. A crumpled leather helmet was banging against the side of the ship. Attached to the helmet was a large piece of shredded meat like a whole beef brisket, only with a bare human arm bone sticking out of it red with blood. The flesh was slapping in the wind on the side of the fuselage, painting it red as though the ship itself was bleeding. In fact, the ship really was bleeding since all the blood drained through the shell holes and spread out under the tail in a wide streak of slowly darkening crimson. Johns winced, and tried to fight back tears caused as much by the strong blast of wind coming through the missing bubble as by his own grief.

"O'Connor is dead too," Johns announced after pulling out O'Connor's jack and plugging in his own. He pulled in the bloody safety strap, then lovingly lifted the helmet and remains up into the other bunk beside Mary.

Almost immediately, blood soaked through the canvas cot and dripped on the floor. "What if we want to sleep," Shultz asked? Johns ignored him.

When Mary came to, she saw the blood and meat on both sides of her. It looked to her like a seal hunt. Normally, people wake up from nightmares, not from pleasant dreams to experience one. She screamed and cried bitterly, trying to yank Nakamura's bloody mask off as though some monster was devouring her head. She did not know how to unlatch the clasps, but her head was small enough that she could pull it off. With all the bitterly cold air circulating around the cabin, even Mary felt cold, so she climbed down shivering. She stripped off her blanket and started to put on her leggings and sealskin boots before passing out again because of the thin air. She was not the least bit attractive—laying naked on the icy floor covered with blue goosebumps. Johns rushed over and put the mask and helmet back on her. He tried to make her understand, when she woke up, that she had to wear them. She kept trying to take the helmet off because oxygen deprivation was giving her a splitting headache and she foolishly suspected that the helmet was causing it. It had not escaped her, that all the men had put on masks just before they died. She did not want to be next. Johns helped her put on her white bearskin parka. It had strange lumps in it because of the repairs she made, but once she was covered, she had better protection from the cold than anyone else.

"This is AC, I'm still waiting for that damage report, Hank," repeated the skipper.

"Scanner to AC, most of the cowling of number two engine is blown away," answered Shultz, who had climbed down and was looking out the lower left bubble. "A lot of skin is blown off the upper and lower surface of the wing around there, and we've got large hole in the left side of the bomb bay, near mission control, and the weapons bay just forward of me. "The rear dorsal gun door won't close. "Its causing a lot of drag . . . "We also got a large hole in the floor of the cabin and several smaller ones."

"Thank you Sergeant," answered the skipper. "I want you to get the drop tank ready to salvo and I want that Dorsal turret door closed. "You can loose the guns."

"Scanner to AC, what if we're attacked," asked Shultz?

"We don't have any gunners left to fire them," snapped Peterson. "Don't question my orders again!"

"Yes sir," replied Shultz. The only way into the turret bay was through the mission control room. He wasn't allowed in there, but the skipper warned him not to question orders, so he removed his parachute and harness, grabbed his tool belt and portable oxygen bottle, then opened the hatch on the right side of the bulkhead, disappearing into the triangular stringers beside the weapons bay. Wong and Whitefeather looked at him as he entered, since wasn't supposed to be in there, but they said nothing. The big Indian made a haphazard attempt to cover the big map on the wall, but it was so spattered with blood, it was not readable anyway.

There was no bulkhead separating the mission control room from the weapons bay. As Shultz climbed up a short ladder to the top turrets, he had a feeling of flying in the First World War. The dorsal gun bay was a huge open cockpit.

Freezing wind buffeted into the hatch. The wind also swirled into the mission control room, but Whitefeather and Wong were oblivious to it in their warm space suits. When Shultz stuck his head out, he was immediately bowled over by the two hundred fifty mile per hour wind. Because of the thin air, it was only as forceful as an eighty mile per hour wind at sea level. He tried to jimmy the sliding hatch with a screwdriver. There was a hole in the side of the ship directly under the hatch, preventing it from closing.

Shultz attached a wrench to the nut holding the chain drive sprocket. The hatch moved when he turned it, but with a lot of resistance. He unbolted the silver turret covers, unlatched the gun breaches, and removed the heavy ammunition belts. After feeding the business ends of the ammo guides over the side, the ten foot belts of six inch shells flowed like snakes until their bins were empty. Once the ammo was gone, Shultz loosened the hold down screws and trigger wires. Lifting each heavy six foot long cannon barrel on his shoulder, one at a time, he rested them on the side of the hatch and shoved them overboard. Theybanged loudly as they tumbled off the side of the ship. With effort, he cranked the door shut with his wrench and the ship was aerodynamically clean again—except for the shell holes which he couldn't do anything about.

Once the hatch was closed, the mission control room seemed very dark inside. Shultz passed behind the Ravens' chairs, smearing the blood spatters on the map into long streaks. Whitefeather and Wong seemed not to notice him. With many contortions through the jungle gym of triangular stringers connecting the outer skin to the bomb racks, he made it to the front of the drop tank and unscrewed the fuel and electrical lines. Plugging in his interphone jack, he said, "Gunner to AC, tank clear for salvo."

"Thank you, Sergeant," Peterson replied. "AC to VO, salvo drop tank."

"VO to AC, roger on that," Shultz heard Newcomb reply. Was the skipper not going to give him time to get back to the aft cabin? Peterson seemed not to remember that on a reconnaissance bomber, the drop tank salvo switch is on the Photonavigator's panel, not the video observer's, so when Shultz overheard Newcomb command, "VO to Navigator, Salvo drop tank," a chill went up his spine!

"Roger," replied Nawrocki! His bowels relaxing in fear, realizing he was not wearing his parachute or safety strap, Shultz ducked under the wing spar and hugged the nearest empty bomb rack with all his might.

In the forward cabin, Nawrocki flicked up the selector switch on Kewscinski's bombing control panel for bomb bay number three and lifted the red cover to flip the salvo switch up. On the bombing control panel, a light lit with a message underneath "BOMB BAY FUEL TANK READY FOR SALVO." Nawrocki then turned the safety switch to "BOMB DOORS ENABLED," and touched the little red hat button on top of the joystick beside the bombsight.

The entire floor of the bomb bay disappeared in an eyeblink as the bomb doors snapped open. A two hundred fifty mile per hour wind whipped Shultz's coveralls like a cat o'nine tails. The blast blew his feet off the catwalk until he was dangling by his arms over the clouds, thirty thousand feet below. He screamed and clasped his hands together in a mutual handshake agreement with himself not to let go. If he did, he would take an entire three minutes to fall to his death. With a bang and a grinding sound, the huge three thousand gallon drop tank fell out of the ship, vanishing instantly into thin air as soon as the wind hit it. The doors snapped shut just as quickly with a thunderclap.

"Tank's away," exclaimed Johns as he watched the big 3,000 gallon green oblong tank fall into the clouds from Nakamura's gunsight blister. "Doors closed," he added as Nawrocki flicked the switch on Kewscinski's control panel to close the doors. "Where's Shultz?"

Turning around toward Murphy, the Colonel asked, "Marv, what's our fuel situation?"

"Not good skipper."

"Do we have enough to make Okinawa?"

"No."

"What about the Gulf of Chi Li?"

"How far is it," asked Murphy?"

Peterson paused, then exclaimed, "That bad huh? He pressed the interphone button on his wheel and said, "AC to Navigator . . . "Duane, how far to the Gulf of Chi Li?" Everyone on the lower deck cringed when they heard that. They all knew he wouldn't be asking if there was enough fuel for Okinawa. The thought of having to ditch in icy winter seas, waiting for days to be rescued, is hardly better than going down in flames. At least, under a parachute, there is a chance to survive—even if it means being interrogated in a prisoner of war camp.

It was peacetime, but they were spies. Would the Red Chinese let them go if they bailed out? The thought of eating Chop Suey and fried rice for the rest of their lives did not seem very inviting. Besides, the Communist revolution had caused a famine and millions of Chinese were now starving. Would spies be treated any better than the average Chinese? Could a six foot, one hundred eighty pound American survive on the same ration that a five foot, hundred twenty pound Chinaman got?

Peterson pondered the options. Perhaps ditching was the best alternative. Most of his men had families. He had to at least try to make it for their children's sake. It was better to be dead than to be missing. At least their wives would have a chance at a normal life if they remarried. It had not fully dawned on those in the nose of the ship what trouble they were in. Those in the aft cabin could see the damage and the dead. No one up front could see the skin missing from the wing or how much fuel had been burned in the fireball.

"Tail gunner to AC, there's a plane below us on a parallel course," warned Sandringham over the interphone as he pressed his face into his radar hood, trying not to shiver from the extreme cold.

"This is AC, what kind of plane," asked the skipper."

Looking down with Nakamura's binoculars, Johns answered, still manning Nakamura's blister, "A TU-2."

"Is it a threat?"

"It's just hanging there below us."

"What does the book say on the TU-2?"

Pulling a book from the shelf under his radar desk, Newcomb opened it, pressed his talk button, and said, "VO to AC, Tupolev TU-2: Two Shvetsov fourteen cylinder radials, ceiling thirty one thousand feet, speed three hundred knots, two twenty millimeter cannons and three light machine guns, crew of four."

"I take it then it is not a threat," asked the skipper?

"I think they're probably just keeping an eye on us Colonel," replied Newcomb.

"Navigator to AC, coming up on Urumchi, sir," interrupted Nawrocki.

"Should we do a photo run, sir," asked Newcomb?

"I'm just trying to get us home," answered the Colonel.

"PN to AC, Sir, if we're flying over it, we might as well photograph it," advised Kewscinski, who had been more or less in a daze since the attack. "If we don't, they are going to ask why we didn't."

"Yeah, looking at it that way, you're probably right," answered Peterson. "Photographic conditions are just about perfect and someone will have to come back here if we don't. "Maybe if that plane out there sees we're just here to take pictures, he'll leave us alone."

"Tailgunner to PN, from where they're flying, sir, I'd say they want to be in the pictures," quipped Sandringham, who was still listening from the aft cabin!

Turning around to face the Black man, the skipper said, "Lorenzo, I want you to go back there too, and get together with Shultz to see if you can get one of those engines re-started." Washington did not like the prospect of spending the remainder of the flight in the icy, unpressurized rear cabin, but if anyone had a chance of repairing the engines in flight he did. As a member of the famous Tuskeegee squadron, he repaired the big Double-Wasps that powered the Thunderbolt fighters. Some of the officers objected to having a "Colored" on board. During the war, Blacks had their own separate units. When Major Johns selected his crew, he chose the best men that were available. Murphy, Washington, and Shultz were among the few veterans left that did not muster out after the war. Washington said, "Yes Sir," and disappeared into the radio room.

After grabbing an oxygen bottle and tool kit from brackets on the side of the ship just under the stairs, Washington followed Kewscinski into the photo lab and removed his parachute. Kewscinski began adjusting the focus on the trimetrigon cameras. He cursed when he saw one of the five huge multicameras had been shot through.

Washington climbed through the starboard hatch from the photo lab into the bomb bay. Major Johns was swinging like an ape, from bomb rack to bomb rack, as he came in the other direction inspecting the damage. They both spotted Shultz at the same time, still hugging the bomb rack. Swinging like Johns, Washington made his way aft and shouted, "He must have run out of oxygen," over the din of the engines.

"No, he's awake," answered Johns. Shultz was shivering. "Are you all right Sergeant," he asked? Shultz looked at him. "How many fingers am I holding up?"

"Three," replied Shultz.

"Good, he's all right," said Washington. "C'mon we have to get those engines restarted." Shultz looked at him in fear. "I think that shivering he's doing isn't all because of the cold," insinuated the Engineer.

"I'm all right," said Shultz. "Just leave me here."

"We can't do that," said Johns. "You're needed out on the wing to help fix the engines. "That's an order!" Shultz gazed at him wide eyed. Johns pulled Shultz's hands apart and he almost fell through the fragile bomb doors.

"C'mon," Washington exclaimed as he caught him! Shultz reluctantly followed the Engineer, ducking under the massive wing spar and standing where the drop tank used to be. High up behind the bomb racks, was a circular hatch that led to the wing.

"Camera doors open," announced Kewscinski.

"That plane is flying right under the camera," protested Newcomb.

"Amazing what gooks will do to get their picture taken," scoffed the Photonavigator!

"Okay we're done."

"Camera doors closed."

"It'll be interesting to see how that Tupolev turns out."

"It'll be out of focus," Kewscinski scolded sarcastically.

"AC to Radio, Hernandez, I want the code sent for plan F," ordered the skipper over the interphone.

"Plan F, sir," Hernandez replied from the radio room?

"That's right, Sergeant, 'F' for 'Failure.' "And, send our speed and position. "They'll be able to guess the rendezvous time from that. "No need to code it, the Commies already know where we are."

"Roger, 'F' for 'Failure,'" Hernandez answered, as he started tapping the sides of his bronze Morse key. Whenever he touched the right button with his index finger, he broadcast a dot; and whenever he touched the left button with his thumb, he broadcast a dash. After a short pause, he announced, "incoming message with our prefix code on it!" Both he and Beaumont grabbed their pencils to write it down. "Radio to AC," announced Hernandez into the interphone, "Sir, they repeated the code for plan 'F' and added 'confirmed.'"

"AC to crew," Peterson announced, "okay everybody, we just made an appointment to ditch in the Sea of Chi Li. "If those Navy boys do their job, there will be someone there to meet us." Everyone looked at the man next to him with a shared feeling of deep foreboding.

"Just so you know," the skipper continued, "it's those pictures they really want. "They'll rescue us just to get those pictures, so nobody needs to worry about getting home." Some smiled coyly at Colonel Peterson's off color joke, being unable to see him. Only Grant could be sure if he was really joking. He looked with horror at the tension in the skipper's eyes. The elephant trunk oxygen mask hid the Colonel's true feelings.

"The incoming reply, sir, said 'message received' not 'rescue on the way,'" corrected Hernandez. Peterson just looked out the window at the clouds twenty thousand feet below.

After the photography, Major Kewscinski started to patch the holes in the forward cabin with some wet toilet paper. It instantly froze as hard as rock when it touched the minus seventy degree metal skin of the ship. "PN to AC, I think I got all the holes, sir," announced the Photonavigator. There was a pause as not everyone was sure what he meant.

"AC to crew, pressurize forward compartments," commanded Peterson. Kewscinski closed the door to the communication tunnel, then turned the re-press valve. Those in the aft cabin were locked out by a thousand pounds of air pressure. Those up front were finally able to take off their masks.

"Sir, why would they consider photos of that little town Tyura Tam so important," asked Grant from the right pilot seat? A red mark surrounded his nose and mouth where his mask had been. "There was nothing there but rail lines and buildings under construction."

"Didn't you see the rocket explosion, son," asked Peterson, as he removed his mask? Everyone had clown-like red marks on their faces.

"Yes Sir, but so what about an exploding rocket? "The rail tracks led to some blackened equipment and stopped. "The ground all around was blackened."

"What do you think would blacken the ground like that?"

"Incendiary bombs, sir, or napalm."

"Why would the equipment be blackened and not destroyed," Peterson continued?

"Okay, flame-throwers, sir!"

"Why would anyone want to burn their own equipment?"

"I dunno sir, maybe it was the rocket."

"What kind of rockets?

"I dunno sir, V-2 rockets, a really big rocket," suggested Grant? The skipper was silent in reply so Grant asked, "Sir, you don't think that big explosion could have been a giant V-2 rocket do you?" Peterson stared straight ahead and remained silent. Murphy, sitting at the engineering console, turned around to try to hear better.

"Why would anyone build a rocket that big, Lieutenant," asked the skipper?

"To put a bomb on it, sir," answered Grant.

"What kind of bomb?"

"An atom bomb?" Grant could hardly believe the words that had come out of his own mouth. He turned white and flopped back against his head rest at the thought of it. Johns had climbed up to the flight deck after relieving himself at the urine tube. When he overheard the conversation, rather than relieving Grant, he motioned for Murphy to move over to Washington's seat, and sat down in the middle chair just behind the pilot's console to listen.

"You've heard stories about how the V-2 rockets would come out of the sky faster than the speed of sound so people on the ground in London couldn't hear it coming," asked the Colonel?

"Yes sir," Grant nodded assurance.

"Unless they happened to be looking into the sky at the right place at the right time," Peterson continued, "there was no way they could possibly know when to find shelter. "The rocket was so fast, there was no time to escape. "People would be going about their daily chores, and a second later, they would be blown to smithereens, without ever having a chance to pray to the Lord for mercy."

"Yes sir," The younger man nodded assurance.

"But the Nazis were more dastardly than that! "If someone was involved in a deadly sin, such as cheating on his wife, or going all the way with a girl without marrying her first, they would instantly be damned to Hell without any chance of repentance." Grant wondered if his commanding officer was accusing him. "The Nazis figured out a way to kill men's souls as well as their bodies," finished Peterson.

"What about the civilians killed by the two A-bombs in

Japan," asked the young officer? "Weren't they incinerated without warning?"

"No, that's different," said the skipper. "They were fighting on the side of evil. "They had plenty of warning to get out of the way and they were going to burn in hell anyway."

"I was told the guy working the APQ-3 on the "Bock's Car" targeted the Cathedral in Nagasaki because it made the biggest radar target," replied Grant.

"Maybe so," the Colonel responded. "But, do you think a real Christian would support Hirohito and Tojo? "God probably wanted that cathedral destroyed because the so-called Christians in there were mocking real Christians."

"Still, but to destroy a cathedral, sir," the younger man exclaimed!

"The APQ-3 antenna was only three feet wide, and the display screen was only three inches wide," explained the Colonel. "They were bombing through cloud. "It's not likely to be accurate, and with an A-bomb it doesn't have to be."

"If they were bombing though cloud, then the people on the ground had no warning, did they sir," insinuated Grant?

"I suppose not," snapped Peterson, angered that the young officer would question him. "So what! "They got what they deserved."

"If the Communists succeeded in building a rocket that could carry a nuclear bomb," interrupted Johns, as he sat in the First Engineer's seat turned around to face them, "they would have the power to kill whole cities full of Americans without warning, and if they don't go to church, condemn their souls straight to Hell. "If they built enough missiles, they could annihilate every city in the USA without warning. "They could destroy every Air Force base before our planes had time to taxi to the runway."

"Do you remember your Bible training about Gog and Magog and the Kings of the North," Peterson asked, "and the Prince of the East and the Beast with Ten Horns?"

"No sir, I'm Jewish," admitted Grant, certain he was about to be proselytized.

"The Soviet Union has ten republics—one for each horn," explained the Colonel with a glare of surprise toward the younger man. Grant studied him with a puzzled look. He had heard the evangelical schpeel many times before. He knew from experience not to argue—especially not with his commanding officer. Peterson continued, "The world was supposed to come to an end when the nation of Israel was re-established. "Your people in Palestine won independence seven years ago. "The hydrogen bomb uses the same power as the Sun—the very same power as God himself. "The Communists are trying to make themselves gods by destroying the world with artificial suns. "They think that they can replace God! "They've closed all the churches and turned them into museums. "They are trying to harness the power of God and divert it toward evil ends. "They are preparing to fight the battle of Armageddon."

"What's that, sir," asked the younger man? These thoughts made Grant sick to his stomach. He didn't have the Sunday school indoctrination to be able to tell if the Colonel was serious or if he was crazy.

"You know the saying: 'curiosity kills the cat,'" asked the Colonel?

"Uh huh," Grant replied.

"Now that you know what you know, you had better take one of these needles. "Just jab it into your leg with your fist, and they won't be able to torture you if we go down. "You might even have a open casket funeral if they return your body in time," suggested Peterson. "You better take one too, Murphy!"

"No Sir, I didn't hear a thing, SIR," Murphy replied!

"Good," replied the Colonel! "Keep it that way. "You'll live longer."

"I think the Commies are going to be pretty careful that we don't make it back," said Johns. "They've probably got something planned for us with that plane following underneath us. "I don't think you'll need to worry about a funeral Gordon, just an autopsy perhaps."

"That's the way those Commies are," asserted Peterson, "they disrespect the dead."

Like spelunkers, Shultz and Washington wormed their way on their bellies over a shallow catwalk above the giant tires in the main landing gear bay, just under the freezing upper surface of the wing. If they touched any metal with ungloved skin, their flesh would freeze to it instantly. Two turbochargers, glowing cherry red in the engine three nacelle, radiated some welcome warmth once they climbed down onto the foot thick silver landing gear leg. The interior of the landing gear bay was spacious, once they squirmed over the tires, but the nacelle was full of ducts for the oil coolers, intercoolers, deicing heat, and engine air cooling. There was barely enough headroom for a boy to stand, if he crouched a little, but no safe place to step, since the fragile gear door was underneath. They had to shinny between the intercooler and engine cooling ducts above them and the oil cooler and intake ducts below. The two dead engines were farther out on the wing. They faced a birdcage of triangular wing stringers where the skin of the plane had been blown away and burned in the fire.

Whitefeather was a Russian expert. He did not understand Chinese, so he left Captain Wong to monitor the Communist broadcasts alone. Most of the gunners were dead. The only gunner left, other than Sandringham, was now out on the wing. Someone needed to keep watch on the remaining engines in case something else went wrong, and identify any aircraft that showed up on the tail radar, so Whitefeather grabbed his parachute and struggled through the jungle gym into the aft cabin. Sitting in the left dorsal gun bubble, he plugged Calabrese's air line into the front of his space suit and was soon comfortable. The wind in the cabin tormented Sandringham, who bravely shivered at his post watching his radar screens. Mary was out of bed and watching the action from the lower left bubble, still wearing Nakamura's helmet and mask.

It was impossible for either of them to tell who was crawling through the wreckage, because both Washington and Shultz had goggles on. Whitefeather admired the bravery of the

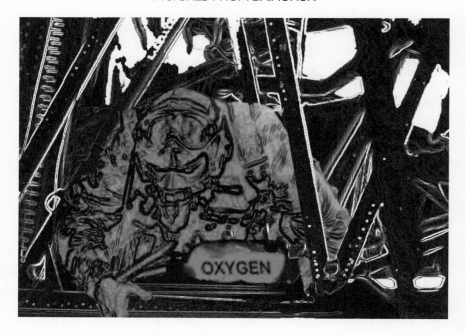

man who gingerly trusted his weight to the twisted metal behind the massive wing spar without a safety strap, pushing a heavy oxygen bottle, fire extinguisher, and tool belt under his chest, while 250 mph winds at seventy below zero blasted above and below him. It was not possible to wear a parachute or safety strap while in the wing, because the passages through the engine nacelles were too small. A parachute would not do much good anyway, with the propellers whirling right behind —though in this instance, the two outboard propellers were feathered because of the fire. It took several minutes for Washington to make his way through the triangular wing stringers, across the fifteen foot gap where the magnesium skin of the wing had burned away.

When Washington made it to the number two nacelle, the middle of the three piston engines in the left wing, he looked back for Shultz. Shultz was not to be seen. Perhaps he was waiting because it would be unsafe for two men to try to cross the fifteen foot span of exposed and damaged stringers at the same time. He examined the electric and fuel lines going into the engine, which were in plain view with much of the cowling blown away. The cold wind was penetrating under his fleece lined leather helmet. Although the collar on his bomber jacket was turned up, the wind felt like a cold knife, slowly cutting a circle around his neck and goggles, deeper and deeper into his face, until it felt like someone had dumped a bunch of ice cubes under his collar and melting icewater was dripping down his back. His wrists felt as icy as the handcuffs of a Southern sheriff moonlighting as a night rider. His feet were already numb with frostbite. "White folks took the Colored man out of the jungle to do this," he murmured, repeating an adage Blacks often used whenever they were forced to do a job that Whites didn't want.

How strange Mary's parka had first seemed, with its thick mittens of polar bear fur sewn onto the sleeves so they would never be lost, and sealskin boots sewn in one piece to her leggings, which opened only in the crotch for going to the bathroom. 'Too bad she can't repair the ship,' Washington thought to himself, shivering.

Where was Shultz? He had not come yet. Washington looked across to the other nacelle in vain. 'Perhaps the man is a coward,' he thought to himself? There was nothing he could do about it, so he continued inspecting the engine. The controls looked charred, but undamaged, and so did the fuel lines. He crawled on his belly through the much smaller outer wing stringers to the outermost nacelle. One of the oil coolers had been hit. Leaking oil had painted the inside of the cowling a sticky, shiny black, so he crawled backward to the number two engine. Even if the number one engine could be restarted, it would probably catch fire and most of the methyl bromide was used up extinguishing the fireball. It was not worth the risk.

"This is Tail Gunner, bandits five O'clock low," Sandringham's shivering lips warbled into his mask as he pushed the interphone button on his console with a thickly gloved right thumb. His hand protection consisted of a white inner liner, a fleece outer liner, a leather cover, and felt mittens. His fingers still felt frozen.

"AC to Tail Gunner, what kind," asked the skipper? "How many?" Whitefeather began looking around frantically.

Sandringham got up and, removing his mittens but not the gloves, borrowed O'Connor's binoculars to look through the dead man's shattered gunsight blister. "Yaks, eight of them," he replied.

"What does the book say?"

"VO to AC, Yak-9P: 1,650 hp Klimov engine; 380 knots at 18,000 ft; 35,000 foot ceiling," replied Newcomb from his desk in the forward cabin.

"They might as well be jets in our condition," scolded Peterson. "Its a damned thing to be shot down by a bunch of plywood, war surplus, Chinese-junk pursuit ships!"

"Well sir, look at the bright side," remarked Newcomb, "they only have one 20 mm cannon and two machine guns. If we can get a little speed, maybe we can shoot them before they get close enough to shoot us."

"All right, lets get some speed and altitude before they get here," the skipper ordered, glaring at Grant, as he reached up to flick the nose door switches and spin up the jet engines that weren't frozen. Grant took that as a hint that he should vacate the right seat to make room for Johns and got up. Colonel Peterson adjusted the rudder trim knob on the console to compensate for the extra thrust. "Sergeant Murphy, we need those engines fixed now!"

"There's nothing I can do, Colonel," the exasperated engineer replied, now manning his console by himself!

Out on the wing, Washington noticed the thunder from the jets starting and the extra speed immediately. He could feel the ship climbing into thinner, colder air. If he was going to get the number two engine started, he would have to work fast, or freeze to death. The fuel line was equipped with a spring loaded valve controlled by a solenoid that needed electrical power to stay open. When the fire burned the wires leading to the breaker panel, the wire shorted out and the valve closed, shutting off fuel to the engine—a good safety feature, but one that he now had to bypass. He twisted the live wires together with much sparking in his thick gloves. He would worry about how to shut down the engine later. If it wouldn't shut off after the wheels were chocked, it would be someone else's problem. Sooner or later, it would run out of fuel. He pressed the breakers in, one by one, to see which ones would stay in. They all did. Apparently, they popped because of the extreme heat. Fuses on an older aircraft would not have done that. The wiring was not really in that bad of shape. The insulation just looked bad, because it was normally white and now it was black or brown—but it still worked. The designers had wisely run the wires on the back of the spar where they would be protected from flames.

Washington needed Murphy to change the prop pitch in order to air start the giant Wasp Major. He puzzled about how to get a message to Murphy. The interphone jack was burned through. Noticing the inlet temperature sensor, he had an idea. The sensor worked on the principle that, the hotter the air was, the less resistance there was in the sensor. He reasoned that if he short circuited the sensor, the temperature gauge would show extremely hot—something that could never happen at altitude, unless there was a fire. He took out his pocket knife and stripped the insulation from the wire. Once he had the wires bared, he pinched them together with his glove.

While scanning his hundred gauges, Murphy saw the inlet temperature needle for engine two jump as though enchanted—or on fire! He gave it a confused stare for a few seconds. He never saw the inlet temperature suddenly increase then fall like that before, then he realized that the gauge was intelligent and communicating to him in Morse code saying: "A-I-R--S-T-A-R-T--N-O-W!" Murphy looked over to the engine. Washington pushed his frostbitten hand up through one of the holes in the cowling with raised index finger and made circles in the air. He had left his mittens in the cabin, since he was working. Murphy knew immediately this tiny black glove projecting above the giant wing meant "start engines." He then put up two fingers in reply, though Washington couldn't see them.

To start the engine, the propeller pitch had to change so it would auto-rotate. Murphy pushed the number two ignition breakers in, clicked up the number two primer switch, then folded down the protective handle to flick up the number two oil dilution switch. He lifted up a red cover on the right side of the desk, and clicked the number two feather switch back to off.

"Tail Gunner to AC, they're coming within range," warned Sandringham over the interphone. "Do I have permission to fire?"

"This is AC, do not fire unless fired upon," commanded Peterson.

"Mike, it's eight to one," interrupted Johns, "we have to fire to even the odds, unless you want us to spend the rest of our lives eating Chop Suey!"

"You never asked me that," shouted the Colonel!

"Pilot to Tail Gunner, permission granted to fire at will," said Johns, worried the tail might fall off from the gun vibrations and more worried that more holes would definitely cause the tail to fall off!

Sandringham pressed his head against the radar hood on his console, which faced the right side of the ship against the rear bulkhead. Inside his hood, were two rectangular screens. On the top screen, the radar antenna swept up and down, revealing the altitude and range of the incoming planes. On the bottom screen, the antenna swept left and right to reveal the direction and range of the approaching planes. A large blip separated into two smaller blips when he turned down the gain control knobs. When the blips approached and crossed the dashed 1,500 yard line permanently marked on the screen to represent the range of his guns, he pushed the radar lock switch for his left antenna. A small parabolic antenna inside a cone shaped blister underneath the rudder changed from an up and down sweeping motion to a slight wobbling motion pointed directly at the incoming planes. He pressed the fire button and the guns replied, "Poom poom poom poom poom poom!"

The gunfire startled Washington. The blades changed their angles in less than ten seconds, after Murphy threw the switch. Washington jumped back from the rotating alternator. Shultz watched from nacelle three as clouds of unburned fuel streamed out of the exhaust stacks. The stone cold engine rotated to life. At forty below zero, oil turns to viscous goo. Gasoline thins it. The oil dilution switch allowed a mixture of gas and oil into the machinery, so the engine would be able to turn.

As the pistons started to fire, one by one, the nacelle began to shake like an earthquake. Washington began to fear the vibrations might shake the engine right out of the damaged wing, and him along with it. There was no telling what damage was done to the spar when the shell hit it and exploded. Many thought it strange that an aircraft would have armor around the fuel tanks and oil coolers, but none for the crew. Now it made perfect sense. What good was armor, if the wing fell off?

As more pistons fired, the engine began to run smoother and the oil pressure came up on one of Murphy's gauges. "Engine two has been restarted Skipper," he said as he flicked off the oil dilution switch and raised the protective handle back in place.

"Good," Peterson replied! "Not a moment too soon. "Full power!" The entire ship shook, as more gunfire came from the tail in three second bursts. Johns, now back in his pilot seat, pushed the throttle lever all the way forward with the others. Murphy adjusted the prop pitch a little shallow and the mixture a little rich, to avoid detonation so soon after a cold start.

With his face pressed against his own more powerful radar screen, Newcomb turned down the gain to see some blips moving under the clouds. "VO to AC, we've got a dozen more bandits, ten O'clock, Skipper," he shouted over the interphone!

Sandringham could not see the attacking planes. When any of the bright green blips moved inside the dashed lines on his two radar screens, he pushed the fire button with his thumb. The attackers were not very maneuverable at such a high altitude. They were like ducks in a robot shooting gallery. The tail radar gunlaying system shot the little planes down, one by one, with little waste of ammunition. The obsolete pursuit

planes did not stand a chance against the sophisticated computer technology of the RB-36. The radar provided information
on the range, speed, and direction to the computer's wheels,
gears, and vacuum tubes, so it could automatically calculate a
firing solution that would lay the guns precisely on target.

Thanks to the excitement of the attack, Sandringham
was no longer shivering. He coolly and casually sat at his
console, gently pressing the fire button with his right thumb as
he selected targets with his left hand, using the joystick under
his desk. The Chinese pilots died anonymously by computer,
one by one.

Sandringham spent more time cleaning and oiling his
guns than any other member of the crew. He was proud of his
one hundred percent fire-off record. Grant was lucky to fire off
even half of his ammo before his guns jammed, if they were cold
soaked. It took a long time to clean and oil two six foot long
guns and grease the feed belts with paraffin, so officers often
ordered others to do it. Sometimes it did not get done.
Sometimes just stacking the giant ammo in the can the wrong
way would cause a jam, or failing tamp the big shells into their
brass all the way.

Washington began to inch his way back through the
fifteen foot bird cage of twisted metal where the explosion and
fire had blown the skin off the wing. A three hundred mile per
hour wind began pulling over the wing through the flailing
propeller as the number two engine warmed up. It vibrated like
a freight truck without shock absorbers on a potholed road. The
exhaust stacks spewed fire like a volcano, thanks to the rich
mixture and whatever was left in the menthol-water injection
tank.

The shaking was too much for Washington's cold hands
to cope with. He lost his grip. He was sucked by air pressure
through the top of the wing above where the flap used to be.
Washington caught himself on the leading edge of what used to
be the wing flap. His feet were only inches from the wildly
churning propeller. Fire from the exhaust heated up his left
boot while his hands and right foot were freezing. The wind was

strong enough to rip ordinary clothes clean off his body, but his thick nylon coveralls and insulated boots held to his frozen legs and feet despite the flogging. The rapidly flapping quilted nylon covered, wool pants liners whipped against his cold legs until they were raw. Washington screamed and cried and yelled into his mask for help, as Shultz waited for him in the warm engine nacelle, which was heated by two cherry-red turbochargers.

The belly guns opened fire. Whitefeather had not been trained to use them, but like most Navajo boys, he was a good shot with a rifle. He instinctively aimed ahead of the approaching aircraft as though he was shooting doves. He did not know that leading the target was the computer's job. If he had simply put the center dot on the target, he would not have missed.

Mary, who had changed places with the Indian when he decided to man the belly guns, noticed that something was wrong. She climbed down the ladder to the lower gun bubble and pounded on Whitefeather's back shouting, "Oonsgewl, vor for hehr paw vingt?" Whitefeather did not understand her and continued firing until a Yak fighter zoomed by. The guns overheated and jammed because he didn't let them cool for ten seconds after every three second burst. What the Chinese pilot must have thought when he saw the American hanging on the outside of the ship! Mary tugged the big Indian's thick rubber pants and pointed at the wing, repeating, "Oonsgewl, vor for hehr paw ving?"

Finally realizing what she meant, Whitefeather yelled into the interphone, "Second Raven to AC, someone's in trouble out there!"

"AC to Raven, who," asked the skipper?

"Washington or Shultz," answered Murphy.

"Someone needs to help them," demanded Whitefeather!

"Third Raven to AC, I'll do it," said Wong, only half worried that the attacking planes would change radio frequencies while he was away from his desk, and more worried about being shot down. Wong disconnected from the

† Undskyld, Hvorfor hr på wing? — Excuse me, why is that man on the wing?

interphone, unscrewed this air hose from the oxygen manifold, got up, removed his space suit, and attached a mask and oxygen bottle to his leather helmet.

Wong's main expertise was decoding messages at a desk in the Pentagon. When he heard that Chinese speakers were needed on intelligence gathering flights, it sounded exiting, so he applied. People would always ask what he did in the Air Force and it was embarrassing to admit that all he did was fly a bomber made of mahogany. Of course, what he really did was Top Secret, and he couldn't tell anyone about it, but being on a select crew gave him a lot of status, not to mention fifty percent higher pay. If he said he flew on bombers, that was usually enough to satisfy most people's curiosity—except for little children who would ask about the more exciting details like "were you ever shot at?" Now he could confidently say "yes," if he made it back alive.

After climbing down into the bomb bay, Captain Wong looked up at the little circular hatch that led into the wing. "I'm going to chain my leg to my desk if I ever get back," he mumbled to himself, as he climbed up the bomb rack where the drop tank used to be. Wong crawled on his belly over the landing gear into the nacelle and startled Shultz, who seemed to be frozen, or perhaps reluctant to leave the warmth of the turbos and oil coolers. Wong's bulky pressure suit would have been the ideal thing to wear in the three hundred mile per hour, seventy below zero winds, but the helmet would not have fit through the shallow catwalk over the landing gear or the tight passageway under the intercooler ducts. One had to be a wee fellow to make it through there anyway.

Wong climbed down over the folded, tree trunk thick, left landing leg and gave Shultz a push. Shultz just stared at him. Shultz decided he had better get back to his guns, since they were under attack, and tried to push past Wong. Wong wouldn't budge. "I have to get back to my guns," Shultz yelled. Wong, only inches away, could not hear him, so loud was the din from the engine drowning out his words. Shultz pointed at the exit. Wong pointed toward Washington hanging for dear life on the wing. Shultz looked into Wong's eyes through his goggles, but saw only a penetrating stare behind the elephant mask, like a motorcycle cop threatening arrest. Wong remained with an outstretched arm, pointing toward Washington like the Grim Reaper, as he sat on the giant landing strut, the largest ever fitted on an aircraft, as a man might straddle a horse.

Washington was losing his grip. He could feel the vibrations from the propeller blades passing by the rubber soles of his frozen boots like a vigorous foot massage. Electrical shivers buzzed through his shins and knees. His right foot was numb. If he let go and was sucked into the propeller, he would be cut to pieces. He yelled at Shultz, "C'mon you yellow Nazi bastard, help me!" He knew the gunner could not possibly hear. The other two men just stared each other down through their expressionless facemasks.

Washington yelled into his mask, "Tell him to help me Lord! "Tell him that a Colored man is worth something! "Don't let my kids grow up without a father!" Then Wong gave Shultz a push. Shultz fought back, but Wong kept pushing him out of the landing gear bay back into the nacelle. Pushing against the folded landing strut with his feet, Wong repeatedly banged and jammed Shultz with his forehead until Shultz was stuck between the oil and intercooler ducts. Shultz couldn't free his head, so Wong pushed harder with his feet until he fell forward into the nacelle on top of the oil cooler ducts behind Shultz. There was not enough room for the two of them, so with nowhere else to go, Shultz squirmed under the cooling fan duct into the damaged wing, toward Washington.

Shultz could feel the incredible wind tearing at his army green coveralls and quilted pants liners. Wong completely blocked the shallow crawl space that led back into the fuselage. Shultz Looked at Washington hanging on above the wing and gulped when he discovered what Wong was trying to get him to do. Was it legal for an officer to force an enlisted man to risk his life? Shultz looked down through a hole in the wreckage at the ground and marveled at the clear view of the lenticular clouds, perched on the mountain tops below like oblong snow-white mushrooms.   Dry brown washes and dark green riverbeds scribbled across lime green, rock speckled valleys—stained black where cloud shadows fell. The high altitude sky was still dark blue with a few stars scintillating, even though it was mid morning.   Small Chinese fighters scarred the sky with wavy contrails, thousands of feet below.   They dove and zoom climbed in an effort to get a shot at the huge ship high above them. Shultz inched toward Washington, taking one step every twenty seconds.   "Hurry up you bastard," Washington yelled into his mask, "or you'll be out here by yourself!" Shultz heard nothing but wind and roaring engines.

After several minutes, Shultz reached Washington. Grabbing at the frozen man's sleeve with his left hand, he couldn't get a grip. Shultz reached back and inserted his fingers behind Washington's leather helmet. Washington could feel Shultz's cold gloves scratching up the back of his collar then up the back of his neck, then pressing against the back of his head deep inside the helmet. Tightened, Washington's oxygen mask dug into his cold face painfully. Shultz grabbed a piece of twisted metal with his right hand and pulled with all his might. Washington could feel his helmet strap digging a deep groove under his chin. He hoped he fastened it on properly.

Washington's frozen hands lost their grip and he was connected to the ship, inches from the whirling pusher propeller, only by the mask and Shultz's arm and fingers under his helmet. Shultz inched back at the same slow pace he crept out, one step every twenty seconds, towing Washington behind him through the bent structural triangles like a lifeguard might rescue a drowned swimmer. The wind beat Washington's frozen body against the damaged wing flap like a flag. Washington tried to grab the twisted metal, but his fingers were frozen into hooks.

When Shultz made it back to the nacelle, he pushed Washington toward Wong. Wong reached out and grabbed Washington, pulling him away from Shultz. As Shultz rose up through the missing skin to allow Washington to pass under-neath, the wind struck him like a speeding truck.   Wong watched him vanish instantly into thin air. Chunks of meat flew from the propeller, painting the rear of the ship with small red speckles. Nakamura's gun bubble became spattered. Mary screamed. Tiny drops of blood flowed across the bubble in streaks. "Second Raven to AC, we just lost one of the men," Whitefeather shouted into the interphone!

"AC to Second Raven, what happened," asked Peterson? Whitefeather just bowed his head down into his knees and vomited into his visor. Mary cupped her sealskin mittens over her oxygen mask as she might cup her hands over her mouth in horror.

"AC to Second Raven, what's happening," asked Peterson again? Whitefeather still wouldn't answer. He unlatched his space helmet and threw it to the floor then attached Calabrese's bloody oxygen mask to the leather helmet he was wearing underneath. "AC to Tail Gunner, what's going on back there?"

Wong jerked Washington through the ducts in the nacelle. They fell in front of the warm turbochargers, which now vibrated like an electric massage chair due to the damage done to the propeller when it sliced through Shultz. Wong moved like a man possessed, as he squirmed past the air ducts to the interphone jack in the landing gear bay. With shaking hands, he plugged in his jack and yelled, "AC, this is third Raven, Washington's hurt, I need help!"

"This is AC, who is this," asked Peterson?

"Third Raven," answered Wong!

The engine interphone lines were on a different channel than the rest of the ship, so only those on the bridge could hear. Peterson switched lines and yelled, "This is AC, Harry needs help!"

"Second Raven to AC, I'll get him, sir," replied Whitefeather. He had plugged in his jack just in time to hear.

"Okay everybody, decompress," commanded the skipper. "Masks on! "Jerry, I want him up here."

"I can't get engine three in sync," interrupted Murphy. "It has to be shut down."

"VO to AC, those Chink fighters are going home, sir," informed Newcomb. Peterson nodded. Johns flicked off the switches for the turbojets in order to save fuel, as he watched the small fighters moving away below.

"AC, You want me to leave Mary and Sandringham all alone," replied Whitefeather?

"Mary?"

"The Eskimo girl!"

"Oh yeah, I forgot . . . the least of our problems. "Bring her up here too." Peterson turned around and said, "go ahead and shut it down, Marv, before it shakes the wing off. "Damn!"

Whitefeather pushed Mary into the communication tube, unplugged her mask, and laid her down on the tube trolley. She became disoriented and lost consciousness almost immediately. The skipper didn't ask for it, but he put the hot coffee pot and some sandwiches between her legs and some sandwich boxes under and on top of her legs and parka. "Second Raven to PN, Care package for you on the trolley," he alerted Kewscinski. Whitefeather then put on an emergency oxygen bottle and scrambled past the gun bay, through the mission control room, and into the bomb bay while Kewscinski cranked the loaded trolley to the front of the ship.

It took a while for Whitefeather to squirm his way into the bomb bay because of the space suit. He climbed up the bomb racks to the round hole leading into the wing. With the suit on, he was too large to fit in the crawlway above the landing gear. With a Herculean effort, Wong shoved Washington with all his might, head first, into the crawl space over the giant tires. Washington had passed out when his bottle ran out of air, so Wong removed the bottle and threw it overboard, but left the mask on as protection from the cold. It dawned on Wong, that with Washington blocking the crawlway, he would die when his own oxygen ran out—which was going to be soon with all of his huffing and puffing.

It had seemed like an eternity before Whitefeather got there. Whitefeather was barely able to reach Washington. He pulled him by the helmet, just as Shultz had done. Wong watched Washington's feet disappear into the crawlway, an inch at a time, and wondered who would rescue him when he ran out of oxygen. If he passed out where he was, standing on the folded landing gear leg, he would fall out of the ship as soon as Johns or Peterson tried to lower the gear.

Manhandling the unconscious Second Engineer left Whitefeather exhausted. He almost dropped Washington through the fragile bomb bay doors. Instead, the unconscious man tumbled headfirst onto the catwalk behind the bomb racks. The big Indian dragged him forward over the bomb doors toward the photo lab. They weren't made to carry the weight of a man, but they were just springy enough to break a man's fall without severely injuring him. By the time Wong climbed through the little round hatch that led to the safety of the bomb bay, Whitefeather and Washington were gone.

Whitefeather began to feel a headache from oxygen deprivation. He slouched down, the exertion of dragging the unconscious Washington over the bomb doors being too great for the limited flow of oxygen from his bottle's frozen regulator. Kewscinski entered the bomb bay dragging a long hose from the oxygen manifold in the photo lab, and the two of them finished the much more difficult job of lifting the heavy body through the tiny circular hatch. Every portable bottle in the ship was frozen or empty.

Feeling tippy when his oxygen ran out, Wong got caught in the triangular braces on the side of the bomb bay near the photo lab and lost consciousness. Fortunately, Kewscinski noticed him in time, and was able to connect another long oxygen hose to his mask and revive him. It would not have been possible for him to drag Wong thorough the hatch into the lab by himself. Once they were all safe inside, they dragged Washington to the lower bunk in the back of the lab and laid Mary on the bunk above him. Washington regained consciousness once his mask was plugged in to the manifold, but he preferred to sleep because the oxygen deprivation gave him a splitting headache.

Mary was blue. "She'll die if she doesn't get some oxygen," warned Kewscinski.

"I'll go back to the mission control room," said Wong. "Give me another bottle."

"There are none left," said Kewscinski.

"What about the forward cabin," suggested Whitefeather.

Kewscinski yelled through the eight foot tunnel to the radio room, "Help, we need more oxygen!" With a lot of banging, Beaumont shoved Johns' emergency bottle through the tunnel to Kewscinski, who passed it to Wong. He shook it to test how heavy it was. It seemed to hold enough oxygen to keep him alive until he passed back through the bomb bay, so he connected his long hose to Mary's mask and disappeared through the hole.

Once all the hatches were closed, the forward compartments could be repressurized and everyone's masks removed. Kewscinski added more water to some of the frozen wads of toilet paper he had used to plug the shell holes. They had come loose when the pressure was relieved. The two little cabins warmed up quickly, thanks to the many bodies there to add to the heat, but they became filled with the pungent smell of urine from men who, out of fear, lost control of their bladders during the fight.

The photo lab had all the charm and ambiance of a hobo jungle. It had been more than a day since anyone had bathed. No amount of talc under the armpits could have absorbed the gymnasium ambiance. Every available square foot of floor was occupied by someone trying to sleep, with Washington and Mary filling the narrow pipe berths in the rear of the cabin. Mary took off Nakamura's bloody helmet and rubbed her temples. Oxygen deprivation gave her a headache. Whitefeather yelled through the eight foot tunnel, "Do you have Washington's coffee cup?" Beaumont grabbed it from the floor of the Radio room where it had fallen, and flung it through the tunnel. Whitefeather poured some of the hot coffee he had sent forward with Mary.

Washington could not move his hands, so the big Indian slowly tilted it to his mouth so he could sip. Washington did not show any sign of appreciation, but at least the look of fear was gone from his face. Drinking coffee is dangerous in an unpressurized cabin because the body loses water at low pressure making the skin feel cold and clammy. Coffee can cause excessive urination, so there is a danger of dehydration, but Whitefeather felt this time was an exception. The frozen toilet paper in the shell holes had used up a lot of precious water, but everyone agreed that Washington deserved an extra ration for what he did. All congratulated him for getting the engine restarted even though the other one had to be shut down, but he laid there expressionless, sipping Whitefeather's coffee, and did not pay much attention to what else was going on.

"Hey!"

"We're passing over the Great Wall of China!"

THE MUTINY
February 1956

Nawrocki the Navigator could see for hundreds of miles sitting at his desk behind the giant front window. The air was so crisp and clear, he could see the Great Wall of China draped snake-like over the snow covered mountaintops into the purple-brown valleys and disappearing into the distance. Snow white glaciers reached down from the mountains like clawed tentacles scratching deep furrows into the valleys below. The Silk Road, the same as was traveled by Marco Polo centuries earlier, meandered through the passes only to straighten out along the plains between them. Except for Russians, China was now closed to Westerners. For a moment, Nawrocki thought he might like to visit China rather than just flying over it, but he quickly changed his mind. Looking over his shoulder, he noticed that Newcomb was not enjoying the view. The VO's face seemed permanently attached to the radar camera. Occasionally, about once every two or three minutes, Newcomb would look down at his desk to update his plot as he nervously tracked the movements of a second Tupolev that was dogging the ship at a lower altitude. Never once did he look out the front window.

China did not have a nationwide radar system, so chase planes followed American reconnaissance aircraft wherever they went. The RB-36 was safe, as long as it remained at high altitude. No Chinese plane could fly so high. Radar guided artillery could only shoot up to twenty five thousand feet—if the Chinese even had any out in the desert.

All of the sandwiches Whitefeather brought with Mary were soon eaten. Newcomb didn't want his, so Nawrocki had two. Most had developed an insatiable hunger due to the excitement, but the survivors of the holocaust in the aft cabin didn't feel like eating either. Washington couldn't eat if he wanted to. His hands and feet were in a great deal of pain. Holbrook went aft and gave him a prick of Morphine to help him sleep.

Bright sun streamed into the greenhouse canopy covering the bridge. Four white vapor trails followed the four tired, but still running engines for hundreds of miles. "Too bad the skipper isn't up to see this," exclaimed Grant, again sitting in the armored command chair. The Colonel had retired to his commander's bunk above the radio room.

Johns grunted in reply, but was otherwise silent. He was thinking about Linda and what he would say to the wives of his dead crewmen if he made it back, then he said, thinking aloud to himself, "And God made the firmament, and divided the waters which were under the firmament from the waters which were above the firmament; and God called the firmament heaven."

"What did you say," asked Grant?

"Military men were never meant to fly so high," answered the Pilot. "We're too close to heaven."

"I've got bad news," said Murphy, looking at the fuel totalizer gauge. "Calculating our fuel situation, we're not going to make it out of China if we remain at this speed and altitude."

"How much time do we have," asked Johns?

"Three hours, tops."

"We're supposed to have enough to remain in the air for two days," said Gordon.

"You guys have been running the jets pretty hard,"

accused the senior APE.

"Pilot to Navigator, is three hours going to get us to the sea Duane," asked Johns over the interphone?

"This is Navigator," answered Nawrocki, "wait a minute . . . no it's not enough." The ship began a slow turn to the right.

"WO to Pilot, you're turning," protested Holbrook.

"I know," answered Johns.

"Don't you think you should inform the skipper before making a heading change?"

"No."

"Why the hell not?"

"Because I know what he'd say."

"What's that?"

"He'd say we have to try to make it. "I say we have to try to get to Burma."

"There's no landing strip big enough for an RB-36 in Burma," reminded the weather man.

"Who said anything about landing?"

"You're planning for us to bail out," asked Holbrook? "There's nothing but mountains and jungle there. "We can't parachute into rocks and trees."

"Do you have any better idea," asked the Pilot?

"If we drop in the drink, at least it will be less painful," recommended the Weather Observer.

"Duane just said we can't make it to the drink. "If the Chinks get a hold of us, it will be very painful indeed."

Holbook unbuttoned the fabric headliner from the ceiling so he and Johns could see each other between the rudder pedals, even though Holbrook was on the lower deck. Johns looked between his feet and their eyes met. Johns talked down to him, "Do you think I want to drown, waiting to be rescued by a bunch of Navy swabos? "At least in Burma, we'll have a fighting chance to make it back. "If we go down in China, we'll be arrested and put on trial as spies and before they do that, there will be daily beatings for entertainment!

"I'll take Burma over China any day," joculated Grant from the armored Aircraft Commander's throne.

"Now wait a minute," interrupted Wong, who was listening in the mission control room, wearing his space suit. "Third Raven to Pilot, you can't just nix the mission like that . . . We've got valuable intelligence data that has to get back to the Pentagon."

"I'm sorry Harry, if we can't make it we can't make it," replied Johns.

"I demand that you wake up the skipper," shouted Wong! The interphone buzzed with distortion. His space helmet had a way of concentrating the sound. Heavy breathing was heard through his open mike before he released his interphone button.

"Mike is tired and needs some rest," replied Johns.

"You can't do this on your own authority," protested Wong. "Jerry are you there?" Whitefeather was asleep on the floor of the photo lab. "Jerry," he repeated, "Jerry!" There was more than a thousand pounds of air pressure on the door of the forward cabins. Like it or not, unless someone inside released the air pressure, Wong was trapped in the unpressurized con- verted bomb bay and there was nothing he could do about it.

"Jerry is asleep," answered Johns, tongue in cheek, as he looked over at Grant in the commander's chair. Grant returned his gaze with a disturbed look.

"Somebody wake up the skipper," Wong pleaded! "We've got a hundred pounds of magnetic tape reels. "We'll never get them out of the jungle!

"I'm just trying to save us, Harry," explained the second in command.

"There's more to this than you know about," complained the intelligence officer. "There is a lot more at stake than just the lives of twenty men."

"Sixteen men," Johns corrected.

Wong continued with an exasperated look that no one could see, "I grew up in Hong Kong. "I think I know this part of the world better than you do. "We can't bail out in Burma. "There is nothing but mountains and jungles, and the natives aren't friendly. "The government has very little control over the mountain peoples. "The Karen tribesmen there are bloodthirsty savages. "They stretch their women's necks and legs with brass coils so they can't run away. "They will sell you to whoever is willing to pay the most for our skins."

"Well then, we'll bail out in India then," Johns replied.

"The TU-2 under us will follow us down. "The Reds don't care about national borders. They'll will find us before the Burmese will."

"Not over the Himalayas," protested the second in command.

"Do you think we'll have any better luck with Nehru? "He's anti-British and anti-American."

"At least we'll survive."

"But our data won't! "Tens of thousands of lives depend on getting this data back to Washington. "The lives of sixteen men don't count for much in an atomic war. "If we don't get this intelligence about the Russian rocket back, our scientists will be unprepared."

"So what," answered Johns! "Our rockets are ten times better than their rockets. "Do you think the Rooskies have better rockets than we do?"

"That's exactly what I'm trying to say," the space suited Chinese American answered! "You saw it yourself."

"Naw, I don't believe it," answered Johns. "Our guys probably have the same kind of rockets."

"What if they don't? "Can you take that chance?"

"I don't believe it," Johns continued. "The Russians don't have the brains to develop rockets. "They must have gotten the technology from us."

"If they got it from us," argued the intelligence officer, "why do you think General LeMay risked all of our lives and this four million dollar ship to get pictures of their launch site. "Do you think they would send a crew to Russia to photograph something we have in our own back yard?" Newcomb and Kewscinski were sitting behind Nawrocki and Holbrook listening. Kewscinski had been asleep in his seat, but the conversation in his headset awakened him. They glanced into each other's eyes for a clue as to what to do. "What if the skipper wakes up and insists on continuing the mission," Wong continued?

The expression on each of the faces in the forward cabin silently seemed to ask the same question. Beaumont, sitting at the radio desk listening to static in the vain hope of detecting a message from the other side of the world, let out a loud yawn and said, "I have to stretch!" He lifted his fists very close to the bulge in the bottom of the canvas pipe berth made by the sleeping chicken Colonel directly above his head.

"Be careful," said Hernandez, who was awake, but laying on the floor and not plugged into the conversation. "You'll wake up the skipper."

"Arrrrrraugh," roared Beaumont loudly, his face contorting in faux pain!

"What are you doing," Hernandez objected?

Beaumont smiled. Drawing back his fist, he punched the bulge in the green canvas as hard as he could. Colonel Peterson, startled, banged his head on a shelf above the berth that held the throttle, mixture, and pitch amplifiers and yelled, "God dammit!"

"I'm sorry Colonel," apologized the Electronic Counter-measures officer. "I forgot you were there. "It won't happen again."

"What is our position, course and speed," hollered the still sleepy chicken Colonel?

"Duane, this is radio," asked Beaumont loudly over the interphone, "the skipper wants to know our position, course and speed."

Johns jumped in his seat as though startled. Wong, still in his space suit smiled, but then beat his visor with his glove because the smile caused an itch on his nose that he could not scratch. He began sniffling around like a rodent, trying to rub his nose against the microphone in front of his mouth, but his almost flat Chinese nose was too small to reach it. He soon began to feel as though there were ants crawling all over his face.

Nawrocki and Holbrook gazed at each other in terror. "Thirty seven North, ninety eight East, one-eight-two mark thirty two at one-niner-five knots," the young Navigator trepidly advised.

"One-eight-two," asked the skipper? There was no reply. Boots thumped down on Beaumont's desk from the bunk above, crushing his notepad and sending his pencil flying. The skipper scrambled up onto the bridge. "Why are we on one-eight-two," he thundered? Grant and Murphy looked at each other in horror.

"We don't have the fuel to make it," explained the second in command.

"I didn't authorize any course change!" The skipper banged his head on the gray canvas covered canopy several times, trying to look taller, until his leather helmet found the astrodome bubble so he could stand.

"Under the circumstances, I can't see we have a choice," defended the second in command. "I didn't want to wake you."

"*You*, didn't want to wake *me*? "If we continue on our present course, we'll end up in Burma!"

"That's the general idea," revealed Johns.

"The general idea," the skipper repeated with fury! . . . and what about our mission? "Our job is to get that rocket telemetry back to Fort Fumble."

"I'm just trying to save our lives," the junior Aircraft Commander explained.

"What makes you think your life is worth anything? "If this stupid move prevents us from completing our mission, I'll have you hauled before a court for insubordination!"

"Think about it Mike," said the second officer, "if we don't make it, we'll end up in a Chinese prison or worse. "At least in Leavenworth, the prisoners are fed."

"I can't believe this," fumed Peterson! "I can't believe you have such a negative attitude. "I thought I knew you! "Where's your patriotism?"

"Mike, were all about to die," Johns pleaded. "This isn't about patriotism. "We don't have the fuel to complete the mission. "The mission is ruined. "It's a failure. "We have got to think about how we're going to survive this."

"You don't know that! "It's impossible to tell how much gas is left in thirty three thousand gallon tanks. "If there is a chance of completing the mission we have to try."

"I don't want to take any chances!"

"Damn you," the skipper cursed! "We just took the most important pictures of any recon mission in the history of the Air Corps! "I never thought I'd hear my best friend turn yellow. "Have you ever thought about what this will do to my career? "We were sent here to do a job!"

"We can't do the job, Sir, I'm trying to save your life," Johns retorted!

"My life isn't worth much! "Do you think I want to live in disgrace? "I flew twenty five combat turns in the B-24, and I survived when my buddies didn't. "Do you think I want to be remembered for cowardice on my last chance to do something really important before I retire? "We were ordered to get those films to the sea or die trying. "I would rather auger in than fail to carry out those orders! "AC to Navigator, what is the course for the Gulf of Chi Li?"

Sliding the vector card through the center of his computer and rotating the outer ring, Nawrocki calculated a new course. "I recommend turning left to zero-eight-eight mark thirty five, sir," the young man answered.

"Turn left to zero-eight-eight, flight level thirty five," commanded the skipper!

Johns folded his arms. "Pilot to Navigator, what is the course to Burma, Duane?" The interphone was silent. Grant looked up at the skipper. Upon meeting the Squadron Commander's stern glare, he immediately unbuckled and hopped out of the left seat, then squirmed around the far side by the window and hopped down the stairs into the radio room. The skipper stepped slowly over the center console and settled into his armored throne, strapping himself in. Stealthily, Grant climbed back up and sat beside Murphy, turning Washington's seat around to face forward. Beaumont sat on the stairs behind Peterson's throne.

Putting his feet on the giant pedals, Peterson flicked the autopilot switch to off and turned his wheel to the left, but Johns was a stronger man and the ship remained on course to the south. His inability to control the ship infuriated Peterson. He jerked at the controls. Each wheel had separate cables running to the control surfaces, so there was some slop between the two control columns. "This is Third Raven, what's going on up there," asked Wong from the mission control room? The ship took a sudden jump, then dove suddenly. His note pad slid off his desk as the rudder and ailerons became uncoordinated. The ship skidded sideways and fell in such a way as to make everyone airsick. "Hey, get it under control," Wong added! The ship gyrated and bucked as they struggled against each other's control cables.

"I order you to come to course zero-eight-eight mark thirty five," repeated the skipper! Johns remained still and held his wheel tighter. Strangely, the ship continued to thump up and down like a truck on a pot holed road. "What have you done," asked Peterson?

"I'm not doing it," defended Johns! The ship began to bounce up and down violently. He pressed his interphone button and shouted, "Something's wrong, everybody fasten your safety straps!" The ship continued to shake.

"What are you doing," asked the skipper?

"Nothing," repeated Johns! The violent shaking continued.

"It looks like we found some clear air turbulence," explained Holbrook over the interphone. "We might have just run into a jet stream."

Newcomb could hear the shouting between the skipper and Johns. Only a thin layer of canvas around the rudder pedals divided the bridge from the lower deck. He began a radar plot to determine if the ship had entered a stream. The radar had a feature that allowed him to freeze the display to position a dot of light on some feature with his joystick. After a few seconds, he could see how the many blips on the ground had moved and thus calculate the true course and speed. He immediately noticed that Nawrocki was off course. The ship would miss Burma by a hundred miles. If it missed by only fifty miles, they would still be over China when they ran out of fuel. To reach Burma would now mean having to fight against a headwind.

"Excuse me Duane," Newcomb said to Nawrocki, "shoot that mountain down there with your sight and tell me if you are on course."

"I'll do it," volunteered Kewscinski. Nawrocki lifted up his desk and switched seats with him.

Kewscinski aimed the bombsight at a mountaintop, then adjusted the wind deflection vector lever on the right side to calculate the true speed and direction of the ship over the ground. "You're right," he agreed. By comparing the true speed with the apparent heading or airspeed, the Photo Navigator determined the speed and direction of the wind. "PN to AC, I think we hit a jet stream, sir," he announced over the interphone.

"Where is it," asked the skipper?

"We're in it," he replied.

"We can't make Burma against this wind, Hank,"

Newcomb shouted through the hole Holbrook made in the headliner above the rudder pedals, "you have to turn."

"Yes Sir," Johns shouted in reply! Gritting his teeth and panting without looking up, he turned his wheel all the way to the lock while stomping with full left rudder and the ship began to do a wingstand. Everyone was pressed into their seats. Johns' eyes moistened as though he was about to cry. The skipper stared disgustedly at the failed mutineer as Johns watched his gyro repeater rotate to the new course.

"You don't know how close you just came to a court martial son," accused the Colonel.

Johns sullenly worked the throttles to find the best altitude, intentionally avoiding the continuous gaze of his commanding officer. Peterson pondered in his mind whether he should relieve Johns.

"Navigator to AC, we've almost doubled our ground speed," Nawrocki announced over the interphone gleefully. "We're doing better than 400 knots to the good. "At this speed we'll be able to make Puchon or Kwangju." A cheer went up from everyone plugged into the interphone. Peterson decided not to relieve Johns. He would have to admit in his report that Johns' mutiny had saved the mission.

The Chinese plane noticed the sudden right angle turn in the white contrail streaking the dark blue sky and turned to follow. At 35,000 feet, the ship was less than 4,000 feet above where the Chinese plane could go. Wong listened to the Chinese pilot's conversation in the mission control room through his "Ferret" antenna, recording it with his tape recorders. Wong chuckled to himself when the pilot reported that the "crazy Yankees" were lost and couldn't fly straight. He laughed out loud when the pilot insisted he could not keep up and that the cruising speed of American reconnaissance bombers had been severely underestimated.

"WO to Navigator, the stream might not lead us to Korea," informed Holbrook over the interphone to prevent everyone from getting their hopes too high.

"Well then, we'll land at Cheju Island," replied

Kewscinski. "It's a beautiful place with spectacular rock formations."

"I hate to disappoint you, but the airstrip at Cheju is not big enough for a B-36," said Newcomb, candidly. "We'll end up hitting the rocks when we try to take off."

"Who says we have to take off," defended Kewscinski, "I'll be happy just to land."

Peterson had been straining his ears to hear the conversation below, lifting the rubber muffs of his helmet. Then he looked at Johns, pressed his interphone button, and said, "AC to crew, these are your orders, we're going to land in the Gulf of Chi Li, so everyone put on their Mae Wests."

There was silence for about half a minute, then Nawrocki asked, "Why ditch a perfectly good aircraft?" Not accustomed to having anyone question his orders and still angry over Johns' insubordination, yet not unaware of the extreme stress the near-death experience had on the crew, Colonel Peterson unstrapped himself from his throne and descended into the radio room. Beaumont jumped down out of his way and sat in his regular station beside Hernandez. Peterson sat on the stairs near the forward landing gear bay that divided the radio room from the forward cabin. Grant, who had been sitting beside Murphy, followed him halfway down, sitting on the stairs leading to the bridge in his normal take-off and landing position. Removing his helmet, the skipper sat lower on the steps leading to the forward cabin so both those in the nose and in the radio room could hear what he had to say. This meant that the heads of the men in the radio room were higher than his. Everyone stopped what they were doing to look at him.

Combing his fingers through his short thinning hair, Peterson began by saying, "Our mission was to photograph a certain target. "Many of us gave their lives in order to do that. "These pictures we took were important enough to risk their lives for—they are important enough to risk all our lives for. "Right John?"

"Yes Sir," answered Kewscinski, saluting, seated against the window just beyond Nawrocki.

"Well, everyone named John is in agreement," quipped Holbrook disrespectfully, as he watched Peterson return the salute. He was seated farthest away.

"So what was it at that little Pony Express station on the Russian prairie that was so damned important anyway, sir," shouted Beaumont down to him from the radio room? "Don't the families of Major Hughes, Shultz, O'Connor, Calabrese, and Nakamura have the right to know what their husbands, fathers, and sons died for?

"Its classified," answered the Colonel, looking up at him.

"Why ditch a perfectly good ship, Mike," challenged the meteorologist? Do you think we are just going to stand around and let you drop us into the drink for no good reason?"

"Those are your orders."

"Do you think you can order us to death? I'm sorry, but I vote to live."

"This isn't a democracy."

"I didn't volunteer for a suicide mission," shouted Holbrook! "I just need the flight time to get my damned fifty percent bonus hazard pay and nothing else. "I don't need to risk my neck!"

"Your wife'll get your pay," answered the Colonel. "You agreed to do this job, so what do you have to complain about? "We've been ordered to get our films and tapes to safety and dropping them into the Gulf the Chi Li is the surest way of doing that. "If we try to get to Korea and fail, then everything will be lost at sea, and someone else will have to go back there and take those pictures again . . . only they won't have the benefit of surprise. "If two recon ships show up at two consecutive rocket launches, the Russians will know we have intelligence about their schedule of launches. "They will almost certainly change their schedule and cut the heads off of the patriots that bleebed. "The next crew will only see a big tarpaulin instead of launch sites.

"Our films are one of a kind," explained the Aircraft Commander. "They're priceless . . . irreplaceable! "They are worth more than all the gold in Fort Knox, all the diamonds in

Kimberley, and all the wedding rings on all the wives of all the men in the Air Force. "We have orders to drop those pictures where we know that there will be a sub waiting to pick them up."

"What exactly are these pictures of," asked Beaumont, the Electronic Countermeasures Officer?

"Tell them what you saw Gordon," the skipper murmured, looking up at Grant, who's feet were dangling above him.

"I thought you said our conversation never occurred, sir," Grant replied, jumping down into the radio room beside his gunsight, where he could see the others?

"It didn't, but what you saw hasn't been classified...yet."

"What did you see Gordon," shouted Holbrook from his seat against the front window?

Grant paused and thought for a moment then said, "It was hard to tell, since the flashes were so brief, but I thought I saw a large piece of machinery at the end of some railroad tracks with some kind of scaffolding around it."

"So what," asked Beaumont, looking up at him from his swivel chair?

"The ground where it was sitting was scorched and burned."

"And," questioned Holbrook?

"It was bigger than two railroad tracks side by side," answered Grant. "It was three times as long as the Diesel locomotive pulling it."

"You mean big enough to carry a really big rocket?"

"Yes."

"How big a rocket?"

"A rocket big enough to hurl an A-bomb," exclaimed the Co-pilot.

"Are you sure?"

"Yes," said Grant.

"Did anyone else see it," asked Holbrook?

"We all saw it," answered the skipper, "you did too and you know it. "You just don't want to admit it to yourself that that's what they sent us here to see. "You just didn't know how dangerous it was 'cause you didn't know what you were looking at. "Not all Russian scientists are Communist," he continued. "Some are patriotic and provide intelligence on what the Commies are doing. "This is Merril's mission. "He is the one that requested it. "It went right up to the Vice President's desk. "Merril told the Vice President that he would risk his own life to get these pictures and he did. "Curt LeMay called me personally and asked if I would lead it and I asked Hank."

"HOLY Smokes," interrupted Newcomb! "It sounds like the Commies are planning world war three! "If they build something like that, they won't even need bombers. "A brainwashed Commie general could press a button on his desk and vaporize New York City in twenty minutes, or Washington or Chicago or Detroit."

"New York, Washington, Chicago, and Detroit simultaneously," corrected Peterson, "with San Francisco, Los Angeles, Cincinnati, and Honolulu thrown in for good measure. "We have to get these films back to warn them so SAC can come back and nuke that place. "They aren't going to drop the bomb on Gordon's word alone, or even with my report to back him up. "The Pentagon needs those films so there will be proof of what those Commies are doing . . . so the entire world will know what the sick Communist mind has planned."

"Can I ask a question, sir," interjected Nawrocki?

"Go ahead, son," replied Peterson.

"What if the Ruskies aren't building an atomic rocket and they are building a space ship to fly to Mars like in the movie 'Conquest of Space?'"

"Why would we want to let the Communists conquer space," asked the skipper? "If they are trying to conquer space, it is even more important that we stop them! "Can you imagine if they built a station in outer space, where they could zoom around the Earth, even over Texas, and rain atom bombs on our children's heads?"

" . . . And they would do it too," added Newcomb! "These radar bombsights are so good, they could bomb from outer space as easily as from the stratosphere."

"What if they just want to fly to the moon or to see some

Martians," the young Navigator asked? That brought a chuckle from the others.

Someone woke up Captain Whitefeather and told him that he should go forward. With Hughs dead, it was Whitefeather who was nominally in command of the intelligence aspects of the mission. "Well then," answered the skipper, as he watched the big space suited Indian emerge from the eight foot tube without his helmet, his long braids hanging in front of his shoulders, "it's even more important that we nuke'em cause they would claim the moon to be their sovereign territory and they wouldn't let anyone else on it. "As for the Martians, they will probably try to convert them to Communism too! "Can you imagine if the Communists ganged up with Martians in a war against us using atomic rockets?

Everyone except Whitefeather nodded in agreement. Surprised at what he heard, the Navajo made a gesture to Grant, who was again sitting on the stairs above him, insinuating that the skipper was crazy, shrugging his shoulders and twirling his index finger beside his head. He then sat on the floor behind Hernandez's seat and whispered into Beaumont's ear about the bad dream the skipper had in the aft compartment. Beaumont bent over to listen, but he did not understand the significance of dreams or how they fit into Whitefeather's Native American religion. He just shrugged his shoulders. The skipper looked in their direction and Whitefeather stopped his gesture abruptly.

Like most people who had spent some time looking at Mars through a telescope, Nawrocki was skeptical about the existence of Martians. "What if they just want to explore, you know, like Admiral Byrd going to the South Pole, or something like that," asked the young Astronavigator?

"Then we should stop them," Peterson continued! "Can you imagine if the Commies had made it to the South Pole first, and claimed it for themselves? "What is there to see in outer space? "There is nothing out there! "They just want to point telescopes down from their station and spy on us so they can see where all of our ships are and aim their atomic bombs."

"I sure don't want them looking down on my wife and

kid," asserted Newcomb, raising his voice. "If we make it back from this trip, I want to be the one to go back there with a TX-17 and nuke that place so bad that they will NEVER be able to build a station in space! "They won't ever fly a man into space if I have anything to say about it! "The first country to fly a man into space will be the United States . . . if I have anything to say about it!"

"And, what if we don't make it back," asked Whitefeather, turning around to face the skipper, surprised by the Bombardier's enthusiasm?

"Then they will have those films," answered Peterson. "Someone else will have to do the dirty work . . . probably one of those new B-52's or a B-47 based in Iran."

"So what happens to us," asked Holbrook, "once we drop the film in the Gulf of Chi Li?"

"There is a submarine there waiting. "The canister has a clicker that the sonar man on the sub can find. "I intend to land this ship right where we drop the canister and the sub will find us when it finds *it*."

"What if the sub doesn't find *it*," asked the Meteorologist?

"Then we die."

"That's it then, we die?"

"If the Rooskies finish building their rockets and manage to build enough of them," the Colonel continued, "we'll die anyway; and so will our families and friends and everyone else you ever knew, because the Communists will destroy the entire world in order to rule over what is left. "Do you know what the Bible says about the Battle of Armageddon? "Do you think it is a coincidence that the Beast of the Apocalypse had ten horns and the Union of Soviet Socialist Republics has ten republics? "The Nation of Israel was re-established just eight years ago in nineteen forty eight. "According to the Biblical timetable, the world will come to an end three years from now if we don't nuke them first!"

"How do you know that we won't be the ones that start the war," asked Whitefeather?

"Because the Bible says they are the ones that will start it."

"So what," exclaimed Newcomb! "Even if they did destroy a few cities, that's hardly the same as the whole surface of the Earth. "We destroyed a few cities in the last war and the world didn't come to an end. "You might even say we made the world a better place."

"These new H-bombs aren't like the A-bomb," explained Peterson. "They work on a different principle. "The A-bomb uses the power of the atom . . . a very small thing. "The H-bomb uses the power of the Sun . . . a very big thing! "It's like an artificial star dropped from heaven down upon the Earth. "It doesn't just destroy cities, it destroys whole countries!"

"General LeMay has been working on ways to drop the bomb for a decade," the skipper continued. "During the war, he ordered all the guns removed from the B-29. "The crews balked and hated him for it. "Who wants to fly defenseless against the enemy, they said? "Curt LeMay has Bell's Palsy which paralyzed his face in childhood so he can't smile. "They said he was an evil avatar who couldn't even smile, sent straight out of hell to destroy the world. "The statistics proved them wrong and that LeMay was right! "B-29s without guns could carry twice as many bombs, which meant half as many missions to do the same amount of hurt to the Japs."

"With the H-bomb, there will be fewer missions yet," interrupted Newcomb. "So why fly without guns?"

"LeMay was right then and he is right now," Peterson continued. "When B-29's were shot down, half as many men were lost. "Without guns, the B-29 was a very clean airplane. "Its speed increased from three hundred seventy to four hundred miles per hour! "There was nothing in the world that was faster down on the deck and no other plane in the world could fly higher. "If the Japs attacked it, the aircraft commander just pushed the throttles all the way forward and flew away from danger."

"What does that have to do with us," asked Holbrook? "We have guns!"

"A rocket is ten times faster than a bomber . . . faster than a bullet. "There is no hope of shooting it down."

"So if the rocket is unmanned," asked Newcomb, "how does the bombardier plant it on its target?"

"He doesn't have to. "A bomb that can destroy a whole country will destroy the cities in a country at the same time." They all shuddered and looked at each other. "If they build enough bombs and rockets," continued the Colonel, "they will be able to destroy the entire free world, and drive over with their tanks to terrorize anyone that is left."

"How can a rocket shot from one side of the world hit the other side of the world," asked Beaumont?

"By flying in outer space," answered Peterson.

"If they shot it up, wouldn't it eventually come back down," asked Hernandez? "How can it turn around and hit under the feet of the person who launched it?"

"It uses the Earth's gravity to turn it around. "If it is shot high enough and also at an angle, it will miss the earth when it falls down and just keep falling around and around the earth." Everyone grunted, but not everyone shook their heads in understanding.

"So, how many bombs do you think it would take to destroy the world," asked Holbrook?

"I figure about a thousand," answered the Aircraft Commander.

"If they built a thousand, don't you think someone would know and tell us? "I find it hard to believe that most Russians would like to see the world destroyed, if it destroyed them too."

"It doesn't matter what they want or like," Peterson explained. "Russians are like robots, they do what they are told. "They have no freedom to resist their government. "Even if they only built a hundred, they could destroy most of the cities in the country."

"How big are these things; could they really build a thousand," asked Newcomb?

"They could build tens of thousands just like B-24's coming out of the Fort Worth plant during the war," answered the Colonel. "Once they had them aimed at us, they wouldn't even have to launch them; they could say, 'submit to

Communist rule or we will kill your children,' and our yellow politicians would submit."

"President Eisenhower would never submit to a threat like that, no matter what the cost," interrupted Newcomb!

"He wouldn't have to . . . the Commies would just nuke Washington and the rest of the upper crust, blue blood, jelly bellies would just cave in," retorted Peterson. "Our only hope is to stop them now and save the World. "We have to get these films back, no matter what the cost, so the politicians can see for themselves that our only hope is to strike first with an all out atomic attack before the Commies get their factories going to mass produce these things!"

"I'm sorry Skipper, I was wrong and you are right," said Holbrook saluting. "You can count on me to help get these pictures to the submarine, Colonel . . . live or die!"

"Right," exclaimed Newcomb! Most of the men grunted in agreement and also saluted. Whitefeather just stood still and said nothing. Peterson climbed back up to the bridge.

"UP SHIP!

"Hank, get us some altitude!"

SACRIFICE IN THE GULF OF CHI LI

February 1956

A flak explosion burst in front of the ship, staining the beautiful clear sky with a puff of black smoke. Johns reached up and flipped the nose door switches to air start the turbojets. "Those yellow Chinks can't shoot us down with planes, man to man, so they're sitting on the ground like cowards shooting flak at us," exclaimed Grant!

The contrails thickened and increased from four to six. With the jets started, the ship climbed quickly, despite having three engines out, because it was almost empty of fuel. The explosions were soon occurring a thousand feet below.

"I've got bad news," said Murphy. "At the present fuel consumption, we've got less than two hours left in the air, and that is assuming we shut down the jets in the next few minutes.

"That is what I meant when I said we would not be able to make it," explained Peterson, as he again reached up and killed the fuel gobbling jets. "To get to Cheju island we would have to fly low and the Chinese will never let us do that. "AC to Navigator, are we going to be able to get to the drop point, Duane," he asked?

"This is Navigator, I think so," Nawrocki replied, "we can glide the rest of the way if we can't."

"I don't want to glide. "I want a low level pass over the drop zone under their radar, so they can't see where we set her down. "John, I want you to wrap up the photography and get the can packed and ready to jettison, we'll need all the films from the gunsight cameras and the tapes from the mission control room."

"But Sir," Kewscinski replied, "this is PN, our flight path takes us right over Peking, don't you think we'll catch hell if we don't try to photograph it? "We're over the Mongolian border right now. "We really ought to be photographing those border installations where that flak was coming from."

"John, you amaze me," replied Peterson. "We've got a badly shot up aircraft with several dead and one wounded and all you can think of is work." Johns winced.

"Just doing my job, sir," said the Photo Navigator.

"Okay, how long will it take you to wrap things up after you photograph the guns?"

"Less than ten minutes, Sir." Kewscinski went aft, inserting his feet through the short, eight foot tube into the photo lab, closing the hatch behind him. He covered the windows of the lab with special shades and pulled a dark green curtain around his desk. One at a time, he removed the big rolls of film, which looked like black torah scrolls, from the giant camera backs and inserted them into his developing tank, a tall metal container with a top that sealed with a couple of buckle clasps. It had a silver crank built into its lid.

The tank had room inside for two film spools, a full one and an empty one, that both turned with the crank. Kewscinski poured in developer through a special plug, then cranked each film back and forth inside the tank from one spool to the other until every square inch of film was treated. A mechanical timer ticked on his desk which rang a bell when each film was done. "Sorry Washington," he said, "films have to be developed promptly after being exposed, or the quality will suffer." Washington did not respond. Kewscinski babbled on, "An undeveloped film can be ruined by light and heat. "A developed film is very durable, once it is dry, and can even withstand a crash if it is sealed in a fireproof container."

After treating each film, Kewscinski dumped the used developer out the Photo Lab urine tube and poured in an alcohol based drying solution, cranking the film back and forth again before dumping that out as well. Once the films were developed, he opened his curtain and removed the shades from the four little windows. The films were piled like ancient scrolls draining into a tray on his desk.

Kewscinski helped Washington and Mary put on their masks. The films had to be dried before they were packed. The most time consuming step, every drop of drying solution had to be blown off both sides of each fifty foot roll with a short hose and nozzle powered by a blast of warm compressed air from the engines' superchargers. This required that the lab be depressurized for the compressed air to work. Low air pressure lowered the boiling point of the alcohol, so the film would dry faster. Kewscinski closed the re-press valve and opened the urine tube dump valve announcing, "Everybody swallow!" Mary and Washington both opened their mouths and held their ears. The drying solution filled the lab with a noxious alcoholic smell as he blasted the films. It made everyone's eyes water and their heads ache even worse. When he was done, Kewscinski opened the repress valve and Mary and Washington again swallowed and held their ears.

"AC to crew, attention all hands, standby to receive your orders," commanded Peterson. "Remember that our buddies didn't die for nothing and we still have a job to do. "Lets make the most of our situation. "We're going to continue taking pictures. "As soon as we get to Peking, we are going into a dive and make a high speed, low level pass over the city. "When that happens, I want Jim and John to retrieve the rest of the films and get ready to salvo the can. "Harry and Jerry, I want you to get all of your tapes and meet John in the camera bay to load them in the can. "Sandringham, you will be in charge of rounding up all the films from the gun cameras and getting them to the photo lab. "Once we salvo the can, I'm going to put this mother into a tight one-eighty and set her down on top of it. "Any questions?"

"Why can't we bail out," asked Grant?

"If we got enough altitude for that, we'd show up on their radar and they would know where we went down," answered the skipper. "It is imperative that they do not make it to the rendezvous point before the cavalry arrives. "I know there are risks, but that is my decision."

"Why can't we rig our chutes with static lines and jump from the bomb bay at the same time you salvo the can," asked Grant?

"A hundred feet is not enough to slow you down from two hundred knots. "That canister can survive hitting the water at forty or fifty miles an hour. "It would kill *you*." Grant did not question the skipper again.

"Oh yeah, Sandringham," the skipper continued, "I want you to remove any personal effects from the dead that might fit into the can. "Captain Whitefeather and Captain Wong might be able to help you with that. "I know it is not a job that I would wish on anyone, but their wives and families will appreciate it and someone has to do it." Sandringham grumbled to himself. Of all the men in the crew, he alone had to remain shivering in the cold, windy, unpressurized aft cabin. His hands and feet were numb—and now he was expected to rummage through frozen dead bodies?

"What about Washington," shouted Whitefeather? "How do you plan to get him out?"

"Put him in forward gun bay."

"What about the girl," shouted Holbrook?

"Same thing," answered Peterson.

"The aft dorsal gun door is jammed," reminded Whitefeather.

"Exit the upper blisters."

"What if the tail comes apart on impact? "It's pretty badly shot up!"

"Worry about it when it happens," advised the Aircraft Commander.

Kewscinski began clicking pictures of the Chinese and Russian border defenses with his port lateral camera, which was mounted on the side of the photo lab. It had a simple window sight. The big camera gave a whir every time it advanced each frame. He needed something to do to focus his mind, since he was worried about he impending crash.

"What do you think Major," Nawrocki asked Holbrook, as they looked out of the mighty front window, watching the Yellow River pass under their desks?

"About what?"

"About what the Colonel said about the atomic rockets?"

"I don't know what to think," answered Holbrook, "it sounds pretty downright evil to me."

"Do you think the Communists want to take over the world," Nawrocki asked?

"I don't know," answered the meteorologist, "they might just want to destroy it."

"Why would anyone want to destroy the world?"

"Its just like the Bible says," explained Holbrook, the King of the North together with the Evil Beast rising out of the sea will wage war on the Earth to torment mankind. "I just wonder if maybe Mike is wrong. "Maybe we are the evil beast that rises out of the sea. "Maybe the 'Whore of Babylon' riding on its back is Broadway, Hollywood, and New Orleans. "Just look at the influence radio and television is having on young people. "If the rockets are as fast as the skipper says they are, and they can just fall out of the sky without warning, a half hour after they are launched, sinners would not have a chance to repent before they are killed. There would be no judgment day and every non-believer in the world would be sent straight to Hell."

"I don't believe that," exclaimed Nawrocki. "God has mercy on sinners. "At worst, they would go to Purgatory."

"Purgatory," asked Holbrook? "What is Purgatory?

"I thought you were a Christian," accused the young Navigator.

"Now, I didn't say I was a Catholic," Holbrook corrected.

"I don't know what you Catholics believe and I was just asking a question."

"Purgatory is the place in the sky just below Heaven where souls wait for those remaining on the Earth to do Penance for them so they can enter Heaven."

"What do you mean penance?"

"Penance is a good deed done in someone else's name . . . sort of like asking God for a favor."

"So, like, we are flying through purgatory right now," Holbrook chided . . . "and your mother is saying, 'God do me a favor, don't let him come back.'"

"That's not funny," Nawrocki protested. "Souls in Purgatory are already dead."

"Maybe you're already dead and you just don't know it," suggested the Meteorologist. "Do you know with certainty that you will go to Heaven when you die?"

"Of course," said the younger man! "I went to mass last Sunday. "I don't wear Rosary beads around my neck like Calabrese, but . . . " He paused for a moment and looked down at the clouds passing under his desk. The brown mountains looked like crumpled brown wrapping paper speckled with white and gray polka-dot clouds. Small green-black rivers and streams glistened with blazing white sunlight along sinuous paths. Except for the desk, bombsight, gun periscope, and radar detection antenna, the giant front window gave an unobstructed 180 degree view. Nawrocki felt he was among the angels, looking down at the cloud topped mountains and wrinkled brown valleys crossed by twisting roads scribbled like tan graffiti under the blue-black, partly star-spangled evening sky. The Great Wall of China, now far to the North, continued to drape from mountain top to mountain top, disappearing into the clouded valleys in places. " . . . I try not to eat meat on Friday," Nawrocki continued where he left off."

"And you think not eating meat on Friday will get you into heaven," asked Holbrook? Taught to look at clouds scientifically, the meteorologist was not as impressed by the beautiful view.

"It will get me into Purgatory, and then my mother will make a donation to the Church in my name, and then I will get into heaven," explained the Navigator.

"What if your mother is killed and there are no people on Earth left to do penance," interrupted Newcomb, who was overhearing their conversation?

Nawrocki got mad: "God would never allow that to happen!"

"The Bible says he will," claimed Holbrook!

"God will never kill all the Christians," defended Nawrocki. "God loves us!"

"He's not going to kill us, we're going to be raptured into Heaven," claimed Holbrook.

"What do you mean, 'rapture,'" asked Nawrocki?

"True Believers will ascend into heaven to face the Lord on the Judgment Day," the meteorologist explained.

"And what kind of church did you learn that in," asked the skeptical young Navigator?

"A Baptist church, of course . . . its in the Bible!"

"If its in the Bible, how come our Priest never talks about it?"

"Ask your Priest! "You can read the Bible for yourself, you know. "Its in Revelation."

"You mean the Apocalypse of Saint John," corrected Nawrocki. "Maybe I'll read it when we get back on the ground."

"I got news for you friend," Newcomb interjected, "but nobody has ever ditched an RB-36 before."

"Are you saying you don't think we're going to make it," asked Holbrook?

"I'm just saying it's never been done in a ship this large."

"What do you mean, 'this large,' Nawrocki the Navigator asked. "The Howard Hughes Spruce Goose was half again larger than an RB-36!"

"That was a seaplane with a giant belly of a hull and it only flew once. "I'd give us a little less than fifty-fifty chance of surviving it," estimated Newcomb. Nawrocki stared at him with an angry look.

"It would be a good time to make peace with the Lord now," insisted Holbrook. "You need to accept Jesus Christ as your Savior."

"I told you I attended Mass just before we left."

"But did you accept salvation?"

"What do you mean, 'did I accept salvation?' "Of course!"

"Salvation is not dependent on some ritual," quipped the Meteorologist disparagingly.

In the photo lab, because of the repressurization, Mary woke up and immediately felt hot. It was evening light. A bright high altitude sun was streaming into two of the four windows of the lab. Jumping down from her bunk, she removed her mask and helmet and stripped off her clothes—revealing as before, not a little of her Danish heritage. Kewscinski, still on oxygen, was amazed at how fast she did this, since she wore nothing under her parka. He crossed himself three times as he sat with his mouth agape. The parka and leggings were secured only by a few thongs. He wasn't present at her previous exhibition in the aft cabin, which was partially concealed by the dimness of the orange glow from the vacuum tubes. She quickly ran out of breath and fainted on her bunk above Washington. Her furry parka served as a mattress to cushion her smooth skin from the cold aluminum sides of the cot. From where Kewscinski was sitting at his camera control panel, he could plainly see between her legs and everything else. Her firm young chest heaved up and down. Even though the cabin was pressurized, she was not used to the thin air.

"Maybe you should send her village some of your Catholic Nuns to teach her how to dress," suggested Washington, who was finally awake on the bunk just under her!

Ignoring him, Kewscinski shouted: "THIS IS OUTRAGEOUS!—GET SOME CLOTHES ON YOUNG LADY!"

"STOP IT," yelled Whitefeather, who was emerging out of the giant mouse hole under Kewscinski's desk from the radio room, where he had fled to escape the noxious alcohol fumes, "she is from a different culture and she doesn't know any better! "Is there another blanket?"

"There might be one in the first aid kit," suggested Kewscinski. Whitefeather got up and opened the white box on the side of the cabin. Inside, was a thin, tightly wrapped bundle, which he unwrapped. He laid the small red crossed square of white wool over the sleeping beauty.

"Wait, what if we need that," complained Kewscinski!

"Shut up Sir," responded the Indian, "or you'll jinx us!" He then put Nakamura's bloody mask back on her.

Kewscinski frowned because the Red Man had failed to follow proper military protocol in addressing a superior officer. "All you Injuns like to prance around half-naked," he accused!

"She said her name was Mary Beorjessen," replied the Navajo. "If she has bad morals, it probably came from the Diablo Blanko† side of her family! "Don't Danes all like to dress naked in their sweat lodges while eating fudge?"

"Danes eat Danish, not fudge," Kewscinski corrected. "The Swiss eat fudge."

"I read in the National Geographic that Danes have a kind of sweat lodge," baited the Indian, "where they beat each other naked with sticks and eat fudge and since they don't wipe themselves, you can't tell their mouths from their sphincters."

"You're thinking of a Swedish sauna," interrupted Washington, overly relaxed from the morphine. "Besides, it's the Swiss that have chocolate, not the Swedes . . . a lot of people get the two mixed up.

"Any way you look at it," Kewscinski continued, "if it wasn't for you heathens, that girl would be a Christian, and she wouldn't behave that way."

"If it wasn't for some lilly White Dane named Beorjessen," Whitefeather shouted, "the girl would never have been born! "Aren't Danes Christians? "Is she not a byproduct of European Christian culture?"

"Of course not," replied Kewscinski! "Danes are Vikings.

† Diablo Blanko — Spanish for White Devil

"They worship Thor and Odin and the Valkiries of Valhalla, just like the Nazis, and they wear giant horned helmets when they rape teen age girls."

"And I suppose their women dance around naked to lure their husbands home," chided Whitefeather?

"Excuse me for saying so Major, Captain," interrupted Washington, "but, you're both full of it!"

"Full of what, Sergeant," asked Major Kewscinski?

"Fudge!"

Their mutiny over, the two aircraft commanders sharing the bridge stared ahead silently, both thinking about a predicament so dire, and a rendezvous with death so certain, that neither noticed the mountain country of the Great Wall descending down to the lush verdant valley of the Huang Po River beneath them. They watched the surrounding hills redden and purple beyond the setting sun. Because it was winter, and the speed and direction of flight was the same as which the world turns, the ground and the ship, together with the sun, all conspired to shorten the day. To Mongol Horsemen on the ground, this might have been a normal eight hour Winter's day.

To the men of 753, the day was shortened from eight to only five hours. It did not seem adequate compensation for the more than twenty two hours of continuous uninterrupted night they had endured while flying over the pole—made permanent for five of them.

Each commander stared straight ahead, embraced by the total illusion of flight that the almost unobstructed greenhouse canopy provided. Only the thick radial window frames and the busy instrument panel punctuated their view of the jagged mountains sending out lengthening shadows beneath them. 753's own shadow, elongated, but not distorted, could be seen darting from hilltop to hilltop, dogged by the bouncing shadows of two Tupolev chase planes, like an eagle harangued by crows.

Peterson and Johns, no longer on speaking terms, silently watched the black terminator advance toward them over the surface of the earth, filling valleys and hills with blackness like a devilish flood. The world's own shadow snuffed out the white cotton puff clouds in the distance, one by one. The nose of the RB-36 was short and low, and could not be seen from inside the ship. The view was like looking out the front window of a cab-over truck. It was both beautiful and threatening. They stared ahead with blank expressions at the effect of the sunset on the ground, eight miles below. Each man, those in the rest of the ship included, had separate thoughts, but together they imagined and reminisced like a choir of thinkers, musing and mulling over identical thoughts, remembering past wrongs against those left at home and reflecting upon their fate.

As The Lord's own big red, fiery thermonuclear ball rapidly dropped beyond the horizon, the mountains below instantly purpled. At the same moment, wispy clouds of cirrus in front of the ship lit up with the golden glow of yellow-red witches' hair, and began jumping toward them out of the violet sky. Behind them, a bright blue line marked the dark horizon.

Johns wondered if this was the last he would see of daylight over the beautiful Earth. How he liked to fly! He thought about Linda and Bobby. The idea of such a young woman like Linda being widowed made him weep quietly to himself. He couldn't help it. He turned his head to the right so his helmet would hide his tears from Peterson, but averted his glassy pupils to the left in order to continue to watch the ugly glowing instruments that hid so many of the slowly darkening clouds below. Johns felt angry for having chosen a flight assignment when he could have had a desk job. He was angry with himself for putting his own selfish thrills ahead of his family. On the other hand, the spot promotion did give him a fifty percent raise in pay which would continue if anything happened.

Bobby adored his father and even bragged at school in front of the other children what a good pilot he was. Would his son have grown up better with a mediocre father rather than a dead hero? He thought of the men who died—who's bodies still lay in the aft cabin. He thought how close he came to death. The projectiles that killed the four men missed him by only a few feet. It could have been him lying frozen on a blood-soaked bunk. Perhaps God intended for him to survive. That was a comforting thought. It gave him hope.

Immediately below and in front of Johns on the lower deck, Holbrook, the Born-again Christian, was sure he was saved. He was certain that in only a few hours, he would be standing before the throne of Christ, which he imagined to be just a few miles above where the ship was at that very instant. Holbrook imagined he would look down from heaven like an angel and see beautiful dawns and sunsets for all eternity as well as even greater wonders that he was sure The Lord had in store for him. He was not the least bit worried about his wife. 'Alice would re-marry,' he decided. That is one of the benefits of being a wife or daughter of the military—there were plenty of single men around. There were plenty of men at the church who would help the family out.

Colonel Peterson was also sure of his fate. After all, he was always right. God would never desert someone of his expertise. Grant, sitting back to back with him, like all young men, thought he was immortal.

In the photo lab, Kewscinski thought about his sins as he

continued to shoot photos with his lateral cameras every five or ten minutes. He made the St. John's cross over his forehead, mouth, and heart, but he did it slowly, so no one would notice. The naked girl had tempted him. He had found her attractive. What would Mary, "Mother of God," think? What would his priest think? What would his wife think? "Jerry," he asked Whitefeather, "would you mind if I told you something?"

Whitefeather grunted and nodded, then laughed as Kewscinski bent down to the floor and whispered into his ear. "Of course you found her attractive," the big Indian exclaimed, sitting up! "Who wouldn't? "I would think you were not normal if you did not find her attractive . . . after all, it isn't every day that a young girl strips buck naked in front of you."

"You don't have to blab it to the world," growled Kewscinski!

"What, are you trying to confess to me like I am a priest? "You don't need to confess to a priest to be saved," Whitefeather asserted. "They just tell you that to get money out of you." As long as you have faith, Jesus will save you. "That is what the priests taught us in Indian school. "After all, you were the one that said I should put a blanket on her, so what do you have to worry about. "If it were up to me, I would have left her just like she was, dressed only in her youthful post-virginal God given glory!"

Newcomb sat at his desk looking at his reflection in the radar screen. He had removed the camera hood, since it wasn't needed at night. He watched his chin beginning to vibrate. He could not understand why his chin was vibrating. He had seen the same vibrations in his son when he was angry or upset. He feared the others might notice, so he replaced the camera hood and pressed his eyes against it so his dangling oxygen mask might hide any possible facial expression.

The bitterness he felt was overwhelming. He felt anger that God was about to let him die. His mind dwelt upon the unfairness, that others back home were going about their daily lives, blissfully unaware of the sacrifice he and the others were making for their safety and freedom. He began to wonder what

Heaven was really like and how he would fit in. Singing hymns and strumming harps was not Jim Newcomb's style. Inside the camera hood, his eyes started to weep.

Newcomb decided that when he got to Heaven, he would have to make some changes. First, he had to have a car. He couldn't be happy without his car. A two hundred twenty five horsepower V-8 Thunderbird would do and a brand new DuMont television set. And he would need a dog—a big growling dog, to warn strangers to stay away. He remembered his old girlfriend who took ill with diphtheria and died when he was just seventeen. Would they be re-united? His wife Shirley would re-marry soon enough. There were plenty of men on base. The idea that someone he never met would be raising his son made him furious! The anger, combined with his impotence to affect the situation, made him weep even more. It seemed terribly unfair. He swore to himself that he would haunt whoever took his place, and breathe terror in the strange man's lungs to make certain his son would never forget who his real father was. His unmanly tears soaked into the padding around the hood until he felt wetness on this cheeks.

Nawrocki thought about his funeral. He realized that if the ship crashed into the ocean, his body would probably never be found. 'That will cut down attendance,' he thought to himself. He thought that his mother might buy a casket anyway, then decided that his dad would talk her out of it. There was nothing he could do about it, so he looked back down at his desk and updated his plot, ignoring the orange-red flaming clouds and purple sky passing in front of him.

Resting on the floor of the radio room, Beaumont pulled from a pocket on the leg of his flight suit, two pieces of wood which he twisted together to form a small flute. He began playing the tune of "Eternal Father Strong to Save". Hernandez pushed Beaumont's talk button and the performance was cable-cast all over the ship. The Chicano had played this prank on the Cajun many times before, to while away the hours during two day picket missions along the Russian border. No one ever told him that they enjoyed his music, but except for Russian propaganda stations, there was nothing else to listen to beyond the North Pole, so they liked it just fine.

"Stop playing that," bellowed Peterson! "We're not dead yet."

Not realizing that everyone was listening, Beaumont was puzzled. He could not understand how Peterson could possibly hear him over the noise of the engines. He began playing the tune to "Up we go into the wild blue yonder".

"That's better," praised the skipper, interrupting the performance when he pushed his interphone button!

Murphy looked at his engine analyzer display with distress. One of the propellers was out of sync. The number six manifold pressure gauge read zero and its fuel pressure was falling. Murphy clicked the switch to feather the prop. "We're out of fuel, sir, we have to throttle back," he shouted! The skipper and Johns stomped on their left rudder pedals to prevent a flat spin. Johns cut power to the three remaining engines as he turned the rudder trim knob, which looked like a big black mushroom sprouting from the center of the console between the seats. All felt a sudden sinking feeling as the ship began to fall out of the sky. Johns nosed into a dive to keep the airspeed up. 753 needed to be going two hundred miles per hour to fly five miles up. At least four engines were needed to do that.

"Can you restart the number six engine," the skipper asked?

"No sir," answered Murphy! "The others are not long for the world. "They all are running off the same tanks."

"There's no fuel left?"

"Sir, you know how it is. "Its impossible to tell how much is actually left in thirty three thousand gallon tanks when the gauge starts to read empty," Murphy answered. "They were running on vapors as they were."

"Dammit," cursed Peterson! "AC to Radio, Hernandez, give a mayday call on hailing frequencies for Puchon."

"Yes Sir," answered Hernandez! He gave Beaumont a kick.

"Navigator to Pilot, turn left to course zero-three-four to transmit, sir," advised Nawrocki. The ship began to bounce in more clear air turbulence as it fell out of the jet stream.

"Roger," answered Johns. He sharply banked the diving ship to line up the long horizontal short wave antenna wire, strung between the top of the fin and the radio room, with the intended receiver in Korea.

Hernandez, who had dozed off, sat up and asked, "what's happening?" The ship began to bounce violently.

Beaumont keyed in Morse over the radio: "S O S, A F 7 5 3, S O S, A F 7 5 3, 4 0 2 2, 1 1 6 0 9 . . . 4 0 2 2, 1 1 6 0 9 . . . S O S, A F 7 5 3, S O S, A F 7 5 3, 4 0 2 2, 1 1 6 0 9 . . . 4 0 2 2, 1 1 6 0 9" The radio crackled with nothing but static. "Nothing," he replied to Hernandez, "we're just out of fuel and the ship's going down."

Alarms sounded at the Air Force base at Puchon. The announcement was made over the public address system: "Ready alert, scramble, scramble, scramble!" Pilots already in their flight suits ran to their planes, a row of shiny single engine jets decorated with American white stars in blue circles and red white and blue epaulets. Under their noses, each plane had a jet intake in the front shaped like a mouth that seemed to always be scowling or frowning. Major Robert Becker hit the engine start button on the side of his F-86 "Dog Sabre." The engine started like a vacuum cleaner, as he climbed the ladder up to the cockpit. He removed his helmet from the seat, and slid down onto his parachute. Three groundcrewmen removed the ladder and wheel chocks. He saluted and released the brakes as he strapped himself in and connected his oxygen mask, steering with his feet as the little plane headed for the runway. "Jack of Diamonds one five one, ready to taxi over," he said.

"Jack of Diamonds, taxi left to runway five right," answered the tower, "cleared onto the active."

"Lucky one thirteen on your tail, Jack," said his wingman. The two of them slowly opened their throttles and leapt into the air.

Wong had been listening to the radio traffic between the ground and the Chinese chase planes as they discussed the movements of the "doya doya Yankee." When Peterson ordered the mayday announcement to be made, Wong's hands suddenly started to shake and he could not control them. Now there were two Chinese planes coming. "I need to crap," he said to himself, and unplugged himself from his post in the mission control room and removed his helmet. The sudden release of pressure made his joints ache. As the ship was descending below 18,000 feet, he felt only a little light headed as he squirmed through the triangular stringers beside the gun bays. When he made it to the toilet in the aft cabin, he found Sandringham already sitting there.

Sandringham was embarrassed because Harry did not tell him he had the same problem. The privacy curtain had been pulled off its rod by the sudden decompression during the attack. Sandringham stuffed his soiled underwear into the chaff dispenser. "Damn, you've used all the paper," Wong shouted over the swirling wind! Sandringham grunted in reply, indicating he was sorry.

After they swapped places, Wong unzipped his space suit and struggled out of it. The icy breeze chilled his bare bottom. He pulled a technical manual from the shelf under the gunner's platform and tore out pages to clean himself and the wool pants liners he wore inside the suit. Sandringham happened to look up and shouted, "Hey, that's classified information you're stuffing into the toilet! "What if the Chinks find it," he asked, oblivious to the fact that Wong was also Chinese?

"THEN THEY CAN EAT SHIT," shouted Wong in reply, angry about the disturbance to his privacy.

"Carry on Captain," said the Sergeant with a laugh and a sharp salute.

Wong felt uncomfortable pulling the soiled fleece against his behind, but there was nothing else he could do." A hell of a way to die," he exclaimed!

"Okay, back on course," commanded the skipper. Johns banked the diving ship in the other direction. "What's that city lit up ahead?"

"Peking, sir," answered Nawrocki. The lights could be seen in the distance under the rapidly darkening sky.

"You plotted a course over their damned Capitol?"

"I thought we were going over to take pictures," explained the younger man. "We need a fix on the city center to dead reckon our way to the rendezvous point."

"DAMMIT! What altitude can we fly at?"

"We can probably level out at ten thousand at this weight on three engines," Johns estimated.

"No, keep on descending," ordered the skipper. "Take her down all the way."

"We're going to buzz the capital city, sir," asked Nawrocki over the interphone?

"At least if they shoot at us and miss, they'll hit Mao Tse Tung's palace by accident," answered Peterson.

"What if they want to kill Mao," asked Grant?

"Then we'll give them the excuse! "Do you have any better ideas," the skipper asked of the younger man?

"Nossir."

"On the deck it shall be," said Johns as he pushed his wheel toward the panel.

"AC to crew, battlestations," commanded Peterson over the interphone! He tapped the alarm bells for a short ring to wake everybody up. "Get ready to go aft and get the tape and films as we discussed . . . and the dog tags from our dead. "Decompress!" The forward dorsal hatch opened and the two gun turrets came up behind the cockpit, as Grant and Hernandez got ready to fight.

Once the ship had descended below 10,000 feet, the air became warmer and they could all remove their masks. Newcomb entered the photo lab. Whitefeather ordered Mary to get her clothes on and helped her pull up her leggings, before disappearing into the communication tube. Kewscinski frantically developed and dried the remaining film from the giant cameras while Newcomb passed through the hatch into the bomb bay. The canister, exactly the same as the ones used by airborne troops, two feet in diameter and about six feet long, was hung from the center bomb rack on the ceiling of the bomb bay near the photo lab. Newcomb inspected the nylon static line attached to its parachute, the other end of which was also attached to a bomb rack. Attaching his safety strap, Newcomb climbed up the beams that reinforced the photo lab bulkhead and, standing near the ceiling, he opened the end of the can.

In the aft cabin, Whitefeather went through the pockets of the dead men. Wong gathered the tapes from the mission control room and carried them to Newcomb, who packed them into the canister with Kewscinski's film rolls. They developed a bucket brigade, as Kewscinski passed his priceless films to Wong, who handed them up to Newcomb. Sandringham gave the film from the gun cameras to Whitefeather, who sent them forward on the tube trolley to Kewscinski. He passed them to Wong, who handed them to Newcomb to place in the canister around the smaller trimetrigon film backs Kewscinski dug out of the floor of the lab, but had not bothered to develop. After the film and tapes, Newcomb shoved the dead men's dogtags, wallets, and wristwatches into the spaces between the other items. The canister was almost full by that time. When Wong gave him some computers Whitefeather had pulled from the dead men, Newcomb asked, "What are you putting those in for?"

"They're personal effects," answered Wong.

"How are you going to know which one belongs to who?"

"I dunno, who gives a damn! "Maybe their wives will recognize them."

Newcomb shoved them between the other items, then wound up the pinger, a kind of clockwork noisemaker attached to the lid, and held it close to his leather helmet to make sure it was working. Wong climbed up to help him clamp the lid on with a large circular gasket, making sure the waterproof "O" ring seal was properly set, then inserted a bronze sealing wire through a lead pill which he bit with his teeth. Their job done, they passed through the circular hatch into the lab.

"You'll probably have a better chance of surviving the crash if you stay here with us," advised Kewscinski, looking through the hatch into the bomb bay. "The skipper can salvo the can with his safety switch."

"Naw, if I'm going to die, I want to die at my post," answered Newcomb, climbing back into the lab, "besides, I have to find that submarine and drop this thing on target. "You can stay here, John. "I just don't want it said that I died for nothing. "Besides, who is to say which end of a ship this size is safer in a crash? "Nobody has ever ditched an RB-36 before. "If the skipper does it right, its the tail that hits first."

"Yeah, but its the nose that hits harder," argued Kewscinski.

"The tail is shot up. "It might come off," warned Whitefeather. "If it does, everybody up front will be a goner. "The safest place is probably right here."

"I appreciate it Jerry," said Newcomb, "but I figure I want my death to be quick and that clear plastic nose lets me see what I'm getting into. "You guys are going to be busy enough trying to evacuate Washington and the Eskimo girl."

"Shucks, she's the only one with waterproof clothes," Whitefeather replied. "Maybe she will rescue us." Everyone chuckled!

"Eskimos can't swim," Washington reminded them.

Wong began to regret leaving his helmet behind in the mission control room. His suit would float if he had brought his helmet.

"Jerry," asked Kewscinski, "if by chance you make it and I don't, will you tell my Mary that I love her?"

"Of course! "You'll do the same for Margaret?"

"I'll say they were your last words."

"You'll remember my Eunice," asked Wong?

"Of course!"

Newcomb stuck his gloved finger in his eye. "It must be the altitude," he said, "I think I got something in my eye." He then turned away from the others and banged his leather helmet against a shelf on the forward bulkhead that normally held the photographic chemicals. As they watched, he deliberately banged his head four more times.

Kewscinski grabbed him by the shoulder and said, "We know how you feel."

Newcomb had his finger and thumb pressed against his eyes. "I'm sorry," he said, "I can't help it . . . I just can't help thinking that I haven't been a very good father to little Jimmy. "This military life, always having to move from base to base. "The boy can't make friends and when he does, we are sent somewhere else."

"I know what you're saying. "My kids say the same thing."

"I just haven't been a good father," Newcomb repeated, "or a good husband to Shirley."

"Who has? "We've all fallen short in one way or another."

"Harry, Jerry," said Newcomb, reaching out with his hand, "it's been a privilege to have flown with you." The four men shook hands. Then Whitefeather grabbed Newcomb violently and patted him on the back. Kewscinski did the same and Wong put his arms over Kewscinski's and Whitefeather's shoulders so the four of them stood there leaning against each other in an embrace, like a bunch of huddling football players banging their helmets together. After a few more back pats and another round of hand shaking, they stared into each other's eyes and parted. Newcomb went forward. Kewscinski strapped Washington and Mary to their bunks as he watched Whitefeather and Wong each disappear through the circular hatches into the bomb bay, then sat down at his desk and strapped himself into his seat.

After taking the tube trolley through the ship's intestine to the shattered aft cabin, Whitefeather climbed up into Calabrese's bloody chair and strapped himself in. Wong passed through the bomb bay and strapped himself into the mission control room beside Hughs.

Johns leveled out after completing the descent. The lights of the city seemed to pass underneath at tremendous speed, despite the fuel efficiency settings of the three remaining engines. Like a skier descending a steep hill, the ship gained momentum as it dove toward the ground. Johns steered for a bright light up ahead. As they flew past, they were able to see it was a picture of a man on the side of a red roofed building.

"Is that Mao Tse Tung," asked Kewscinski, looking through the big front window?

"Who else could it be," Newcomb replied?

Nawrocki updated his plot and said, "Navigator to AC, come to course zero niner three to the drop."

"Thank you Duane," replied Peterson, "zero niner three."

"It looks like they've made him into a kind of god," remarked Kewscinski. "He's the only thing in town that's brightly lit!"

"Tail Gunner to AC, Those Tu-2's are coming within range," said Sandringham through the interphone. "Should I shoot them down?"

"This is AC, are they making any aggressive moves," asked the skipper?

"Inbound bogies, two, no, four," shouted Grant from his left forward gunsight bubble!

"Yes, shoot, activate chaff dispenser," commanded the skipper. "We can't let them follow us to the drop zone." Sandringham adjusted the gain and tune knobs as he gazed into his two radar screens and pressed a little button on the console with his thumb. The jarring sound of a large motorcycle being kick started came from the tail. Murphy, Hernandez, Grant, and Whitefeather, watched the tracers arcing through the night at the Chinese plane's flashing navigation lights. There was an explosion.

"GOT'EM," yelled Hernandez from his right forward gunsight bubble! "They never had a chance!"

A Chinese shopkeeper relaxed as his wife stirred her wok in his tiny back-room brick apartment. A large aircraft passed low overhead with a deafening noise. He went to the door to see what it was. An explosion knocked him to the ground. He turned around to see his wife and daughter engulfed in flames. His store was full of wreckage. He watched his 12 year old girl run out of the building with her hair on fire trying to remove her burning clothes.

Sandringham flexed the joystick under his console to the left and again thumbed the fire button. The motorcycle sound started again. "Got em," said Whitefeather, as he watched the flaming Tupolev crash onto the roof of a factory. Sandringham flicked a switch to activate the automatic chaff dispenser in the tail compartment.

"Co-pilot to Tailgunner," announced Grant, "all right Pete, that makes you an ace!"

"This is AC, Where are the bogies," asked the skipper?

"This is VO, they're sortie-ing behind us where we dropped the two chase ships," answered Newcomb, his face pressed against his radar camera. "Wait, they're coming! "They're fanning out in a search pattern. "The ECM is working! "Wait, there are four more. "No, eight more closing four hundred knots at three O'clock! "There are four more inbound at eleven O'clock!"

"That's Cavalry," cheered the skipper!

"NEPTUNE ONE FIVE NINER CALLING AIR FORCE SEVEN FIVE THREE OVER," a voice announced over the cockpit radio. "AIR FORCE SEVEN FIVE THREE, THIS IS NEPTUNE ONE FIVE NINER OVER!"

"This Is Air Force seven five three eastbound niner three," answered Peterson, pushing the comm button on his wheel. "We've got bandits six o'clock and three O'clock over!"

WHAT RANGE," asked Neptune?

"VO to AC, that'll be ten miles to six O'clock and three miles to three O'clock and closing," interrupted Newcomb over the interphone.

"Neptune this is seven five three," answered Peterson, "They're right on us, angels two, eight of them, with four more ten miles behind us!"

"ROGER, STANDBY! "THIS IS NEPTUNE CALLING RAZORBACK AND TITTYTWISTER, OVER!"

"RAZORBACK CHECKING IN!"

"THIS IS TITTYTWISTER, GO AHEAD!"

"TURN RIGHT TO TWO EIGHT FIVE, DOZEN GOOKS ANGELS TWO, TWENTY MILES CLOSING. "BELLYFLOP VECTOR TWO SEVEN EIGHT ANGELS

ONE, EASTBOUND NINER THREE."

"TALLYHO TWO EIGHT FIVE!"

"TITTYTWISTER TALLYHO."

"JACK OF DIAMONDS ONE FIVE ONE AND LUCKY ONE THIRTEEN CHECKING IN!"

"Bellyflop buster niner three cherubs two," advised Peterson!"

"ROGER BUSTER, STANDBY, WERE SUPERSONIC," said Major Becker. "WERE ON GOOKS ONE, TITTYTWISTER TAKE GOOKS TWO!"

"ROGER GOOKS TWO!

"They're coming up fast," warned Newcomb, as he gazed into his camera. "Closing at four hundred knots."

"Break left," the skipper yelled to Johns! Everyone was pressed into their seats as the ship stood on its left wing.

"We don't have the altitude for this," Johns yelled back, "or the power to climb out of it if we screw up the turn!"

"I know," said Peterson.

"Tail Gunner to AC, they're passing by our tail," yelled Sandringham!

"This is AC, FIRE," commanded the skipper, pressing his interphone button! More motorcycle sounds came from the tail. Murphy and the gunners watched the tracers arc toward the glowing flames from the tailpipes of the fighters and miss.

"They're turning toward us," said Hernandez!

"Break right," commanded Peterson! The ship stood on its right wing as Johns turned, his eyes glued on the wingtip blowing dust off the darkened housetops below. It took both of them to handle the sluggish controls at such high speed.

"They're turning to follow," yelled Whitefeather! "They're firing!" Tracers ripped into the right wing and caused an explosion. Johns ducked to protect his night vision.

"There goes the rest of our fuel," yelled Murphy. "Fire extinguishers on five, feathering five." He reached over and mashed the fire extinguisher switch on Washington's console with his left hand and flicked the number five feather switch. "Two and four running on vapors!"

"Tail Gunner to Nose Gunner, they're disengaging," yelled Sandringham! "Ready in front!" The MiG's made easy targets. Their tailflames, trailing from their afterburners, lit up the sky. Holbrook gripped the handlebars under his periscope, pressed his right eye against the sight, and squeezed his trigger. A black rubber cone covered his left eye as he leaned his forehead against it. The skipper and Johns were blinded by the bright muzzle flashes of the nose turret guns waving in front of them. They had to climb, so as not to dash into the ground.

After the Chinese planes flashed by, a great deal of flak and tracers rose from the ground like fireflies and exploded around the ship. Hernandez and Grant fired the dorsal guns, filling the bridge with psychedelic dancing lights as the greenhouse window frames made differing crosshatch patterns on everyone and everything under the waving muzzles blasting over their heads.

Everyone's ears were ringing. More afterburner flames descended from above. "CEASE FIRE, CEASE FIRE," yelled Peterson, pressing his interphone button! "THOSE ARE FRIENDLIES! Holbrook did not hear. Newcomb had to pull him away from his sight by the shoulders.

The tail flames were noiseless as they zoomed by. Long fiery streaks shot from their rocket tubes, exploding like fireworks in the distance. Loud sonic booms shook the ship. The supersonic jets sent shockwaves in every direction.

"They're disengaging," announced Grant!

"SORRY TO LEAVE YOU BELLYFLOP, BUT WE'LL BE ON VAPORS IF WE DON'T HEAD BACK; RAZORBACK OUT!"

"TITTYTWISTER DISENGAGING; GOT TO GO HOME; MAY THE GODS OF WAR BE WITH YOU, GOOD LUCK!"

"HAVE A SAFE TRIP HOME; JACK OF DIAMONDS OUT," added Major Becker as he turned his Dog Sabre toward Puchon.

"Thanks boys, hope to see you stateside; bellyflop out," answered the skipper.

"THIS IS NEPTUNE, CAN YOU MAKE THE RENDEZVOUS POINT? "WE HAVE TWENTY MINUTES TO SEE YOU DOWN."

"Roger Neptune, bellyflop in ten minutes. "Rendezvous in five minutes," answered Peterson. "Jim, John, get ready to salvo can one," he added, switching thumb buttons on his wheel.

"Roger Mike; bomb door safety switch enabled," answered Kewscinski.

"Hey where did all the lights go," asked Newcomb? He pulled his face away from his radar camera long enough to notice that the view through the front window had suddenly gone dark.

"We're over water," explained Nawrocki. "Four minutes to drop! "Can you help me with these skywave corrections, sir," the young navigator asked Holbrook as he adjusted the knobs on his LORAN receiver to center the sawtooth waves on his screen? The Meteorologist began frantically attacking the grooves in his adding machine with his stylus as Nawrocki read off the time delays in milliseconds. Newcomb resumed pressing his face against the radar camera.

"Tailgunner to AC, there are more blips closing from behind," warned Sandringham.

"When will they get here," asked the Colonel?

"They're closing fast . . . ten seconds. "I don't have any ammo left."

"Shit," replied the skipper! "Neptune this is bellyflop," he said, pushing his comm button. "We've got more company. "You might not want to stick around."

"BELLYFLOP THIS IS NEPTUNE, WE WILL TRY TO DRAW THEM OFF OF YOU, OVER!"

"Can you tell me the wind vector?"

"ABOUT THREE THREE ZERO."

"Roger, I will orbit to three three zero after the drop. "Are you ready," the skipper asked, switching buttons again without letting go of the wheel?"

"I've got a blip," said Newcomb.

"That would be it, sir," said Nawrocki.

"VO to AC, turn right to one-two-zero, now! "Can salvo in thirty seconds!"   Johns and Peterson nervously banked hard to the right. "Standby, we're on it," added the VO, his face in the radar camera. "Ten, nine, eight, seven, six, five, four, three, two, one . . . "   A red light went out on the bombing control panel. A clunk in the back of the ship was heard. "Can one away; make your orbit!"

"Bomb doors closing," announced Kewscinski! Another clunk was heard. The parachute opened instantly to slow the canister as soon as it fell.

The skipper banked hard to the right as he turned into the wind. The Navy version of the B-24, an old PB4Y-2, momentarily joined the flying battleship in formation. With only four engines, the PB4Y-2 was less than half its size. Peterson pulled back the throttles as he leveled out, then rang the emergency bells and yelled, "LIGHTS, FLAPS, PREPARE FOR DITCHING, PREPARE FOR DITCHING!"   Johns clicked the switches, but many of the flaps were damaged. "PREPARE FOR DITCHING, PREPARE FOR DITCHING," repeated Peterson nervously, ringing the emergency bells!

"Keep turning right to zero zero zero," demanded Newcomb, "you're heading too far away!"

"Tell me when to flare Hank," ordered the Aircraft Commander, his hands shaking. "Murphy, remove the astro-dome!" The remaining APE turned around and unlatched the plastic bubble and threw it under Washington's desk. A strong icy wind swirled around the bridge. None of them could see the black watery grave they were descending into. Johns concentrated on looking for the reflection of the landing lights in the water's surface. Tiny dots of light along the horizon made the water seem blacker than the sky. Nawrocki and Holbrook removed their parachutes and put on their Mae Wests. They fled the forward compartment and sat on the floor of the radio room beside Grant, Beaumont, and Hernandez, who were folding down the gunsights and removing the Plexiglas sighting bubbles so they could make an easy escape. A cold strong wind swirled through the radio room with a deafening roar.

Kewscinski removed his parachute, put on his Mae West, then unstrapped Washington and Mary from the bunks. Though Washington could barely walk, the Photonavigator shoved him up through a tiny circular hatch above his desk into the forward gun bay under the turrets. Wong inserted one last tape inside his space suit, then got up from his radios and swung like Tarzan through the bomb bay to the photo lab where he met Whitefeather and Sandringham, who had evacuated the aft cabin through the communication tube. Everyone climbed up on Kewscinski's desk and through the hatch into the now crowded open forward gun bay.

The wind in the gun bay was terrific. The raised gun turrets overhead seemed to deflect the blast downward like giant air scoops. Washington sat beside Mary with his back against the forward bulkhead. The hood of Mary's parka violently lashed Kewscinski's back, as he took position between her knees, facing aft. Whitefeather sat down between Kewscinski's knees, beside Wong and Sandringham, who were together in a row between Washington's knees like a bunch of tobogganers. A folded life raft filled the space between the two groups.

"We're passing the target," yelled Newcomb, still at his post!

"One hundred feet," Johns read from the altimeter. Neither man trusted it. Two days had gone by since it was set. Murphy watched his gauges with alarm as the remaining engines began to sputter. "We're coming in much too fast," warned Johns! The arrows on the gauges fluxtuated wildly as the engines began to stall and roar intermittently.

"There's nothing to be done," replied Peterson. "If we stall, we're goners!

"DO IT, SIR! "There's no fuel for another pass," shouted Murphy!

"This is VO, FLARE, FLARE, FLARE," shouted Newcomb, pressing his interphone button! He scrambled onto the toilet behind his radar desk as the landing lights danced off of a patchwork of white ice floes covering the surface. He quickly buckled the safety strap around his hips and bent over in crash position.

Whitefeather pressed his feet against the aft bulkhead of the gun bay, crushing Mary and Kewscinski firmly in place. Sandringham did the same with Wong and Washington as the belly of the ship hit the ice with several loud thuds. Murphy, facing aft at his console on the bridge, watched in horror as the giant tail ripped completely off, taking the aft cabin with it, as it flipped over several times like a showery jumping jack.

With their goggles pulled down, those in the gun bay looked like insects, their closed squinting eyes betraying expressions of absolute fear. Great plumes of white water and ice shot up on either side of the nose as it hit, then water came over the top of the bridge canopy and drenched them.

A six foot wall of ice and water slammed through the Plexiglas nose, inundating the forward cabin and causing the ears of everyone in the radio room to pop. The floor bent upward until Newcomb's legs were trapped between the radar desk and forward landing gear bay. Cold water like the shower room of a boy's gym covered everyone in the radio room, spuming through the autopilot chassis and electronic counter-measures equipment, shorting out the electronics. M-80 firecrackers in secret fail-safe mechanisms began to explode like gunshots, sending flying glass from the many vacuum tubes all over the cabin. The rectangular black boxes that still had their covers puffed up into a pumpkin shape like giant popcorn. The cabin filled with smoke as everyone's deafened ears rang.

Newcomb yelled for help. Holbrook swam forward as water and chunks of ice filled the radio room. He grabbed Newcomb off the toilet by the shoulders and tugged until he fell backwards into the icy water. One of Newcomb's legs was pinned. He began flailing his arms and kicking at the ceiling with his other leg, screaming "HELP, HELP! "HELP ME!" Hernandez reached forward and tried pulling him, but he could not be budged. The water rose fast. When Newcomb's head went under, Holbrook abandoned him and swam toward Grant's open gunsight bubble.

The six in the gun bay scrambled up from between the turrets and threw the folded life raft between them onto some floating chunks of ice. Sandringham jerked the lanyard to inflate it, pulling it toward the ship. Those in the radio room climbed aboard using Grant's folded down gunsight as a ladder. Those on the bridge frantically removed their chutes, put on their Mae wests, and stomped on the throttles, thrust reversers, and autopilot switches as they squirmed up through the astrodome hole on top of the canopy.

"Help Washington up," yelled Whitefeather! He and Wong grabbed the wounded man by the armpits and dumped him headfirst into the water, falling into the water on top of him. He was not wearing a life jacket. With quick thinking, Grant grabbed Washington's foot and pulled him aboard. The last to abandon ship, Kewscinski looked down into the radio room to hear Newcomb scream.

"Sons of bitches, DON'T LEAVE ME HERE," Newcomb yelled in a garbled tone as icy waves sloshing between the exploding black boxes covered and uncovered his head! "YOU MOTHER-FUCKERS HELP ME!" Then there was silence as the troubled waters covered the top of his helmet for the last time. Churning bubbles boiled out of the underwater radar bay as more fail-safe mechanisms exploded. Green phosphorescent marine life glowed for miles around, for a second or two, after each pounding blast. A surreal glowing, undulating icy landscape surrounded the ship as it disappeared under the ice, taking poor Newcomb with it. The interior of the open-topped gun bay glowed bright green, lit by luminescent plankton as it sank beneath the floes.

Wong and Mary swam toward the darkened raft. She did know how to swim. Both had waterproof garments. The polar bear fleece and the space suit performed equally well to keep them dry as they climbed aboard.

The ship's shiny wings reflected a green phosphorescent glow as they creaked and groaned, accompanied by an occasional bang of rock and roll, whenever ice punched holes through the thin magnesium sheet metal. The swells slowly wrinkled and tore the empty gas tanks so they would fill with water and sink. They hissed and gurgled as the air trapped inside escaped. The rivets of the main spar popped as the waves bent and folded the giant waterlogged wings, slowly tearing them to pieces.

The remaining gasoline reeked a terrible odor as it floated up onto the surface between the floes. It colored the phosphorescent green glow beneath into beautiful swirling rainbows at the surface, but irritated eyes and noses, filling lungs gasping for breath with the fear that the very air they breathed might, at any moment, explode into a fireball and burn their very hearts and souls.

Fail-safe charges continued to burst, boiling columns of hot bubbles from below. With each pop and bang, everyone winced, expecting the sky to ignite. Only by grace of God, was there enough wind to dissipate the vapors and prevent a fiery conflagration. The silvery left turbojet pod on the right wing was the last part of the ship to sink. It lifted high above the surface like the arm of a swimmer beckoning them to join poor Newcomb. It loomed over the little raft like a giant sea monster, illuminated from underneath by green planktonic bubbles floating to the surface from the remaining air pockets, and from drowning Jim Newcomb's lungs as he expelled his last breath.

Once the jet pod sank, all were overwhelmed by the sudden silence. The gunfire and the exploding fail-safes that made everyone's ears ring were now replaced by the quiet lapping of the sea on the sides of the raft, accompanied by the bump and thump of ice floes grinding, men groaning, and bubbles fizzing from the still sinking wings beneath. In the distance, the thunder of jet engines could be heard as MiG's returned to their bases after their encounter with the PB4Y-2. It had been two days since the engines were first started back in Fort Worth. To some, the most powerful airplane engines in the world just make noise. To the crew of 753, the throbbing din was comforting and reassuring. It is the squealing sound that an engine makes when a propeller hits the water and the bearings seize up that brings terror. All felt profoundly disappointed, depressed, hopeless, powerless, and ashamed to have been shot down. The mission failed. Friends died for nothing. Forty thousand gallons of gasoline and six hundred gallons of oil were wasted for nothing. One minute they were the most important men in the world, crewing the greatest thing ever to fly. The next, they were useless jetsam floating alone on a dark icy sea.

As their eyes adapted to the darkness, it seemed that there were never so many stars—not even on a West Texas Autumn night. The sea seemed to be alive. It glowed green with plankton around the grinding floes, in a strange patchwork of light and dark. It was hard to understand how the horizon on such a black moonless night could be seen by zodiacal light alone. A bright green line divided the green-black icy sea from the starry yellow-black sky. Perhaps from among the stars, the glistening souls of departed comrades gazed down upon them. The Milky Way seemed to be a streak of solid white against the black velvety sky. Was that the firmament spoken of by Moses? Perhaps heaven had been visible all along, but could not be seen because of street lights. The bright belt of Orion twinkled through the clear air turbulence of the jetstream, below which steadily glowed the bejeweled nebula of Orion's sword.

All grunted and groaned, not out of pain, but out of despair. If only mothers had the power to rescue their adult children from such escapades. Except for frightened heavy breathing, no one talked. There was nothing to say. Washington and those in the radio room who had fallen in the water were shivering from cold. The others tried to comfort them, but no one was foolish enough to offer dry clothes. If someone died of exposure, it was bad luck. No one who's clothes were dry would offer to share their fate.

"Everybody try to form a heap to keep those with wet clothes out of the wind," commanded Johns! He was a real 'take charge' kind of guy—a real leader! Most were glad to have him as a friend. Peterson was not sure he wanted him as a subordin- ate, but now it did not matter. When men outgrow childish pranks and begin to take responsibility for their actions, there are times when they don't want to admit their shortcomings—that they are vulnerable and defenseless and really still need their mothers. This is why a leader like Johns is so loved by his men. A man like that can take responsibility and offer some comfort in times of personal vulnerability. He can comfort his men the way a father comforts his son. He can unite the group into a cohesive family unit that together is stronger than the sum of its members. On the other hand, there was Peterson.

The yellow, oval shaped raft was designed to hold twelve. Sixteen men huddled in a pile in the center. The bottom of the raft was wet. It didn't make sense for a man with dry clothes to be on the bottom, so those with dry clothes piled on top of the wet men to try to keep them out of the wind. Mary, thanks to her polar bear fleece, was the only one who didn't feel cold. She stood on top of the pile like a captain on the deck of a ship—a deck made of men!

Kewscincki quietly said some Hail Marys and crossed himself several times, begging St. Christopher to save him. Holbrook prayed for his wife and children and tried to make peace with the Lord as best he could. Grant, who thought he was immortal, smiled and acted like it was a great adventure. Most of the others were glad just to have survived the crash. Beaumont again twisted together the two parts of his wooden flute and began playing "Eternal Father Strong to Save." This time, no one complained.

After several hours, Mary was the only one still awake. The concept of night and day made little sense to polar people. In Thule, it was always night or always day. In spring and autumn, it was always twilight. Fully alert, she noticed a streak of foam on the surface about a half mile away and stood up to get a better view. Wong groaned as her sealskin boots dug into his back. "Vad hedder deddert," she asked? She could hardly believe her eyes. The sea erupted with boiling water. Wong could understand her, but he was too numb with cold to care. Like the others, he just groaned. The black silhouette of a submarine silently appeared on the horizon. Mary jumped

† Hvad hedder det der — What is that there?

down off of the raft and scampered from ice floe to ice floe toward the submarine yelling, "Yelb, yelb, day hasder! "Hender ayn laiger! "Kurr my till ayn laiger†! "Hender ayn laiger!"

Wong was beyond shivering or caring about what she was saying. He was just glad to have her off his back. Mary sometimes stopped and waved her arms to keep her balance. The Gulf of Chi Li does not normally freeze in winter, but when the jet stream propels an icy storm system out of Siberia, even China can be held hostage by its frozen embrace. The ice was clear and thin.

† Hjælp, hjælp! Det haster! Hente en læge! Vær så venlig, kør mig til en læge! — Help, help, its urgent! Bring a doctor! Please, take me to a doctor!

"Hjælp, hjælp!

"Vær så venlig, kør mig til en læge!"

THE SUBMARINE
February 1956

A groaning, crackling sound combined with deep rumbling from engines, not unlike those of a railroad locomotive, woke Grant and Johns.

"The sub," yelled Grant!

"Get the flare canister," ordered Johns!

Grant found it. His numb hands hurt as he unscrewed the lid. "Anybody have any matches," he asked?

"Aren't there any in there?"

"I can't find them in the dark," said Grant. "Wait a minute." The flare had a special waterproof abrasive cap that could be removed to strike the end of it like a giant match. Grant lit the flare. Its warmth in his hands was a welcome relief from the cold. A searchlight on the sub began scanning the surface and lit up the raft. Then it began scanning in the opposite direction.

"Why aren't they coming," asked Holbrook, shivering?

"There not here to rescue us," Peterson explained, "they're here for the canister."

"How can they find it in this blackness?"

"By listening to the pinger with their sonar."

"I sure wish they'd hurry up," complained Wong.

"They must have found it," said Peterson, or they wouldn't have started their engines."

After what seemed like an interminable amount of time,

the conning tower of the submarine loomed over the tiny raft. The silhouette of an Eskimo stood in the very bow with an arm stretched out toward them. Grant lit a second flare because the first had burned out. The idling sub engines seemed to shake the water between the floes. A searchlight shined on the undulating yellow pancake. Water boiled behind the sub as its propellers backed down to stop. Abruptly, the spotlight went out.

"Ahoy there, extinguish that flare," a voice yelled from the sub! Engines could be heard coming from the opposite direction—higher pitched than the idling engines of the sub. Grant threw the flare into the water. It took a while for everyone's eyes to adjust to the darkness again. A number of dark figures were involved in a commotion on the deck. Soon, a number of white faces seemed to be supernaturally hovering out in the blackness. As they grew larger, they sprouted black uniforms, a black rubber boat, and black painted paddles. They moved over the floes like a giant bug. Four legs on each side lifted it up and propelled it forward over the thin layer of ice.

"Heads up," a disembodied white face shouted! A line fell over the raft. "Secure that," the Cheshire head commanded!

The Air Force men looked at each other, not sure what to attach the line to. "It's just like the Air Force to build a boat with no way to attach a line!" commented the disembodied face. The other Seals laughed, but those being rescued were not in any mood for jokes.

"It's okay, we got it," advised Johns. All who were able grabbed the line and started pulling it in.

"ALRIGHT, PULL," the black suited Seal yelled toward the sub! There was a loud "heave ho" coming from the deck as a group of sailors in black coveralls pulled the heavily laden rafts toward them, hand over hand. As eyes adapted to the dark, the deck gun could be seen pointing at the sound of the approaching engines. A black rectangular shape appeared to be moving closer, silhouetted by a backdrop of zodiacal light. The ice hindered its movement. There was a flash, then a whistle, followed by an ear splitting explosion in the water just behind the sub, and thunder from both sides.

"RETURN FIRE," said a voice over the public address system. A man sitting in a chair attached to the deck gun seemed to be pedaling bicycle pedals, with another set of pedals for his hands. Depending on which way he pedaled with his feet, the gun would turn left or right. By pedaling with his hands, he could make the gun go up or down. Without warning, the gun fired with an ear popping bang! "HURRY UP, ALL PASSENGERS BELOW," the voice from the speaker commanded, barely audible over the ringing in everyone's ears!

"We need a litter for a wounded man," shouted Johns!

"There's no time for that," said the Seal, "Which one is he?" Peterson pointed at Washington. "bring him here," ordered the Seal. The men dragged Washington toward the black boat. The other seals dragged him aboard. When the rafts were alongside the sub, men on deck began helping those in the boats climb aboard. They lifted Washington by his armpits and lowered him through a hatch. "C'MON YOU LUBBERS," the Seal shouted. "Hurry, or you'll be bobbing on the surface by yourselves!"

Another explosion in the water showered the sub. The deck gun replied with another ear piercing crack! Whitefeather was the last one aboard. Before he could regain his balance with both feet on deck, the rafts were cast adrift. The engines, which had been growling like an idling locomotive, suddenly stopped. "Ahoogah, Ahoogah," sounded an old fashioned car horn as the loudspeaker commanded, "DIVE, DIVE, DIVE, DIVE!" With much hissing and bubbling, waves began washing through holes in the deck as everyone struggled with numb hands and feet to climb up a ladder on the side of the conning tower. "Down the hatch," the Seal yelled! "HURRY!"

The deck gun boomed one last time, before the gunner jumped off and climbed up on the tower. Wong sat on the edge of the hatch, but a Seal shoved him down into the boat, causing him to bump his ice cold elbow on the hard steel. He lost his balance and fell as he cried in pain. His space suit offered little protection. The ladder was vertical and about 16 feet tall. Wong fell feet first, but before he reached the floor of the conning tower, a sailor punched him in the gut, shoving him aside. He fell against the other men crammed in the tiny compartment, his deflated space suit taking twice as much space as the others. "When the Chief says hurry, he means HURRY, shouted a man in a black sailor suit at the top of his lungs, his voice echoing godlike in the tiny steel chamber!

The Air Force men marveled at how quickly the gunners descended the ladder. First their feet would appear, but instead of stepping on the rungs, they would slide their boots on the sides of the ladder, in a type of controlled fall, until their feet caught on the hatch below. They grabbed the rungs only to keep themselves from toppling backward when their toes hit. Each man descended two stories, from the bridge atop the conning tower into the control room, in just two seconds, jumping out of the way just in time to keep from being clobbered by the man above. The last man pulled a lanyard and slammed the hatch closed, then hung with his full weight from the rope, his free hand twirling a hatch handle that looked something like a car steering wheel to engage the dogs that made the hatch water tight.

As the sub descended, ice could be heard grinding on the sides of the conning tower. The floor began to tilt down toward the bow at a steep angle, but this made the ladder easier to descend since it was no longer vertical—more like the ladder on the side of a house.

The control room was painted pastel green and it was filled with green painted equipment. The walls and ceiling were covered with pipes and tubes and valves painted a rainbow of different colors.

"All passengers aft to the Mess," commanded a sailor, which was repeated by another. Colonel Peterson disobeyed and insisted on meeting the gray shirted Captain. Captain Rodgers was bent over a plotting table where a chart of the sea bottom was spread. The chart was elaborately marked with obstacles and listening devices the Chinese had placed to prevent infiltration of American subs during the Korean Conflict. In the lower front corner of the control room, a pimply kid steered a control wheel much like that of an aircraft, as he studied the sonar to keep the sub off the shallow bottom.

"All passengers aft to the Mess," the Captain repeated to a sailor, "then rig for depth charges!"

"Eye eye sir, the sailor replied. He grabbed Colonel Peterson by the arm and said, "come with me!"

The Mess was a small cafeteria with two tables running lengthwise toward the back of the boat. The walls were covered with woodgrain paneled cabinets, but the ceiling was white, with the same rainbow colored tubes and pipes running fore and aft. The tables and benches were covered with Air Force men trying to remove wet clothes. They stank. It had been days since any of them had bathed or talced their armpits. Sailors continually walked through on their way from one end of the sub to the other. Some plugged their noses as they passed. There was no privacy.

Washington had fallen asleep as soon as he was laid down on the table, but woke instantly when Whitefeather and Wong tried to remove his boots and gloves. Because the morphine was wearing off, it caused him some pain. Colonel Peterson was so exhausted by the ordeal, he just laid down under one of the tables and fell asleep. "COLLISION ALERT, RIG FOR DEPTH CHARGE," ordered a voice on the intercom. A loud boom shook the whole boat. It was frightening, but the Air Force men were too tired to care. Thanks to the ice, the sub could go faster beneath the surface than the Chinese patrol boat could above. There were two more loud booms, but they had no hope of catching the sub.

A blue staff car descended the winding dirt road that lead to the subdivision just across Lake Worth from Carswell Air Force Base. "US Air Force" was written on the side in yellow block letters. It stopped at Phyllis Peterson's white, flat topped bungalow. The comforter of widows and orphans, wearing dark winter blues and carrying his cap under his arm, rang the doorbell. "Hello," Phyllis answered, "Chaplain Edwards, what brings you here?" She was wearing the same frilly white apron with red polka-dots she wore at the ladies' breakfast two days earlier, over an aquamarine house dress.

"Can I come. in," he asked? The television was on.

"Of course," she answered, a little nervous about the unexpected visit.

"There's been a crash."

Her friendly look of greeting was instantly replaced with one of horror. The clergyman's words seemed to come from nowhere, as though the Devil himself had whispered in her ear. She looked away and paused, stumbled, then danced quickly over to the television and turned it off. She seemed to turn to stone and had difficulty moving. Slowly turning, she looked down at her spiral area rug in the middle of the floor.

After what seemed like a minute she asked, "Is Mike all right," starring wide eyed at his portrait on the wall with tears dripping onto her nose? She knew if her husband was all right, the Chaplain would have said so immediately. She could not bring herself to look him in the face. 'Crashes only happen to those who screw up,' she remembered the Colonel saying among her husband's last words to her.

"He's missing," answered the Chaplain.

"Where did he go down," she gathered the courage to ask? She could not look him in the face.

"I don't know, but I understand there is a Navy search team looking for him right now."

Conflicting thoughts raced through her mind: 'At least he did not go down in Russia,' she thought to herself; 'if the Navy was involved, he must have gone down at sea, but he would not have much chance in winter; 'on the other hand, an RB-36 can fly halfway around the world without refueling; 'if he went down in the tropics, there was still hope.'

"Thank you for telling me," she said to the Chaplain fighting back more tears as she was finally able to look him in the eyes.

"I'm sorry. "I can't stay," the chaplain replied, "I have to visit the others. "We'll have a service this afternoon at the First Congregational Church at Two, once I get everyone together."

Phyllis arrived at the church wearing her black dress. Linda Johns was already there in similar attire. Both women broke into tears and embraced each other. Mary Kewscinski and Shirley Newcomb, wearing a brown and a dark green dress respectively, rose from a pew and joined their chorus of tears. All wore stylish black hats from which hung a black speckled net that partially hid their faces.

"You always prepare for the day that they don't come home, and when they don't, you hardly know how to act," said Shirley.

"Hank just loves to fly," said Linda, "He didn't want to take this mission, but he couldn't turn it down." She glowered at Phyllis since it was her husband Mike that persuaded him.

The little church was light and airy with tall pointed windows on pastel blue walls, and a white high peaked ceiling from which a wooden cross hung at one end. The light fixtures were of brass, but because the service was to be multi-denominational, the altar had only a simple red cloth, with two candles, a Bible, and a menorah on top. The menorah was placed there for the benefit of an officer who was Jewish. Margaret Whitefeather and Eunice Wong sat in the back wearing similar black hats. No one knew who they were. Their husbands had only recently been transferred. Eunice was obviously Chinese, but no one knew what to make of Margaret. She was big girl like Loretta and could have been anything. Nets hid their faces.

The enlisted men's wives assembled on the other side of the aisle. Gladys Murphy, Maria Hernandez, Mary O'Connor, Rita Shultz, and Esther Calabrese. A number of wives from other crews filed in to give their friends support and there was much tearful embracing. Off-duty officers and Airmen began to fill the little church to capacity.

When Chaplain Edwards arrived, he asked Margaret and Eunice to move to the front to sit with the other wives who's husbands were lost. A school bus pulled up in front and two dozen kids poured out into the little church. The kids stormed up the aisle, Bobby Johns cheerfully yelling, "They let us out

early, Mommy!" The mothers tried to explain that their fathers
were missing and that it was hardly a joyous occasion, but the
flying naval vessels often remained aloft for two days without
landing. Tours of Duty always took at least a week. It had been
less than three days since 753 had departed, so the children felt
nothing was unusual. A ten engined battleship roared overhead,
returning from a two day mission patrolling the Soviet border.
The kids ran joyously outside to try to follow the one hundred
fifteen mile an hour giant down the street.

A Black woman, dressed in black, with a black net
obscuring her face, nervously looked to the left and the right as
she entered the church. She carefully sat down in the rear
asking, "All right, all right?," as if she needed permission of
everyone she met, before she could sit. No one asked her if she
wanted to move to the front. Realizing that some of the kids
were hers, she called them near. A white woman got up and
moved when three tiny Black faces sat down beside their
mother.

An old lady, wearing a small pillbox hat, began playing
the Air Force Hymn on a wheezy reed organ. Many of the
officers who were veterans of the war and Korea knew it by
heart. They sang loudly:

> *Lord God protect the men who fly*
>
> > *from unseen dangers in the sky*
>
> *be with them always in the air,*
>
> > *in darkening storm or sunlight fair*
>
> *and keep them in thy watchful care*
>
> *from unseen perils in the air*

They sang as if rehearsed—many at the top of their lungs.
A rumor had passed through the crowd that 753 had gone down
at sea, so they sang the Navy hymn as well:

> *Eternal Father, strong to save*
>
> > *those cast adrift on restless waves*

Command the mighty ocean deep
   that gales and storms and torrents keep
away from them who cry to thee
   when cast in peril on the sea

The crowd did not do such a good job singing the second verse, not because they did not know it as well, but because many were rendered speechless by tears and unable to sing.

Chaplain Edwards, wearing a black gown and stole, said a short opening prayer and then introduced General Allen, who stood beside him in a blue uniform. The General began by addressing the base personnel who had filled the church to standing room only. "I'm going to make this short," the General began, "then the rest of you can get back to work. "The Navy has informed us that fifteen been rescued by one of their subs. "Because communication with subs is restricted, we do not yet know the identity of the survivors."

A gasp rose from the crowd. Everyone knew that there were twenty on board. If fifteen were rescued, then there must have been five fatalities. In tears, the ladies all studied each other's faces as if they could somehow discern, by psychic premonition, which of their husbands had been killed, and which would be returning home, simply by observing each other's facial expressions. They did not know if they were crying for themselves or each other.

"Excuse me, General, do you have any information about where they went down," asked Linda Johns, raising her hand?

"The location of the crash is classified," answered the Wing Commander, "but I can tell you it was in a politically sensitive area and that search and rescue operations have ceased."

"If no more are being rescued," asked Shirley Newcomb, "does that mean some of our husbands won't be coming back?"

"I regret to say yes."

"You can't tell us which," a voice interjected from the back of the church?

"I'm sorry to say, no," answered the General. "If I knew, I would certainly tell you. "We won't know more until the sub surfaces to transmit more information or makes it back to port."

"Excuse me General," Maria Hernandez asked, "do you know anything about the cause of the crash?" Phyllis cringed at that question because the Air Force usually listed unexplained crashes as "pilot error." The last thing she wanted in life was to be the widow of the screw-up that got the rest of their men killed.

"No, I'm sorry," answered the General, "we won't know that until we conduct a full investigation. "Chaplain, I'm turning it back to you."

"Now we will say a prayer for the missing men," announced Chaplain Edwards reverently.

When Peterson awoke, he looked up from the floor of the Mess at the different colored pipes on the ceiling and saw a blue-shirted sailor standing over him. He could hear Beaumont playing something on his wooden flute. "Colonel Peterson, the sailor asked?

"Yes."

"The Skipper would like to see you in the Ward Room." Colonel Peterson could see that the watertight doors were open. He got up off the floor and followed the sailor through the crowded control room to the front of the sub. The ward room was a small, wood-paneled niche behind a very narrow door, about the size of the dinette in a camping trailer. The outer pressure hull of the boat curved dramatically upward, so the wall and the ceiling merged into one, just as on an RB-36. Those on the far side of the dinette could not sit fully upright. Captain Rodgers and Lieutenant Commander Nelson, the Executive Officer, were gracious enough to sit in the head bumping cramped seats. Johns was already seated, so Colonel Peterson sat down beside him.

"I understand you lost six men," the Captain began.

Colonel Peterson fought to remember that in the Navy, a Captain is Equal in rank to a Colonel and a Lieutenant Commander is the same as a Major. "I thought we lost five," he said.

"Newcomb didn't make it," explained Johns.

"What happened to him?"

"He stayed at his post."

"That's stupid, he knows better than that!"

"Knew better," asked Johns? "If he hadn't yelled to pull up we all might have been killed. "Maybe he didn't think we were going to make it and he wanted to die at his post."

"Your Darkie, Washington, is in a bad way," informed Captain Rodgers, "we have to make a decision about his fingers and toes."

"Did you pick up the can," asked Peterson?

"Yes, we have it under guard in the forward torpedo room."

"They sure do," Johns interjected! "They got two guys with carbines that won't let anyone near it."

"Is it likely someone will be able to steal it from a submerged submarine," the Colonel asked?

"I was ordered to keep it under guard so I keep it under guard," explained Rodgers. "In the Navy, orders are orders, no matter how ridiculous they may seem."

"It's like that in the Air force too," the Colonel replied, "but at least when you take off, you are fooled into thinking you're free as a bird." Rodgers laughed. "At least my men didn't die for nothing," said Peterson! "They usually say 'pilot error' in situations like this. "If I have the film, I can prove what I did."

"Oh yea," exclaimed Johns, "there will be no problem proving it!"

The Captain smiled and said, "We listened in on the radio traffic just before you went down."

"It sounded like you had a run in with some fighters," inquired Nelson?

"That isn't the half of it," answered Johns.

"Were you shot down?"

"Not exactly."

"That's classified," interrupted Peterson.

"Of course," agreed Captain Rodgers.

A loud cheer rose from the Mess. The four of them got

up and rushed aft to see what was causing the commotion. Though the sub was filled with equipment, all painted lime green, the Mess was an exception, with wooden paneling and white tables and floor. In the corner, Mary, who felt hot, was giving another performance. The submariners were clapping and cheering and yelling "Baby, baby, oh baby!"

"Does anyone have a blanket," demanded Whitefeather?

A blue shirted sailor replied, "She can use my blanket if I can use it at the same time!" To this, a chorus of sailors offered her their blankets and stipulated that they must be able to strip it off her whenever they liked.

"Unusual sort of crew you have Colonel," commented Rodgers.

"She was a stowaway," explained Peterson.

"Kind of like the Captain's woman," Nelson asked? Rodgers laughed so loud that Peterson could see the back of his throat!

This made the Colonel upset. It is bad enough to have lost an aircraft and six men, but to have a stowaway, or any other unauthorized personnel on board, suggested incompetence. "She hid in the nose landing gear bay," he explained.

"She wanted to see America," Johns added. These excuses only made Rodgers laugh louder.

Peterson cringed and said, "She was very nearly killed. "If we had not found her, she would have frozen to death," he continued, pointlessly.

"Yes, but if she had not run to us across the ice," Rodgers chided, "you would have frozen to death."

"I can't say it is bad for morale, but she is certainly not freezing now," commented Nelson. "In fact, she doesn't look frigid at all."

"I'm sure a search plane would have spotted us by morning," argued Peterson.

"You don't understand," explained Nelson, "our orders were to get the canister and return to port immediately. "In the Navy, immediately means immediately . . . no time to search for floating sky boys. "It's very unusual for the Gulf of Chi Li to ice over, even in February. "It would have prevented us from finding you. "If it wasn't for her, you would all be thawing out in a Chinese morgue or a prison camp if you survived the night."

"I'll tell you," Rodgers laughed, "its the damndest thing a sailor ever expects to see. "If you look out across the waves on a black ocean, miles from land, and you see a beautiful girl running toward you, walking on water; then you *know* you've been away from home port too long! "I think you should consider her your guardian angel. "God must have sent her to protect you. "GET HER A BLANKET," he barked at a sailor!

"Toolee is not a favorite assignment in the Air Force," apologised Johns. "The men assigned there are not always of the finest character. "We think she might have been the girlfriend of one of the men who transferred out and she is just trying to see her common law hubby."

"You mean common child molester," accused Nelson? "She doesn't look much older than fifteen or sixteen, if that much!" A sailor got a blanket out of a cabinet and threw it at her. Whitefeather pinned it on her.

"Make sure she keeps it on," ordered the Captain! "If she causes any more commotion . . . " Rodgers stopped, realizing he had no real authority over the passengers, then added, "I'll have to mention it in my report!" He could not have made a more serious threat, from Peterson's point of view. The Colonel was worried how it would play out between General LeMay and General Allen. "Where is Thule anyway," asked Rodgers?

"In Greenland," answered Peterson.

"So she is an Eskimo? "Do all Eskimos have such groovy figures?"

"I couldn't tell you," answered the Colonel, "we only stop there for fuel."

"I think you had better look at your Darkie," said Rodgers, pointing at the table on the other side of the room. "The Pharmacist's Mate has him sedated and he has given him penicillin, but he has gangrene."

Roberts, the Pharmacist's Mate, lifted the bandages and said, "It's spreading. "They have to come off."

"His fingers," asked the Colonel?

"Yes!"

"Can't it wait until we get to a hospital? "He's a mechanic. "He won't be able to do his job without fingers."

"We won't be in port for a day and a half," answered Rodgers, "even then, it takes several hours to get berthed."

"By that time, it could spread to his hands and he could lose his hands," insisted Roberts. "Look at his fingers, they're black like claws! "They are useless to him anyway. "They have to come off."

"Don't all Negroes have black hands," asked Peterson?

"Not Black black; their palms are white. "When I said Black, I meant black . . . black like death!"

The Colonel shuddered and asked, "Are you going to cut them off yourself?"

"No, the cook has volunteered. "He is the best with a cleaver."

"Who is the cook?"

"That's Meyers, right behind you." Meyers was a big man with a paunch wearing a white sailor suit.

"Doesn't it make you a bit queasy, asked the Colonel?"

"No sir," answered Meyers smiling.

Another sailor standing behind him quipped, "Cookie's serving frozen Nigger fingers for morning mess!"

"I like to see a man who enjoys his work," Peterson commented, snidely. Meyers smiled a goofy look.

Meyers and Roberts rolled Washington on his belly and told him to bite on a towel. Peterson couldn't bear to watch. Meyers took three practice swings much as a golfer might before a delicate putt, then "CRACK!" He swung with all his might. Washington groaned.

"There's blood," Roberts said, "it's a good sign." He wrapped up the stump of Washington's left hand.

"You've done this before," asked Peterson?

"There was a buddy of mine lost his hand trying to repair a camshaft," Roberts said, "someone cranked the engine when they shouldn't have and he got caught."

"Did it happen during the war?"

"No, just a stupid camshaft," explained Roberts. Meyers stood with the cleaver dripping with blood and a queasy look on his face. "Lets do the foot." There was another crack. "Good job, Meyers! "If you need to heave, don't do it on the patient." After bandaging Washington's right foot, the Pharmacist's Mate said, "Lets do the other hand."

"I don't think I'm feeling too good," said Meyers.

"You have to do it. "You know there's no one on board that can swing that ax half as good as you!"

"I think I'm too nervous," apologised Meyers.

"It's all right, the fingers we can do one at a time. "You only need to cut the tips off this time!" There were several more cracks, then Meyers turned around and lost his lunch all over the white linoleum floor. The fifteen sailors crowding around to witness the amputation had dwindled to just two. Only six remained in the usually very crowded mess hall.

"Don't worry about that, Meyers," said Captain Rodgers, "the main reason they put mess halls on naval vessels is to have a place to put the wounded!"

The two "surgeons" traded places and Roberts bound the fingers. There were more loud "cracks," then Roberts asked Meyers to do one over again because he judged there was insufficient blood flow and he had not cut off all of the gangrene.

The church emptied out quickly after the service. The ladies who were first to arrive also found themselves the last to leave. The children were outside playing a game of tag which was accompanied by somewhat louder yells and screams than usual. This bothered the ladies in the church, but no one complained.

Some of the ladies noticed a Black woman sitting in the rear by herself. No one had asked her to join the other wives. Linda went over to talk to her. "You must be Mrs. Washington," she said.

"Please, call me Polly."

"I'm Linda Johns."

"Yes, I know. "I've seen you before. "My husband was very grateful to the Major for asking him to fly with him. "He was passed up for many flight assignments and then your husband said he wanted Lorenzo and he was ecstatic, really thrilled to be allowed to fly." She looked down at the floor.

"Hank didn't pick your husband because of his color; he said your husband was the best mechanic on the base and he was the one he wanted."

"I'm sorry," said Polly, "I just had a premonition that Lorenzo might have been one of the ones that did not return." She continued to look at the floor and then looked up straight in Linda's eyes and said, "I knew it would only be a matter of time before Sergeant Washington was recognized for his fine work. "I used to tell him whenever he got discouraged, that my mother told me you can do anything if you just keep on trying. "Larry used to dream of flying so much, he crewed for the Tuskeegee squadron, you know, the Colored squadron, but he never got to fly. "He thought they might let him fly if he did good work, but it seemed like the better he got as a mechanic, the more they needed him as a mechanic, and then your husband came along and got him his wish and now that he has fulfilled his life's dream, he's dead."

"Don't say that," cried Linda! "You don't know that!"

"That's what I think. "That's all."

"It does no good to think about it. "Either they rescued him or they didn't and nothing you think is going to change it."

"What about the Chaplain praying for all the men as though they were all still alive when he knew that some of them couldn't be alive?"

"That's what Chaplains do. "It is better to pray for someone who is dead than not to pray at all. "If you don't pray because you say he is dead already, it's like telling God that you don't care."

"Larry prayed and prayed that he would get to fly and now he got his wish and look where it got him."

"Oh stop it Polly! "He's probably fine!"

"But I don't know that!"

"So maybe he's not, but it is important not to give up hope."

"We won't know until we know and until then we just have to pray." Linda's eyes filled with tears and the two women embraced. "I'm sorry your husband was on Hank's flight."

"Oh, I'm not blaming Major Johns," the Colored Woman said, "Larry would have flown with whomever asked him. "I think it was his destiny."

"Who knows about anyone's destiny?" Linda replied?

The following morning, Phyllis Peterson was awakened by her teen-age daughter. She did not bother to set the alarm clock and she did not sleep well.

"What are we supposed to eat for breakfast," asked Denise?

"Fix some peanut butter and Jelly," her mother commanded, as she lay alone in her queen sized bed.

"Peanut butter and Jelly for breakfast," the girl asked?

"Yes, fix whatever you want!"

"What am I supposed to wear for school?"

"Wear whatever you want." Her mother then changed her mind. "You don't have to go to school today if you don't want to."

"Is that because Daddy isn't here?"

"Yes, because Daddy isn't here." Phyllis rolled over with her face in her pillow so her daughter would not see her cry.

A scream came from the neighboring bungalow, followed by two shrieks and another scream. Phyllis jumped out of bed and ran to the front door to see what was the matter. A dark blue Air Force staff car sat in the dirt driveway of Loretta Hughs' house. Loretta and her husband Merril had just moved in from Washington DC. It suddenly dawned on her that Major Hughs was on her husband's ship!

"Get my robe," she shouted at Denise! She fastened the belt of her frilly, cherry red robe with small white polka dots, and padded down the sidewalk in fuzzy pink slippers, slamming the screen door behind her.

Covering her curlers with her hand, Phyllis glanced right and left, worried that the neighbors might see them as she ran quickly to Loretta's whitewashed bungalow.   She looked through the dark green front door and saw Loretta kneeling on the floor wailing and pounding General Allen on the chest with her fists. Chaplain Edwards held her by the hips. Jerking open the door, Phyllis ran inside without knocking. Loretta could not control her sobs.   She was screaming something, but it was impossible to make out what she was trying to say.   General Allen had watery eyes too. He tried to deflect her blows by holding onto her elbows. Loretta had obviously received some bad news. Phyllis grabbed her around the neck and squeezed her hard.   Loretta stood up, turned, and struck the General's shoulders right and left with the bottoms of her fists.

Chaplain Edwards' presence there could mean only one thing.   Phyllis felt relieved because, as wife of the ranking officer, if her husband, the Colonel, was among the dead, the Chaplain would have come to her first. Still, she felt a twinge of fear and had to ask, "Is Misses Michael Peterson on the list of homes to visit?"

"No, she's, I mean, you're not," revealed Chaplain Edwards. General Allen stared at her, not quite knowing what to do or say as she pulled Loretta away from him.

"Thank you, thank you," sobbed Mrs. Peterson softly, with tears running down her cheeks.

"I'm sorry," said the General to Loretta, who was still bawling, "We have other homes we must visit." Though several feet away, Loretta continued to attack his dark blue uniform with tears.

"Would you mind telling us where you are going to call next, asked Phyllis, "I would like to do something."

"No, I'm sorry," replied Edwards. "Regulations require that I notify the next of kin first."

"Couldn't you tell me what house you plan to stop at next?"

"No, I'm sorry," apologised Allen . . . "regulations! "I have to go."

As he and Edwards left, Phyllis dragged the sobbing Loretta, who would not let go, over to the door to watch the car depart up the hill. Her heart leapt for joy when the car drove past Linda Johns' house. Mike and Hank were such good friends, she thought to herself, and Hank and Linda usually came over every other Thursday for Bridge. If something happened to Hank, Linda would have to move and she would lose a friend. It was so nice to have someone to talk to when Mike was away.

She wondered who else would be next to receive the comforter of widows and orphans. She gasped and could not hold back her tears as the staff car turned into Shirley Newcomb's driveway.

"Poor Shirley," Phyllis exclaimed! She yearned to go to Shirley, but Loretta would not stop crying. She did not have anyone else. There was an open, half empty bottle of Gin on the table of the sparely furnished whitewashed dining room, which still contained half-unpacked cardboard boxes stacked against the wall. There was only one glass beside the bottle.

THE FUNERAL
March 1956

The submarine did not stop in Korea. It continued on to Yokohama, Japan, where all of the survivors were given physicals and debriefed at the Air Force headquarters in Tokyo for two days. Men from the new Central Intelligence Agency sat in on the debriefings. Once they were cleared to return home, Peterson and his men were led onto a big KC-97 bound for Kiska and then on to Seattle.

A full week after the crash, an army-green four-engined C-54, a relic of the Berlin airlift, reached the old hangar at the end of Runway 35 after landing back at Fort Worth. A large crowd had gathered inside. The men were in full dress Air Force blues. The women wore mostly black with black speckled nets under their black hats. A number of children had been called out of school. Most of them wore Sunday suits. Others, who had not been to school for several days, had brand new clothes with the creases still showing—either all white for the girls, or all black for the boys. Several black limousines and large black hearses were parked outside the building.

Virtually everyone on base, except for the Air Police, had stopped work to attend the ceremony. As the nose of the plane entered the hanger, its whirling propellers seemed to break the silence with an unusual amount of noise. A man stood in front giving hand signals since it was not normal for a ship to enter the hangar under power like that. Once the groundcrew set the chocks, a moveable stairway was positioned in front of the door. The first to come down was Sergeant Sandringham. His girlfriend ran forward to greet him, then broke down in tears. She grasped him tightly by the waist and bawled against his chest. He embraced her—genuinely surprised at her reaction, since their reunions were usually joyous. He asked her if something was wrong. The others descended to equally teary joyous hugs except for Whitefeather, who turned around and grabbed the front of a wheelchair pushed by Colonel Peterson. Major Johns kissed his wife Linda passionately.

That all the White men would descend first, was nothing unusual to Polly Washington. She expected her husband would emerge after the others. When she saw a Black face in the wheelchair, she froze, then burst into tears. She ran to the foot of the stairs with her hand over her mouth. "What's the matter with Daddy, Mommy," asked one of her three little ones, who ran after her?

It took Captain Whitefeather and Colonel Peterson about a minute to bump Washington down the steps. There was a special truck with a scissors lift for unloading cargo that they could have used, but Washington wanted to go down the same way as the others, even if it was a little uncomfortable. He just stared at the ground and did not look at his wife.

"What is the matter with him," asked Mrs. Washington?

"He lost his fingers and toes to frostbite," answered Colonel Peterson.

"We would not have made it back if he had not managed to repair a shot up engine in flight," said Whitefeather.

"A short circuited fuel cut-off valve," explained the Second APE, dourly.

Polly Washington embraced her husband, but the bandaged hands beat on her back like clubs. The embrace gave no comfort, The metal arm of the wheelchair dug into her knee. "Damn them, damn them," she quietly cursed, as she held his neck kissing his head. Washington was surprised at her reaction. He was curious who she was so angry with. She glared at Peterson.

The flight engineer of the C-54 descended the stairs with a large box. Colonel Peterson reached into the box and pulled out smaller boxes and gave one to each of the widows. Each woman received a wallet and some pictures, a watch, if her husband had one, and a pair of dog tags. They all burst into tears. Whitefeather pulled out a metal canister too large for the smaller boxes and gave it to Loretta Hughs, whom he knew personally. She opened the canister and fainted when she saw her husband's dried blood on the tape reel.

A command was given to order arms. "Right shoulder ARMS," was heard. Six riflemen marched in behind a two man color guard, one with the American Flag, and the other carrying a yellow flag emblazoned with a flapping eagle standing on the three black crosses on yellow bend, blue shield of the 8th Air Force, 7th Bombardment Wing. Under the shield was written: "MORS AB ALTO"—Death from Above! Behind the color guard, followed forty-eight air police wearing white gloves and spats, marching in close double-file. The men ascended the stairs into the plane. After what seemed like a very long time, they emerged carrying six coffins. It was obvious there was nothing inside the flag draped wooden boxes. The coffins seemed as light as feathers. They were sealed as classified material, which was often done when the cause of death could not be revealed. Pinned to the flags on top, were floral bouquets, the names of the men the coffins represented, and Air Medals as decorations.

Esther Calabrese, a thin wisp of a girl, barely older than sixteen, screamed and fainted when her husband's coffin reached the ground. She had to be revived with smelling salts. It made no difference to the widows how much of their husband's remains had been returned. Some corpses return from war missing heads and arms and legs. Some soldiers and flyers return alive and whole, but missing their sanity. Even if a body is chopped to pieces by a whirling propeller or sucked like sausage out of a tiny hole in a pressurized cabin to be devoured by wolves, the military becomes creative at finding left over remains, even if it is only blood and tissue samples from the

Air-hospital. Being poked and prodded is a familiar and indispensable part military life. Unless a soldier, sailor, or airman is officially listed as missing, there will always be some blood, hair, saliva, or fingernail clippings to fill a coffin with. After all, when one gives one's life for one's country, one gives one's entire body and soul. What is wrong with the Air-hospital giving a little bit back for a hero's burial? Were not several families in Russia and China doing exactly the same thing?

The honor guard carried the mostly empty coffins with great solemnity to expandable funeral carriages that were set up. Words were said that no one seemed to pay any attention to, then the coffins were picked up again and put into the six hearses. Six riflemen fired six rounds three times and taps was played by a bugler. The crowd followed them out of the building, Linda and Phyllis towing the weak kneed Esther, who seemed unable to lift her teary face from Linda's shoulder. A sound, first like a swarm of bees, then like a squadron of Japanese planes attacking Pearl Harbor, came from behind some trees and three B-36 bombers, with thirty engines and eighteen propellers whirling, roared overhead at treetop level. A single B-47 Stratojet flew above them almost straight up, performing a split-S, before diving out of sight followed by peals of thunder from its six engines. Everyone was amazed that such a large plane could make such maneuvers. All of the widows, including Esther and Loretta, looked up, weeping.

"I never thought I'd see a bomber do the missing man," quipped one of the wives.

"Isn't that Ready Alert Five," Colonel Peterson asked General Allen?

"You would be guessing right," the General answered.

"Should they be doing that with a TX-15 on board?"

"They have to practice sometime," answered the General.

A young lieutenant in dress blues approached the two men and saluted, accompanied by Lieutenant Grant. The ranking officers returned the salute. Offering his hand, the unknown officer said, "Hi, I'm Tony Avery."

Colonel Peterson ignored the outstretched hand and

embraced the younger officer around the shoulders. "What happened to you," he asked? "We were so worried!"

Avery answered, "After the second photo run when the flak came up, I high tailed out of there! "They scrambled some MiG's, but they weren't able to catch me. "I had some altitude on them and dove for the deck to outrun them before they completed their climb. "After about an hour of being scared out of my wits, I climbed over the border and rendezvoused with our other ship. "I kissed the ground when I finally touched down in Morocco." Overhearing that, General Allen decided right then and there to recommend all of them for The Distinguished Flying Cross.

"How'd you log your flight time," asked Grant?

"I told the truth," answered the young fighter pilot. "I took off in Washington State, landed two days and four hours later in Morocco, then refueled and took off for home, landing back where I started twenty eight hours after that."

"Eighty hours in a single engine jet with only one stop?"

"Why should I lie? "If they don't believe me, I'll just tell them I had been abducted by Martians. The psychiatrists will really be confused when I tell them what the fuselage stringers inside the bomb bay looked like." Grant and General Allen both laughed.

Outside the Oval Office, in Washington DC, a particularly beribboned Air Force general sat down to wait. On his shoulder were four stars just above his pilot's wings. "Who is he in there with," the general asked?

"Andrei Gromyko, the Russian Deputy Foreign Minister," answered the receptionist.

"What is he here for?"

"I'm sorry General, I can't say." The door flew open and the black browed Russian stormed out without a word. "The President will see you now," said a secretary.

The general thanked her gruffly and expressionlessly with cheeks that hung in a permanent frown like those of a bloodhound.

"Well hello Curt," welcomed President Eisenhower. "What do you have for me?"

"I've received those pictures of the Russian Rocket site you wanted."

"The one you think is important enough to launch a preemptive strike on?"

"Yes sir."

"Well, I'll put them in my in-box, I'll look at them later."

"Later Sir? "It cost the lives of sixteen men to get them, six on my RB-36 and all ten on the PB4Y-2."

THE COMMENDATION

March 1956

"Colonel Michael Peterson to see Senator Symington," announced a spiffy officer in a spotless silver-gray summer uniform with an Air Force blue cap under his arm.

"Yes, go right in," said the horn rimmed secretary from behind one of three burl walnut desks in the corners of the sky blue reception room, "they're waiting for you." General LeMay, chief of SAC, the Strategic Air Command, and General Allen, commander of the 7th Bomb Wing, rose from sky blue armchairs on either side of an American flag. Pictures of the Senator shaking hands with Presidents and world leaders were hung on richly paneled walls opposite a huge hutch full of law books.

The Senator got up from the tall red leather swivel chair behind his desk and extended his hand. Colonel Peterson saluted, feeling intensely proud of being asked to accompany General Allen to Washington. He shook hands with the Senator. "A pleasure to meet you Colonel," said Symington. "You were saying," he added, looking at Allen without letting go of Peterson's hand?

General Allen continued his conversation which had been interrupted, " . . . and the shape fell just two hundred seventy eight feet from the funnel, bombing through cloud from twenty miles away at forty thousand feet . . . less than a ship length!"

"Wow, that's great," said the Senator!

Allen continued, "The Captain of the destroyer counted down the seconds with a big smirk, 'cause we never saw or heard any plane. "He thought we'd given up or had a technical glitch. "As he counts 'five, four, three, two,' suddenly the thing hits the water like a thunderclap, at supersonic speed, and showers us with a cloud of spray. "The Captain's jaw drops and he says, 'Damn, that thing is dangerous!' "The sea boiled for two minutes where it hit. "Even if it was just a twenty ton block of concrete, it still would have sunk us if it fell any closer."

Senator Symington laughed with glee, "I'll bet the Navy isn't going to want to try that again! "So this is the man that proved us right about the B-36," praised the Senator, finally looking Peterson in the eyes?

"Yep, he's the one," said Allen, smiling at the Colonel.

"I want you to know Colonel, that you put egg all over Art Radford's face." Without letting go, Symington squeezed Peterson's elbow and shook his hand again. "Admiral Radford called the B-36 a billion dollar blunder. "He said it could not even defend itself from straight wing Navy Banshees and you proved him wrong." Peterson smiled. Symington finally let go of his hand. "You be sure to stand your ground when we meet the President."

This was a surprise! The Colonel became somewhat weak in the knees and stood like a fish with his mouth agape. "You heard right," insisted the Senator, "you are going to meet the President!" Colonel Peterson stood dumbfounded. He did not know what to say or what to do with his hands. He hadn't expected to be hailed as a hero. Suddenly, a feeling of joy rose in his chest and he beamed uncontrollably, like a small boy given a large lolly. The two generals nodded while the Senator returned the grin.

How he wished that Phyllis and Denise could have been there. How proud they would have been! Washington DC was such a beautiful city with the cherry blossom buds glowing red in the late winter sun. It would have been a wonderful vacation for the family.

"Just make sure you don't let old Radford get his buck teeth into you," Symington continued. "He's known for tearing men apart."

After a short limousine ride, a Marine in white braid and spats opened the door of the Senator's shiny black car. The White house was bigger than he had imagined it. The walk down the long corridor to the west wing made it seem even larger on the inside than it looked on the outside. Peterson had a dour look, so General LeMay said expressionlessly, "Cheer up Colonel, the President may have something for you."

"Yes Mike," added General Allen, "you might get a picture with the President for your 'I love me' wall." Peterson smiled and dodged into a restroom to straighten his jacket and tie and rub the creases out of his gray trousers. He took out a toothbrush he carried for the purpose, and brushed any flakes or hair or dandruff that might have fallen on his shoulders.

As he entered the pastel blue conference room, also known as the Cabinet War Room, Peterson was surprised to see so many ribbons and brass buttons surrounding the huge table. Paintings of former Presidents hung on the walls, opposite a huge bay window, through which leaf-bare cherry trees outside sent a kaleidoscope of squiggly shadows over the collage of polished mahogany, leather briefcases, manila folders, yellow note pads, typewritten papers, and braided officer's sleeves.

Newspapers and Televisions in 1956 only showed black and white, so seeing the Generals and Admirals of the Joint Chiefs of Staff in person came as a pleasant shock. The Air Force grays contrasted with the Navy's black and gold. The Army and Marines wore their own slightly different hues of green. The chest of each man displayed an extensive war record.

In the far corner, Peterson recognized Vice President Nixon as one of the few that was not in uniform, along with the stern, silver haired Secretary of State, John Foster Dulles, and the balding former Chairman of General Motors who was now Secretary of Defense, Charles E. Wilson. How funny Nixon looked in profile, he thought. Peterson had never seen a picture of him that wasn't straight on from the front. In fact, he had a hard time recognizing many of the Admirals and Generals despite having seen pictures of them. Without their caps, Peterson realized, for the first time, that two of the Joint Chiefs were bald.

He did not recognize the President at first, because General Eisenhower was wearing large black eyeglasses and scratching his ear with a fountain pen. Like most people, Peterson had the impression that those in highest office sat rigid and still like kings and queens all the time, as they do in photographs. General Eisenhower and Nixon were looking at some kind of document put in front of them by their many secretaries, both male and female, that hovered over them. The President's end of the table had four telephones.

"Glad you could finally make it to the top, Mike," said General Allen.

"Excuse me," announced General LeMay to the assembled crowd of brass, "this is Colonel Mike Peterson, commander of my Four Hundred Ninety Third Strategic Reconnaissance Squadron. "He is the one who flew the mission to bring us the pictures." The President glanced for a moment in his direction, but went back to what he was reading. The Vice President stood up beaming a broad smile, and walked toward him around the table. A number of the Generals and Admirals stretched out their braided sleeves to shake hands. He saluted each one. They returned his salutes, but Peterson was surprised at the informality of the War Room. No one saluted anyone else except the uniformed secretaries and clerks of the various Chiefs. He felt he should salute everyone who looked in his direction, but no one was paying any attention to him. They would glance at him, then look away before he could get his arm up.

There was a certain body language in saluting. One could always tell when a salute was coming by observing a certain ridgidness in a person. It seemed that whenever he wanted to salute, the General or Admiral would look away. He felt a tap on his shoulder and turned. The Vice President was standing right behind him with a broad smile and an outstretched arm.

"Can I get you anything, coffee," Vice President Nixon offered, shaking hands vigorously, his other hand on the Colonel's elbow? Peterson felt his arm turn into a wet rag. He weakly smiled in reply. The Vice President snapped his fingers and a cup of coffee instantly appeared. "Please sit down," he insisted, offering a red leather chair. "Attention everyone, attention, can I have everyone's attention," Nixon announced, as he moved to the end of the table opposite the President? "We have here the man that survived combat alone against four MiG-17's." Everyone, including the President, instantly stood up and applauded.

"I'm sorry to hear you were shot down," said a graying, weathered looking Navy officer with a toothy grin, sitting next to the President with a three inch wide gold stripe wrapped around the cuff of his sleeve. In addition to the three inch stripe, there were three one inch wide gold stripes and a gold star most of the way to his elbow.

"That's Admiral Radford, Chairman of the Joint Chiefs of Staff," whispered General Allen into Peterson's right ear.

"Excuse me Art," corrected General LeMay, "Colonel Peterson was shot *up* not *down*." The hound faced General patted Peterson's shoulder.

"Hold your horses, Curt," demanded Radford! "Let me ask the Colonel if he was shot up or down . . . "You lost your four million dollar ship didn't you?" He stared challengingly into Peterson's eyes. The toothy grin had not changed, but now it looked menacing.

"Yes Admiral, we had to ditch due to lack of fuel." Peterson felt the sudden need to go to the bathroom, but he was trapped.

"And one of my submarines had to rescue you," the Admiral continued with the same grin?

"Yes Sir!"

"How long had it been since you took off from Greenland until the ditching?"

"Thirty five hours, sir, about a day and a half aloft."

"Would you mind describing the circumstances of the loss of your ship," asked The Secretary of Defense, Wilson?

"We were low on fuel. "We had to ditch," Peterson repeated.

"We know that," snapped the Admiral. "What I'm talking about is your encounter with the MiG's. "You should have had enough fuel to make it back. "What happened? "Did you fail to stick to your profile?"

"We were heading one-zero-three over the Tien Shan mountains trying to get out of Russia," answered Peterson. "Our deceased Electrical Gunner, Staff Sergeant James O'Connor, called over the interphone that he saw four MiG's on an interception course coming at us from two o'clock low. "I fired up the turbojets, but only three of them lit."

"Do you blame the faulty engine for your failure to adhere to your mission profile," asked the Admiral?

"Yessir," the skipper replied. "I initiated a diving right turn, and they passed underneath us, then a zoom climb, but they turned and were able to outclimb us."

"Is that when you realized these were MiG-17's and not MiG-15's?"

"Yessir. "They overtook us on both sides and cut us off with high and low scissors. "I turned into the first group with a diving left turn. "The first group passed underneath or rather South of us as we were by then heading East."

"Then the second formation got you," interrupted the Admiral?

"Yessir. "They peeled off into a high yo-yo. "I had to stop the turn and dive to keep them from getting an angle on us."

"Your defensive armament didn't do any good, I take it?"

"We believe we shot two of them down, sir, but I can't confirm it. "Our gun camera footage was not returned to us."

"You didn't mention it in your report."

"I mentioned in my report, sir, that we observed that one or more of the fighters was struck, but without the films, I can't prove it. We saw them tumble out of control and disappear below the cloud deck."

"Any other Aircraft Commander would have called that a kill," interrupted LeMay. "The Colonel is just being modest."

"And how many hits did you take," asked Secretary of Defense Wilson, ignoring the beribboned Air Force General?

"More than we could count, sir," said Peterson. "Most shells passed through the skin without exploding."

"So you have an unconfirmed kill and they have an unconfirmed kill," insinuated Radford?

"Yessir," answered the Colonel! LeMay and Allen winced.

"I would say you are a very lucky man," exclaimed the Admiral.

"Yessir, I believe I am," answered Peterson.

"So it was the loss of your two port engines that caused you to burn additional fuel," asked Radford?

"The chase planes, the Chinese fighters, and the radar guided artillery all played a part in that, Admiral," answered Peterson. "We were forced to fly at a higher than normal altitude."

Just then, the Vice President interjected, "I think now is as good a time as any, don't you," nodding at the President?

"Sure Dick," agreed Eisenhower.

"C'mon," requested the Vice President, waving the Colonel toward him. Peterson pushed back his chair and moved toward the President's end of the table. LeMay's secretary, an airman, replaced the chair under the table. Then Nixon beckoned him all the way to the other end, where the President was standing. Peterson Saluted.

The President saluted back. "I understand you were awarded the Distinguished Flying Cross during the war," inquired a smiling General Eisenhower?

"Yes Sir," the Colonel replied. His knees felt like jelly, so he stood at attention, not quite knowing what to do with his hands.

The President lifted his left hand and took a small blue velvet case out of the left front pocket his jacket and opened it. Then he said, "I thought you ought to have one with an Oak

Leaf Cluster on it." The President held the decoration out in front of him. Someone grabbed Peterson by his right elbow and thrust his arm forward involuntarily. General Eisenhower grabbed the limp outstretched hand and shook it warmly while passing the small box with the decoration to his other hand and saluting. Colonel Peterson returned the salute, as did every officer and enlisted man and woman in the room. The Colonel, by then beaming with joy, saluted everyone else and they saluted back. He felt a hand on his shoulder.

"Excuse me Sir," said an Air Force sergeant with a large flash camera and a braid under his arm.

"Smile," commanded LeMay, something he couldn't do himself. The flash blinded everyone. Standing behind the President, General LeMay ordered, "Take another!" Everyone stood still while the photographer clumsily pressed a button in back of the camera to eject the flash bulb. He cranked the film several times and inserted another bulb while everyone waited. After the second flash, the Colonel was finally able to turn around. The hand on his shoulder belonged to none other than the Vice President himself!

"I wish I could give you a Bronze Star," said Nixon, "but we can't admit we had a battle without first admitting we have a war."

"If it were up to me, I would give all of you a Silver Star," praised LeMay.

From behind the Vice President, Admiral Radford came forward and asked, "Would it have made a difference if you were flying a B-52 instead of a B-36?"

"Yes," answered Peterson. "They would never have caught us."

"What if they were MiG-19's instead of MiG-17's?"

"Based on what I have been briefed on," Peterson speculated, "the MiG-19 has twice the fuel consumption of a MiG-17, so they would have had only have one chance to hit us."

"What about the B-36?"

"The MiG-19 against the RB-36 at altitude? "Same thing sir, they would only have one shot."

"What about the B-70?"

"Sir?"

"The nuclear powered bomber?"

"I'm sorry Art," LeMay interrupted, "I'm afraid the Colonel has not been briefed on that."

"He has clearance doesn't he?"

"Yes, but he doesn't have a need to know."

"I want to ask him his opinion about some things."

"You mean the Convair Crusader," asked Peterson? LeMay glared at him with a look of surprise.

"Yes," answered Radford.

"I've only watched it taxi and take off. "I don't know anything about how it could be nuclear powered. "It looks just like a regular B-36, sir. "It's one of the ships damaged in the Labor Day tornado of fifty two but with a new radiation proof nose on it."

"It's equipped with a prototype nuclear reactor for the X-6," informed the Admiral, "but the X-6 engines haven't been installed under the bomb bay yet."

Peterson paused with a look of wonder and said, "I don't know what to say, sir. "I've been trained to load, arm, and drop atomic weapons, but I have no idea how an A-bomb could be used to power an aircraft."

"The J-53 nuclear engine works just like any other jet engine," explained LeMay, "only instead of a combustion chamber that burns kerosene or aviation gas, compressed air is blown through the reactor core and superheated so it does not need fuel."

"That's incredible," the Colonel exclaimed!

"Assuming the B-70 has the same performance as a B-52," interrogated Radford, "do you think the Russians could shoot it down?"

"The Convair Crusader has a massively armored cockpit," Peterson replied, "but otherwise it is structurally identical to a B-36, so I would guess they could, sir."

"Thank you Colonel Peterson, that's all I wanted to know," said the Admiral.

LeMay did not look very pleased about the information his uninformed subordinate was telling the Admiral, but it was difficult to fathom what he actually thought because of the palsy in his face. He whispered something to General Allen. "Why don't you spend some time at the Smithsonian Colonel," suggested Allen?

"I'd rather stay," Peterson objected.

"I'm sorry Mike," Allen insisted. "They won't even let me stay. He shook hands in congratulation. "You did a great job. "You've given them quite a problem. Peterson took that as his cue to leave. "Have a nice time in the museum. "We'll meet back at the Hotel." LeMay was glumly tapping his foot, but he reached over and shook hands one last time, as Peterson saluted. The two Air Force Generals saluted back as he disappeared down the corridor.

Peterson did not make it to the Smithsonian. His head was so swollen with pride, he felt ten feet tall. He floated through the air like a giant parade balloon all the way to the Washington monument, then floated over a mile back to Capitol Hill before settling onto a park bench in front of the Capitol Building to rest his sore feet. From his perch in front of the Capitol Building, the view down the Mall was spectacular. The cherry blossom buds were just starting to bloom between the impressive Museums rising above the trees on either side. The lawn in the center was wide enough to land an RB-36. Peterson tried to imagine the reception he would receive as he climbed down out of his giant ship in front of the Smithsonian after nuking the rocket site. From then on, anyone looking down the mall from the Capitol would see his huge RB-36 enshrined in a glorious glass air and space museum bearing his name and the names of those who died.

Looking at his decoration and narcissistically smiling, he felt a twinge of guilt. Because the crash was officially recorded as caused by an engine problem, the others would not be receiving the decorations they deserved. They would only get the Air Medal. If he had survived, Merril Hughs would have been the one to meet the President, not him. Thinking he might like a picture of himself standing in front of the Capitol, he suddenly realized his photographer had been left behind in the War Room.

Долэс, Лемэи, Эызьнхоур, & Радфорд

Dulles, LeMay, Eisenhower, & Radford
decide the future of mankind

THE PRESIDENT'S DECISION

March 1956

"Well gentlemen, what are we going to do about that rocket site," the President asked the remaining officers?

"What was it, an R-5M," asked Radford?

"Much bigger," insisted LeMay, pointing at Nawrocki's photo in his folder. "If this explosion went off over the DC area, it would stretch from here to the Capitol building."

"That's the silliest thing I ever heard," ridiculed the Admiral. "That's almost a mile!"

"Not as silly as your Commander Tatom's statement before the House Armed Services Committee that he could survive an A-bomb bomb exploding at the other end of the North South runway of the Washington National Airport wearing nothing but his Navy blouse." The other Joint Chiefs chuckled.

"Okay Curt, I see your point. "It was a big fireball . . . a rocket big enough to reach the United States, if it hadn't blown up. "So what do you propose we do about it, nuke the site?"

"Yes!"

"It would start a war."

"We're at war," asserted LeMay! "This is war! "They're pointing their weapons at us. "The Japanese fleet has just left port! "The only reason the shooting just hasn't started yet, is we have twenty bombs to their one."

"They could still retaliate against a Naval asset," argued the Admiral.

"And our bombers would retaliate against one of their naval . . ."

"Just what he said, Curt, a war," interrupted Wilson, the Secretary of Defense.

"You wanted to bomb Dienbienphu two years ago," LeMay accused, "why not now, when the future of the world depends on it? "The sooner we get World War Three started the better. "If we don't act now, they'll soon have parity with us. "Do you think they will want to start a naval war when we have ten ships to their one?"

"I was in favor of using conventional bombing in Vietnam," defended Radford, "not atomic weapons. "What if your plane doesn't make it? "What if one of your B-52's breaks an arrow on Soviet soil? "Then they really would have parity with us."

"It won't happen. "We'll use a B-36 armed with a TX-16 Jughead. "If they don't make it, we'll say they flew off course in bad weather and when they take it apart, they will only get obsolete technology. "Besides, there is not much left when a B-36 crashes."

"I know," exclaimed Wilson, "that's the only reason we loosened your chain enough to do this much."

"And you two wouldn't even have had authorization to do that if it wasn't for this damned heart," interrupted President Eisenhower, pointing at his chest. "How do you know the Jughead is obsolete?"

"Because the Russians air-dropped a one point nine megaton H-bomb from a Tu-16 Badger bomber last November," Wilson blurted before LeMay could answer. "Now they're trying to build the largest bomb ever, twenty to sixty megatons to make artificial lakes to water their cattle."

"Sounds like radioactive cattle to me," scolded the President. The other Joint Chiefs chuckled.

"Magnesium burns fiercely and the special plastic liner

would be long gone by the time they found it," explained LeMay. "All they would get is chunks of depleted uranium from the radiation tube, and a world war two plutonium core made with technology they already possess. "They won't be getting one of our lithium-deuterride weapons."

"Anyway, it seems they've already figured out how to make those," commented Wilson snidely.

"So, what if the ship does make it," the President continued? "How do we explain it? "Foster?"

"Who knows what Russia will do," answered Dulles, the Secretary of State? They explode A-bombs wherever they want. "How will anybody know its ours? "It's just a dusty hill on the Steppes of Kazakhstan that isn't even on the map. "Officially there is nothing there."

"The Brits will know its our bomb," asserted Wilson. "They took dust samples from the Mike Shot. "They will get samples when the radioactive cloud passes over India on the subtropical jet. "The Jughead uses the same technology."

"The British are our allies," defended Dulles. "Why should they complain? "If they say anything, we'll just tell them that the ship went off course and no one was killed except a few sheep and shepherds in a place that doesn't exist. "There will be nothing left of that city, but a big crater that will fill with water and become a lake. "They'll name it 'Lake Tyuratam.'"

"And what if we do nothing," asked the President?

"Then Krushchev will have a weapon that can take out our entire defense structure without warning," responded Dulles, "Maybe even destroy every city in the country."

"That isn't even the biggest problem," advised Nixon, "if Stevenson's people get wind of this and leak it to the press, it could affect the election this November. "How to you think the average man on the street will react when he finds out there are nuclear missiles pointing at his kids?"

"Not to mention how every woman voter would feel," quipped Wilson.

"That, gentlemen, is unacceptable," shot back Eisenhower, pounding his fist on the table! "Stalin gave his word when we met in Berlin, that he would develop an exact copy of the V-2 and nothing more."

"Krushchev has broken that word," accused the Secretary of State!

"But this, this makes even our Atlas program look small," asserted Wilson. Even if our own rockets are successful, they'll be too little too late. "If they develop intercontinental ballistic missiles before we do, they could launch a pre-emtive strike on us just to prevent us from testing our technology."

"Only if we don't launch a pre-emptive airstrike on them first," Nixon interjected. "Even Adlai would agree with that."

"That's why Stalin agreed not to develop this," explained Radford. "He knew we would never stand for it. "Krushchev is reckless!"

"That's not the only problem," added Dulles. "Krushchev just gave a secret speech at last month's Twentieth Party Congress denouncing Stalin."

"Denounce Stalin," the President stammered, wide eyed with raised eyebrows! "Are you sure? "Why wasn't I told?"

"C'mon Dave," answered Nixon, "I only found out about it yesterday. "Remember, you've just had a heart attack and your blood pressure needs some rest. "If this is true, it will give us all hand tremors."

"Don't go on about my heart," snapped the President. "I'm fine! "Now what about this speech?"

"We only found out about it a week ago," apologised Dulles. "We can't confirm it yet or I would have brought you a complete report. "We're negotiating with one of Gomulka's people over in Poland to try to get a copy. "The scuttlebutt is that Nikita Sergeievich was very critical of Stalin for being caught unprepared in forty one, you know how Churchill's man Cripps warned him in April, a whole two months before Barbarrossa, and he thought it was a Limey trick?"

"Devil forbid that Ioseph Dzukashveelee would ever be tricked," mocked Eisenhower, calling the bloodthirsty dictator by his former name! "Give the man a little advice, and you could count on him to do the exact opposite every time."

"So you think Khrushchev is not going to make the same mistake," asked Nixon, "that these rockets are his way of being prepared . . . for what . . . war? "Why would he want weapons of mass destruction?"

"I think the reason he refused our Open Skies Initiative in Geneva, was that he was working on this," asserted Dulles.

"Or, that he didn't want us to know how deficient they were in conventional arms," suggested Radford.

"Or that he didn't want us to know he was diverting his entire defense budget into this one sick program," fumed Nixon.

"Who did this Foster," asked the President? "Who built this rocket? "Was it the Germans they captured after the war?"

"No," answered Dulles, "the Nazi missile men are more anti-Communist than we are. "They're firmly on our side. "We think the designer's name is Korelov, Sergei Korelov, but we're not sure. "Even his name is classified."

"Who is he? "What kind of man is he," asked the President?

"He's Russian, but he was a political prisoner for six years, living in one of Lavrenty Beria's gulags," added Dulles. "He was rehabilitated after Beria's arrest and execution in fifty three. "He is said to be one tough individual. "One of the few independent thinkers they have."

"A political prisoner," questioned Eisenhower? "So the product of this independent thinking is to build rockets to destroy the world? "I thought Beria was in charge of their atomic program."

"Figure that," exclaimed Wilson! "We know very little about him. "He appears occasionally before launches, but no one even knows where he lives."

"Apparently he's still a prisoner," speculated Dulles, "but he refused to work for Beria as a matter of principle."

"So he is a man of sound moral character," asked Eisenhower? "If he is a dissident, can he be turned, or grabbed in a covert operation?"

"We've tried, but none of our people can get to him," answered Dulles. "We just don't know enough about him. "His main design bureau is called Zvy-oz-dny Gorodok about forty miles north of Moscow."

"So," the President gazed at LeMay with a piercing glare, "since you can't turn him or nab him, you want to nuke him?"

"Yessir," answered the expressionless hound faced General, "I'm asking for permission to pre-emptively disable the larger of his two test facilities. "We've never countenanced the possibility of destroying Zvyozdny Gorodok. "It is a scientific research facility of no military value other than in the minds of the people who work there. "The launch site, on the other hand, is like a gun pointed at our children's heads."

"I agree with Curt's rationale," said Radford. "We have the moral right to act pre-emptively when we are threatened."

"A moral duty," corrected Nixon! "If we don't act, Stevenson will. "I can see Adlai now, getting up on the stump and saying we let this happen or that your heart attack paralyzed the White House while you were in the hospital or some stupid thing like that."

"The question is how," insisted Radford?

"What is the future of this," asked the President? "What does this man Korelov, or whatever his name is, have planned for us if we do nothing?"

"He wants to launch a man into outer space," answered Dulles. "Steve Robinson, at the CIA, seems to think he cares nothing about missiles, except that they provide a source of funding for his man in space program."

"That's speculation," argued LeMay! "Everything they have done so far suggests that this is a weapons program only, not a man in space program.

"You're right," continued Dulles, "all of their funding comes from the NKVD, but there's more to it than that."

"I have to agree with Curt," seconded Radford. "These nuclear ballistic missiles are the weapon of the future. "Any armed force that does not have them, cannot hope to prevail in a conflict. "This man in space stuff is just a smoke screen. "We have to act."

"So if we destroy the launch facility and not the design

bureau, won't they just build a new facility," asked Eisenhower?

"Of course," answered the Admiral, "but by that time our Polaris submarines will be undergoing sea trials and they won't be able to disable our ability to retaliate."

"We're also working on nuclear hardened silos for our Jupiter and Redstone rockets," added LeMay. "Once we have those installed in Turkey, we'll be able to knock down their launch sites as fast as they can put them up."

"So what you are really talking about is slapping their hands a bit to distract them until we can catch up with them," asked Eisenhower, "then nuking them over and over again until they cry uncle?"

"That's the general idea," agreed LeMay. "If they move their bombers to the forward staging bases on Kola and Kamchatka, I'll have every bomber in the air in orbit over them, ready to wipe them off the face of the earth as soon as they try to take off."

"Well I'll tell you what I think," the President volunteered, "if someone dropped an A-bomb on me, I sure as hell would put whatever program I had into full gear and get back at them as soon as I could . . . even if it killed me."

"The point is to wipe out whatever program they have . . . . . . *before* it becomes a threat, even if it kills *them*," insisted Dulles!

"What you're talking about is starting a war," accused Eisenhower!

"If you are scared to go to the brink, you are lost," said Dulles.

"What do you think, Chuck?"

Wilson put his face in his hands and ran his fingers through what was left of his hair until his hands clutched the back of his neck to let out a sigh. The others watched him in silence. The setting sun sent long tangled shadows across the table of the war room. The walls seemed to glow an orange color. "I didn't take this job to start a war," said the aging Secretary of Defense. "I joined this administration to prevent one. "I don't know much about weapons. "I'm not even sure I know how an A-bomb works. "But I know one thing . . . its not the number of weapons you have that counts, its how fast you can get them to the enemy. "My DUKW amphibious truck was not a powerful weapon," continued the former Chairman of General Motors, "but it got the real important weapons off the ships and up to the boys at the front, sooner."

"And I would have given you a medal for that if you were military," praised Eisenhower. "That's why I asked you to do the Defense job. "You understand that what wins wars is logistics."

"What I'm saying, Dave," clarified Wilson, "is that with these new intercontinental ballistic missiles, there are no logistics. "If the enemy can bring the battlefield to your weapons before you can bring your weapons to the battlefield, then you aren't going to have any weapons."

"What's bad for General Motors is bad for the country," Nixon quipped? Radford frowned. Dulles placed his hands on his forehead.

"But, once we have replaced all our B-36's with B-52's and B-70's," LeMay interjected, "even our air fleets will be invulnerable. "By then, nothing they do will matter."

"That's not what I heard," argued Radford, "Your lucky Colonel Peterson just told me that the B-52 would have no better chance of surviving combat with the MiG-19 than the B-36 would, and the B-70 would do no better than the B-52 would."

"You didn't tell him that the B-70 will have a delta wing twice as big as a B-58," the hound faced General replied, "and that it can cruise fourteen miles high at better than Mach three for months at a time until the oxygen, food, and water runs out. "No fighter or missile will be able to touch it. "Besides, I'm talking about surviving A-bombs, not fighters."

"What I was trying to say, Curt," defended Radford, "is that all bombers are obsolete. "They are a waste of taxpayers' money. "The B-70 will have to be made out of titanium to get the performance you want. "Do you know how expensive that stuff is? "You might as well make them out of gold." Eisenhower wrinkled his nose. Dulles and Wilson folded their arms and stared at him seriously. "By the time you get them flying," Radford continued, "the Ruskies will have supersonic jets and missiles capable of catching them. "Each of your B-52's costs eight million dollars . . . twice as much as a B-36 . . . more than a dozen fighters! "Just wait until August," the Admiral went on, "I'll bet getting rid of them will be a plank in Stevenson's platform."

"Bomber parts are built in too many swing states," corrected Nixon. "We couldn't cancel those programs if we wanted to. "Too many people would be laid off. "Even if all they could do was carry freight, we would still have to build them." The other assembled Chiefs chuckled glibly.

"What do you think a nuclear tipped torpedo would do to one of your submarines, Admiral," baited the hound faced General?

"They'd have to find it first, which isn't easy to do," countered Radford.

"They can follow your submarines right out of port," argued LeMay.

"Do you think a B-52 would faire better in an atomic blast," responded the Admiral? "Of course you can bury your missiles in the ground," he continued, "but can you take them to the enemy? "Your rockets aren't big enough to reach Russia from the United States. "Under your plan, the most powerful nation on Earth will be Turkey!"

"A nuclear air to air missile costs more to produce than a B-52 does," LeMay retorted. "If they tried that, I'd send a few hundred SM-73 Bull Goose decoys ahead of the B-52's without any weapons at all, and let the politburo incinerate their own people when they try to shoot them down. "We wouldn't even need bombers. "They would nuke themselves."

"I thought you just canceled that program last month," asked Dulles?

"That was the Buck Duck," corrected LeMay. "The Bull Goose is a whole new ball game: "Launched from the ground, five thousand mile range, delta wing, J-83 engine, inertial navigation, traveling wave tube amplifiers, it's some of the finest technology mankind has produced."

"But it can't do anything," exclaimed Radford! "It has no weapons. "What good is it? "What about fighters?"

"Even if they had a dozen fighters for every bomber," LeMay argued, "some would get through, because most of the fighters will be wasting fuel and ammunition on wild 'Bull Goose' chases."

"I still say you're still going to need a lot more bombers if they start mass-producing fighters," claimed Radford. "We can't bet the future of the world on a tiny number of gold plated miracle weapons that will be outnumbered a hundred to one on the battlefield. "How do you know the thing will even work? "What if they develop the ability to distinguish the decoys from the bombers, then zap, zap, zap . . . all your bombers are gone?"

"That's why we funded the B-52," explained Wilson. "The B-52 is made of relatively cheap aluminum, not titanium or magnesium. "It burns relatively cheap kerosene, not uranium or plutonium, and it requires only a fraction of the maintenance of a naval vessel. "It can get into the air within fifteen minutes of an alert, and survive an atomic blast once it's airborne. "Without vibrations from piston engines, its airframe ought to last thirty years or more. So, despite its high initial cost, in the long run it is a good investment that will eventually save money."

"If there ever was a gold plated weapons system, Art," accused LeMay, "it's your Polaris submarine project. "One cheap war surplus mine or torpedo from a tin plate dictator will send it to the bottom where the warheads can never be recovered, or worse, where they can be recovered and make whoever finds them the most powerful man on Earth. "Bombers have conventional warfare capability," he continued, "missiles don't. "The B-70 will be able to fly for weeks, even months if necessary, without ever stopping for fuel. "It's shielded cockpit will protect the crew from any explosion it might encounter, short of a direct hit, and with the smaller, lighter bombs we're developing, like the TX-21, we can convert the bomb bay into a combination recreation room, galley, and food pantry with enough oxygen and fresh water in the wings to keep them flying until the engines wear out. "You promised Senator Symington at your confirmation, way back in June of Fifty Three, Art, that you would treat all the armed services equally," accused LeMay, "but so far all you've done is protect your ruinously expensive pet projects." Radford stared at him wide eyed in shock. Everyone else stared at the Admiral.

Nixon gulped, then broke the silence: "Yes, but won't the food spoil and become radioactive," he asked?

"Irradiated food is good for you," claimed LeMay. "Atomic radiation kills bacteria. "We could hang whole sides of beef from the bomb racks and it would never spoil. "Someday, someone will figure out a way to pipe orange juice through an atomic pile, and we'll be able to have fresh squeezed orange juice for breakfast every morning without having to squeeze any oranges." No one laughed. LeMay lacked the ability to turn up the corners of his mouth to suggest humor. His eyes twinkled. Those who knew him understood that he was trying to make a joke. But to others, he looked sinister—like a predator ready to pounce.

"I've played Santa long enough," Radford exploded! "I've given you flyboys all the toys on your list in the hope that one of them might pan into something, but some of your ideas, Curt, are just crackpot stupid! "How do you think the average Joe Voter is going to feel when he finds out you have a hundred unshielded nuclear reactors flying over his house showering radioactive exhaust on him? "They'll think you're nuts," he fumed!

"They'll feel safe," maintained LeMay, "like being protected by an invincible defensive shield. "The atomic engines will only be used over uninhabited regions, such as Canada and the North Pole. "At altitude, the B-70 will be invulnerable to attack. "The Russians would have to melt all the ice in the Arctic to destroy all of them."

"What if one crashes," asked the President?

"Our drop tests with simulated lead cores indicate that the uranium, which is a very heavy metal, will stay in one piece and bury itself in the ground," the hound faced general asserted.

"Unless it hits the side of a mountain and vaporizes into tiny particles," argued Wilson.

"There is very little population density in mountainous areas," defended LeMay. "We can fence off the crash site."

"For twenty thousand years," asked Eisenhower? "I agree with Art. "There are too many nature lovers in the Congress who will oppose giving you the funding."

"They will cost less than aircraft carriers and submarines and they can provide early warning ability," pleaded the hound faced general. "Having an atomic powered bomber continually in the air over their launch sites will give us enough warning to get our B-52's and B-58's out of the way before they can be destroyed, and maybe even nuke the missiles out of the sky as soon as their tailflames appear above the clouds."

"I think the whole point of flying bombers over their launch sites," interrupted Dulles, "is to blow them to smithereens *before* they can destroy the United States . . . *before* they can be launched . . . correct that . . . *before* they are ever installed!"

"Yes," seconded Wilson. "All this talk about atomic powered airplanes or submarines and hundreds of unmanned drones carrying no weapons at all is just too expensive. "What about fighting poverty? "Are we going to ask the American taxpayer to do without the better things in life, like cars, phonograph records, electric dish washers, and internal plumbing to pay for weapons that God forbid we will ever use?"

"Stevenson will have us by the throat in November if we do," interjected Nixon. "The big campaign issue will be why we didn't do something to prevent this."

"How can we prevent it," fumed Radford bitterly? "Russia is the biggest country on Earth. "Not even the new ultra high altitude reconnaissance aircraft Lockeed is developing will be able to keep an eye on all of Russia all of the time."

"That's why we need nuclear powered aircraft, Admiral," claimed LeMay, "its the only way we are going to be able to keep tabs on them." Radford winced.

"How are the airborne reactor tests progressing," asked

Eisenhower?

"As I said in my report, sir," replied the hound faced General, "our first test was on February thirteenth. "We just had our second data flight on the twenty sixth. "The ASTR airborne reactor was critical for about four hours of the eight hour flight over New Mexico. "We had a glitch on the twenty first, so that flight only lasted twenty five minutes. "The J-53 engines for the X-6 are still having some development issues, but two out of three ain't bad for so early in the program. "The airborne reactor looks like it's going to be a complete success. "We ought to be running them off the Fort Worth assembly line by the hundred in three or four years, once we work the bugs out of the engines."

"That . . . will . . . be . . . too . . . late," objected Radford in staccato, pounding his fist on the table. "They will have their intercontinental missiles installed by then." Everyone looked at each other, grimacing.

"He's right! "We must act now," demanded Dulles! "What is the point of building new weapons if we lack the courage to use the ones we have? "Sure there might be a retaliation, but you have to weigh that against the economic cost of funding weapons programs we don't want or need. "People die of poverty too, you know."

"And presidents who raise taxes loose elections," reminded Nixon.

"Ever since the Labor Day tornado of fifty two," continued the Orthodox Presbyterian Secretary of State, "I've been wondering if the Lord wasn't trying to tell us something. . . all those B-36's scattered around like that . . . one two hundred ton ship lifted up and thrown almost a half mile, its wings and tail ripped completely off, its fuselage torn in half with a flick of God's finger, all within a few seconds! "That was just a month before the Mike Shot, right when our boys in the Pacific were just setting it up. "Everything was ready for the big one, concrete bunkers and a wooden bridge across three islands for the data tubes, and then this tornado strikes, wiping out *in seconds* two thirds of the only bombers in the world that could carry the

new super weapon . . . *eighty two* flying battleships, with twenty
five severely . . ."

"So what," interrupted Nixon! "We wiped an entire
island off the face of the earth that had been there since the
beginning of time and replaced it with a mile wide crater two
hundred feet deep, and all God could do was send a little
tornado."

"It was a warning," said Dulles!

"Every ship but one was repaired and even parts from
that were recycled," argued Nixon!

"But look at the timing, Dick," insisted Dulles . . . "all on
Labor Day . . . the Communist *holy* high holiday. "And what did
we do? "Did we learn anything from that?

"What are you saying, that the Commies created the
tornado with cloud seeding?

"NO! "God sent the storm as a warning, but within a
week, we were flying sorties and one of the wrecked ships was
converted for atomic propulsion with an additional two hundred added to the fleet! "Now we have this missile problem."

"So, what you're saying," asked Wilson, "is that we
should not have tested the Super?"

"God gave man stewardship over the Earth," answered
the Presbyterian Secretary of State.

"God gave America the atom bomb to kill the heathen
Japanese," the Quaker Vice President fired back, "and he gave
us the Super to wipe out the godless Commies. "It is our moral
duty to fight evil using the tools Our Lord has provided."

"But now they have a super," reminded Wilson. "How
do you explain that?"

"Evil begets evil," said Dulles.

"It was our own atomic scientists that gave it to them,"
accused Nixon.

"The same devils that gave it to us," observed Dulles!

"After he tested their super," countered Wilson, "Academician Kurchatov walked in to ground zero and broke into
tears when he saw all the withered trees and said, 'this must
never be used.'"

"How could you possibly know that," asked the Quaker Vice President?

"One of the 'devils' at Los Alamos told me."

"Are you telling me they talk to each other?"

"I knew it," exclaimed Dulles!

"Kurchatov wrote them," explained Wilson. "They're colleagues, you know . . . in the same business, so to speak. "He said 'this must never be used,' and he meant it. "That's why they used a de-rated bomb in an air burst to minimize fallout. "They didn't want to have another incident like with the crew of that Japanese trawler."

"And their censors cleared the release of that kind of information," asked Dulles?

"I don't know," answered Wilson.

"Is this devil willing to help us," asked Nixon, "or is this just devil's propaganda to break the morale of our devils?"

"It doesn't matter," LeMay asserted. "They created it, so now it must be used."

"I've heard about as much of this as I'm going to take," bellowed the President, grasping his temples between his fists. "I called you here for some suggestions about how to resolve a crisis and all you can do is argue about the funding of weapons programs that won't be built for at least five years and how holy and righteous the God damned Russians are! "Let me know when you have any better advice than to nuke them or to do nothing. "This meeting is over!" The President threw down his papers, rose, and stormed out of the room. At that very moment, the sun went down.

Лемэи

LeMay

THE NEW SHIP
April 1956

Hank Johns began to wonder if he would ever get another ship. Not many pilots get a third try after two wrecks in five months. Most are sentenced to a desk after just one crack-up. At four million dollars a ship, his was an expensive habit. The entire crew lost their spot promotions. Hank had to go back to being just ordinary Captain Johns. He was ordered to attend a meeting with General Allen to discuss his future in the Air Force.

Linda made him wear his dress grays to the dressing down. "The best defense is to look your best," she said as she ironed his blouse and trousers. It was a good thing. General LeMay, himself, was attending the meeting. When Hank saw him in the windowed conference room, he paused to try to overhear what Colonel Peterson and General Allen were saying. Eavesdropping is not becoming to an officer, but sometimes higher-ups talk louder than usual to give the man waiting outside some inkling of what was about to happen. The officers murmured quietly, so he knocked. Peterson waved him in. Johns snapped to attention as soon as he entered and saluted.

"Close the door," ordered Allen. Johns closed the door quietly. "Do you know General LeMay?"

"It is a great privilege to meet you sir," said Johns, saluting. LeMay returned the salute expressionlessly with a piercing gaze.

"Have a seat, Hank," said Peterson. Johns sat down as quietly as possible, though the windows surrounding the conference room seemed to amplify every sound. The rattle of his chair dragging across the floor seemed deafening. Not wanting to meet his boss's boss's boss straight in the eye, he peered over LeMay's shoulder and compared him to the portrait on the far wall, beside that of the President and Vice President. The square jawed, black haired man in the portrait was wearing a blue winter uniform while the wrinkled, gray haired man before him was wearing a gray suit and smoking a cigar. Only the cap, laying on the table, was the same color.

"I've come here to offer you another ship," began the beribboned hound faced General.

"Thank you Sir," Johns heard himself reply. Johns' heart leapt in his chest when he realized he was being offered another ship, but he kept comparing the officer before him to the portrait on the wall and wondered if people were really as bad as their reputations or appearance suggested.

"If you agree to accept this command," the expressionless General continued, tapping ash off the end of his cigar, "I have a personal request to make of you."

That such a high ranking General would take a personal interest in him, gave a feeling of importance that relaxed all nervousness. "What ever you want sir," Johns answered without hesitation. He beamed a broad smile, no longer afraid to look the expressionless general in the eyes.

"Before I tell you what I want," said LeMay, pausing to take a drag from his cheroot, "I want you to understand that what you photographed on your last reconnaissance is classified at the highest level.

"Yessir," answered Johns!

"Officially, what you saw does not exist."

"Yessir," answered Johns!

"It never has existed and it will not exist for much longer."

"Yessir," answered Johns!

"Do you think you can get another ship to the same target?"

"Yessir," answered Johns.

"I want you to accidentally lose a TX-16 Jughead on that target. He blew a smoke ring.

"Yessir," answered Johns, suddenly breathing heavily because of the General's incredible bluntness? "Sir, may I ask what you mean by accidentally?"

"What General LeMay means," interrupted General Allen, "is that he can't order you to carry out this mission and neither can I."

"Nor can I," seconded Peterson. Hank gazed with surprise and astonishment into the eyes of each man as he spoke.

"You want me to start a nuclear war?"

"No, of course not," said Allen. "We just want you to accidentally lose a weapon over someplace that doesn't exist."

"What do you mean 'doesn't exist,' asked the younger officer? "There's a city there . . . at least ten thousand people. "I've seen it!"

"Officially, it doesn't exist," said Allen.

"Its just like the little village on Eniwetoc," explained LeMay. "They didn't have property deeds to that land. "They were living on US government property without permission, so we moved them off." He again tapped the cigar on his ashtray.

"But sir," Johns asserted, "they were living there a thousand years before there was a US government."

Peterson was horrified at his subordinate's insolent reply. Before he could bawl out his junior officer, LeMay spoke: "I know how you feel about that, and your objection is noted, but the target we are talking about has not been in operation for more than a year and the only natives to the area are cattle, sheep, goats, and nomadic Cossack horsemen." He took another drag and continued, "Believe me, if there was any other way, we would do it, but this site threatens my family and yours. "It's a loaded gun pointing at our nation's head. "If you don't want this assignment, that's fine. "I'll ask someone else." Johns tried to interrupt, but LeMay kept talking, waving the cigar around, painting the air with a smoky contrail: "We have to do this now, before it is too late. "Think of your little Bobby. "What kind of world will he grow up in if we let the Russians complete their plans? "We're going to have to fight them sooner or later. "The sooner we get World War Three started, the better."

Johns felt an icy steel blade working up and down his back. "I don't want to start a war, sir," he replied. His intestines twisted into a knot.

"I'm asking you to prevent a war that will destroy the United States," the General continued. "Somebody has to do it and you, Major, are the best qualified for the job." LeMay leaned back, chomping the shortened stogie between his lips.

Johns clasped his hands and looked down at the Captain bars on his shoulder. Surely General LeMay could see he was only a Captain, he thought to himself. "If you don't want the job," said Peterson, "Captain Rashid is retiring after twenty years as maintenance chief. "I can put you in charge of his bays. "We'll be getting B-52's soon, so we'll need to train a new man anyway. "I'm sure you will consider parts requisition a challenge with all new aircraft and completely new suppliers. "You know what the Boeing company is like to deal with. "You can't just walk across the runway to get parts from Seattle."

"I'm sure you understand why we can't put you in command of one of those B-52's," added General Allen. "We can't allow someone who is reluctant to deploy a nuclear weapon to command a B-52 because, frankly, that's the job. "I know all about your insubordination toward Colonel Peterson over China . . . it's not in his report, but between you and me, we can't trust a man like that. "See Mike's new ribbon? "You'd 'ave gotten one just like it if it wasn't for that stunt you pulled. "If deterrence is to work, the enemy must be absolutely certain that we will use all of our weapons against him."

"Indeed," said LeMay, tapping the ashtray again, "I'm sure it will give you a lot of satisfaction watching the new birds take off knowing that you are in command of the men that maintain them, but consider this: "If the man I pick to replace you is unsuccessful, the Bears will be coming to pay us a visit, and here you will be." He snuffed out his cigar into the ashtray with much force. "Think about your wife and son." He clasped his now empty hands together as though in prayer. "If you agree to accept this job, you will walk out of this room a major, not just a brevet major, and when you return with your new ship, Colonel Peterson will be waiting with some silver posies to pin on your collar. "It will make a big difference in your pay envelope."

Johns looked at LeMay's clasped hands, then down at his own clasped hands and asked, "Sir, do you remember the name of the guy who shot the Arch Duke at Sarajevo in Nineteen Fourteen?"

"Gavrilo Princip, I think," offered General Allen. "The Duke's name was Francis Ferdinand. "Why?"

"They will remember my name too."

"No they won't," asserted LeMay; "they will remember mine!"

"Okay," said Johns. "Since it seems to be a done deal no matter what I do . . . " The Generals and the Colonel immediately rose and shook hands with him.

"Major," announced LeMay with a salute! "You'll have your new orders in a few days. "If we do this at a time of our own choosing, you can give your family warning to get out of town."

"No sir," Johns replied. "Please, I don't want Linda to know about it." He returned the salute as they left the room.

Everyone in Johns' crew, except Washington and Holbrook, were flown to Tucson, Arizona, on a KC-97 to take command of a B-36 "J" model that belonged to a unit that was converting to B-52's.

Grant, Johns, Kewscinski, Nawrocki, and Beaumont did not see any of the sleek shiny new silver ships when they descended the stairs from the freighter. Murphy, Sandringham, and Hernandez brought up the rear, burdened with the officers' duffels as well as their own. The base looked like a junkyard.

PICTURES FROM BAIKONUR

Fifty B-36's and RB-36's were crowded together at one end of
the runway with their engines and tires missing. Behind them
was a long row of propellers leaning against each other, hub to
hub, like cord wood. A crane snorted black clouds of smoke as it
lifted a giant rectangular plate of rusting steel, looking
something like a giant cleaver, into the air over the tail of one of
the flying naval vessels. With a mighty crash, the cleaver
descended and the entire tail of the giant ship fell to the ground!
Everyone stared dumbfounded. "Oh god," look what just
happened," exclaimed Beaumont!

"Ouch," commented Kewscinski!

"Somebody's going to be in big trouble," predicted Grant.

"Captain Johns," a young officer running toward him in
dress grays asked? "Captain Johns!"

"That's me," he answered!

"I'm Jeff Lewis, your new engineer, Sir!" The young man
clicked his heels and saluted. Johns and the others returned the
salute. "Our ship is over there, sir." He pointed. A single B-36
could be seen in the distance, parked at the other end of the
runway.

"What's going on here," asked Johns? "That crane over
there just hacked the tail of that ship off!"

"What is this place," asked Grant?

"Davis Monthan Air Force Base," answered Lewis. The
cleaver lifted again and, with another crash, sheered a horizontal
stabilizer off of the fallen tail.

"I know that," snapped Johns! "What the hell are they
doing to that ship?" Without hesitation, the cleaver lifted and
sheered off the other stabilizer, causing the severed tail fin to
roll over on its side accompanied by a sound of grinding,
crunching metal.

"They're recycling aluminum," explained Lewis. The
giant cleaver fell with another crash and severed the tailfin from
the remains of the aft cabin. The front half of the damaged ship
just stood there on its three landing legs without complaint or
any expression of pain, its tail completely missing. "Colonel
Andrews, my last AC, says we're going to be flying the same

ships, sir. "They're just going to look different." Mercifully, Lewis had arranged a crew van so Johns and his men would not have to walk the entire distance. Two green Army bulldozers began crushing the shiny fallen metal between their blades. The men climbed into the van. As the van sped away, the dozer blades crumpled the precious metal into giant balls of tin foil.

Almost invisible, parked behind the giant B-36, was a pregnant RB-47H. Grant immediately noticed Whitefeather standing nearby. "Jerry, Jerry," he shouted, running toward him! The B-47 was the world's most beautiful plane. It was a six engined bomber that thought it was a fighter. It had a clear canopy on top, just like a fighter, and it could do aerobatics. The reconnaissance version had a grossly swollen bomb bay to provide space for three Ravens and their black boxes. Another unsightly black painted bulge in the tail looked shockingly feminine, like the cookie of a naked woman, covering the ferret antennas under the tail.

"What are you doing here," asked Whitefeather, saluting and shaking hands with Beaumont and Kewscinski?

"Same thing as last time," explained Johns, "picking up a new ship."

"Oh my god," exclaimed the Navajo! "They picked you." Beaumont and Kewscinski muttered to each other about the insult.

"And what are you doing, if it's not classified?"

"Same thing as last time, same as you," replied Whitefeather, sticking his thumbs under the bronze posies on his collar to show he had also been promoted. "How do you like my new junker?"

"What do you mean junker," asked Johns? "It's a real Pretty ship."

"Pretty cramped, you mean. "Sorry I can't give you a tour, but just getting from one end to the other is a struggle with all the black boxes we carry now. "Heaven help us if we have to bail out. "At least the cabin is pressurized so we don't have to wear those clunky Navy pressure suits.

"You just have to wear those tight itchy Air Force pressure suits," commented Grant without adding "sir."

"Uh, huh," the big Indian nodded to the junior officer without taking offense.

"What the hell is going on here," inquired Johns? "Why is that crane deliberately destroying that ship over there?"

"I'm just here picking up a junk ship to take on our mission, same as you," the Indian explained. "It's none of my business what goes on here. "Like they say in intelligence training, 'don't ask, don't tell.'"

"C'mon Jerry, don't pull that security crap with me. "What do you mean, 'a junk ship?'"

"Okay, I'll tell you," the Indian explained. "There would be a Congressional investigation if we lost a four million dollar reconnaissance bomber like 753, so we have to fly junkers."

"Seven fifty three was no junker," debated Grant!

"Yes it was," Whitefeather insisted. "Officially, it was scrapped here back in February. "Its engines and propellers are right over there." He pointed.

"None of this was going on last time we were here," said Johns. If seven five three's engines are still here, what engines were we flying with?"

"They came from those birds over there. "Nobody is going to notice if a few engines and propellers turn up missing," Whitefeather explained. "This recycling only started in February. "Seven fifty three was one of the first RB-36's to arrive. "Fatigue cracks in its wing spar was the official explanation, I think. "Most of those are older "D" models." He pointed at the hobbled ships. "There's absolutely nothing wrong with them. "LeMay just wants new ships, and he needs the aluminum out of the old ones."

"What about your RB-47," asked Grant? "It's practically brand new."

"Same thing," explained the Indian, "fatigue cracks. "A hundred thousand pounds of aluminum ingots showed up here when 753 crashed, along with twenty seven miles of electrical wire, so nobody would notice the short fall."

"Showed up how," asked Kewscinski, "from where?"

"Nobody knows. "The ship wreckers said they came to work in the morning and there it was, sitting on the ground."

"I don't believe it," exclaimed Johns! "Did they swap out the engines in our new bird too," he asked Lewis?

"Yessir," the young engineer answered, "they needed overhauls anyway."

"So you guys are telling me that LeMay is a crook?"

"I wouldn't say he's a crook," objected Whitefeather, "but you don't get to be a big chief General like that, without knowing how to work deals. "He's just doing what he's got to do to get the job done, that's all. "The Congress would be throwing fits, if they knew we were flying missions over Russia. "They'd cut off our funding."

Johns frowned. "I agreed to do this for him, because he made a personal request," protested the recently promoted, but naïve aircraft commander. "I never thought there was anything dishonest about it. "I assumed the higher up's knew everything."

"They need deniability for diplomatic reasons," explained the Raven. "Anyway, this is one of the ships that flew diversion for us last time. "We're going to do it again, so I'll be up there with you, just not in the same ship." Some other officers approached. "You know my pilot Greg Simmons," Whitefeather stated, nodding toward them.

"I don't believe I do."

"You flew together in Operation Red Wing." The officers saluted. "This is my old boss, Major Hank Johns," said Whitefeather.

"You must be Jenkins and Beauchamp," guessed Johns, returning the salutes. "I think I remember you." They shook hands.

"They work for me now," boasted Whitefeather proudly. The others introduced themselves.

"What about Harry," asked Beaumont; "where's he?"

"He got his own ship. "He left yesterday. "We're still grounded with some fuel leaks on our *new* engines, but they ought to have them fixed by tomorrow."

"This way, Sir," interrupted Lewis," pointing to an officer beckoning under the giant B-36.

Johns' new ship was B-36J-5-52-2811. Compared to 753, it was Spartan. As a featherweight III model, it did not have a photo lab, Ferret antenna blisters, or guns except a single turret that could hold two 20mm cannons in the tail. Its dull magnesium skin made it look dowdy compared to Whitefeather's shiny B-47, even thought it was practically brand new. Less than three years old, 811 was one of the last ships to come off the Fort Worth assembly line. Johns saluted the man standing under the ship.

"I'm Lieutenant Colonel Andrews," the man introduced himself as he returned the salute. "This used to be my ship." The others in Johns' crew also saluted.

"A pleasure to meet you," replied Johns. They shook hands.

"I'm here to give you the grand tour," Andrews explained, "while I wait for the ship that dropped you off to refuel and fly me and my men back to Rapid City."

"Ten hut," commanded Johns! The crew fell into two rows with Grant, Kewscinski, Nawrocki, Beaumont, and Lewis in front and Murphy, Sandringham, and Hernandez in the rear. "Sir," he shouted, turning around to face Andrews and saluting, "by the orders of General Curtis LeMay of the United States Strategic Air Command, I assume command of this aircraft."

Andrews returned the salute and replied, "I stand relieved and relinquish command." The two aircraft command-ers clicked their heels and saluted again.

"Men, bring the ship to life," commanded Johns! They fell out and lined up at the nose gear doors.

After climbing up through the forward landing gear well, Sandringham rode 811's trolley through the eighty four foot long intestine that led to an empty aft cabin. He found the cabin stripped, with no bunks, galley cabinets, food warmers, coffee pots, or even a floor. It looked like a silver skeleton inside. "You should look at this," Sandringham yelled back through the tube!

"There's nothing in here!" A single, three foot tall, K-17 aerial camera stuck up like a giant green mushroom where the floor used to be.

Since the new ship only needed one radio operator and there were no gun turrets, other than the one in the tail belonging to Sandringham, Hernandez was assigned to be a rear scanner. On a normal aircraft, with forward facing engines, the flight crew could watch for fires. Since the engines on the B-36 faced to the rear, it was necessary that someone watch them from the aft cabin. Hernandez became the lead scanner and back-up tail gunner. He regarded that as a demotion from his former position as radio operator.

Beaumont grumbled that he had plenty of jammers to operate, but without parabolic Ferret antennas, he could not locate enemy aircraft or figure out where enemy transmissions were coming from. Becoming an ordinary radio operator was a demotion for him too. He was now an officer doing an enlisted man's job.

Kewscinski took over as Video Observer, since there were to be no more reconnaissance missions. The cameras on all remaining RB-36's were being removed. It was rumored that a new single seat spyplane had been developed that could fly higher than the RB-36. Who would have thought that a twenty man, ten engined flying battleship would be replaced by a single seat, single engine jet? 753's experience with MiG-17's proved that ordinary reconnaissance missions over Russia were just too dangerous. Kewscinski regarded it as a demotion to become an ordinary bombardier after being a Photonavigator.

The metallic, stripped-down skeleton of a cabin gave Sandringham and Hernandez a ghastly feeling. Turning around and not seeing any bunks in a place that used to be crowded with happy, joking poker players made the hairs on their necks stand on end. The cabin had a cold clammy feeling, as if the ghosts of the dead gunners were haunting the new ship.

Hernandez stared out of his blister, from which the gunsight had been removed, hypnotized by the spinning propellers as Johns taxied to the active runway for takeoff.

Sandringham sat at the other bubble reading a magazine. The upper gun bubbles were replaced with flat aluminum covers, making the aft cabin and radio room considerably darker inside. The catwalk that used to hold the upper gunner's seats high over the card table was still there, but it was bare naked metal. There were no shiny food cabinets underneath. Instead of Shultz and Calabreze looking down over the card table, the big cabin was dark and empty like a ghost town church. The light that came through the two remaining blisters was blinding. Eyes could not easily adjust to the view inside after looking outside the ship. Inside, they saw only blackness.

Up front, a Farrand Y-1 periscope was installed in the center of the forward cabin for Kewscinski to aim the bomb, instead of a Norden bombsight. Unlike the periscope on a submarine, this one poked through a small bubble under the nose of the ship. Without the periscopic gunsight in the way, the view from Nawrocki's navigation desk was more spectacular than on 753, but the view of the ground was less, since the optically perfect bomb sighting glass had been replaced with an opaque oval of green aluminum to reduce weight. Another smaller periscope dangled down in the middle of the bridge where the astrodome used to be. It had a built in bubble sextant for shooting fixes, but it robbed what little standing headroom there was between the seats. It made the bridge seem smaller.

As Murphy revved up 811's engines on the warm up pad, Lieutenant Colonel Andrews climbed up to his old flight deck to say goodbye to Lewis.

"Coming with us," asked Johns?

"No," said Andrews, "I just thought I would like to experience the roar of the engines at full throttle one last time."

"So what's this I hear, a B-52 commander waxing nostalgic for old shaky" asked Johns?

"Well, I'll tell you," answered Andrews, "I have eight throttles that I must advance very slowly to avoid flame-outs. "At full power, the engines make the most mournful humming and whistling sound. "When I release the brakes, the takeoff roll is imperceptibly slow. "The acceleration is so poor, that you watch the fence at the end of the runway, wondering if you'll ever have enough airspeed to get over it. "Then suddenly, she lifts straight up, like an elevator, without rotating or nothing, levitating into the air like psychic power."

"So you don't have to pull back to rotate," asked Johns?

"You better not! "The brute has power assisted controls," replied Andrews. "You'd be standing on your tail if you did!"

"What about landing," asked Grant?

"Same thing, you come in with your nose pointing down," said Andrews, "no flare, just level out for touchdown, and in a crosswind, you crab the landing gear to come in sideways."

"Gee," said Grant! "That's neat!"

"You must have had someone at SAC pulling strings, to get two new ships in two years," Johns insinuated.

"The B-36 is obsolete and it doesn't matter if you crash another one because they're all going to be scrapped anyway," Andrews rebuffed. Hank just smiled at the insult. His mission was classified. He couldn't tell Andrews where his old ship was really going.

Recognizing he made a faux pas, Andrews just said, "Bye Lewis," and climbed down through the nose gear.

With only enough fuel on board to reach Fort Worth, 811 leapt into the air just seconds after turning onto the active. Johns pulled up in just a few ship lengths, climbing at a thirty degree angle just like a fighter, then banked in a hard right turn over the Bachelor Officer's Quarters so Andrews could experience the ten engined roar of the B-36 one last time. "That ought to make the jet jockeys jealous," said Grant as he retracted the gear.

Lewis joined the crew to replace Washington because the B-52 needed only one flight engineer. There was no room for him on Andrews' new ship, so he remained assigned to 811. When a millionaire buys an old mansion, he sometimes keeps the same butler since nobody else knows how anything works. It was good to have someone aboard who knew the bird's special quirks. Each ship was different. True to form, 811 soon lost oil pressure on the *new* number five engine and it had to be shut down. This created a controversy as to who the chief APE would be. Murphy had a dozen years experience flying B-29's over Japan and Korea. Lewis had been in the service less than a year, but as an officer, he out-ranked the more experienced Murphy. Johns decided that on the ground, Lewis would be Chief Engineer; and in the air, Murphy would. All heartily agreed with the compromise. As an officer, Lewis would be better at requisitions.

When Johns climbed down from the forward landing gear well, Colonel Peterson was waiting with a jewelry case just as LeMay had promised. "Congratulations Hank," he said with a salute, as he presented Johns with Lieutenant Colonel pins.

"All right," exclaimed Grant, clapping his hands, believing Captain's bars might not be long in coming to his own collar. Hank would have preferred to have received them at a ceremony that Linda and Bobby could have attended, but security concerns about the mission prevented that.

"I got a wire from the Davis-Monthan tower claiming you guys cracked a little plaster in their BOQ," accused the Colonel. "Were you guys in a hurry to leave or something?"

"The ship's former AC said he wanted to experience the roar of the engines at full throttle one last time," explained Grant.

"Colonel, if I may," the youngest officer interjected as he emerged from the nose gear well, saluting, "My name is Lewis. "Lieutenant Colonel Andrews, my former AC, said that the '36 is obsolete and it doesn't matter if we crash another one because they're all on their way to Arizona to be scrapped. "I asked Major, I mean, Lieutenant Colonel Johns to fly over the BOQ so I could wave goodbye to my shipmates properly, sir."

"So they made you mad and you got stupid," asked Peterson, glaring at Johns?

"Yes Sir," the new light colonel replied, saluting!

"If you try a stunt like that here in Carswell, I'll put you in charge of the maintenance detail to repair the damage, and you won't fly again until its fixed," Peterson shouted in mock rage. "Is that clear?"

"Yes Sir," answered Johns, clicking his heels in a salute! He grinned at Lewis as soon as Peterson looked away.

THE JUGHEAD
April 1956

The weapons pit was a tunnel entrance that led to an ammo bunker deep underground. It was covered with one inch steel plates that opened to meet the doors of the aft bomb bay. The TX-16 was carried through the tunnel on a large hydraulic carriage that rode on old aircraft tires. It took quite a bit of time to get the hydraulic lift into position and clamp the huge weapon in place. 811 had special oversized chain slings hanging between the bomb racks to support it. The new ship was not capable of carrying conventional bombs. All of the conventional bomb racks had been removed to save weight.

Once the chain slings supporting the giant, five foot diameter, twenty five foot long, twenty ton "Jughead" were safety suspended from the ship's massive weapon shackle, special stabilizer pads were screwed against the bomb to keep it from rocking from side to side during flight. With a nuclear weapon on board, Sandringham or Hernandez had to stand guard around the ship at all times. Even though the plutonium core was not installed, the uranium radiation tube and special plastic lining inside the casing were highly classified. It had to be watched. The Air Police took over on the four O'clock and graveyard shifts, but guard duty during the day fell to the aircrew.

Because the only enlisted men left were Murphy, Sandringham, and Hernandez, and because Murphy outranked the others, there were only two men privileged to march back and forth to protect the dud bomb. Hernandez's dad loaned him a shiny blue Smith & Wesson .38. They were not permitted even to put their rifles down, unless they had the sidearm strapped to their belts.

What a difference nuclear weapons made! When the first B-36's were stationed at Carswell, there was not even a perimeter fence. The Air force felt that if taxpayers anted up four million dollars to buy a new ship, they had a right to come and see it if they wanted to. Now, if an unauthorized person approached and did not raise their hands when challenged, Sandringham and Hernandez were ordered to shoot to kill.

Everyone was fitted for new T-1 heated partial pressure suits. These were not the same bulky, Navy style space suits as before. Each was tailored individually to fit like a second skin. There were webbing straps connected to air hoses that ran along the sides of the torso, arms, and legs. Once a man strapped himself into his seat, laces had to be pulled to tighten the suit. At altitude, air pressure would inflate the hoses along the sides, stretching it tight against the body to prevent blood from pooling in the legs.

Without a pressure suit, it would not be safe to fly above fifty thousand feet. Blood boils at sixty three thousand feet, causing human flesh to swell and burst. In order for a B-36 to fly that high, all excess weight had to be stripped from the ship. Pressurized air is heavy. An unpressurized cabin weighs less. The fuselage was not strong enough to contain sea level pressure at that altitude, anyway. If the ship needed to climb away from Soviet fighters, the suits would keep Johns and his men alive for about ten minutes, before blood plasma began shooting out of their pores.

The day before the mission, a bunch of men in yellow rubber suits came and replaced the lead practice core with a real one made of plutonium. Everyone had to wear film badges from then on. No unauthorized personnel were permitted near the bomb bay after that.

The following morning, Hank watched a van marked "DANGER—LIQUID DEUTERIUM" parked alongside the ship. A green canvas skirt was draped around the aft bomb bay. Clouds of vapor leaked from under the skirt. Hank lifted the skirt and entered the bomb bay, dropping it behind him. A great cloud of ice vapor flowed out from underneath. The cloud was so thick, Hank could see only a few feet. Like a rocket ready to blast off, the large bomb was covered with a thick layer of ice. A yellow suited man on a tall ladder fueled the bomb through an ice caked rubber hose. Hank inspected the heavy retarding parachute, tightly packed between the four stubby tailfins, and the wiring harness for its all important heater. If the chute froze and did not open when the bomb was released, the ship would not have time to escape the blast. He lifted up the skirt and exited the bomb bay.

A ground power unit idled loudly, providing the heater with power. Peterson was waiting outside. "Time to saddle up," said the Colonel. "You better get that badge developed."

Grant was late for the pre-flight briefing. Johns found him in the locker room nursing a black eye. It took him a long time to pull on his new G-suit so Johns helped him. "Shouldn't you get that checked by a flight surgeon," he suggested?

"Do you want to replace me," snapped the young man in reply?

"No," said the new Aircraft Commander! "Tell me what happened."

"Two cowards wearing hoods jumped me from behind my back. "They threw me to the ground and started kicking like sissies!"

"Were they military?

"They were wearing hoods!"

"What did they say," asked Johns?

Grant paused, glaring at his commanding officer. "Nothing but crap," he cursed! "Lets go, I wanna have a crack at them Rooskies! "I'm sorry I'm late, Sir."

President Eisenhower had taken an entire month to decide what to do about the Russian rockets. This gave Gordon time to see Shirley Newcomb. He told her that he would be there for her if she ever needed help. She telephoned the very next day. Jim's car, a brand new Chevy convertible, was still at the base. She asked him to drive it home for her. Little Jimmy hadn't figured out what had happened to his father. When his daddy's car pulled into the driveway, he expected his father would walk through the door—and there was Gordon. "Daddy, daddy, daddy," Little Jimmy yelled with a confused stare. Shirley burst into tears and was all broken up about it for about an hour. Grant comforted her all the way to third base.

Newcomb had not taught Shirley how to drive. She needed a ride back to the base to accompany the casket back to Jim's parents in Mississippi. She treated that empty coffin as though the Major was really in there. Grant didn't tell her what really happened and she didn't ask. He lived on base in the Bachelor Officers' Quarters, so when she returned, he was already there to drive her home. They often ate at the Big Apple on the North side and sometimes he would take her to the Cattlemen's Steak House in Jim's car. Some of the guys used to ask how he ever got his hands on such a girl or a car as pretty as that. He told them that he inherited her and the car from a friend. That was always good for a few laughs until they realized he was not joking. It was dangerous for a Jew to be dating a widow woman in Texas—especially a recent widow.

Wearing matching frilly pink, polka dot dresses, Phyllis Peterson and Mary Bjorggessen arrived at the base in the Colonel's car. Peterson escorted Mary past the armed guards to Johns' new ship. Mary lifted her knee way up high to ascend the ladder into the nose, revealing, as before, not a little of her Danish heritage. The guards bent over to watch. Peterson handed her a small suitcase full of clothes Phyllis had bought for her, and a military issue nylon parka. Her old one made of polar bear fur was consigned to the lobby display case in the administration building, which enshrined many 7th bomb wing memorabilia.

Peterson did not say goodbye. He was glad to see her go. Mary had become a bad influence on his daugher Denise, who had become very popular with the boys at school even though she was not very pretty. Inviting Mary to stay in his home had been a big mistake. "What are you doing," he snapped at Hernandez, who was on a ladder painting on some nose art.

"Decorating the ship as ordered, Sir," the young man answered, saluting with his paint brush holding a can of black paint in his other hand.

"Victor agreed it would be a good name since it means the same in Spanish as it does in English," explained Johns.

General Allen showed up in his dress grays to offer a salute as Grant and the others climbed aboard. He noticed the nose art, but said nothing. There was no photographer this time. Everyone was on edge. All knew where they were going. Few spoke. Hawley wasn't planning to follow 811 down the runway with his hot rod either. "You crashed my ship and I don't care if you smash up another one," he shouted angrily from his engine start position under the wing as Johns climbed aboard. The recently promoted Aircraft Commander just grunted in reply. Hawley had heard scuttlebutt going around the base, that Johns was ordered to bail out over Iran so that the radioactive evidence of what he was about to do would plunge into a deep fisher on the floor of the Gulf of Oman. He could not bring himself to care about a ship that was about to be destroyed.

All had been warned not to discuss the mission. Nothing else was on their minds, so they said nothing, except what was read from the preflight checklist. Beaumont strapped Mary to the toilet cover for takeoff. She was thrilled to watch the houses pass underneath the giant front window as 811 roared over Lake Worth. Shirley waved at Grant from Linda's front porch as the ship roared overhead, until they were forced to cover their ears. Linda grinned widely when she read the nose art. Shirley was in tears.

Johns wanted to get some altitude to see what the new ship could do. The rated ceiling of the B-36J was 48,000 feet, but that was with a normal fuel and weapon load. On a one way mission, relieved of its burden of fuel, the ship could fly much higher. The plan was to fly so high that Soviet fighters could never reach them. Above 50,000 feet, fighters were essentially ballistic and the big ship could easily turn out of the way of their guns. Also, the higher they were when they released the bomb, the more time they had to get away before it vaporized everything within miles.

Pressure suits dug into groins and became very uncomfortable as the hoses along everyone's' arms, sides, and legs inflated. Each suit had a small athletic cup built into the cod-piece that opened to use the urine tube. It was strangely similar to the type of underwear worn by medieval knights under their armor. At altitude, the pressure on this thing was excruciating and it could not be scratched. The clear visor prevented any relief for an itchy nose or face. Grant was in considerable pain from the bruises as his face swelled. He began to imagine horsefly maggots were biting his nose and cheeks because no mirror was available to reassure him that nothing was there. It was impossible for anyone to get an itch anywhere but the face and groin because of the tightness of the suits. The lack of blood circulation made everything tingle as though one's entire body had fallen asleep. It might have been considered an effective method of torture if they hadn't volunteered for it.

"We're at fifty thousand feet indicated altitude," announced Grant over the interphone.

"What's that city coming up ahead of us," asked Johns?

"That would be Minneapolis or Saint Paul," answered Nawrocki.

"Calculate simulated bomb run for one thousand foot airburst."

"Are you sure we ought to be doing this with a live core," asked Kewscinski?

"The weapon shackle is locked, isn't it?"

"Yessir."

"Why not then? "The worst that can happen is that we blow ourselves up."

"And half of Iowa with us," remarked Grant.

"Yes Sir," answered Kewscinski, "calculating bombing solution for one thousand foot airburst." The wheels and gears inside the bombing navigation computer whirred and clicked as the associated vacuum tubes flickered on and off. "Whoa, we're coming up on it sooner than I expected. "Initial point in only thirty five seconds, thirty four, thirty three . . . "

"Roger, that was quick! "Turning autopilot over to you," interrupted Johns. Grant flicked the autopilot switch.

When Kewscinski finished counting to zero, the ship lurched violently upward. "Bomb's away," announced Kewscinski! Nothing happened.

"Autopilot off," said Johns. He turned the ship into a wingstanding chandelle maneuver until the horizon was a vertical streak from the top to the bottom of the windscreen. Then at 57,000 feet, the wings buffeted and the ship fell out of the sky.

"Dammit," Johns cursed!

"You stalled," accused Grant. The ship shook violently.

"Remember, we'll be a hundred thousand pounds lighter when we do it for real," reminded Kewscinski, "so we'll probably be all right. "I wouldn't do anything different."

"I don't want to take no chances," said Johns as he wrestled the ship into a dive to try to regain control. Everyone was pushed into their seats as he pulled out of the dive at more than four hundred knots.

"Boom," shouted Kewscinski through the interphone loud enough to cause crackling distortion that hurt everyone's ears! Nothing happened.

"Did we survive," asked Johns?

"We are still in the danger zone," warned Nawrocki.

"Let me see that," demanded Kewscinski! The oxygen hose, suit heater wires, and straps securing him to his seat made it impossible for him to get up from his desk. Nawrocki lifted his chart off his desk and passed it to the VO. "We're no closer than we were last time. "It's the same as before . . . bashed in bomb doors and radome, fire in the aft cabin."

"Scanner to AC," announced Hernandez, "the fire is out."

"Thanks Victor for that added element of realism," Johns chided. "You didn't puke all over your visor this time did you John?"

"No sir," answered Kewscinski. "The lecture you gave me about that last time must have sunk in, Sir."

"See that it doesn't happen again."

"Yessir!"

"Resuming course for Thule."

"Radio to AC," advised Beaumont, "Mary isn't wearing a pressure suit, you know. "I think you should head the ship back down."

"Oh yeah, the least of our problems," answered Johns. "Thanks for reminding me."

Because most of the insulation had been removed to save weight, the temperature inside the ship quickly dropped to minus seventy degrees above fifty thousand feet. Humidity from human breath froze on the curved walls and ceiling, giving the bare metal interior a frosty look, like the palace of the Snow Queen. Little icicles seemed to be forming on the skeleton stringers overhead. Exhaled breath from underneath face masks made a fog thicker than cigar smoke. Pants liners, coveralls, and bomber jackets were pulled over the pressure suits. Large felt mittens covered their hands and feet. The only comfort came from the deicing outlets for the windows. The air coming through them was supposed to be warm, but it cooled off to just above freezing by the time it made it through the vacuum cleaner hoses. It didn't help much.

Fortunately, the suits had built-in electric underwear. A little knob on the wall controlled the suit's temperature, much like an electric blanket. This underwear required another set of wires that made everyone feel like cyborgs connected to a machine. Oxygen hoses, interphone wires, suit heater wires, urine tubes, and safety straps, all reminded each man that he was no longer an independent being, but an inseparable part of the ship. The ship became alive, being made partly of human flesh utterly dependent on it for survival. The only truly human person on board was Mary, who was passed out on the toilet.

Above fifty thousand feet, even one hundred percent oxygen is not enough to maintain consciousness without positive pressure, so Mary's unpressurized mask and leather helmet, which she wore under the hood of her new nylon parka, were not adequate to keep her alive for very long. The cold temperature of her arms and legs, almost frozen because the thin military surplus artificial insulation did not keep her as warm as her polar bear fleece, kept her blood from boiling. Beaumont dragged her off the toilet and laid her ice cold flesh down on the equally cold, bare aluminum floor of the radio room.

Without foam insulation to absorb some of the sound, the roar of 811's engines was intense. Communication in a normal voice was impossible, except over the interphone—that is, if the mechanical tinny sound the headsets in the new hard shell helmets made could be considered normal. The low air pressure made everyone's voice sound deeper. Combined with the electronic distortion from the interphone, everyone seemed to talk like robots, making it hard to tell who was speaking unless each man announced his designation first. Everyone missed the jovial atmosphere of 753. Shultz's and O'Connor's wildly exaggerated stories from the war led one to think the two of them had beat the Japs by themselves. Now there seemed to be very little for anyone to talk about. What had become of the world?

THULE
April 1956

"Ape to AC, Losing manifold pressure on six," an unfamiliar voice growled over the interphone. It was Lewis.

"Hank, we've lost fuel pressure on six," added Murphy.

"Feather six," said Johns. "We must have gotten some ice in the fuel lines."

The outermost propeller on the right wing slowed to a halt as Hernandez announced, "Scanner to AC, six fully feathered, three diamonds," over the interphone.

"We've got more problems on four and five," warned Lewis.

"Continuing descent," said Johns.

"We've lost pressure on five," informed Murphy. "The entire fuel manifold must be affected."

"Feather five," ordered Johns.

Red topped green auroral curtains rose over the flat topped mountain called Old Dundas to welcome Johns' new ship to icy Thule. Everyone was nervous. Losing any more engines would be deadly, but not any more deadly than continuing the mission. It was impossible for a B-36 to fly with all the engines on one side shut down. In the 1954 movie "Strategic Air Command," the star, Jimmy Stewart, who himself was a decorated B-24 pilot during the war, ordered, "Feather one, two, and three, full power to jets three and four, full power to four five and six." Without power assist for the rudder, a B-36 would be spinning like a helicopter if anyone actually tried that.

"AC to crew," announced Johns, "I've decided to attempt a power off approach, so everyone assume crash positions. "Starting jets three and four." He set the flaps at the minimum setting so he could adjust the glide angle if engine four quit as Grant reached up to start the jets.

Everyone sighed with relief when the gear bumped down a little harder and faster than normal. "Reverse three and four," ordered Johns. "Full power!" Grant complied by flicking the appropriate switches on the center console as Murphy pushed two of his six throttles all the way. The command car had to chase the sliding ship. It took almost half the runway to stop. When 811 finally came to a halt, everyone's pressure suit was so stiff that it was hard to climb out of the seats. Mary was in pain. The altitude, combined with sitting too long in one position, had given her blood clots in her legs.

It was almost the end of winter. The sun, just under the horizon, bathed the base in twilight. The ice on the runway had been pounded to a thickness of two feet of bone jarring rough-ness. Each of the landing lights seemed to be sunk into a small pit where the ice had melted due to the heat. Johns had to be careful not to steer too close to the side of the ramp, or he might fall into one of the holes. He did not have the power to climb out of them. Although everyone was cold and all dreamt of the hot chocolate awaiting them in the "O" club, Johns taxied unusually slowly. The fighters all had studded snow tires. 811 didn't.

Thule was like no other base in the world. All of the buildings, except the aircraft hangars, were converted from walk in freezers. All of the pipes and plumbing from electrical, fuel, and sewers ran six feet above the permafrost on scaffolds covered with thick insulation. Many of the prefabricated freez-er buildings were brought in from the sea in one piece on a giant Diesel-electric Snow Train—a one hundred seventy foot long, fifteen foot wide, articulated overland train that rode upon sixteen ten foot tall snow tires.

811 was not met by a fleet of fuel trucks like 753 was before. A hose was attached to the filler pipe in the forward bomb bay from another pipe suspended above the ground. A pump over in the garage filled every tank in the wing at once, or tried to.

"Stop, stop," Murphy yelled with much cursing, as he climbed up beside the bomb bay to tighten all the hose clamps. The super cold air surrounding the cryogenic bomb had shrunk the rubber expansion joints, causing fuel to gush out of the bomb bay like a shower bath. Sergeant Davis climbed into the wing and brought out a mayonnaise jar filled with 115/145 octane gas. Little icicles dangled from the lid. There definitely was water in the fuel. It would take the ground crew at Thule three hours to unfreeze the fuel filters.

When the fueling was complete, Davis had 811 pushed aside by a giant tractor and hoses were inserted into the nacelles from six heating units. A message had been received that there was fog over the target. Of course, Kewscinski could have bombed with radar, but what if he made a mistake? The cost of a navigational error would be incalculable, and the possible loss of life to innocent civilians, unthinkable. The mission had to be put on hold.

Four Air Police with carbines escorted three Eskimos toward the ship. Colonel Cox had been sacked and demoted to Major because of the stowaway. He never was a full Colonel. He had only worn birds on his shoulders because of his spot promotion. LeMay was merciless to officers who fell short of his high standards. What if she had been a spy? Where thermonuclear weapons are concerned, there is no room for slackers. Colonel Mathers was now the Base Commander.

Despite the pain in her legs resulting from high altitude, Mary descended from the nose doors wearing her new parka and immediately ran to meet her family. They greeted her in tears. The Air Police marched them off the base permanently, with little fanfare.

Everyone ran through the icy wind straight to the "O" club, which doubled as the officer's and enlisted man's club since the base was so small. The little bar was not a bad place to relax, for a base so far north. It even had a pool table and a one lane bowling alley. Two heavily padded Air Police remained to guard the ship—not an enviable job in minus forty degree weather. Inside, Sergeant Davis, Chief of the groundcrew, introduced the men of 811 to the B-36 drink. He prepared it in a mayonnaise jar and carried it over to Murphy, who was immediately concerned about the amount of crushed ice and a light yellow tint in the "fuel." "Which tank did you drain that from," asked the old APE?

"Taste it," replied Davis.

Murphy slowly unscrewed the lid, expecting the worst. he dipped his little finger in the concoction and touched a drop onto his tongue. The old man's prunish face slowly transformed into a smile. It was the first time he smiled since the crash. He put the mayonnaise jar to his lips, drank about a quarter of it, and said, "I hope there's nothing alcoholic in there."

"Oh no," replied Davis, "just six shots of 115 proof gin and four shots of 145 proof vodka, one for each engine, and Tom Collin's Mix to give it the right color."

"What about the crushed ice," asked Murphy?

"Oh, that really did come from the fuel filters!"

Murphy passed the jar to Lewis, who seemed to truly respect the old man even though he outranked him. The ice did not have enough time to dilute the liquid, so Lewis was thrown into a fit of coughing when he tried to drink it.

"The B-29, B-50, C-97, and C-124 are all the same as a B-36," explained Davis, "only they get only four shots of Gin instead of six and no vodka."

"Well, I'll take a B-36 over a B-29 any day," replied Murphy, already feeling friendlier. "What does the B-52 get—eight shots of vodka?"

"Something like that," said Davis, "but we haven't seen one here yet. "Fighter jocks get only one shot straight up unless its one of those F-89 Scorpion fighters. They get two."

Johns, Kewscinski, Nawrocki, Beaumont, and Grant were having dinner with Colonel Mathers. The Colonel looked very old and experienced. His hair was white. Lewis preferred to eat with the enlisted men because of the way Grant treated him. One would think that two officers about the same age would like each other, but it was not so. Grant regarded Lewis as an inferior to be ordered around. Both had received the same spot promotion to First Lieutenant, but Grant didn't think Lewis had been in the service long enough to deserve it. He had only graduated from Air Force ROTC at Nebraska State instead of West Point. The bruises on Grant's face made him more irritable than normal.

Also dining with Mathers, was Colonel Bill Jacobsen who was in command of the squadron of Lockheed F-94 Starfires that infested the base. He seemed a little young to be a full chicken Colonel, but fighter pilots had an advantage on the promotion list. He probably received a spot promotion the same as everyone else did. A number of higher ranking jet-jockeys joined them at the officers' table. The shiny metal walls of the freezer buildings reflected sound so much that everyone could hear what everyone else was saying. "Do you think you're going to get the go-ahead," asked Mathers?

"I think so," replied Johns.

"You know what they'll do to us. "They'll figure out your flight originated from here and they'll nuke this place."

"I hope not. "I guess that's why they sent Bill," replied Johns, casting an eye over toward Jacobsen. The fighter commander looked down pensively at his steak and rehydrated mashed potatoes.

"We don't have much of a bomb shelter," Mathers admitted. "They dynamited a hole in the permafrost and sunk a freezer barracks weighted with a three foot thick roof made of concrete rebar and then filled the hole with ice, rock, and water. It's one giant ice cube now."

"It'll be a giant lake if they blow up an A-bomb over it," said Jacobsen. "If two of them get through, all the meltwater will vaporize and you'll be sitting ducks for the third one."

"A mortar round could kill us then," said Mathers. "They can get us if they want to."

"Do you think you can take on the Bears," asked Johns?

"Oh, the Bears are easy meat for the Starfires," answered Jacobsen. "We have radar and we can find them in all weather. "Its the My-3 Bison I'm worried about."

"Have you ever intercepted one?"

"No, I've never even seen one. "We get Bears almost every day, not always at the same time, but always when the photography is best. "They started overflying us regularly about two months ago."

"No doubt. "How long has it been since one flew over," asked Grant?

"Since yesterday," replied Mathers. "It would be coming about now if there is going to be one today," he added, looking at his watch. As he looked up at the clock, an alarm sounded and all the fighter pilots, including Colonel Jacobsen, jumped up from the table, abandoning their food. "C'mon outside, you'll get a look at it." Everyone jumped up and ran to the barracks to get their cold weather gear as a muffled sound of jet engines starting was heard in the hangar next door.

The insulation of the freezer barracks so completely deadened the sound, Grant did not cover his ears when he opened the door. The afterburners of the blunt nosed straight winged fighters shooting down the runway, with tailflames blazing, clapped a thunderous roar the moment Grant pushed the handle. The air was so cold, the fighters left vapor trails down the runway.

It was noon, so the sun peaked above the horizon, but it would not stay up permanently for another few weeks. At altitude it was daylight, so the giant Russian bomber and its contrail were easy to see. The officers were looking through binoculars at a silver glint in the distance in front of a long vapor trail stretching to the horizon. The vapor trails of the fighters circled higher and higher until they intersected the trail from the bomber, The two vapor trails soon twisted together in a pretzel shaped knot.

Grant asked Johns if he could borrow his binoculars. They got a close up view of the Soviet Bear bomber. It was an ugly plane. It had the swept wings and tail of a B-47 on a long slender fuselage, as slim as a pencil, studded with moles and warts. Instead of jets, it had counter-rotating turboprops, two propellers on each of the four nacelles, turning in opposite directions like wild egg beaters. The only decoration on the shiny aluminum skin was a red star on the tail fin. The eight flailing propellers seemed ominously threatening, considering it had the range to reach Texas with it's A-bomb. The four Starfires provided reassurance by boxing in the Russian ship, two on either side of it, ready to shoot it with rockets if it should stray too close to the base.

"I wonder if the men inside are comfortable the way 753 used to be, or if they are being tortured like we are now on 811," asked Grant? Johns looked at his partner, but did not comment. Nobody knew the answer to that but the Russians.

The glasses fogged up quickly, so not everyone got to see. After only a few minutes, everyone ran back inside, stopping at the barracks only to remove the cold weather gear before ordering hot chocolate in the "O" club. Kewscinski stayed out to try and see the big plane's camera ports.

"He'll go all the way to Boston if he can," said Mathers, sitting back at his steak dinner, which by then was cold.

"They go that far," asked Johns as he resumed his seat?

"They go all the way down the Newfoundland coast and cross through the Belle Isle Straits, before turning toward Iceland and back to Severomorsk where they are based. "Bad luck they spotted you on the ground."

"I would say that's very bad luck indeed," said Jacobsen.

"Bad luck for all of us," asked Johns?

"Do you know if your orders came from the President, or just from LeMay," asked Mathers?

"I couldn't tell you if I knew," answered Johns.

"Is it possible the General is doing this on his own," asked Jacobsen?

"General LeMay won the war against Japan," Johns asserted. "He is a man of the greatest character. "He would never go against the President's wishes or our country's best interest."

"I didn't mean to question his character," apologized Jacobsen. "I've never met him and I don't really know much about him, but the thought that there might be a loose cannon at SAC really bothers me."

"LeMay is not a loose cannon," Mathers interrupted. "There is more to this than you know," he continued. "There have been some rocket tests in the desert in New Mexico. "Some people think the Russians have been doing tests too, eh Hank?"

"I'm not at liberty to discuss the nature of my mission," answered Johns.

"No, of course not, but any fool can guess what it is," exclaimed Mathers! "Don't worry Hank, nobody is going to leave this base until you get back and no radio traffic goes in or out without my say-so. "I think maybe the President and the Congress don't fully appreciate the trouble we'll be in if the Russians put nuclear bombs on rockets. "I think maybe General LeMay is going to put a stop to it, even if it means his career."

"Well, let me put it this way," said Johns, "if I return, you'll know I've failed." The other officers gasped.

Ticks of an alarm clock out in the hall bounced off the walls as they tried to sleep. A man snored like a steam shovel a few bunks away. These, combined with the constant din of ventilation fans and hot water surging through recirculating pipes, kept Johns and his crew up all night. When the clock finally rang, it seemed to blast a deafening roar. Ten restless men struggled out of their bunks in the freezer barracks.

After a cold shower to wake up, skipping breakfast was the recommended order of the day. The new pressure suits had no way to take a dump. They were too tight to be removed and donned easily in flight. Attempting to use the toilet would be a chilling experience in a minus forty degree cabin. If someone ate breakfast and later had to go to the bathroom, there would be no place for the feces to go and there would be problems.

Instead, everyone took a red vitamin capsule that packed all the nutrients of a day's worth food into a pill about an inch long. In a different package, a similar sized green capsule in a special wrapper was filled with cyanide. The flight surgeon gave each man a supply of caffeine pills laced with amphetamines to help him wake up. These were regular "pill" pills and could not be confused with the capsule containing cyanide. It was these caffeine pills that allowed B-47 and B-52 pilots to stay in the air for days with in-air refueling. The new jets did not have bunks for off duty crew like the RB-36 did. The bunks had also been removed from 811. All were now expected to pop a pill if tired, instead of sleeping.

The toilets at Thule were of the naval variety, which had to be pumped rather than flushed. There were not many of them to be shared by such a large number of men. Every man in Johns' crew had experienced mornings when he didn't feel like going to work. On this day, all were tempted to call in sick even though they knew they were perfectly well. The flight surgeon waited for them outside the cubicles to detect fakers. The most important decision each man had ever faced in his life was whether he should go along to nuke the Rocket base at Tyura Tam, or try to fool the flight surgeon into being allowed to stay behind and be nuked when the Bison bombers came to retaliate. A long line of glaring eyes were waiting outside the bathroom. The airmen assigned to the base had no idea of the difficulty Johns and his men suffered as each sat by himself on the stool, waiting for his suppository to kick in, and pondering whether he should claim to be sick.

For Johns, the decision was especially hard. He could call the whole thing off and pass the weighty responsibility onto someone else. What would Peterson say to General Allen about him then? Would he be accused of cowardice? Would it mean the end of his career? Could he enjoy being maintenance chief, or would he have to leave the Air Force? What would Linda say? Continuing the mission actually seemed to be the safest thing to do.

The groundcrew had not been informed of the trouble they were in. They were angry at the flyboys who seemed to be taking too long to do their business. Each man wanted to be sure his bowel was completely empty so that there would be nothing unclean inside, should he have to stand before his maker. Even if they survived the mission, it would be a long time before they parachuted into Iran. There were no American style, sit down toilets there either. Johns' legs tingled from sitting on the throne too long as he hobbled to the ready room to lace on his pressure suit.

The amphetamines in the caffeine pills were beginning to take effect as they strapped themselves into their ice cold seats. Grant felt like Superman: "Its a bird, its a plane," he yelled, "its a B-36 about to burn you Commie rocket men off the face of the Earth!" Hernandez and Sandringham didn't think that was funny. "You should have taken two pills," the young pilot added with a shout! The heating units had been blowing so-called warm air into the cabin all night, but it didn't seem to make any difference. After more cajoling from Grant, everyone but Johns popped another pill. In a few minutes, morale was not a problem.

The maximum weight takeoff was uneventful. Other than counting off the pre-flight and climb-out checklists, nobody said anything. Some tapped their thighs as though they were listening to music even though no music could be heard. For several hours the interphone was silent. Then Nawrocki announced, "I know you've all been here before, but we're passing the North Pole again." There was nothing but silence in reply. Ice passed under the ship, illuminated by a green auroral glow. Some of the ice blocks were as big as houses and cast a long shadow. There were pressure ridges and valleys with an occasional black fissure where freezing cold water was welling up through the crevasses.

"Gordon," asked Johns, "I have a favor to ask."

"Sure skipper," whatever you want, the co-pilot quipped!

"I know you've been seeing Shirley Newcomb and all, but if for some reason I don't make it, do you think you could call on Linda to see if she is all right?"

"Oh yeah Shirley," the co-pilot replied as he smacked his visor trying in vain to rub his black eye. "I love Shirley! "What a woman!"

ZHUKOV

MARSHAL ZHUKOV
April 1956

In a richly burled, well lit office at the Kremlin in Moscow, three Americans in ordinary business suits stood before a large flame birch desk topped with several different colored telephones. Standing on a red carpet, gazing at the beautifully carved, ornate gilded ceiling, Ambassador Mumley shook the hand of Marshal Georgi Zhukov, the Soviet Union's most decorated soldier, now the gray haired, balding Minister of Defense. General Zhukov was better looking than the average man his age, with a firm square jaw and a determined look of confidence in his penetrating blue eyes that made the Americans feel small in comparison. His sharply tailored green uniform had gold epaulets and three gold stars hanging from three red ribbons of three Hero of the Soviet Union Medals above the many other ribbons and medals clustered on his breast. Four Russians wearing plain black suits stepped behind the Americans as their leader shook hands and kissed the General's cheeks in traditional Russian fashion. "You requested a consultation Georgi Konstantinovich," the Ambassador asked sheepishly? He did not notice that his secretary and translater were being pulled by the elbow out of the room by two of the four Russians.

"I have a surprise for you," said the military man in halting, heavily accented English.

"What is it?"

"You must close your eyes."

The two remaining Russians approached the Ambassador from behind and covered his head with a black leather hood, pulling the drawstring tight around his neck. The two American aides yelled for help.

"Stop that! "What the hell are you doing," shouted the Ambassador, feeling lightheaded and unable to breathe, his voice muffled by the hood? "Let me go!"

When the hood was finally lifted, Mumley found himself laying beside General Zhukov, now wearing his coat and officer's cap, on the leather back seat of a huge black Zil limousine. The car stopped. The chauffeur opened the door. The General helped the American keep his balance as he staggered out of the car. Mumley lifted his hands to his temples to rub a splitting headache. The hood must have been doused with ether, he reasoned.

Some guards saluted as the two of them ambled together into a large, plain brick building. Under well lit, white painted steel girders stretching across the ceiling of an aeronautical laboratory, stood a beautiful young woman wearing a red space suit. Behind her was a hypobaric chamber that looked something like a giant, ten foot long green bug, connected by heavy black hoses and electrical cables to several gray boxes and other scientific equipment covered with Cyrillic writing. White curtains separated it from the rest of the laboratory.

"What is this," asked the Ambassador? "Why did you bring me here? "Explain!" Two soldiers, standing guard, raised their carbines slightly to suggest he should not try to move in closer for a better look.

"We are in Zvyozdny Gorodok," said Zhukov. "This is Svetlana Periscova. "She is competing to become the first woman to fly into outer space. "Svetlana is the pilot who shot down your reconnaissance bomber seven hundred fifty three."

Svetlana's ice blue eyes twinkled with pride. She had not been told that the combat had been a victory. The grueling interrogation concerning Sergei's death had left her questioning her choice of careers, but now she could cheerfully thrust her voluptuous chest forward with pride as she stood at attention. The idea that she might be selected to be the first person to fly in outer space was a thrilling revelation. Sergei would be so proud of her! Perhaps she would be reunited with him among the stars.

"Where are my secretary and translator," asked the Ambassador?

"They were unavoidably detained," answered the General.

"Air Force 753 was not shot down," Mumley corrected. "According to my report, the attacking MiG's were shot down and the bomber had to ditch due to unrelated engine trouble."

"You may believe what you want," replied the General, "but, as you can see, Svetlana is here and your bomber is not."

Mumley scowled, "We have film from the gun cameras that clearly shows two MiG-17's breaking up with no survivors." He frowned at Svetlana until he noticed tears welling up in her eyes, which caused her to look away. Lana did not know who Mumley was or why she had been told to put on the pressure suit. She yearned to be home with her mother.

"Perhaps this is something you two would rather discuss over lunch," suggested the General. "You are dismissed," he said to Lana in English. Saying nothing, she saluted, then turned and left. Zhukov said something to an aide in Russian and turned to the Ambassador. "We have fine dining in this building. "Won't you join me?"

"I'm sorry, I have a headache," answered Mumley, "but under the circumstances, I suppose you are giving me no choice."

"After you," the General insisted. "I must apologize for these security precautions, but it was important that I show this to you. "I could not allow you to know of our location. "Would you like some aspirin? "I must make an unprecedented request. You have an important decision to make." They walked down a short hallway full of young men in white doctor smocks, all of whom snapped to attention and saluted. General Zhukov returned the salutes automatically and instinctively, without breaking his stride. "When we realized that your reconnaissance bomber had successfully penetrated our airspace, the Politburo decided I should show you what we are doing here. "We wouldn't want anything destructive to happen to our great adventure."

"What are you doing," the Ambassador asked? "What adventure?"

They entered a dark luxury dining room. Red drapes attempted to hide gray cinderblock walls. In the middle, a white linen covered table was dressed with fine silver. Four green suited waiters stood behind plain metal chairs. The General gestured to sit. Two of the waiters pulled out chairs for them as the others took their coats. This seemed strange. Mumley could not remember putting his coat on. As he sat, he

felt his wallet and keys out of place, as though someone had rifled through his pockets.

"I hope you don't mind our blue plate special," said the General. "I took the liberty of ordering for you, fois gras, caviar, and borscht. "Very democratic." He gestured and Svetlana entered with a snappy salute. "Dobri Svetlanka, mnyeh drooga, vince, vince†," uttered the General, returning the salute without getting up. The Ambassador instinctively rose as a waiter pulled out a chair for her. She wore a red banded, black billed, green Russian officer's cap that seemed wider than her shoulders. It had a shiny round red and gold star badge in the center as its only decoration. She removed it and tucked it under her arm, unleashing a cascade of blonde hair that was not evident inside the space helmet.

† Добрй Светланка, мне друга, внс, внс — Good Svetlana (affectionate nickname), my girlfriend, sit, sit

The Ambassador pondered the strangeness of her drab green uniform—buttoned along both sides like that of a band cadet, with two vertical bars and a little airplane on each side of her tight Mandarin collar to indicate that she was a captain and a pilot. Her long sleeved, worsted wool tunic was strangely wrinkled around her chest, as though it had originally been cut single breasted, but had been converted to double breasted to accommodate her ample chest. Atop her left breast, the simple gold star and red ribbon of the Hero of the Soviet Union Medal was her only decoration.

Lana placed her cap on the table beside Zhukov's. The green brims and black bills of both caps were identical. Only the size of the red hat band was different. The smaller band on Svetlana's cap made the brim seem ridiculously large compared to the crush cap preferred by American pilots.

The Ambassador was not used to seeing women wearing tall boots and trousers. Tucked into polished black leather knee boots, her puffy green worsted wool knickers seemed several sizes too big, as though they were meant to conceal an obese amount of cellulite—something her trim athletic figure obviously lacked. Mumley scanned her from her grossly inflated hips to her narrow unpadded shoulders, then felt embarrassed as his gaze met her icy blue eyes staring right back at him. She placed a napkin on her lap. He had never seen a woman dressed in such a preposterous fashion. What was he to make of this strangely pear shaped petite blond warrior?

"During the war, when she was a young girl," informed the General as he wolfed down some salmon and caviar hors d'overes a waiter had placed on the table . . . "Jump in," he insisted, putting food on her plate, then continued without losing his train of thought . . . "Lana was one of my Night Witches. "One time, she was shot down behind enemy lines in her obsolete PO-2 biplane. "To avoid capture, she took off her helmet and flight suit and ran through the snow, wearing only a sweater and a cotton dress." He took another bite. "Rather than taking her prisoner," he continued with his mouth full, "when the Hitlerite soldiers saw her combat boots, which were only issued to pilots, they stripped her and stretched her nude body over a hay stack, holding her by her arms, legs, neck, and breasts. "They rubbed their frostbitten hands all over her smooth young skin and repeatedly enjoyed her delicate virgin womb until the snow of the motherland was stained red with her warm virgin blood."

Lana's features hardened, but she offered none of the shame and embarrassment a Western woman would if such a personal secret was discussed so openly. "She escaped and lead her squadron back to them the following night," boasted Zhukov, "armed with two one-hundred kilogram bombs. "Her bombing navigation was so exact, that when the Hitlerite position was overrun the following day, not one Hitlerlite soldier was found alive. "She may have lost her virtue, but she was awarded the Hero of the Soviet Union Medal . . . a worthy trade!" Svetlana looked down at the napkin on her lap with an expression of despair.

"An interesting story," replied Mumley, feigning relaxed indifference, not sure he wanted to concede that the pretty woman sitting before him was in any way credible.

"Svetlana is just like the Motherland," added the General as he lifted another hors d'overe. "She does not lie still and enjoy it when she is being raped. "She retaliates and kills her attacker. "Please tell the Ambassador about your combat with the American bomber Lana," ordered the General.

"Prah-stee-tyeh, myah pa-English-kee etah nyeh khah-rah-sho† ," the humiliated fighter pilot replied.

"Don't worry, he understands pa-Rooskie," Zhukov replied energetically.

"Ya bawrots-ya za mir," she began nervously. "I fight for peace," she repeated in heavily accented English. "Strana hochet mira. "The country wishes peace. "Ne ctan-oo opee-soe-vat Orenburg-skyu oo-sadoo, naw potchtee wlee-sheel-sya jeez-nee‡." Mumley did not understand her joke

† **Простите, моя по-английски ето не хорошо. — Excuse me, my English is not good.**

‡ **Не стану описывать оренбургскую осаду, но я почти лишился жизни — I will not try to describe the seige of Orenburg (Pushkin), but I was almost killed.**

so she continued, "Tovarich Leonov, 'Von wlyetit camawlyet Amerikanski, vector dvah dyeh-vyah-nostah,' roo-kovo-dee-le! "'Chtah sss vami, bistrah, bistrah,' ohn raz-gova-ree-val! "Ya klinool ee obrazo-vala, nee sss togo, nee sss sego . . . " She described the combat in great detail, moving her hands as fighter pilots do to show the maneuvers of her plane.

Ambassador Mumley did not understand Lana's Ukrainian accent very well and he had not seen the gun camera footage, but he read an account of the battle. Clearly, if Lana had not been there, she was well coached, and she was definitely a fighter pilot as she claimed. It would not have been appropriate for her to wear a Hero of the Soviet Union Medal if she had not earned it, even for a bogus NKVD sponsored diplomatic disinformation campaign. As he looked into the glazed icy blue eyes telling the story with cold indifference, he began to feel he should not immediately discredit what the adorable young woman in the strange green uniform had to say.

Suddenly Lana burst into tears crying, "Sergei oomreht poss-le trusosti bejalee sss polya beet-voeet," and stopped! Not fully understanding the language, Mumley had not been paying attention. He thought he had heard her saying something about her wingman being shot down, but he was thinking more about what he was going to say to the General. Her lecture gave him some time to think. He offered her his handkerchief, but she refused it, preferring to wipe her eyes with her fingers. She smeared the clear salty drops on her trousers, even though she was wearing a napkin on the other knee. "Prahsteetyeh," she said as she rose from the table, grabbing her long tresses with her right hand and scooping them into her cap, which she pulled over her head with her left hand in a well practiced motion. She dropped her napkin on the floor as she stood and saluted, before padding briskly out of the room.

"Sergei, her lover, was shot down," said the General. A waiter stooped to pick up the napkin. "You may tell the commander of your reconnaissance bomber seven hundred fifty

† Сергеи умреет после трусости бежали с поля битвы! — Sergei died after the coward fled from the battlefield!

three that he has a confirmed kill. "Perhaps you will now believe
me when I tell you that we know about your plans to bomb our
new rocket site at Leninsk near the village of Tyura Tam, also
near Baikonur. "Our own reconnaissance aircraft has photographed your bomber on the ground at Thule." The Ambassador smiled incredulously at the outrageous accusation. Zhukov
continued, "We know about the successful ground level
penetration and the risking of several lives on a civilian airliner
that your flying battleship flew dangerously in formation with to
get past our radars. "You are trying to do this again with a
doomsday bomb."

"How can you possibly know that," Mumley snapped?

"We have our sources," insisted the General.

"Even if it was true, there's nothing I can do about it
here," the Ambassador replied.

"There is a car waiting to take you back to your embassy,"
said the General.

"Shall we not finish this fine dinner?"

"No, we should go now." The General clapped his hands
and the dinner disappeared in the hands of the waiters. "After
you." The General showed the Ambassador to the door as other
waiters helped them with their coats.

Svetlana was waiting in the car. She said nothing as they
sat down next to her. Although he was a married man, Ambassador Mumley could not help but feel a little aroused sitting next
to such an athletic, attractive, and unattached woman. He
wondered if the General might be discretely offering her services
to get what he wanted. Two other cars, another Zil and a Chaika
pulled ahead and behind.

With a siren blaring, the small motorcade bumped and
thumped over the rough cobbled Moscow streets at better than
one hundred miles per hour. Mumley was terrified, as the car
lurched violently from side to side. It made sharp turns at
impossible speeds. The General and Svetlana relaxed comfortably as though such reckless driving was normal. There were
several close calls with pedestrians and donkey carts.

Upon arriving, they and two other Russians rode the elevator to the top floor of the embassy and went directly into Mumley's richly paneled office. Mumley's secretary and translater were waiting. "What's the name of the new Air Force Attaché again," demanded the Ambassador?

"That would be Lieutenant Colonel Stiles," answered the secretary.

"Get him up here!"

"I demand that you contact the President," insisted Zhukov. He and Lana sat before an elegant birdseye maple desk topped by four telephones in front of a library of book shelves. The two other Russians stood behind.

"Hold your horses," said the Ambassador as he motioned for the other men to sit. "We don't even know what this mission is about." When Stiles entered, he said, "Send the following message to Art Radford, CJCS . . . begin . . . "Art, we have a situation, stop. "Marshal Zhukov is in my office right now and he thinks you have a mission to preemptively disable one of their rocket sites in Kazakhstan, stop. "Go! "Send it now!" Stiles rushed out of the office. The two Russian aides pulled chairs from against the wall and sat behind Zhukov. Mumley's aides did the same. They stared at each other with icy silence until Stiles returned and placed a message on Mumley's desk. "Art Radford is on his way to the White House," informed Mumley. General Zhukov gasped and began to pant heavily, holding his chest as though his heart was palpating.

НЙКСН

NIXON

HOW TO START WORLD WAR III

April 1956

In Washington, a black limousine pulled between the red budded cherry trees guarding the west wing of the White House. A Marine opened the door of the car. Admiral Radford walked briskly into the war room, stopping only to remove his black Navy overcoat, which he handed to a secretary. Nixon and the President were already inside with Wilson and Dulles, meeting with some of the other high brass.

"Well somebody unzipped their pants and shot their shit over to the Russians," said Radford as he barged into the meeting.

"Do they know the route," asked Eisenhower?

"I don't think so," answered the Admiral, "Bernard was not very specific."

"You know that makes this a high risk mission."

"We contemplated that, that's why we chose an expendable aircraft."

"What do you mean expendable," asked the President?

The Vice President interrupted before Radford could answer: "These are the same clowns that got radiation exposure from the Cherokee Two Shot in Operation Red Wing. "They were supposed to stay fifty miles away until after the blast and then collect dust samples, but the damn fools blundered almost directly over the fireball as it went off."

"Oh God," uttered the President! "Somebody told me something about that, but no one told me how that all turned out. "So these guys got sick?"

"According to the flight surgeons, they'll develop enlarged thyroids, hair loss, and impotence just like those Japanese fishermen after the Bravo shot . . . the whole radio-active shebang," answered the Vice President.

"Damn," exclaimed Eisenhower! "So you decided to send people who are going to die anyway?"

"It beats dying of cancer," quipped Nixon.

"I doubt they're going to get cancer," the Admiral contradicted, but at least they know what they are getting into. "There is nobody more experienced at surviving a nuclear blast."

"Well, you make sure that Aircraft Commander is a Lieutenant Colonel by the time he gets back and even if he doesn't get back," ordered the President.

"Eye eye Sir," said the Admiral. "It's already been done. "I'll call Curt and make the arrangements for some kind of ceremony if they don't make it back."

"You don't think any of them could have gotten their wives pregnant between then and now do you," asked the President, "you know with the radiation exposure I mean?"

"Doubtful," answered Radford.

"So what do you want to do now, scratch the mission?"

"We can't," protested Wilson, the Secretary of Defense. "If we scratch the mission we are left with the same problem: "The Russians will have threatening technology that we will eventually have to deal with one way or another. "We'll never get another chance with Khrushchev out of the country."

"He's still in London?"

"Not for long," interrupted Dulles. "We just got word that he and President Bulgannin are leaving."

"I thought they were supposed to stay with Anthony for two more days at Chequers," stated the President incredulously. "I can't believe they'd break up a summit meeting because one of our bombers is sitting in Thule."

"Its not that," said Dulles, "there's been a spy incident."

"What now?"

"A certain Commander Crabbe from the Royal Navy was found drowned in the Thames just downstream of the Russian cruiser. "The diving lung he was wearing went missing and the cruiser is weighing anchor as we speak."

"Jesus! "So the god damn Russians have one of those now," cursed the President?

"That's not the worst of it," continued the Secretary of State, "Khruschev bragged to Mrs. Eden, you know, Winston's niece, that his R5 rockets can now reach London. They have Academician Kurchatov with them."

"My god! "Telling the Prime Minister's wife, Churchill's niece, that he can destroy London with the father of the Soviet A-bomb standing right beside him," Eisenhower shouted? He lowered his head into his hands with a look of despair. "That's bold! "Real bold!"

"Remember your blood pressure Dave," insisted the Vice President. "This guy obviously does not believe in subtle diplomacy. "What are you going to tell Bern?"

"Oh jeez, this is getting out of hand," said the President. "Lets call it off."

"We might not be able to," said Radford. "They're on the other side of the North Pole by now. "The signal will be lost because of atmospheric skip."

"I don't care! "Have all stations broadcast the recall code immediately!"

"Eye eye Sir," obeyed Radford. He saluted as he got up and left the room.

The President pressed a button under the table and said, "Send a message to Bernard Mumley in Moscow." He hung up the phone. A red phone on the table buzzed and he picked it up and said, "Begin message . . . Hello Bern, stop. "Everything is under control, stop. "There are no missions to concern yourself about, stop."

Lieutenant Colonel Stiles barged into Mumley's office and gave him a manila folder. "This just came in off the teletype, sir," he said. "I think it's an emergency war plan file on the mission you were talking about. "I'm sorry I didn't tear the sheets apart. "I thought you would want to see it right away."

The Ambassador first looked disturbed as he read the top sheet, then he looked surprised when he flipped through the others. They were joined together, top to bottom, in a long strip. "Why would he say there were no missions to concern myself about and then send this huge dossier which looks like they're trying start world war three?"

Stiles looked puzzled. "The dossier arrived before the message, sir," he explained.

"It did," asked Mumley quizzically?

Stiles nodded. "It came from the CJCS," he added. "The top one is from the White House.

Okay, send a reply," ordered the Ambassador, "Send . . . "Georg† is here personally in my office, stop. "He wants to talk, stop. "I think you had better listen, stop. "Will you talk to him, question mark? "Go!" Stiles ran out of the room. The General and the fighter pilot watched him leave.

The Ambassador and Zhukov starred at each other for another minute of icy silence until Stiles reentered and placed another message on Mumley's desk. The Ambassador frowned and said, "the President says there is nothing to discuss."

Zhukov raised his hand to his forehead and rubbed his eyes. Mumley studied him and said to Stiles, "Send another message. "Begin it . . . Dave, comma, this isn't just a missile program they've got there, stop. "It is much more than that, stop. "It is a man in space program, stop. "A few hours ago, comma, they took me to Zvyozdny Gorodok to see it, stop. "They have got the entire Red Air Force clustered around that missile site near Tyura Tam, stop. "One ship will never make it, stop. "You must call it off, exclamation point! "Go!" Stiles rushed out of the room.

Several minutes passed before Stiles returned. Mumley offered his guests coffee, but they refused. Finally, Stiles returned and placed a message on Mumley's desk. It read, "WE WILL NOT HAVE ANOTHER CHANCE WITH K. & B. OUT OF THE COUNTRY. Z. WILL NOT REPLY IN KIND WITH K. & B. IN LONDON. WE THINK IT IS AN ACCEPTABLE RISK. THE SHIP AND CREW ARE

†**Georg — pronounced Gay'org**

EXPENDABLE. RESPECTFULLY YOURS, DICK." The Ambassador turned pale and his hands shook when he read it.

"God," the Ambassador blasphemed! He pounded his desk with his fist. "They're serious!" Zhukov's hands began to shake as he closely studied he expression on Mumley's face. One of his aides whispered in his ear. Recognizing it might send the wrong signal diplomatically, the General steeled his expression, and drummed the arm of his chair with his shaking fingers, trying to look impatient. The Ambassador saw right through the posturing. Zhukov was obviously nervous and Mumley could see that.

"Send another message," Mumley hollered at Stiles. This time he wrote it down himself. Stiles again left the room. Zhukov and Mumley starred at each other silently. When Stiles returned, the message read, "DEAR BERN. I DO NOT THINK GLORY IS THE RIGHT WORD. IT DOES NOT MATTER IF THEY SUCCEED OR FAIL. THE PURPOSE OF THIS EXERCISE IS TO INTIMIDATE THEM A BIT, SORT OF LIKE GOLIATH BEATING HIS SHIELD. TELL Z. THEY MUST STOP WHAT THEY ARE DOING, OR ELSE. RESPECTFULLY YOURS, DICK."

The Ambassador shook his head nervously and said, "They are refusing to cancel the mission."

"What," the Russian answered! "You can't be serious! "Do you know what this will mean? "This will mean war!" Lana underscored his words with a look of fear across her pretty face, followed by steely determination.

"The Vice President said you have to stop your missile program," the Ambassador said flatly. "If this mission for some reason does not get through, next time we will send a B-52."

"This is outrageous," shouted Zhukov! "We will not stop our space program just because the yankee imperialists give us their command. "Do you think we Slavs were born just to be ordered around by your master race? "Svetlana will become the first woman to fly into outer space. "It is her destiny. "Nothing you can do will change that." Lana starred into the Ambassador's brown eyes with her jewel-like ice blue eyes firmly and emotively.

"What do you intend to do," asked the Ambassador?

"Shoot it down of course," answered Zhukov! "What would you do?"

"And if you can't shoot it down?"

"Then we retaliate!"

"Send another message," Mumley gruffly commanded Stiles! He wrote it down. "Here," he said, as he gave it to him.

Stiles read it. It said, *"Dear Dick, You know what happened to Goliath! Signed BM."* "Yes Sir," obeyed Stiles, saluting! He bent down and whispered into Mumley's ear.

"I think you should at least try to intercept it and divert it before it enters your airspace," advised the Ambassador after Stiles left the room.

"The Soyuz Soviet-ski Socialistic-skya Republic is the largest country on Earth," reminded the General. "Our northern border is a frozen waste. "It is not possible to deploy interceptors there. "If you would tell me the flight plan and the route the bomber will follow, it may be possible to send Lana to find it before it enters our territory and turn it back, but I should warn you, if your ship enters, we will shoot it without question."

"I want you to know that I personally feel this mission is a mistake," confided the Ambassador. The information you requested is classified and I don't have access.

"Then I suggest you get in touch with someone who does have access," insisted the General.

Mumley turned to Stiles and said "Send a message to Curt LeMay in Omaha. "Say, Marshal Zhukov knows about the mission to Tyura Tam, stop. "He will intercept peacefully outside border, stop. "Need flight plan, stop." Stiles immediately left. When he returned, the Ambassador read the message. It said: "L. IS TRAVELING TO THE NATIONAL WAR COLLEGE TO GIVE A SPEECH TITLED, "DECISIVE VICTORY IN A NUCLEAR WAR." HE IS CURRENTLY ENROUTE AND CANNOT BE REACHED. WILL FORWARD MESSAGE WHEN NEXT IN CONTACT. SINCERELY, HQSAC."

Mumley placed his forehead in his hands looking glum. He studied the message for a long time. Zhukov studied Mumley's face. The Ambassador closed his eyes, then pinched the bridge of his nose and said, "He's on his way to the National war college to give a speech titled, 'Decisive Victory in a Nuclear War.'" Zhukov gasped. There was a long silence, then Mumley said to Stiles, "Send the same message to General Allen at Carswell Air Force Base in Fort Worth."

When Stiles returned and gave Mumley a new message, the Ambassador jumped all over him and shouted, "What do you mean General Allen has the day off! "He's a wing commander. "He isn't allowed to visit his momma's favorite juke joint without the President knowing about it!" Mumley looked down and studied the open file folder on his desk. "Repeat the same message to Colonel Michael Peterson at the same location." After Stiles left the room, Mumley looked up and remarked to Zhukov, "For a country about to start a nuclear war, there sure are a lot of guys on vacation."

Svetlana murmured something to Zhukov in Russian. "Who can blame them," answered the General? "If I were them, I would like to flee as far into the countryside as I could."

When Stiles returned, he slowly shook his head. Mumley stared at him angrily and asked, "No answer?" Stiles shook his head. "All right," Mumley continued, "I want you to arrange a person to person telephone call to General Allen or Colonel Peterson at home. "They're assigned to Carswell Air Force Base, so if they live off base, they should have listings in the Fort Worth Texas telephone directory."

"A transatlantic telephone call," the Lieutenant Colonel asked in disbelief?"

"Yes! "Just like we did with the President."

"That will take some doing, sir."

"Then you had better get started! "And if you can't get though to either of them, I want you to ring the home of Lieutenant Colonel Henry Johns, the guy who, according to this dossier, is in personal command of this mission."

"Yessir," answered Stiles. He left the room.

THE HOUSEWIFE
April 1956

Linda Johns was washing some negligée in her bathroom sink when the telephone rang. "Long distance person to person call for Major or Mrs. Henry Johns," announced the operator."

"I'm Mrs. Johns," answered Linda.

"One minute," said the operator.

"Hello, Mrs. Johns," a barely discernible scratchy voice said through the static in the long phone line. Linda had never heard such a bad connection before. It sounded like the voice of a clown, with sirens and bells ringing in the background.

"Can you speak up or turn those bells off," she asked?

"This is Lieutenant Colonel Frank Stiles of the United States Embassy in Moscow," the voice said, "Ambassador Mumley would like to speak to you."

"All right," Linda answered, certain it was some kind of joke.

"Hello, Mrs. Johns, I'm Bernard Mumley, the Ambassador to the Soviet Union in Moscow, would you mind if I asked you a few questions," the clown voice asked with more bells and sirens?

"Okay," she answered sheepishly with a wide grin.

"Hello," the Ambassador repeated, "would you mind if I asked you a few questions?"

"OKAY," she hollered!

"It is imperative that you answer my questions honestly," the clown continued. "Your husband's life may be in danger."

"What is this about? "Is Hank in trouble," shouted Linda, waiting for the punch line?

"He is in grave danger. "I must speak to Colonel Michael Peterson immediately. The clown changed into a threatening robot in mid sentence. "Do you know where he can be found," asked the robot? The sirens blaring through the receiver grew louder. Linda suddenly felt afraid. For a moment she was at a loss for words.

"He isn't here," she said, wondering why anyone would expect to find the Colonel at her house.

"Do you know where he is," asked the robot?

"At home, unless he and Phyllis went somewhere," she guessed. "I think it's his day off."

"Can you get him? "He doesn't have a telephone."

Beginning to worry that the call was not a joke, Linda answered, "I can try, but it will take a long time. "He lives down the hill. "Can I call you back?"

"No, don't hang up," implored the robot! "Just leave the telephone receiver on a table and go and get him."

"Are you sure? "The operator said it was long distance."

"Don't worry," I'm paying for it, the robot insisted. "Go get Colonel Peterson now!"

"Okay, I'm laying the phone on the desk." Linda put down the receiver and ran out the door, across the lawn, and down the hill to Phyllis Peterson's house.

She was out of breath when she arrived at the Petersons'. She knocked violently. Phyllis came to the door. "Phyl, there is a man on the telephone who wants to talk to Mike," she shouted through the screen. "He has a really weird voice and he says Hank is in trouble."

"Mike," Phyllis yelled, "Mike!"

"I'm in the back," a male voice yelled.

"Come to the door," shouted Phyllis. "Hurry!" Colonel Peterson was out of uniform, wearing just a white tank top undershirt and some old, paint spattered, green Army Air Corps pants.

"Mike," said Linda, "there is an ambassador on the phone

who says Hank is in trouble, you need to come and talk to him quick."

"An ambassador? "It must be some teen-ager playing a prank."

"Please Mike, just talk to him," begged Linda. "He's got me really worried!"

"Mike, go," said Phyllis, "it will only take ten minutes."

Linda ran back to her house. The Colonel walked slowly up the brown grass hill behind her, carefully avoiding the tall green tufts of winter clover where rattlesnakes sometimes hide. As Peterson approached the Johns' bungalow, Linda waved and said, "Come in, come in," and then said into the phone, "He's here." She gave the phone to Peterson.

The Colonel said, "This is Mike Peterson." He grunted several times, then said, "Sir, I'm not at liberty to discuss that information. "I'm not even sure I know who you are. "I'm sorry."

"Your men are in trouble," shouted Mumley five thousand miles away in front of the surprised Russians. "They're being set up for an ambush. "They'll never make it to their target. "I need a coded message sent with the waypoint coordinates from eight eleven's emergency war plan route."

The handsome old General and beautiful fighter pilot watched him speak with studied interest. Zhukov nervously clasped and unclasped his fingers. Svetlana, her elbows on her knees, nervously twirled her hat in her hands, occasionally batting her long blonde hair back behind her shoulders as it fell forward.

"I'm sorry I am not at liberty to divulge that information," answered the Colonel into Linda's phone. "This is some kind of loyalty test right? "Are you one of J. Edgar Hoover's men from the FBI? "Where are you calling from?"

"This is not a loyalty test," the robot threatened, turning back into a clown! "I'm calling from Moscow."

"An overseas telephone call? "That's impossible!"

"We have a full duplex connection over the short wave,"

the clown explained. "We usually talk this way only with the President."

"Even if what you say was true, I couldn't beam a recall code from here," said Peterson. "There's too much skip. "You need to contact Omaha."

"LeMay is out to lunch, so is Allen, so are you. "Don't you see SAC has no intention of issuing a recall order," the clown implored over the sirens, bells, and whistles?

"No, I don't see!" Peterson furrowed his brow. "This is damned preposterous! Linda became upset. She would never have allowed such language in her home under normal circumstances. She glared at Peterson with a look of both worry and anger. "How do you know the Russians found out about it," asked Peterson?

"Marshal Zhukov, the Soviet Minister of Defense is right here in my office right now along with the fighter pilot that shot you down."

"Oh yeah," quipped Peterson? "That bird was shot down by my co-pilot, Lieutenant Gordon Grant. "You can ask him about it when he gets home. "We both saw it on fire and tumbling out of control."

"Nevertheless, she survived . . . and if you don't get me those recall codes," threatened the robot, "your co-pilot won't be coming back!"

Not sure he heard correctly, Peterson asked, "What do you mean, 'she?'"

"The pilot that shot you down was a woman," teased the clown.

"This is fucking ridiculous," Peterson shouted! "I don't know who you are, or who put you up to this, but if I find out and it turns out you are military, you will be marching the stockade for a long long time!" He slammed down the phone. "I'm sorry Linda," he added.

"Wait," shouted Mumley as he heard a loud click! He looked up from his desk and met the General's eyes with a look of despair as he slowly hung up the phone.

"What will you do now," asked Zhukov?

Mumley picked up his phone and said, "I was cut off. "Ring that number again. "Connect me as soon as it answers!"

A half hour later, Linda Johns' phone rang again. She answered. The operator told her it was a long distance call and asked her to wait.

Before she could speak, another clown voice said, "This is Colonel Stiles again. "Please don't hang up. "Your husband is in great danger!"

"You must think I'm just a naïve little housewife," answered Linda. "Let me tell you we've been in the military a long time and we've had these pranks before. "Colonel Peterson didn't believe you. "What makes you think I will?"

"Let me connect you with the Ambassador. "One moment . . ."

"Misses Johns, Did your husband ever tell you how he came to lose his last two ships," asked Mumley over the bells and sirens?

"No. "Of course not. "My husband would never discuss classified information."

"The ship was not the only thing destroyed."

"What do you mean?"

"I shouldn't be telling you this over an unsecured phone line," said the Ambassador, reading from the dossier on his desk, "but according to your husband's medical records, he has been exposed to radioactivity."

"Are you still there," Mumley asked?

"Ugh huh," said Linda. She wiped a tear from her eye. "If this is a joke, I swear you will pay for this," she threatened.

"Are you all right?"

"I think so," said Linda. "Hank never said anything to me about any radiation. "I expect, if it were true, we would hear from his flight surgeon, not from somebody I've never met over the telephone."

"I'm sorry to have to be the one to tell you," said Mumley. "The Vice President is worried that if your husband

gets cancer, a lot of other servicemen might become afraid of
nuclear weapons and leave the military. Then there would be
no one left to fight a nuclear war. He asked your husband to
volunteer for a dangerous mission that he might not return
from.

"Hank is the type of officer who will to do anything for
his country," volunteered Linda.

"Something has gone wrong with his mission and it is
very important that Colonel Peterson send me the coded information I need to set it right. "Your husband belongs at home
with you, not flying halfway around the world with an 'H' bomb
slung behind his seat." Mumley was becoming a robot again.

"Flying around the world with an H-bomb slung behind
his seat is his job mister," countered Linda, "and he does it very
well."

"Do you think they will let him fly when he gets cancer,"
asked the robot? The question made her weep. "Even if he
survives being shot down over Russia," the torturous voice
continued, "they will put him on trial as a spy and you will never
see him again." The robot changed back into a clown.

"What can I do about it," asked Linda?

"Convince Colonel Peterson to send me the information
I need," insisted the clown. "Tell him as long as the message is
coded, it won't fall into the wrong hands. "Can you do that?"

"I'll tell the Colonel you called again," said Linda.

"I'm hanging up the phone now," said the clown. "Go
find Colonel Peterson."

"Okay," said Linda. She waited for a click and hung up
her phone.

Mumley looked into the eyes of the Russian General
and clasped his hands, then leaned back, spreading his elbows
with his hands behind his neck, giving him a quizzical look as if
to indicate that there was nothing more he could do.

"You were unsuccessful," asked Zhukov?

"The future of the world is in the hands of a West Texas
housewife."

Zhukov frowned and said, "During the Hitlerite seige of Leningrad in the Great Patriotic War, we had many incidents of cannibalism. "More than eight hundred people were found with human flesh in their possession, and that was just the ones we caught. "One housewife had the bodies of three infants in a large sack. "I had to order a twenty four hour guard on all of the cemeteries. "This is the way it will be in both of our countries in two, maybe three, months." Mumley stared at him intently. "STILL," Zhukov shouted abruptly, "WE ATTACKED!" The Ambassador's aides jumped in their seats. "We drove the fascists back," he continued. "I ordered skis mounted on my Yak fighters to destroy them from the air. "I assure you Ambassador, whatever your President has planned for us, no matter how badly we are harmed, even if we are starving, I will retaliate!"

Linda hurried back to the Petersons'. Phyllis opened the door. "Linda, what's the matter," she asked? They embraced tearfully.

"The Ambassador called back again," Linda wailed. "He said Hank has cancer and he is going to be shot down and be tried as a spy if Mike doesn't give him the information he needs. "He said as long as the message is coded, it won't fall into the wrong hands. "Why can't he do something?" Linda grabbed Phyllis and sobbed on her shoulder.

"Mike is in the back yard," said Phyllis. "I'll have a talk with him. "Why don't you just sit down in front of the television? Phyllis pulled Linda over to her husband's big easy chair and pushed her down into it. "I Love Lucy will come on in about an hour. "You just relax. "I'll ask Mike." As the television warmed up, the picture got larger and larger until a black and white test pattern could be seen.

Phyllis ran into the back yard shouting, "Why can't you send that message? "Linda is very upset. "Its for an ambassador, for Christ's sake!"

"That was no ambassador," answered the underdressed squadron commander, angered as he tried to relax in a hammock stretched between two trees on the shore of the lake. "A real ambassador would use normal channels. "It was probably one of Senator McCarthy's people from the Committee on Un-American Activities, or one of J. Edgar Hoover's people from the FBI trying to see if I would divulge classified information. "Hank and I had an argument on our last trip. "I didn't mention it in my report, but I told General Allen about it. "If word about that got around, someone at the Pentagon might question if Hank was the best qualified for this mission. "This is some kind of test. "Sending a message like that would prove that I didn't trust Hank or that one of us was a Commie or a traitor."

"And what if it really was a real ambassador," asked Phyllis? "Are you just going to let Hank and the rest of the boys be shot down and captured?

"It couldn't have been. "It's impossible to make a phone call like that from a foreign country. "In fact, I read in the paper that they are supposed to try to lay a submarine telephone cable across the Atlantic this summer. "Maybe next year it will be possible, but I'll bet only millionaires and presidents will be able to use it." "Whoever it was that called her was stateside . . . that's for sure! "As for Hank, he knows the risks."

"What if they sent the call by radio? "How can it hurt to send a coded message?"

"I really would be a Communist sympathizer if I did that. "The Russians might have broken the code. "That could have been a Communist agent just as easily as the FBI. "Now that you mention it, the connection was bad enough, I could believe they had sent it over the short wave."

"That explains it then. "So send it in a new code."

"I can't without authorization from General Allen or General LeMay, so that's the end of it."

"NO THAT'S NOT THE END OF IT," shouted Phyllis! "You don't know what I went through while you lost on that submarine. "I couldn't sleep for three days! "When they said only fifteen had been rescued, they wouldn't tell us who. "I cried and cried; I was so worried. "When the Chaplain finally came next door to Loretta, I was actually relieved to hear that

Merril was killed because it meant you were all right.

"Loretta cried so much," Phyllis continued, "she collapsed completely. "She couldn't walk or get off the floor. "I had to drag her into bed. "She wouldn't let go and I had to spend the night with her since she didn't have anyone else. "Do you know she threatened to kill herself? "And now they are doing the same thing to Linda! "I don't care if it is the Committee on Un-American Activities, what they're doing to Linda is evil and wrong and you are not going to just lay there in that hammock while she cries her eyes out! "Do something!"

"What do you want me to do," the Colonel barked angrily, "jeopardize my career? "It's a hoax!"

"I don't care if it is a hoax," Phyllis threatened, "its a damned cruel thing to do to a woman who's husband is away on a mission and you are not going to have dinner, breakfast, or lunch tomorrow until you do something about it!"

"WHAT DO YOU WANT ME TO DO," he hollered? "ITS MY DAY OFF!"

"I don't know, something, anything, start an investigation!"

"Look honey, its just a few more months and we'll have our twenty five years in, then I can retire and we will be free. "We can do whatever we want, even move to the Bahamas if you want. "We could even buy that shoe store in downtown Fort Worth you were telling me about, and set Denise up in a good business. "I don't want to risk all that now. "I've worked too hard for too long."

"How could you live with yourself, knowing your best friend had died," asked Phyllis? "Do you think you could enjoy retirement? "It would haunt you. "Who do we know in the Bahamas?"

"This is silly," argued the Squadron Commander. "There is a lot that haunts me . . . from the war . . . buddies killed. "I have best friends all over country, 'cause we move so much. "I'm tired of it Phyl. "I've done my part. "I could get a job at Convair, and with our Air Force pension, we could live really well, even buy this bungalow if you want to."

"Oh Mike, I don't want to live here with atomic bombers flying over the house all the time, rattling the dishes so loud I have to cover my ears. "I want to live somewhere safe. "I'm tired of sleepless nights waiting for you to come back from your damned missions."

"Well, we'll move away then, or we can travel," answered the Colonel. "We can buy one of those trailers to tow behind the car and live a vagabond life, but we need our military pension to do it. "There's just too much risk to break the rules."

"What about Linda and Bobby? "How will they live?"

"They'll be fine. "Hank'll be fine. "You'll see, and if anything did go wrong, Linda would get a pension just like Shirley and Loretta."

Phyllis burst into tears. "How would I ever love you? "This isn't the man I married! "Lieutenant Michael Peterson would never have put his own selfish needs ahead of his men. "He would have done what he knows is right."

"This is bigger than all of us Phyl. "I wish I could tell you where Hank is going and what he is doing, but I can't. "Its a very important mission. "You could even say that it is so important that the future of the world depends on it. "It's that important!"

"I know its important, honey, but Linda's feelings are important too. "It's wrong for them to put her through this."

"What I am doing is what is right. "Things have changed Phyl. "You don't know how dangerous Russia has become. "If you did, it would frighten you out of your wits. "I think it's terrible what they're doing to Linda, but it has to be done to protect our country. "What Hank is doing will protect all of us. "It's a really heroic thing he is doing. "I even asked to lead the mission myself. "The sacrifices Hank and Linda are making is just part of being in the modern military. "It's no different than in the war. "This is war. "We're trying to prevent the battle of Armageddon!"

"They are asking for too much, Mike."

"The Bible does not say The Tribulation is going to be easy, honey. "The world is an evil place. "Don't you think those Jews that died in the Nazi camps had plans too? "Didn't they plan for their retirement? "Look what happened to them! "There are powers bigger than us, beyond our control."

"Are you saying the Communists can defeat the United States," asked Phyllis?

"They can only defeat us if we let them," asserted the Colonel. "God gave us the power to make the world however we want it to be. "It is our duty to prepare it for the coming of Christ."

"If you are so powerful, then why can't you help Linda?"

"The opinion of a squadron commander doesn't count for much," replied Peterson. "Only the Joint Chiefs have that power. "I'm sorry, there is nothing I can do."

"I can't live like this," Phyllis replied meekly, her voice trembling, not sure how her husband would respond to such a threat: "You have to do something," she added tearfully."

"There's nothing I can do," he answered.

"You can go to the base and talk to somebody. "Maybe someone will listen. "Maybe you can call the Joint Chiefs."

"And what if it's nothing," answered the Colonel? "I'd have egg all over my face. "I'm telling you it's a Devil's trick!"

"Do you really think they would take away your pension over a phone call?"

"They could demote me for wasting their time."

"So what, if our pension is less if the world is coming to an end? "We're talking about Linda!"

"But Phyl, don't you see, I just met the President. "The President! "That means I'm next on the promotion list. "By next year, I could be a brigadier! "Do you know how much difference that will make in our pay, our retirement? . . . and they'll listen to me then. "I'll have a say!"

"You'll be a great general, Mike, but what kind of general abandons his men? "It was Merril's mission. "He was the one who should have met the President, not you, but he died, and now Loretta is a widow, forgotten. "If the President trusts you enough to make you a general, shouldn't they trust you to ask questions when something strange is going on? "Wouldn't it be worth the piece of mind to know you did all you could, no matter what the price? "The best generals put their men first."

"The best generals put their country first," corrected the Squadron Commander!

"What if that man really is an ambassador and he really did call you over the radio and the President found out you did nothing to help him? "How do you know someone in our government isn't making a big mistake by ordering this mission?"

"Okay," Peterson answered with pursed lips, "I know a way to settle this. "I'll go to the base and send a message to the Air Force attaché at the embassy in Moscow. "I'll have to wire the Pentagon to find out who that is. "If the Ambassador's code name is not on the reply, I'll wire the attaché that someone impersonating the Ambassador has been tormenting the wives of my flight crews, and suggest that I am sorry to bother them and that I'm only conducting an investigation. "When General Allen bawls me out for wasting their time, I'll hear not one more word about this from you. "Agreed?"

"Agreed," said Phyllis.

"Get my uniform ready!"

"It's already spread out on the bed."

An hour later, Stiles burst into the Ambassador's office. "We just got a message from Colonel Peterson," he shouted!

Send the same message as before with my code name on it," ordered Mumley.

Zhukov and Svetlana had been fidgeting in their seats for almost two hours. They jumped to attention when Stiles returned, shouting, "I have the flight plan! "Someone at the CJCS sent a confirmation code."

"Give it to me," demanded Zhukov!

"Just a minute," insisted Mumley! "Was it Radford," he asked Stiles?

"I don't know, sir," answered Stiles. "It was from his office."

Mumley read the grid coordinates from the coded message and compared it to a small emergency war plan chart which his secretary retrieved from a desk drawer. Stiles converted the coordinates into latitude and longitude. "Get me a map," demanded the Ambassador! A secretary found a Mercator projection of the Soviet Union on a bookshelf behind him and unfolded it. Stiles marked an "X".

Ambassador Mumley read Peterson's message aloud, "I WANT YOU TO KNOW, MR. AMBASSADOR, THAT I AM RISKING MY CAREER TO GIVE YOU THIS INFORMATION." Then he looked up, faced Zhukov, and asked, "Do you give me your word that you will intercept our ship outside of your border and escort it safely away from your airspace?"

"Yes Bernard," answered the Russian, "that is what we have agreed." He and Svetlana rose. Mumley offered his hand.

The General shook hands as he received the map and passed it to Svetlana.

"Vee mnyeh mozheh-teh pahkah-zaht na kahrt-yeh gdyeh do waypointy," she asked?

"What are the waypoints," translated Zhukov? "Where will they be coming from? "Lana must be able to distinguish it from diversionary aircraft, if you send a squadron of B-47's and tanker aircraft like last time."

Mumley beckoned to have the map back. He drew two dots connected by a line through the "X" on the map and gave it back to the General. The General took one look and thrust it into Svetlana's chest.

"Noo, polnoie hod†," he barked!

"Yest Tovarich," Svetlana answered with a snappy salute! "Ya na ekhat na okhotoo‡!" She folded the map, gathered her hair, scooping it under her cap, then clicked her heels and saluted sharply as she turned and left.

"Von, marsh∗," ordered Zhukov! The beautiful pilot ran out of the office headlong, with much clomping of boots, and disappeared down the stairs.

† Ну, Полный ход! — Well, full speed!
‡ Ест Товаричь! . . . Я ехать на охоту! — Yes, (I have it) comrade! . . . I leave for the hunt!
∗ Вон, Марш! — Out, March!

С
С
С
Р

ЗУКОВ!

CONVERSATION WITH THE ENEMY

April 1956

"Can we finish our dinner," asked the Ambassador? "We too have a fine dining room."

"Of course Bernard," said Zhukov. "If Lana does not find your bomber, it may be some time before we are again able to dine together.

The Ambassador lead Marshal Zhukov down a hallway dressed with photos of the many historic meetings between American and Soviet leaders. Through a heavy wooden door on one side, was a small carpeted wood paneled dining room with a long rectangular mahogany table in the center. Mumley motioned with his hand for Zhukov to enter first, then stood in the doorway to prevent his aides from entering. With a nod, he signaled his secretary and translator to leave and beckoned Stiles to come in. The kitchen staff was not prepared at that time of the night, so they waited. Mumley pulled out a seat for the General and nodded at Stiles, who pulled out his own seat. "How long will it take Svetlana to get to the point of interception," asked the Ambassador?

"About as long as dinner," Zhukov answered as he took his seat, "then I must go to the defense ministry to prepare for the alternative if Lana fails to find your bomber." He unfolded his napkin. Mumley and Stiles did also.

"Fois gras, borsht, and caviar," ordered Mumley, as the waiter finally entered the dining room after a stifling silence. The waiter clicked his heels and exited through swinging double doors. "Where did you learn English, Georg?"

"In Spain," Zhukov answered. "There were Americans under my command . . . pilots."

"Oh yes," said Mumley, "they flew there to fly the 'fly,' the legendary Moska."

"Da, you know your history very well," complimented the General. "The Ilyushin Sixteen was the most advanced airplane in the world at the time. "Pilots came from all over the world to fly it."

"How did our people compare to your pilots?"

"Some were very good, like Albert Baumler, Frank Tinker, and Whitey Dahl. "I also attended an English course at Moscow University in preparation for last year's meeting with your President in Geneva."

"Yes, so you could refuse the President's Open Skies Initiative in a language he could understand."

"We cannot allow you to fly your bombs over our territory. "We have already seen what your bombers can do . . . in Korea." Zhukov turned to Stiles and said, "I understand you were a pilot in the war against the Japanese."

Flattered that the Soviet Defense Minister would be knowledgeable about his personal history, Stiles was surprised and hardly knew what to say. "I only lasted one mission," he answered meekly. "My B-29 was shot down during the firebombing of Tokyo. "It was my first mission."

"Tell me what it was like," demanded the General.

Stiles was nervous at being the center of attention. Mumley stared into his eyes piercingly, as if to warn what would happen if he said the wrong thing. The Ambassador knew from experience, that in a negotiation, Russians liked to feel out their adversaries weaknesses with social conversation. He began to regret allowing such an inexperienced officer to sit down at such an important diplomatic meeting, but he needed Stiles' personal knowledge of Air Force procedures. Not knowing what else to say, Stiles told the truth: "I was scared out of my wits. "The city was lit up like a forest fire with a hundred searchlights whirling around like a dozen Hollywood movies premiering at once."

"Hollywood movies," asked Zhukov, confused? "So the search lights found you?"

"As my bomb aimer was steering the ship to a black patch of ground that was not yet on fire, they coned us like an Indian teepee," Stiles continued.

"Aha, a cone of light beams."

"Yessir."

"What happened next," asked the Russian?

"Then there was a loud whump, whump, whump, and the ship rolled upside down! "I rang the alarm bells and climbed up through the bomb bay."

"Climbed up?"

"The ship was inverted."

"You were not hurt," asked the General, as the waiter placed two bowls of beet soup on the table in front of them?

"No sir, I landed on a tile roof, but my chute caught some wind and pulled me off, so I fell into the street. "It was the fall from the building that hurt, not my landing."

"What did the enemy do to you?"

"Fortunately, I was on the upwind side of town. "A large group of children surrounded me and started poking me with sticks and kicking. "Some old men wearing kimonos grabbed me by the arms, and I was dragged along by the mob to a police station, with my parachute carried along behind me like a bridal train."

"A train?"

"When women are married in America, they wear a long dress that drags on the floor called a bridal train," explained Mumley.

"Aha! "The daughters of capitalists and imperialists used to do that here in Russia also, like kings and queens. "It is a waste of scarce textiles. "You were then put in prison," the Field Marshal asked the light Colonel?

"I was sent to bury the dead," answered Stiles. "Over a hundred thousand people burned to death in that raid. "There were no bomb shelters in Japan. "The Emperor told them they would never be bombed. "People ran to the canals around the Imperial Palace and threw themselves into the water until the canals were packed full of people. "Most died of smoke inhalation. "As water was pumped out of the canals to fight the fires, the bodies were left standing upright as though they were still alive . . . a river of thousands and thousands of blackened heads and naked bodies, stretching for miles as far as the eye could see. "The smell was terrible."

"That is nothing," replied Zhukov. "In Kiev, we mined the buildings so that we could explode them if they were captured. "Eight thousand fascists were killed in that way, along with one hundred thousand of civilian traitors. "They were afraid to enter the buildings to bury their dead. "The wind was blowing from the West to the East, where we defenders were positioned. "For weeks, the stench got worse until enough dogs, rats, and ravens multiplied to devour the bodies. "In Stalingrad, there were so many frozen bodies that when spring came, we had to stack them up in a big pile with petrol and railroad sleepers mixed in to burn them. "That too makes a certain smell.

"I remember seeing one young girl," the Defense Minister reminisced, "a virgin of thrirteen or fourteen who was raped to death and left out in the open to freeze. "Her body froze naked in a provocative position. Her skin was pure white like a marble statue or a fallen angel with just a small dab of dark red frozen blood that had dripped from her tiny bare little womb. Three men placed her on top of the pile with her tiny nipples pointing at the sky. This drew the attention of other men who, thinking she might be still alive, were attracted by her smooth white skin, which sparkled in the sunlight because of the frost. When they lit the fire, her body thawed out. Her beautiful smooth skin browned and shriveled and emitted thick black smoke as it burned. "I fear we may both endure this sight and smell again if my Lana does not find your bomber."

"I was made to remove the bodies from the canal," continued Stiles, as though he had not heard anything Marshal Zhukov had said. "The Japanese had all removed their clothes as though they were taking a bath. "Ashes from the clothes were in a long pile of blackened soot along one side of the canal. "They were mostly women and children. "I had to pile up the bodies from some kind of school for teen-age girls. "I was made to lift the naked bodies out of the mud at the bottom of the canal. "Their legs had sunk knee deep in the muck and were held in place by suction. "Their faces were painted white, but blackened gray with soot. Their blood had pooled in their legs, so their normally yellow Japanese skin was drained white as if they were Caucasian.

"To get them out," continued the Lieutenant Colonel, "I sat on the shoulders of the girls behind them, and reached under their arms and breasts with my hands, pulling very hard. "This only made the ones I was sitting on sink deeper into the mud. "It was difficult because their bodies were so smooth and slippery. "The police were yelling and crying and pointing their pistols at me the whole time. "The only place I could get a grip on them was between their legs by putting my fingers in their pubes. "Some old women standing on the bank screamed when they saw what I was doing. "They couldn't decide whether to be angry or sad. "They just kept screaming. "I couldn't understand what the police were shouting at me." Stiles looked down at his plate. "They knocked me unconscious."

Zhukov laughed. "Do you have any children Colonel?"

"I have two daughters, General."

"Are they here in Moscow?"

"Yessir. "The little kids were the hardest for me emotionally, though they were easier to throw into the wagons."

"It seems you are well aquatinted with the horrors of war," said Zhukov. "It is too bad that I must make you do this again. "When we next meet, I will arrive with a bottle and we will drink a toast to Svetlana's success, or I will come with a gun, and you and your family will be arrested and brought to Khazahkstan to wash our dead for burial."

"We must drink a toast that Svetlana will be successful," suggested Mumley, pounding his chest with his fist as though he had indigestion. "Waiter, some vodka!" The waiter brought a crystal decanter and poured.

"Na okhotoo," cheered the General as he lifted his glass! "To the hunt!"

"To Svetlana, may she be the first Russian woman in space after the first American woman," toasted Mumley!

"To beautiful Svetlanka," replied Zhukov, "who will be the first woman to fly in space before the first American man or woman."

"To Svetlana," seconded Stiles, trying to be polite as he lifted his glass. They drank, then slowly slurped the blood red soup, consuming more than the usual amount of vodka.

"Georg," asked Mumley, "why are you doing this? "Why are you so intent on flying people into outer space? "There is nothing out there to see, not even air to breathe."

"Why are you so intent on violating our national borders with your flying naval vessels," answered the General?

"You have nuclear weapons. "We have to know if you are preparing for an attack."

"You have answered your own question," said Zhukov.

"So this great adventure, as you put it, is mainly for reconnaissance? "Your people will spy on us with telescopes and cameras from stations in outer space?"

"Just as you violate our borders to spy on us with your flying battleships," Zhukov explained. "America is the most powerful country on Earth. "I would even say you are invincible. "We must know when your bombers are coming so that our population can be prepared to take shelter."

"We do not violate your borders," Mumley asserted. "We fly above the internationally recognized three mile territorial limit."

Zhukov glared with anger and explosively shouted, "Not when you thunder over homes and churches at treetop level and endanger civilian airliners. "The Soyuz Soviet-ski Socialistic-skya Republic claims a two hundred mile territorial limit."

That's ridiculous! "Suppose we claimed a three hundred mile limit or a thousand mile limit. "How far into outer space do you plan to go to fly over our territory . . . to the moon? "Surely you know that any rocket powerful enough to carry a man over American territory is also powerful enough to carry an atom bomb. "If you will not permit us to fly over your territory, how will we see when your rockets are coming?"

"You will not see them."

"In other words, you leave us no choice but to destroy them preemptively before they are launched."

"Nyet mnya droog†! "You will see them only if you attack."

"C'mon Georg, you know this is a provocation. "The United States is a Democracy. "What do you think the American public will do when they discover there are atomic rockets aimed at their children, just twenty minutes away? "The people will go berserk! "They will demand to laugh our heads on poles if we allow you to get away with this. "No president could remain in power if he did nothing to counteract such a threat. "You leave us no choice but to destroy your test site before you are able to manufacture this technology."

"And what about our people," answered Zhukov? "You install your bomber bases in a ring all around our country, in Turkey, in Iraq, in Iran, in Korea, in Greenland, not to mention Germany and Japan. "Do you expect us to do nothing in the face of this threat? "How are we to defend ourselves from your B-47 and B-52 jet bombers?"

"The same way we defend ourselves from your Tu-95's and My-3's."

"Our aircraft are not a threat to you. "We have no forward bases for them to land or to refuel. "For our pilots, attacking the United States is tyurtam, suicide."

"They've done that before."

"They had to. "The facist bombers had to be stopped."

"That is why the Soviet Union has no friends. "You have no respect for life. "You threaten the world with Communist aggression." Stiles' hands began to shake.

† **Нет мне друг — No, my friend!**

"We have never attacked anyone," argued Zhukov. "In fact, last year we ceded our base in Port Arthur to the Chinese, but if you would kindly let our aircraft land and refuel from your base in Thule, we would be happy to violate your borders the same way you violate ours."

"Port Arthur is just two hundred miles from Peking," the Ambassador chided! "Of course you should have returned it. "Why did you wait so long? "What about Finland, Estonia, Latvia, Lithuania, Poland, and Romania? "Shouldn't they also be free from external rule?"

"They are just four hundred miles from Moscow. "What would you have us do, leave them in the hands of the fascists or allow you to build bases there as well? "We have annexed only those lands which were historically part of Russia. "It is against Marxist and Leninist thought for one country to invade another. "The people there were enthusiastic about socialism."

"Just as the people of Korea were enthusiastic? "You never gave those people any choice. "More than half of the POW's we captured did not want to return home to a Communist system. "The Lithuanians who spoke out against your conquest were arrested and sent to Siberia or shot!"

"That was in the past," apologized Zhukov. "Remember, I was the one who arrested Beria and I enjoyed that very much. "He was a monster who also killed many loyal Communists."

"And then you shot him without a trial."

"I didn't shoot him. "Batitsky did. "He was tried by the Supreme Soviet. "He was even able to vote to save himself, but he was outvoted. "The evidence against him was overwhelming. "Did you know that he raped the daughter of Malenkov's own driver? "The girl was only in the seventh grade! "We even obtained a list of one hundred young virgins he raped. "He used the same procedure on all of them. "He offered them wine with a sleeping potion mixed in it and raped them. "He was not man enough to win their hearts through chivalry. "He was incapable of making love. "He wanted only to see blood. "Pavel told me that Lev crawled and begged for mercy before he shot him. "Blood flowed out of Lev's twisted brain like a faucet and spattered Pavel's uniform. "Pavel stripped off the uniform and burned out the cell because it could never again be washed clean, stained with the ideas of a man like that."

"That is what is wrong with the Communist system," asserted Mumley. "A man like that would never rise to power in a democracy and I can't get a straight answer from the man who replaced him, because he keeps changing the subject!"

"Kak da? "Chtaw wle Truman? "Ya read in Pravda that President Truman's own wife Bess refused to live with him at the White House, the most beautiful palace in America! "He authorized the use of atomic weapons and napalm on unarmed civilians. "Is that less of a crime?

"That was war."

"He invaded Korea and altered the outcome of the Korean Civil War, installing a puppet government that the Korean people did not want."

"South Korea is a democracy! "If they wanted Communism, they would have voted for it. "Kim Il Sung tried to force communism upon them."

"Nyet! "The people of the South welcomed the Korean army as liberators, driving the American imperialists out of their country. "We did not force the Koreans to accept Marxist Leninism. "We did not send troops there. "Only MacArthur's unprovoked aggression at Inchon prevented the Koreans from driving your army into the sea."

"You sent your pilots there. "It was only the Chinese invasion that prevented us from liberating all of Korea," asserted Mumley!

"General Eisenhower would have negotiated a peace and ended the war," argued Zhukov. "He is a chivalrous man, a man of honor who can be trusted to keep his word, as he did in the Great Patriotic War . . . but your system is corrupt. "Mao Tse Tung warned you what would happen if you attacked north of the thirty eighth parallel. "Truman would not listen. "All he could understood was force. "He allowed the basest of men to float to the top of the sludge heap of your bourgeois society like Nixon, who accused as a traitor anyone who suggested that the war should end, and who now violates our borders as soon as his president feels a heart murmur."

"Richard Nixon is an honorable man," Mumley defended. "The only dishonorable thing he ever did was accept a little puppy named Checkers as a gift from a friend. "He even went on national television to apologize. "He is not even in the same party as Truman. "He's a Republican, just like Ike! "Are you saying that President Truman should not have dropped the atomic bombs on Japan?"

"Yes! "I was in Manchuria. "It was only a matter of weeks before Manchuquo fell and we occupied the entire Korean peninsula. "Then Truman dropped the bombs and ended the war . . . and now Nixon threatens to do the same to us as Truman did to the Japanese . . . no discussion . . . no negotiation . . . no warning . . . not even an ultimatum. "Boom," shouted Zhukov, throwing his hands up explosively! Mumley winced. Zhukov continued, "Nixon sleeps in the same bed as Dulles, one of the hell hounds of the Earth, vomiting vile putrid filth out of his beastly mouth. "He hides under the coat tails of McCarthy only to emerge brushing off the hairy dandruff when his beastmaster is denounced!"

"Look Georg, Dick Nixon can't to anything without Dave's approval. "This isn't just Nixon's doing. "America is not like Russia where men like Beria can run amok without the rest of the Politburo knowing about it. "In our country, we make decisions together."

"Nyet! "Nyeh prava. "Nixon is an enemy of Communism. "Everyone knows he will succeed Eisenhower to the Presidency. "We must be prepared for his reign. "Look at what he has already done to your greatest artists, singers, film makers, and poets with his so called Committee on Un-American Activities, blacklisting and impoverishing those whose only crime is to believe in the correctness of Leninist and Marxist thought. "Does he intend to destroy Russia to abolish correct thinking all over the world?"

"You are developing rockets to destroy us and correct our correct thinking," answered Mumley, placing his hands firmly on the table. "You leave us no choice but to stop you. "Stalin promised Ike at the Moscow victory parade, back in forty five, that he would develop only a copy of the Nazi V-2 rocket and nothing more."

"I know," replied Zhukov. "I was there."

"Is that correct thinking? "Why did you go back on your word?"

"It was not my decision. "The rockets were developed in secret by Beria without the permission of the Central Committee. "Where Malenkov's signature was required, he merely wrote, 'This is not necessary,' and his subordinates were too frightened of him to disagree. "I disagreed and I was exiled to a teaching command. "Nikita Sergeievich believes that conventional weapons are obsolete, that only nuclear explosives will matter in the war of the future."

"And what if the people of Germany or Hungary decide they no longer want Soviet troops on their territory and civilians start attacking your soldiers in the streets to drive them out? "Will you use your nuclear rockets to correct their incorrect thinking?"

"I do not know. "I just follow orders. "It is a decision for the entire politburo to make. "The Germans have killed far too many Slavs in the past, for us to allow them do as they wish. "We must protect Communism."

"If you lack conventional warfare capability, how will you do that?"

"I think Nikita Sergeievich is making a big mistake."

"He was the one who rehabilitated you."

"He needed me to arrest Beria. "If I were not here in your embassy, I would not be able to say this freely. "Beria has been dead more than two years and his eyes are still watching and his ears are still listening. "I fear for the future."

"You are the most decorated soldier in world history," praised Mumley. "If you are not safe, who is?"

"MacArthur says that in America, 'old soldiers never die, they just fade away.' "Zhukov says that in Russia, old soldiers that have outlived their usefulness, suddenly disappear without trace. "I cannot think of the words in English to describe the feeling that goes through my mind when the son or wife or daughter of one of my comrades who taught me all that I know, how to attack, how to defend, how to survive battle, how to command men, how to be a man, asks me the question, 'father, husband, or uncle has disappeared, can I find him, bahlshoy pahzhaloostah†?' "I relax my face to smile and say, 'maybe he is having a love affair, 'perhaps he will turn up in a few days,' and then he is never seen again."

"But the elimination of your superiors helped you rise through the ranks."

"Da, Ya benefitted from Stalin, but I would give up all my medals and rank just to know my comrades were safe. "They were like fathers to me. "Look at the cost! "Hitler would never have been able to invade Russia if they were still alive . . . and then, a few years later, there were twenty million of our people dead."

"Stalin wanted to be the greatest leader in Russian history and I guess he succeeded," quipped the Ambassador.

"No Bernard, you are wrong! "Hitler forced him to fight. "He did not have enough food to feed our army, so he ordered them to attack. "Damn him!" Zhukov threw another shot of vodka into his mouth straight up.

"But then you defeated Hitler," said Mumley, pouring Zhukov another drink.

Zhukov continued, "Ioseph Stalin Dzukashveelee fell to pieces and hid in his dacha for several weeks, until we brought him some good news from the front that would lift him out of his melancholy. "When we arrived, he thought we were there to kill him."

"If you disagree with Khrushchev," asked the Ambassador, "how long can you remain in power?"

"I don't know."

"Who will replace you?"

"No one will. "Wars will be fought by civilians or political commissars pushing hidden buttons under their desks. "Nikita Sergeievich says he no longer needs Generals or armies."

† большое пожалуйста — big please

"And what will he do when he has a disagreement with Dick Nixon or Adlai Stevenson, or whoever wins the next election?"

"Attack!"

"Why?"

"To defend Communism! "Nikita Sergeievich does not believe in Malenkov's policy of peaceful coexistence. "He thinks Lenin was right, that war between capitalism and socialism is inevitable."

"Is that why Malenkov was replaced?"

"Malenkov was not replaced, he was outvoted. "He wanted to cut defense spending to improve the standard of living for the average worker. "He called those of us who believe in a strong defense, 'steel eaters.' "He thought that because you Americans supported us in the Great Patriotic war, the United States was an ally and would leave us alone to develop our economy, so we no longer needed such a large armed force. "He lost some of Tovarich Lenin's zeal to spread Socialism throughout the world."

"And so the Politburo sided with Khrushchev?

"We received word of your Bravo device, a doomsday weapon, the largest explosive ever created, the only possible purpose for which is to destroy Russia. Then your overflights of our territory began with the largest military aircraft ever built, the only aircraft capable of carrying the super weapon. "Our best interceptors, at the time, could not fly high enough to reach them." Zhukov swallowed another drink, then explained, "Malenkov was ashamed. "He had to step down. "Why do you develop such an invincible weapon if you do not mean to destroy us? "The only possible use for such a weapon is genocide. "It is not to wage war, but to wipe the entire Slavic race from the face of the Earth! "It's diabolical!"

"It is to make war with us impossible," Mumley asserted! "So you are saying this conflict is our fault, that we are to blame, that the Bravo shot caused Malenkov to be replaced by Khrushchev and Bulganin? "How could that be? "Malenkov stepped down a whole six months before the Bravo test. "You were the first to drop a deliverable thermonuclear weapon from an aircraft."

"Da! "Yes! "You have given us no choice but to prepare for war! "We knew about the test of Bravo six months in advance. "Patriotic American scientists kept us informed. "We even knew about your decision to blow up your bomber crew as human test subjects so see if they could survive the blast. "I will say your own words back to you: 'No president could remain in power if he did nothing to counteract such a threat!' "Our people would 'laugh our heads on poles if we allowed you to get away with this!' "Even your own academician, Oppenheimer, spoke out against it. "As your own words so wisely prophesied after the fact, Malenkov could not remain in power. "He had to admit he was wrong. "Socialism must be defended! "It is happening again in your country just as it happened in Germany. "First, the right thinking artists, poets, and journalists are blacklisted, exiled, or impoverished, so they are unable to speak out against the government, then a massive military build up occurs in secret, then reconnaissance flights, then genocide!

"You're being preposterous," accused Mumley!

"When the Hitlerites invaded the Rheinland in violation of the Versailles treaty," Zhukov continued, "they came with bicycles and fabric covered biplanes. "Who tried to stop them? "The French said Herr Hitler was not a threat, so they built a road through the impassable forest of the Ardennes. "'It would be good for trade,' they said. "Trading with the enemy would appease them. "The next time the Hitlerites came to the border of France, they came with armor and dive bombers and they did not stop at the border. "They drove their tanks on that road all the way to Paris. "Now you cross our borders in flying naval vessels armed with miniature suns and you say you are not a threat? "You ask us why *we* re-arm?"

"I asked you why you need stations in space and missiles that can destroy our cities in twenty minutes, before an end to a crisis can be negotiated or resolved," argued Mumley?

"When the Hitlerites broke their treaty, aircraft should have been in the air immediately. "Even if they were only riding bicycles, the violators should have been shot at once. "The French said they could not fly their planes because of bad weather. "What is worse, bad weather, or suffering total defeat by Fascists?"

"It was the Soviet Union that negotiated an agreement with Hitler, not the French," asserted the Ambassador. "You saw them violate one treaty. "By entering into an agreement with Hitler, Stalin betrayed the French."

"When the French failed to defend their treaty," countered Zhukov, "we had to protect ourselves. "We could not be allied with a weakling that changes governments every six months."

"So now you want the power to change our government in only twenty minutes? "That's insane!"

"My counterpart, James V. Forrestal, your first Secretary of Defense was insane," accused the Soviet Defense Minister. "What if, instead of throwing himself out of a window, he had ordered an atomic attack?" Mumley stared at the beribboned Field Marshal with his mouth agape, not quite knowing what to say. "Now your President has named after him the largest, most powerful naval vessel ever built, the USS Forrestal, a super aircraft carrier that carries ninety nuclear armed jets. "Is insanity now to be admired in America? "Are your young men to enter manhood following this example? "Are your young soldiers to be encouraged to throw away their lives in pointless suicidal attacks on us, like your former Secretary of Defense threw himself out of a window, so they can die in glory believing the world's largest ship will be named after them? "You ask why *we* re-arm? "We arm ourselves so you will know with certainty what will happen in only twenty minutes when your next psychotic or neurotic Secretary of Defense decides on a whim to send twenty million of our people into oblivion!"

The fois gras arrived. They paused to eat. The waiter quickly left the room. Neither was sure that he ought to continue the conversation. They both looked at their plates angrily while making a show of violently attacking the liver paté with their forks and knives, cutting the bread upon which it had been spread into small bits with a loud clattering of silver against porcelain. Stiles could not eat. He excused himself and sat in a spare dining chair in the corner of the room. Both antagonists knew that any further conversation would lead to an argument and ruin the meal, but Mumley had been waiting his entire career to corner one of the powerful Politburo members privately, and ask him to explain the Soviet Union's almost inscrutable behavior. He broke the silence and asked, "How can you defend Communism after Stalin and Beria and all that they did?"

"The people are better off," answered the Field Marshal, eating quickly with his mouth full.

"Not the ones who were killed," replied the Ambassador.

"Some deserved to die," explained Zhukov. "They were capitalistic exploiters."

"You said yourself, that not all of them were guilty."

"Many were merely accused, but when there is a shortage of food, removing them from their jobs is the same as death, anyway. "Better to shoot them first, so they will not be forced to turn to a life of crime and ruin their family names."

"The food shortages were caused by forced collectivization," accused Mumley.

"I cannot say that socialism is perfect," explained the Field Marshal. "It was an experiment that had never been tried. Mistakes were made, but the people are better off now."

"How can a person be better off dead?"

"Those who survived are better off."

"How?"

They stopped eating and put down their silver. Zhukov looked into Mumley's eyes and said, "Adolph Hitler wrote in his book that he wanted to cast out the foreigners because they were controlling and manipulating his people. "He said their sons had an unfair advantage in life over his people's sons . . ."

"He fed poison to his sons," Mumley interrupted with an equal stare, "then he shot himself."

"That was later," admitted Zhukov. "But before his rise to power, the sons of the bourgeois were thirty times more likely to obtain an education than the sons of workers and peasants. "One in every three educated persons was a Jew, even though they were only one percent of the population. "Here in Russia, before the October revolution, the son of a peasant had no chance for an education, no matter how intelligent he was. "Can you imagine a very bright person forced to perform hard manual labor, without reward for his efforts, having no hope of improving himself or his family or is country? "The mediocre sons of the bourgeois were well enough educated, but they inherited so much wealth, they never desired to become productive citizens. "They ate twice as much food, they did not do any work, and then they called on others to empty their chamber pots! "They desired only to control and manipulate others. "What do you think we Bolsheviks did about that?"

"You killed them!"

"Da, we shot them! "What good is an academician or a professor at university if we cannot afford his tuition? "He is good for nothing. "We shoot him! "What good is a medical doctor or a banker or a lawyer if we cannot afford their fee? "They are good for nothing. "We kill them! "Today, we have standardized tests so the best minds get the best education. "Now only patriotic individuals who put the needs of their country ahead of their own greed are educated. "How do you think it was that a farm girl like Svetlana became a jet pilot? She was tested and was found to be the best. "In your country a woman is tied by her apron strings and cannot hope to succeed."

"We had many female flyers in the war," Mumley corrected. "They were called WASP's, Women's Auxiliary Service Pilots. "They did not fight, because it was feared that if they were shot down they would be captured and raped."

"Because you did not give them a chance, they did not reach their full potential," replied the General. "My top woman ace at Stalingrad achieved eight confirmed victories before she patriotically gave her life in defense of her motherland."

"If you had not ordered Svetlana into combat, she would not have been raped and she might have been able to marry instead of taking a lover."

"You are a fool, Bernard! "What do you think happened to all the Ukrainian farm girls who did not attend aviation training?"

"They evacuated?"

"Evacuated where . . . to eat what?"

"To Russia, Siberia? "I don't know."

"It has been almost a hundred years since you Americans had a war on your soil. "You Americans have forgotten what real war is. "Why, I read in Pravda about an infant who was given a million dollars on the day of his birth to ensure that he would never become a productive citizen. "When war came and he was called up to fight, his father obtained for him an officer's commission. "While others rotted in the jungles of the South Pacific or froze in the snows of Alaska, he lived in a luxury apartment near the Pentagon in Washington. "Do you know the latest medical research has proven that the cause of mental illness is too much food and not enough work?"

"Not everyone in America lives in luxury Georgi. "We had a civil war once. "Anyone who did not volunteer to fight was made to wear a white feather. "The wealthiest were the first to join up."

"That is not the same. "When your homeland is invaded by foreigners, there is no place to flee. "We burned the fields and storehouses to prevent the seed grain from falling into the hands of the fascists. "Our own farmers tried to stop us. "They said they would have nothing to eat. "We shot them, or they turned traitor and fled into the arms of the Hitlerites. "By the time the war was over, half of the men Svetlana's age had been killed. "Today, because of that, half of all the women like Svetlana remain unmarried. "And now your reconnaissance bomber seven hundred fifty three has killed her lover. "That is why Svetlana has no husband. "They killed her last chance for love, her only chance to bear children. "What do you think she will do when she finds your bomber?"

"Georg, you frighten me. "You talk as though you are not in complete control of your subordinates." They stopped eating and gazed in each other's eyes with fear.

RADAR-BOMBARDIER'S *Station*

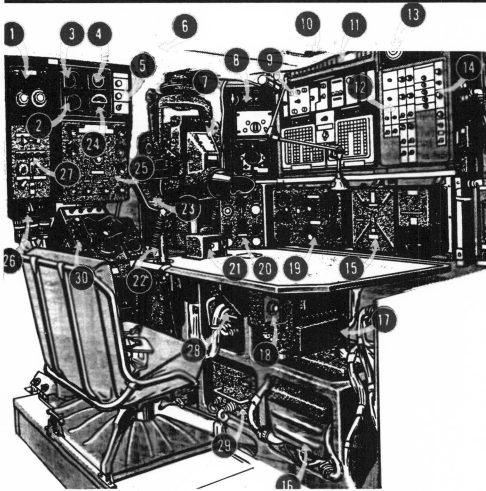

1. LINE OF SIGHT CONTROL	16. RADAR SYNCHRONIZER
2. TIME TO GO INDICATOR	17. JUCTION BOX
3. GYROCOMPASS	18. VARIABLE AUTO TRANSFORMER
4. AIRSPEED INDICATOR	19. NAVIGATION CONTROL
5. RADAR PRESSURIZATION CONTROLS	20. BALLISTICS CONTROL
6. RADAR CAMERA CONTROL	21. TURN CONTROLLER
7. RADAR SCOPE CAMERA	22. TRACKING CONTROL
8. OXYGEN & INTERPHONE CONTROLS	23. RADAR INDICATOR
9. BOMBING CONTROL PANEL	24. RADAR PRESSURE GAUGE
10. RADAR CONTROL UNIT	25. RADAR INDICATOR
11. CIRCUIT BREAKER PANEL	26. BOMB BAY DOORS SAFETY SWITCH
12. AUXILLIARY BOMBING CONTROLS	27. PRIMARY CONTROL
13. BOMB INTERVAL RELEASE CONTROL	28. SERVO AMPLIFIER
14. CAMERA CONTROLS	29. RECTIFIER POWER UNIT
15. POLAR NAVIGATION CONTROL	30. BOMBSIGHT PERISCOPE

"I can see
Russia!"

REVENGE
OVER RUSSIA
April 1956

A faint green auroral curtain showered over the heads of Johns and Grant through 811's greenhouse canopy. Nawrocki was standing between their seats shooting stars with the periscopic sextant. The pep pills had worn off and everyone felt scared, no longer like supermen. But amphetamines have a lingering effect, so Johns and Grant felt somewhat like "Batman and Robin."

Two six engined KC-97 tankers with all of their propellers turning formed up with the ship. "I wonder what they're here for," asked Grant?

"I don't know," said Johns, "They can't refuel us."

Two pregnant six engined RB-47H's joined the tankers. "I wonder if Harry and Jerry are in those jets," asked Grant?

The tankers lit their jet engines and disappeared in the distance, dragging the RB-47's along with them like dragonflies making love. "I don't know," answered Johns. "They must be taking on fuel before we enter Soviet airspace."

The permafrost of the Siberian Tundra was the same shiny green color as the ice, but it had a different character. Instead of fissures and pressure ridges, it was billiard table flat and smooth with occasional black rocky outcrops interrupted by pure white windswept frozen lakes. "I can see the shoreline," said Nawrocki, we're entering Russian airspace." The coastline was marked by huge blocks of ice shoved up on shore by mighty storms centuries ago.

"AC to crew, oxygen check," commanded Johns over the interphone, "beginning climb over Soviet airspace. "Everyone check to make sure your suit heaters are working. "Better go below," he advised Nawrocki. The Navigator obeyed.

"Radio is working," said Beaumont.

"VO to AC," everything good here," insisted Kewscinski.

"Navigator okay," said Nawrocki, after he plugged in his jack at the navigation desk.

"Tailgunner all right," added Sandringham.

"Scanner good," replied Hernandez. Murphy and Lewis turned around with their thumbs up.

"This is First Officer," announced Grant, "All heat and oxygen manifolds are working. "Beginning climb to flight level fifty."

Johns reached up to spin up the jets. "Gordon, why didn't you tell me about those men jumping you like that," he asked? "You were wearing women's makeup to the briefing to cover up that black eye, weren't you."

"It was Shirley's idea," admitted the young co-pilot as he flicked on the spark switches. "I didn't want to miss the flight."

"What was that all about anyway?" Johns looked down at the panel as he advanced the jet throttles to idle.

"Just some good old boys who didn't want me going out with Shirley for some damn reason," answered the younger man as he watched the needles on the jet tach, temperature, and pressure gauges slowly rise.

"What did they say?" Grant was silent. "C'mon Gordon," Johns continued, "as your commanding officer, I have a right to know what that was about. "What did they say?"

"They said that us 'Commie Jews should keep our hands off of pure White Aryan Women.'"

"And they hit you?"

"No, I told them my skin was whiter than theirs."

"Then they hit you?"

"No, one of them said that if his skin was darker than mine, it was because I didn't do any work, that all us Jews are parasites that control and manipulate people to live off the work of others. "The other said that I must be a Russian Jew and that I must be a Commie to have skin so white. "I offered them to look at my freckles and told them I was an Air Force officer and I was going to bomb the Commies."

"What did they say then?"

"That's when they hit me. "Shirley screamed for them to leave us alone." Johns reached up and advanced the jet throttles to military thrust.

"What did they do to her?"

"Nothing. "She pounded them with her fists, but they were big guys. "They kept asking when I was going to bomb the Soviet Union. "I told them tomorrow . . . I mean yesterday. "I mean, the day before yesterday I told them tomorrow."

"You told them about the mission," interrupted Lewis, who was sitting back to back with Grant?

"They were just a couple of good old boys," said Grant, turning around.

"You didn't tell them where, did you," asked Johns? He pulled back on his wheel to begin the climb.

"Of course not! "I told them I was going to destroy a Commie rocket site."

"Dammit Gordon, you should have reported this," insisted the Aircraft Commander.

"There was no harm in it," the young man continued. "They just thought I was just another Jew-boy shooting off his mouth."

"What if they were Commie agents? "How many rocket sites do you think the Ruskies have anyway? "Maybe they only have just one. "You might have told them where we are going and gotten us all killed!"

"No way," exclaimed the young co-pilot!

"If I didn't half believe you, I'd turn this ship around and head back."

"Don't do that," said the immortal young hot shot bomber pilot, "I wanna have a crack at them first!"

"You talk like maybe they were Commie agents."

Before Grant could answer, Lewis blurted in, "If the mission has been compromised, I think we should turn back."

"Shut up Lewis," said Murphy. "Watch your panel."

"You may not have noticed, Marv," the youngest man responded, "but I outrank you. "I have the right to state my opinion to my commanding officer."

"Your opinion is noted," answered Johns.

"I didn't sign up for ROTC, sir, just to get myself killed," continued Lewis. "If this coward has told enemy agents where we are going, in my opinion, we should turn back."

"What do you mean by coward," asked Johns? "You have no idea what Gordon and I have been through . . . and Marv and the others. "You just joined this crew less than a month ago. "Don't be calling people cowards until you've seen some action yourself so we can see how you behave under pressure."

"I'm sorry sir," Lewis apologised. "I was wrong to call him a coward.

"Anyway, they weren't enemy agents," Grant explained.

"Does it matter," the newest man replied? "You should

not have said anything. "Did they break your arms and legs or pull your arms out of joint? "Did they torture you with electric shocks? "Did they threaten to crush your family jewels? "No, they just gave you a little slap on the cheek and you blabbered all about the mission."

"Shut up Lewis," ordered Grant! "You may not have not noticed . . . but I outrank you."

"No you don't!"

"Why would they attack you without provocation if they weren't Communist agents," asked Murphy?

"Why do you think," answered Grant, "because I'm Jewish! "Why else? "What other excuse do they need?"

"Well so what! "I'm Irish," interrupted the old Master Sergeant. "If someone calls me a Mick, I shake my fist. "If they hit me, I hit'em back, or go down trying. "There ain't no point in arguing with stupid people. "If they get in your way, you don't say, 'please sir, would you please step out of the way?' "You whack 'em, and if they're still in the way, you keep on whackin'em until they're out of the way! "There's no point in arguing with stupid people!"

"Why would they care about your religion," asked Lewis? "If all they wanted was information about your pecker, then there was no reason to tell them about the mission!"

"Shut up Lewis," hollered Grant! "I was with a White woman. "There are a lot of good old fashioned Texas boys who don't think a Jew should be dating a White woman."

"I don't either," asserted Lewis!

"INCOMING PLANES," Hernandez yelled over the interphone from the right scanning bubble in the back of the ship!

"I knew it," hollered Lewis!

"Whoa, it's too soon," exclaimed Sandringham, as he jumped in his seat to stick his head in the left gun bubble. He had dozed off.

"Where," asked Johns?

"Now we're going to be killed," said Lewis! "We're not even up to altitude yet."

"Four MiG's coming down on top of us," warned Hernandez, bending forward and looking over his shoulder to see up through the right bubble. Sandringham looked, but could not see them.

"Holy Jesus, what have you done to us," accused Lewis, scowling at Grant?

"Watch your panel," commanded Murphy!

"Battlestations," Johns yelled into his mike as he rang the alarm bells! "Get those radars on!" He released his interphone button. "Looks like you're not going to get your chance to have a crack at them," he added with a nod, looking at Grant. "We're outnumbered."

Sandringham was the only one who could honestly be said to have a battlestation. He moved from the left scanner's blister to his tail radar gunlaying system console. Hernandez looked out of his blister and noticed the ship was surrounded, just as the Russian Tupolev 95 Bear bomber had been boxed by the F-95 Starfires on the previous day. Two MiG's took positions on each side of the ship.

"How did they find us," yelled Kewscinski over the interphone, who up to then had been trying to sleep?

"They dove down on us," explained Hernandez, who was waving at the Russian pilot just outside his blister. Amazingly, the Russian pilot waved back.

"I'm scratching the mission," announced Johns. "Duane, plot a course back to Thule. He turned off the autopilot and began a slow turn to the left, trying to avoid a collision with the fighters. Gunfire was heard.

"Jesus Christ," they're firing on us, cursed Lewis, looking out the back window of the bridge.

"Watch your panel," ordered Murphy. Johns rolled the ship back to the right. The pilot who waved at Hernandez opened fire.

A shower of tracers lit up the night in front of Lana as she pulled the trigger for her two smaller cannon. She was smiling behind her mask. Svetlana was thinking about the next Hero of the Soviet Union medal that would be pinned on her chest when she returned with the huge trophy. 'What a fat prize it will make,' she thought to herself! Surely, she would win the competition to become the first woman in space!

Flying in space was something Lana had never imagined a woman could do. When Zhukov ordered her to put on the space suit, it was too big, and very uncomfortable. One of the engineers inserted wooden wedges into the soles, like elevator shoes, to make the suit fit. She could not walk very well in it. She had to stand on the tips of her toes like the young shepherd boy, David, donning Saul's armor to face Goliath. Still, women weigh less than men. It made sense that the first person in space should be a woman. After all, she might meet God or an angel up there. A mild mannered Russian woman might be better received than a propaganda spuming godless Communist. Perhaps she would meet Sergei. How proud he would be of her!

The American Ambassador had mentioned, while they were waiting at the embassy, that 811 was a featherweight III model with guns only in the tail. As long as she stayed forward of its stabilizer, the huge bomber would be as helpless as a cargo plane. Because it had already entered Soviet airspace, Lana had permission to shoot it down if it did not agree to be captured. What satisfaction for Sergei's parents to put on trial the very same spies that killed him! Visions danced in her mind of bringing the Americans before Zhukov in chains.

"Look at their load out," exclaimed Hernandez. "It looks like they're firing nothing but armor piercing tracers."

"Maybe they know we're featherweighted and all the bullet sealing panels have been removed from our tanks," suggested Lewis.

"How could they possibly know that," asked Johns? He looked at Grant. Gordon starred back innocently.

"I guess they're planning to poke us full of holes until we have to land and plug the leaks," said Murphy.

   "They must want to capture us," said Grant. "The tracers must be just to scare us. "Do you intend to surrender?" Johns looked at his instruments. "I guess this reveals the wisdom of removing all the guns," added the young co-pilot as he fondled the Colt .45 automatic he was issued, which he carried in a holster under his left arm. He mentally compared the size of its large diamond checked grip to the somewhat smaller smooth Bakelite gunsight firing handle for his pair of six foot long 20mm cannons he used to command on 753.
   "Two more targets approaching, eleven O'clock, warned Kewscinski, with his eyes pressed into his radar camera. "Wait, that's four more targets."
   "Sandringham," said Johns, "I don't want you to lock radar on any of them unless I give the word."
   "Yessir," the gunner replied, "no radar lock until I receive word." Four more MiG's flashed past and turned behind the ship. The helpless tailgunner watched the green blips disappear from both of his radar scopes. They took up position above the other fighters. Two flew on ahead and waved their wings to

indicate that Johns and Grant should follow them. Johns continued on course. Another shower of brilliant tracers sprayed in front of the ship.

"You're not going to surrender are you," asked Grant for the second time?

"Turn on the formation lights," replied Johns.

"Why?"

"Don't question my orders. "Do it! "We don't want them to hit us."

"C'mon AC," pleaded Lewis, feeling warm liquid trickling into his tight codpiece, "lets get out of here. "I want to go home!"

"Well it looks like we're not going home," Johns snapped!

"Watch your panel," commanded Murphy!

"We've dragged this bomb all this way," said Grant, "lets finish the job. "We've got to teach them Commies never to mess with us again. "Lets nuke'em!

"No," exclaimed Lewis!

Johns looked at his young co-pilot in the face for a long time, then looked down at his instruments. His face seemed contorted in agony. Visions danced in his mind of the POW camp in Korea, the gassy cabbage he had to eat, and the cold clammy mud, how much he enjoyed the digging of fortifications and repairing roads to keep warm, and the extra rations he received when he worked. He tried to imagine how Linda and Bobby would adapt if he was made a prisoner again. What if he was put on trial and sentenced to life in prison as a spy? Would she divorce him and remarry? Would it be fair to keep her waiting? What would be the reason to go on living? The best outcome would be death by firing squad. He and Linda would both be better off if he was dead, rather than being captured.

Angry that the bomber did not alter course, Lana decided to teach the Americans a lesson. She advanced her throttle to full power. Flames shot from her afterburner. Passing under the ship, she abruptly pulled back on her stick. Looking in her rear view mirror, she laughed as she saw a man sitting at a desk, his eyes wide with fear, illuminated by her tail flame as it passed only a few meters ahead of his front window. She then yanked back her throttle to deploy her brakes, smiling behind her mask as the giant ship altered course to avoid hitting her and following her other fighters exactly as she intended.

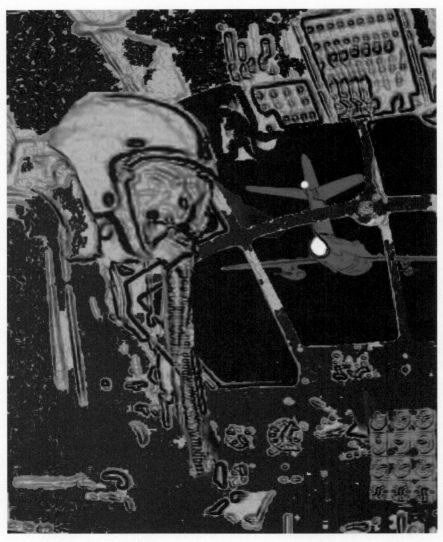

"Jeezus," shouted Johns, as the nose of the ship bucked like a diving board!"

"Son of a bitch phlumped us," yelled Grant as his helmet hit the canopy! "We got us a real hot-shot fighter jock!"

"Motherfucker," exclaimed Kewscinski as he tried to rub his face shield where his forehead had banged against the radar camera! "He's trying to get us all killed."

"And himself as well," added Nawrocki, his eyes temporarily blinded by the bright blue kerosene tailflame brushing the window.

"What are you going to do," asked Grant? "Are we going to surrender?"

Johns' expression hardened. He said, "Hell no!" Looking straight ahead, pressing his interphone button, he commanded, "Major Kewscinski?"

"Yes Sir," shouted a voice on the lower deck?

"Unlock weapon shackle." Hernandez and Sandringham, both shaken by the near collision, gulped and looked at each other with fear through the dark aft cabin as the four turbojets under the wings roared and thundered at full power. Johns dove. The Russian fighters increased their speed to keep up.

"Yes Sir," responded Kewscinski, "unlock weapon shackle.

"I don't believe this," wailed Lewis!

"Lieutenant Nawrocki," asked the VO?" Nawrocki was sitting right beside him, but he pressed his interphone button anyway as a matter of protocol.

"Yes Sir," replied Nawrocki over the interphone?

"Unlock weapon shackle."

"Yes Sir," Nawrocki responded, "unlocking weapon shackle."

"NO," yelled Lewis!

Nawrocki unstrapped himself from his seat at the navigation desk and nervously made his way around Kewscinski into the radio room to enter the bomb bay. He looked over his shoulder out the window, afraid the ship might be phlumped again while he was not strapped down. The ship shook like a freight train as fighters took turns flying directly in front, doing better than three hundred knots. Johns climbed and dove repeatedly, trying to stay out of their jetwash to no avail. Loose items in the cabin floated weightless in mid air at the apex of every climb, only to be dashed against floor or ceiling as the pounding jetwash shook the ship like an eighteen wheel truck slamming through a three foot pothole. The four fighters had little difficulty staying in front. They took turns tormenting the clumsy giant, like the balls of a juggler falling, one by one, on the head of a clown. In the aft cabin, Hernandez and Sandringham looked at each other with eyes wide open. They no longer needed pills to stay awake.

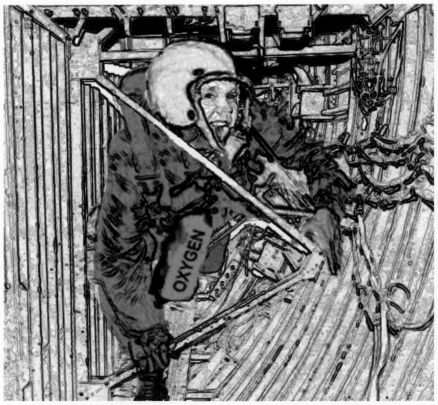

Nawrocki arrived in the bomb bay badly bruised. He was thrown up off the narrow, six inch wide, catwalk several times as he climbed through the jungle gym of triangular braces beside the radar compartment. Under normal circumstances, these obstructions made moving around the ship merely difficult. Now, they painfully dug into his ribs.

Swinging like Tarzan from girder to girder, Nawrocki made his way to the back of the ship. As he slithered up beside the layer of ice coating the huge green cryogenic bomb, he was grateful the nuclear capsule had been inserted on the ground, however dangerous it had made the simulated release over Minneapolis seem to be. Screwing in the twenty pounds of plutonium and its associated shielding while being phlumped would have been impossible. Removing the two, half pound, shackle safety pins was hard enough. Nawrocki was careful not to touch the emergency cable release, or the twenty ton weapon might crash through the beer can thin magnesium bomb doors like they were not even there—leaving him dangling by his safety strap like a paddle ball, dashed against the bomb racks by a bone chilling sub-zero three hundred mile an hour wind.

Nawrocki deftly inserted each pin under his glove and touched it to his wrist to make sure it was warm and that the rack heaters were working. As soon as he pulled the pins, the ship was phlumped again, causing the bomb, almost as heavy as a Sherman Tank, to visibly bend and twist the ship's internal girders like a nervous draft horse trying to escape its halter. He began to fear that the oscillations might trip the manual release cable.

Like an acrobat, Nawrocki quickly swung down and inspected the bomb's tail chute static lines and the wiring harness for the chute heater. He removed the outer felt mitten from his left hand and felt the chute with his glove to make sure it was warm, then climbed back through the jungle gym of triangular braces to the forward cabin. If the chute became frozen and failed to deploy properly to slow the descent of the bomb, the ship would not have time to escape the ten megaton blast.

When Nawrocki emerged from the bomb bay, he gave Beaumont the thumbs up and nodded. "Radio to AC," announced Beaumont, "Weapon shackle unlocked."

"No," shouted Lewis!

"Shut up," ordered Murphy!

Johns repeated Beaumont's message, "Roger, weapon shackle unlocked."

"AC to VO, John, did you mark the location on your radar plot where those fighters came from," asked Johns over the interphone?

"Yes Sir, I did," answered Kewscinski as he removed the clear Lucite targeting map for Tyura Tam from his radar camera and replaced the hood, "there's a blip right in front of us. "They appear to be taking us there."

"Beaumont!"

"Yessir," answered the radio man.

"Send an uncoded message relating our status and position."

"Uncoded, sir?"

"Yes, and end the message with Linda, I love you."

"I love you?"

"Yes Lieutenant."

"You love who?"

"Linda! "Just do it."

"Yessir!" Beaumont began tapping his Morse key. The cabin glowed red, lit by the tailflame of a fighter passing dangerously close in front. The nose of the ship bounced like a diving board as the jetwash struck with earsplitting thunder.

"Jeesus," cursed Grant!

"Goddammit," yelled Kewscinski!

"AC to VO!"

"Yessir," Kewscinski's voice was heard.

"Calculate bombing solution for one thousand foot air burst."

His face shield pressed against his radar camera, Kewscinski nervously searched for the knobs to position the bright dot of light on the target blip. Although years of repetitive simulations had ingrained the location of every knob and switch into his brain, he had a hard time finding them—the ship was bucking so much. When he reached up, his arms flapped involuntarily like those of an orchestra conductor. Nervous, Kewscinski was afraid of clumsily knocking the wrong switch. "Are you sure you want to do this, sir," he asked?

"Follow your orders!"

"Are you real sure?"

"It's the only weapon we have," replied Johns!

"Okay then, I guess we're doing this for Jim Newcomb." With concentration, Kewscinski flicked up the master power switch on his bombing control panel. The wheels and gears in the bombing navigation computer whirred and clicked as lights on the tops of vacuum tubes went on and off, filling the forward cabin with kaleidoscopic flickering Christmas lights. A yellow and a red light lit up on the bombing control panel for the center rack in bomb bay four. If the ship was armed with a full load of five hundred pound conventional bombs, every light on the Christmas tree would have been lit. Since there was only one bomb on board, only one yellow and one red light was lit. Kewscinski swallowed hard, wishing he could have kept his old job as Photonavigator so he would not have to make such a decision, and turned the bomb door safety switch beside his optical aiming periscope from "DOORS SAFE" to "ENABLED." Then he announced, "Pre-combat checklist . . . "Weapon shackle unlocked . . . "For Merrill Hughs, bomb door safety switch is enabled . . . "For Jim Newcomb, bombing solution computed for one thousand foot air burst, automatic release . . . sighting, radar . . . chute on safe . . . nose fuse safe for electrical salvo."

"Roger," replied Johns, "weapon shackle unlocked, bombing solution computed for one thousand foot air burst, sighting radar, nose fuse safe for electrical salvo. Lieutenant Colonel Johns thought about what Kewscinski had said, "for Jim Newcomb" and "for Merril Hughs," and added, "For gunners Shultz, Calabrese, Nakamura, and O'Connor, set rack three to salvo the chute for ballistic release, recalculate bombing solution for free fall trajectory, and set nose fuse to armed." His hands began to shake.

"Oh God! "No," cried Lewis!"

Hernandez and Sandringham again looked at each other to share the same expression of fear. Sandringham looked ghastly, his face painted green by the light from his radar screens.

Kewscinski's hand wobbled as he flicked up the nose fuse and chute control switches. A white light lit up, illuminating a message underneath that said "NOSE FUSE ARM." The yellow and red lights for Rack Three also lit on the bombing control panel.

"I guess this means we're not going home," he said to Nawrocki, who looked back at him with eyes frozen in a wide stare, not quite believing what they had been ordered to do. Kewscinski stared back, his hand still touching the chute control switch as though his arm was frozen. The continuing oscillations of the ship through the fighters' jetwash did not budge it. The wheels and gears inside the computer churned to recalculate the bomb's planned trajectory, flickering the vacuum tubes on and off all over again. Kewscinski looked back at his panel. The shaking of his hands had stopped. The white light also illuminated a picture of Mary and the kids he had taped above it. "Hank, we'll never make it," he protested!

"Yes we will," insisted the Aircraft Commander. "Remember we sat for a day in Thule letting all that liquid deuterium evaporate. "Its going to be a much smaller blast than

LeMay intended."

"I'm telling you it's suicide," insisted Kewscinski, "even if you make the break perfectly, we'll never survive this."

"Don't worry about how I do my job," replied Johns testily, "you just do yours. "We don't have the altitude for a braked release and you know it. "Even if we did, those fighters would just follow us, madder than hell, as soon as it went off."

"I want to go home," Lewis pleaded!

"What do you plan to do," asked Gordon?

"We're going to nuke that base and those fighters are going to fly right into the blast!" Johns stared straight ahead firmly and added, "We survived the Cherokee Two. "We can survive this. "We've been through it before. "They haven't . . . in any case, they will be closer to it when it goes off than we will. "Just be ready with the fire extinguishers like last time."

"You're crazy," accused Kewscinski!

"We're being probed by RGA," warned Beaumont.

"Can you jam it," asked Johns?

"I think so," the lone Electronic Countermeasures Officer replied.

"Activate chaff dispenser."

"Yes Sir," replied Sandringham, as he flicked a switch on a black box beside his chair.

"Kewscinski?"

"Yessir," replied the Video Observer.

"Is the computer tracking yet?"

"It's tracking the target," answered the VO. "Do it if you want, but if we somehow come out of this alive, I'll have you know that I'll be putting in my report that I voiced my disagreement."

"I didn't ask for your opinion," hollered Johns angrily, without bothering to press his interphone button, "I asked you 'is the computer tracking yet?'"

"I told you, YES," shouted Kewscinski equally loud through the thin fabric under the rudder pedals! Then he pressed his interphone button and added in a normal voice, "Bombing solution calculated for one thousand foot air burst ballistic, rack three set to salvo the chute for free fall trajectory, nose fuse armed."

"Is that right Nawrocki," shouted Johns!

"I don't know Sir," the Navigator replied over the interphone as he leaned back to look at the lights on the bombing control panel, "I can't tell, but it looks right. "The yellow and red lights for rack three are lit."

"Roger on that, beginning bomb run," replied the Aircraft Commander icily over the interphone. "One thousand foot air burst ballistic, chute to salvo, nose fuse armed. "Gordon break left, now!" Johns and Grant turned their wheels hard to the left and pulled with all their might, then stood on their left rudder pedals as they were pressed into their seats with almost three times the force of gravity. Nawrocki watched the horizon become almost vertical in the front window as the four MiG's that had been in front continued on toward the target. Kewscinski struggled to keep his visor pressed against the radar camera, watching to make sure the computer continued to track the target blip as the ship maneuvered during the bomb run. Lewis opened the clear plastic front of his mask and cried.

Svetlana was surprised when she saw the giant bomber turn suddenly away. When she saw the red, white, and blue navigation and formation lights turn on, she thought it was going to surrender. Now, she saw the lights go out. All of her fighters remained on course toward the base as the ship veered away. Angered, not having time to call them back to regroup, she opened her throttle, rolled on her side, and pulled back on her stick to follow. She groaned as she was pressed into her seat with six times the force of gravity. Explosions blew up under the nose of her plane. Artillery from the base was firing at her men! "Stop, stop," she yelled into her mike, which means the same thing in Russian as it does in English!

"Break right," ordered Johns, as concussions from the flak shook the ship! They steered hard to the right, then pulled on their wheels, standing on their massive right rudder pedals.

"Mama," Lewis cried, "get me out of here!"
"I told you to shut up," hollered Murphy!

"Dammit," shouted Svetlana, which also means the same thing in Russian as it does in English. She passed under the sharply turning ship—its right wing reaching down like a scimitar to cut her in half in a scissors maneuver. She pushed her throttle full forward to light her afterburner and pulled back on her stick to loop inverted into a high yo-yo as she listened to the controller at the base ordering her men to turn around. She tightened her sphincters to fight the loss of consciousness. Such turns often left her light headed and caused some pilots to black out.

"I've got a target," yelled Sandringham! "Permission to fire?"
"Lock radar but don't fire," ordered Johns.

Lana heard the chirps in her radar detector turn into a constant tone. She broke into a sweat as memories of being shot down flooded her mind. "Sergei tagda Ya," she said to herself as her mind was filled with a memories of him carving their initials into a juniper tree along with the Russian for "together forever." Now Sergei was dead. She momentarily forgot where she was. The blood draining from her brain during the turn must have affected her judgment.

Concussions from the exploding artillery jarred Lana to tears—her poor men! Positioning them in front of the bomber was a bad idea. The base could hardly be blamed for protecting itself once the bomber began its bomb run. Why didn't she call her men back? Would their wives now also be without husbands because of her rash decision? What would she tell them? She thought about Linda, the woman who's name was written on the nose of the ship. Why would a woman reveal her husband's location so that another woman could kill him? Now, it was Svetlana's duty to shoot down "Lovely Linda" so that lovely Linda Johns could become a widow—just like her.

"Initial point in forty three seconds," announced Kewscinski! "Turn to two one six, now! "Remember, we need three hundred knots to send this thing ballistic."

"Dive, dive," yelled Johns! He and Gordon pushed their wheels forward into the instrument panel. Everyone on board seemed to levitate above their seats. Papers, pencils, and duffelbags floated in the cabin. Kewscinski, Nawrocki, and Murphy all watched the needles in their separate airspeed indicators creep past thirty, pressed into their seats as Johns and Grant pulled out of the dive. Lewis, his face in his hands, bent over in a fetal position until his helmet banged against the turbo boost selector switches.

"God damn you," shouted Murphy as he grabbed Lewis by the neck and shoved the young man's helmet under the console between his knees.

"Target in sight. "Switching to optical for automatic release," announced Kewscinski, his hands again shaking. He pressed his eyes against the periscope to the left of his desk. He turned his control knob to position the crosshairs onto the well lit huts and hangar buildings sticking up from the snow. The lights on the buildings went out. His hands stopped shaking. "You're skidding," he protested! "Give it some right rudder. "Get some of the slip out!"

"Autopilot over to you," said Johns.

"We're going to miss the target," yelled Kewscinski!

"Anywhere within five miles is fine, John. "Just be ready for a breaking left turn as soon as the computer releases the weapon."

"Those fighters'll fly right into it," added Grant!

"Switching back to radar," announced Kewscinski. "Bombing navigation computer in full automatic control."

"Roger, bombing navigation computer in full automatic control of the ship," repeated Johns. "Activate menthol water injection." Murphy flicked up six switches on his right engineer's panel.

"Pop up in one minute, seventeen seconds," shouted Kewscinski. "Ballistic release in one minute, forty two seconds."

Upside down and pointing at the ground, Lana grit her teeth and squeezed both triggers as the giant bomber passed through her glowing greenish yellow gunsight. Her instrument panel shook with every blast of her three cannon. She failed to lead the target and tearily watched her precious, foot long ammo explode uselessly on the ice below. "Dammit," she cursed again, as she pulled back her throttle to deploy her drag brakes while rolling upright to pull out of the dive.

Hernandez watched the tracers explode. "They're opening fire," he yelled over the interphone.
"I lost the target," said Sandringham, looking right at him.
"The fighters are coming back," warned Nawrocki, from his desk against the front window. Hernandez crossed his heart in Catholic fashion. They heard a tone in their headsets warning that the initial point had been reached.

As she pulled out of her dive, just meters above the ground, Lana passed under the huge right wing. She watched blue alcohol flames erupt from the dozen exhaust stacks above her as she shoved her throttle forward to retract her brakes. When she looked back at her panel, she noticed the icy permafrost coming up rapidly and cursed herself for not watching her altimeter. Lana knew she had nothing to lose and that she was better off dead, but what would history record about the first woman in space if she flew stupidly into the ground? In ten thousand years, would archeologists thaw out her beautiful white body like the decaying flesh of a frozen mammoth? Would they probe her voluptuous smooth breasts with needles? Too much was happening at once. Lana could not rid her mind of the memories of Sergei. She kept remembering running barefoot through the woods near her mother's collective farm near Kiev, and rolling with him in the wildflowers. He pulled the scratchy burrs and flax seeds from her flowery kerchief and gray cotton dress.
The four jet engines under the giant's wingtips glowed

red as they passed above her.   Instead of wildflowers, she
smelled pure rubbery oxygen coming through her mask, which
felt wet against her face because tears were soaking down into it
from under her goggles.

Lana was momentarily within range of the tailguns and
could hear the chirps in her radar detection set change to a
continuous tone. She advanced her throttle all the way and
pulled back on her stick to fly up into the bomber. One way or
another, she decided, the bomber was going to come down.
They could pin the medal on her coffin, if any scrap of female
flesh could be found after the explosion.

The bomber grew rapidly larger. Lana held her gaze
steady. There was no doubt she was on a collision course. The
flying naval vessel grew to several times its original size. It
seemed to hover motionless—a black silhouette with flaming
exhaust under the green auroral curtains above. As she got
closer, Lana gazed wide eyed at how truly large it was. The
mighty silver wings above her seemed to extend to both
horizons at once. How could the Americans build such a large
aircraft, she wondered? Would her fragile, clear plastic canopy
be enough to knock its bomb loose; or would her tiny little plane
just bounce off its belly?

The huge American could not possibly avoid her. She
was in its blind spot. No one on board could see her approach or
warn the pilot to turn out of her way. It was too late to change
her mind about tyurtam. She was committed. Changing course
now would just cause her to hit a less vital part of the ship.
Aircraft can fly without an engine, horizontal stabilizer, or even
a wingtip, but not without a tail. If she could hit the bomb bay,
she might cause an explosion that would blow the giant
American to smithereens or damage the bomb inside so that it
could not explode, even if they decided to drop it.

The massive weapon shackle was the single most highly
stressed part of the ship. Just a simple oscillation, Lana thought,
such as a collision with a small aircraft would make, might be
enough to collapse the girders that connected the tail with the
rest of the ship, and cause the entire monstrosity to crush into a

ball and tumble harmlessly to the ground. "Ya bawrots-ya za mir, naw oom-yer-yet za rad-yi-noo†," she shouted as her last words, quoting Pushkin! When the big ship touched her glowing greenish yellow target ring, she yelled, "Ka Sergei," and pulled both triggers. The night was alive with fireflies swarming in front of her little plane as her round yellow glowing instruments became a blur of vibration. She closed her eyes and prayed.

Before her shells could hit, the huge ship lurched suddenly upward, causing her to miss. When she did not feel the expected impact, she looked up and saw the bomber climbing away. The bright tracers arced up and then fell toward the airbase, exploding on the ice in the distance. With both hands, Lana pulled her stick back hard between her legs to follow the huge American up. She was directly underneath when the aft bomb doors snapped open, bathing her shiny, red starred silver wings with a shower of bright white light from inside the green painted bomb bay. Her lungs stopped when she saw vapor and blocks of ice flying off the huge green cryogenic bomb being blasted clean by the three hundred mile per hour wind. Noticing the red and yellow warning messages emerging from under its crackling coat of ice, a chill, as she had never felt before, turned her spine to jelly and made her heart jump in her chest. "A message stenciled in big yellow block letters warned, "SANDIA NATIONAL LABORATORY."

"Batyoushkee," Lana screamed into her mask! "Pomeiloete‡," she shrieked, panting! If only she had not disobeyed orders and intercepted the giant bomber outside the Soviet border like she was supposed to! Now, instead of getting a medal, all of her planes would be destroyed, along with the base. It was too late to shoot it down. Instead of the name Svetlana Periscova being known throughout history as being that of the first woman to fly into space, her name would be replaced by a fading blue number tattooed on a lumpy

† **Я бороться за мир, но умереть за родину!** — **I fight for peace, but die for the fatherland.**
‡ **Батюшки . . . Помилуйте!** — **Dear father . . . Have mercy!**

breastbone above shrinking sagging breasts, as her healthy muscular body slowly starved in a Siberian Gulag—if she survived the blast.   Too much ambition is a curse, she remembered from Tolstoy.

Lana depressed the radio talk button on her throttle and yelled, "Brosteh! "Me pri smertee! "Vyehr-nyeetyehs nahzahd ka Moskova†! "Vyehr-nyeetyehs nahzahd ka Moskova! "Polnoie hod! "Polnoie hod," she commanded! Her left hand shook as she advanced her throttle fully forward—too fast and she would flame out and not be able to escape the blast; too slow and she would be caught by the fireball and incinerated. Flames erupted from her afterburner as her head and shoulders pressed into the back of her seat.

"Whoa, look at 'em go," exclaimed Hernandez, over the tone the computer produced to remind them not to touch the controls once the initial point was reached! "They're bugging out! "They're running like scalded dogs with their tails on fire!"

"Where are they going," shouted Johns?

"Every which way out of here!"

"The RGA has stopped transmitting," said Beaumont.

"CEASE FIRE, CEASE FIRE," Johns hollered into the interphone. "JOHN, ORDER ARMS, STAND DOWN YOUR WEAPON, CEASE FIRE!"

Kewscinski flicked the master power switch to off and yelled, "HANGFIRE!" The red lights on the bombing control panel and the computer's vacuum tubes went out. The tone in the headsets stopped.   Everyone tensed their bowels in expectation of the violent lurch that results when a twenty ton weapon leaves an aircraft. Nothing happened. The ship kept climbing beyond the release point. Johns rolled the ship into a wingstanding chandelle maneuver, being careful not to stall and fall to the ground with the immense weight of the bomb still on board. The thick wing bent visibly upward as the jet pods oscillated wildly—belching clouds of black smoke which was

† **Бросьте! Мы при смерти — Quit! We're about to be killed! . . . Вернитесь назад к Москвой — Go back to Moscow!**

visible against the green tinted ice below. Contrails followed the ship in a beautiful fan shaped pattern ahead of a starburst of smaller jet contrails heading in the opposite direction.

Kewscinski did not know what would happen when he turned the power back on. If the bomb released under the ship with the nose fuse armed and the chute set to salvo, the ship would be vaporized. Nervously, he flicked the nose fuse switch and turned the bomb door switch to "SAFE," then twirled the target offset knobs so the computer would not try to release the bomb and announced, "I'm going to try to close the bomb doors." Closing his eyes tightly, he made the Saint John's Cross over his forehead, mouth, and chest, then flicked on the master power switch and winced.

A thump was heard. Everyone jumped in their seats. "Bomb doors closed," announced Hernandez. Kewscinski leaned back in his seat and stared at the ceiling, his mouth wide open with an expression of deep relief.

Murphy lowered his left knee to let Lewis' head up from under the engineering console. Shaken, the young man clipped his clear visor back onto the front of his mask and turned on his oxygen even though the ship was at low altitude. Murphy did not object.

"What's the course for Thule," Johns asked?

"Due North, or about twenty degrees magnetic," answered Nawrocki.

"Lock weapon shackle," ordered the Aircraft Commander.

"Yessir," answered the Navigator as he got up from his desk behind the clear plastic nose of the ship.

Though only the officers were informed about the mission, rumors flew among the enlisted men at Thule that the base would soon be on full alert and that there was a threat of an imminent nuclear strike. When an incoming aircraft was detected on radar, alarms sounded. The order was given to scramble all planes. Sergeant Davis and his entire ground crew nervously donned nylon parkas, felt mittens, and "Mickey

Mouse" boots to brave the cold. All of the fighters that were not red tagged for maintenance roared down the runway in pairs, two by two.

When the last plane left, Davis and some of his men decided they would rather be killed instantly, than cower in a bomb shelter awaiting the inevitable. Many wanted to see what kind of plane the Russians were sending to kill them. To stay warm, they danced in place up and down and twisted like a bunch of teen-agers listening to rock and roll. A thundery droning sound in the distance got louder and louder. Some shivered with cold. Others shivered with fear. The Catholics crossed themselves. The Protestants pressed their palms together muttering prayers.

Tailflames streaked overhead accompanied by thunder-claps. Arms rose into the air with a chorus of cheers as "Lovely Linda" suddenly materialized over the runway lights. Shiny apparitions shrieked low over the runway at almost the speed of sound with tailflames blazing, followed by thunder. The roar of a thousand lawnmowers filled the icy air behind a blizzard of newfallen snow—stirred into a cloud by six huge aerobraking propellers.

The waiting men ran toward the giant ship as Johns taxied toward the fuel stand. Every member of 811's crew was caught on their shoulders as he tried to descend from the forward landing gear doors and ceremonially carried into the tiny "O" club—even Lewis. Each enjoyed the best meal to be had at the base, a frozen T-bone steak with rehydrated mashed potatoes and gravy. Everyone celebrated by passing around B-36's.

Ten hours later, Linda Johns and Mary Kewscinski ran through the perimeter fence at Carswell Air Force Base, escort-ed by The Colonel and Phyllis Peterson. Linda grinned as the most powerful weapon in the world met her namesake. They greeted their husbands with warm teary embraces when they emerged from its landing gear doors. Shirley Newcomb, follow-ing not far behind, welcomed Gordon home the same way.

In the Oval Office of the White House, a beribboned hound-faced general listened expressionlessly to the rantings of the black browed Russian Deputy Foreign Minister as a translator whispered into the President's ear. "Now Andrei," answered Eisenhower, "how can we help it if one of our planes goes off course? "You know how difficult it can be to navigate over the polar sea. "I realize the pilot almost overflew one of your bases and I assure you he and his navigator will be disciplined for that, but the important thing is that when he realized his mistake, he turned around. "Your people were never in any danger. "I can assure you Andrei, we are in *complete control.*" Twinkles appeared in the General's sad eyes.

On August 27th, 1957,
the very day that Henry Ford II announced the existence of the Edsel,
the Soviet Union declared to the world that it had developed a ballistic
missile capable of delivering a thermonuclear bomb anywhere in the
United States of America.
The announcement was not considered credible.
On October 4th, 1957,
Sputnik, the world's first artificial satellite, was successfully launched
from the Baikonur Cosmodrome

. . .

the rest is history.

BIBLIOGRAPHY

Russian Reference Grammar — Nicholas Maltzoff, Adviser on
Russian Courses, United States Military Academy — Pitman, 1965

Hugo's Russian Grammar Simplified — McKay, 1959

Berlitz European Phrase Book — Berlitz 1974, 1985

Khrushchev Remembers — Nikita S. Khrushchev, Strobe Talbot
Little Brown, 1970

B-36H Pilot Manual AN 01-5EUG-1 — United States Air Force,
Convair Corporation, October 1st, 1953

Convair B-36 — A Comprehensive History of America's Big Stick
Meyers K. Jacobsen, Scott Deaver, James H. Farmer, Chuck Hansen,
Robert W. Hickl, Ray Wagner, Bill Yenne — Shiffer, 1997

B-36 Peacemaker, SAC's 'Long Rifle' of the 1950's
Wayne Wachsmuth, Lt. Col. USAF — Squadron/Signal, 1997

Convair B-36 Peacemaker, Warbird Tech Series Volume 24
Dennis R. Jenkins — Specialty Press, 1999

Magnesium Overcast — Dennis R. Jenkins — Specialty Press, 2001

Dark Sun, The Making of the Hydrogen Bomb — Richard Rhodes
Simon & Schuster, 1995

GLOSSARY

AC — Aircraft Commander

ADDING MACHINE — A type of miniature abacus with sliding bars inside instead of beads as on a full size abacus. The bars had notches on the sides which represented numbers. A stylus was inserted into a groove in the top of the machine to move a bar down for simple addition or up to carry the decimal. Some machines, such as the Arithma Addiator, were also capable of subtraction. They easily fit into a shirt pocket. They were not capable of multiplication or division, so a separate circular slide rule, called a computer, had to be carried to perform all of the functions of a modern pocket calculator.

ALARM BELLS — These were operated by pressing a button on the pilot's instrument panel. They made a loud sound like a telephone ringing. Several short rings was a command for all crew to plug in their interphone jacks and listen to orders, even if they were asleep. A continuous ringing meant abandon ship.

ALDIS LAMP — A type of big flashlight

B-17 — The Boeing B-17 Flying Fortress was the most famous bomber to bomb Germany in World War II. It had four 1200 horsepower engines.

B-24 — The Consolidated B-24 Liberator was the most numerous bomber to bomb Germany in World War II. It had four 1200 horsepower engines.

B-26 — The Martin B-26 Marauder was the most dangerous medium bomber to bomb Germany in World War II. It had two 2000 horsepower engines, which made it almost as powerful as a B-24, but its small wing reduced its range and bomb capacity and made landings difficult. The Douglas B-26 Invader was known as the A-26 in World War II. It had two 2000 horsepower engines and as many as 20 machine guns for strafing airfields, as well as bombs. In the Korean War, it replaced the Martin B-26 and became known as the Douglas B-26. In the Vietnam war, it was also known as the F-26.

B-29 — The Boeing B-29 Superfortress was the largest bomber used in World War II. It had four 2000 horsepower engines. A B-29 named "Enola Gay" dropped the first atomic bomb on Hiroshima. A B-29 named Bock's Car dropped an atomic bomb on Nagasaki.

B-36 — The Consolidated-Vultee B-36 was the largest combat aircraft ever built. It had six 3500 horsepower engines and four 4700 pound thrust jets. It could carry two 15 megaton hydrogen bombs—enough to decimate most countries

B-47 — The Boeing B-47 Stratojet was the world's first swept wing bomber. Though it was larger than most W.W.II heavy bombers, its six, fuel-guzzling, 7,200 pound thrust jets limited its range and bomb load. With a crew of three, it was considered to be a medium bomber.

B-50 — The Boeing B-50 Superfortress was an improved B-29 with four of the same 3500 horsepower engines used on the B-36 and RB-36. Later models were also equipped with two jet engines under the wing tips for faster speed over the target.

B-52 — The Boeing B-52 Stratofortress is the eight engine heavy bomber which replaced the B-36. It is still in service.

B-58 — The Convair B-58 was a four engine, delta wing jet bomber. Its weapon was carried in a streamlined external pod which also contained fuel. It was capable of a supersonic dash over the target and could launch its weapon straight up while in an aerobatic loop for better ground penetration. When the pod fell back to earth, it would strike the ground at supersonic speed.

B-70 — Intended as a large, six engined, supersonic delta winged bomber, the North American B-70 was never built because its atomic jet engines were thought to create too much pollution. Two XB-70's, equipped with conventional jet engines, were completed in 1964 as high altitude Mach 3 research aircraft.

BEARS — Soviet Tu-95 "Bear" bombers

BOMBING NAVIGATION COMPUTER — These primitive, bulky, non-programmable analog computers used a thin rubber wheel on a metal turntable to multiply and divide using logarithms. Later, variable voltage vacuum tubes were used to replace the wheels and gears. Because steering an airplane and releasing a bomb is an analog process, these electro-mechanical computers did just as good a job as modern digital computers, but they were less reliable because vacuum tubes were prone to burning out, and each computer could only perform one function. These computers were capable of projecting a dot of light on a radar screen to indicate the place the bomb would hit, so the Video Observer needed only to move the dot of light across the radar screen to select a target and the computer would automatically snap open the bomb doors and plant the bomb there.

BOMBING SOLUTION — A mathematical equation to determine the proper time to release a bomb to hit a target, given the altitude, speed, temperature, and humidity of the air. The calculations were normally performed by a bombing navigation computer.

BRAVO SHOT — This was the world's first lithium-deuteride bomb. The Mike Shot proved that enough deuterium would convert to tritium when bombarded by neutrons from a fission reaction, that a separate flask of tritium was not needed to initiate a fusion reaction. To make the bomb safer and more portable without the need for a cryogenic vacuum flask, the deuterium was bonded to lithium to form a solid. The lithium was enriched to 40% lithium 6 in the hopes that the remaining lithium 7 would not interfere with the fusion of the deuterium. What scientists could not have known, is that when lithium 7 is struck by a neutron, it emits two neutrons to become lithium 6, an unstable nucleus capable of fusion. Instead of some of the deuterium absorbing the neutrons to form tritium, there was an abundance of neutrons and lithium 6 as fuel, so the Bravo Shot "ran away" to three times larger than expected, irradiating a Japanese fishing boat and nearly killing the crew of the "Ruptured Duck."

BUBBLE SEXTANT — An instrument for navigating by the stars. The height of three stars above the horizon is measured to determine three lines of position. Location can be determined on a chart where the three lines intersect.

BUCK DUCK — A type of small decoy carried in the bomb bay of a B-36 bomber. It was not thought to sufficiently resemble a B-36 bomber on radar to justify production. A later version, called the Quail, was produced and used on B-52's.

BULL GOOSE — A large, long range, delta winged, jet powered unpiloted drone that used traveling wave tube amplifiers to reflect a radar blip similar to that of a B-58 bomber. It would be launched by rocket boosters prior to an attack. These decoys would be deployed to lure enemy fighters away from the vulnerable bombers.

C-54 — The Douglas C-54 Skymaster was the military version of the DC-4 airliner. It had four 1,200 horsepower engines.

CHEROKEE SHOT — The first American air dropped hydrogen bomb. A prototype TX-15 was dropped from a B-52 during Operation Red Wing on May 1956. This was not the first air-dropped hydrogen bomb, however. To minimize fallout, the Soviets dropped their first lithium-deuteride bomb from a Tu-16 Badger twin engine jet bomber on November 22nd, 1955.

COMPUTER — A circular slide rule that could multiply and divide with three digit accuracy using a logarithmic scale printed on a rotating outer ring. It had a sliding vector card through the middle to help solve navigation problems. It was not capable of addition or subtraction, so a separate adding machine had to be carried to perform all of the functions of a modern pocket calculator.

CRYOGENIC BOMB — A hydrogen bomb fueled with liquid deuterium, such as the Mike device or the TX-16 Jughead.

DEUTERIUM — A type of hydrogen used in bombs with a neutron as well as a proton in its nucleus. Ordinary hydrogen has only a proton.

DIAMONDS — The cowl vents on the RB-36 were annular rings which retracted into the nacelles in front of the propellers. Three diamonds were painted on the side so that the gunners and scanners could tell that they were fully closed for landing in cold weather, or if no diamonds were visible, fully open for take off in hot weather.

DOG SABRE — A North American F-86D equipped with a radome in the nose that looked like the nose of a dog. It was armed with retractable rocket tubes underneath the cockpit.

DUKW — An amphibious two and one half ton truck designed by General Motors at the request of the Army. When the Army refused to accept the vehicle, a prototype was used to rescue a Coast Guard crew that had become stranded on a grounded freighter. Congress ordered the vehicle into production over the Army's objection. Later, one third of all the men and material carried ashore on D-day was hauled in DUKW's as well as almost all of the material that crossed the Strait of Messina during the invasion of Italy.

EMERGENCY WAR PLAN — A carefully calculated schedule of aircraft arrivals over their targets so that they will not be destroyed by each other's bombs. One of the world's first digital computers was used to calculate this schedule prior to launching a preemptive strike, using data obtained from reconnaissance aircraft concerning the status of Soviet radar installations.

F-86 — The swept wing North American F-86 Sabre Jet was the best American fighter of the Korean War. Those equipped with radar were known as "Dog Sabres" because the radome in the nose looked like the nose of a dog. It was the first fighter to have an all-flying horizontal stabilizer that made supersonic dives survivable. It was armed with six .50 caliber machine guns or rockets. It was the only American fighter that was a match for the Soviet MiG-15, though the MiG had a higher ceiling with almost double the rate of climb.

F-89 — The Northrop F-89 Scorpion was a straight wing, two seat, twin engine, all weather interceptor. It could not fly high enough to intercept bombers, so instead of guns, it was armed with air to air rockets and MB-1 Genie nuclear tipped air to air missiles.

F-94 — The Lockheed F-94 Starfire was a straight wing, single engine, all weather interceptor with two crew. It was armed only with unguided rockets, but it was an improvement over the F-89, because it had an afterburner to reach the altitudes at which bombers flew.

F-100 — The North American F-100 Super Sabre was the world's first supersonic jet fighter. Unfortunately, it could not exceed the speed of sound while carrying underwing ordinance, so it was armed only with four 20mm cannon for supersonic flight.

FEATHERWEIGHT III — With the introduction of the MiG-17 into Soviet Air forces, B-36's were considered vulnerable to being shot down. In an effort to fly above the new fighter, the Featherweight III program removed all cockpit armor, bullet sealing pads, galley equipment, crew comfort items, and all guns except the tail guns from Featherweight III aircraft. Only a few RB-36's were not converted.

FENCES — Vertical wall-like structures mounted longitudinally on the upper surface of an airplane wing to prevent air from flowing sideways during low speed flight. The devices help prevent stalls.

FERRET ANTENNAS — These rotating parabolic dishes in radomes under the fuselages of RB-36's, RB-47's, and other aircraft, were used to locate Soviet radar installations. Because ground based radar units used vacuum tubes that were prone to constant failure, the safest route for bombers to enter the Soviet Union was constantly changing. Ferret aircraft would monitor the activity of Soviet Radar defenses by deliberately crossing national borders to get them to "light up," or turn on their radar, then fly along the border to wait for one of the radar stations to malfunction. Only when a gap in the Soviet Radar net was detected, would it be safe for American bombers to enter the USSR.

FILM BACK — A detachable cartridge holding film which was attached to the back of a camera.

FICON — FIghter CONveyer, a GRB-36 flying aircraft carrier. A single RF-84K could be carried in its bomb bay, though the wings of the fighter projected outside the ship. Takeoffs and landings with the fighter suspended underneath were possible, but not normally done because the fighter could not easily be unloaded for maintenance.

FIRING SOLUTION — A mathematical equation to determine the proper direction to point a gun when firing on a moving target, given the altitude, speed, temperature, and humidity of the air as data. The calculations were normally performed by a gun laying system computer.

FORT FUMBLE — The Pentagon

GAMMA RAYS — Very short wavelength radiation, shorter than X-rays, normally produced only by nuclear reactions and lightning.

GULAG — A Communist concentration camp

GUN LAYING SYSTEM COMPUTER — These primitive, bulky, non-programmable analog computers used a thin rubber wheel on a metal turntable to multiply and divide using logarithms. Later, variable voltage vacuum tubes were used to replace the wheels and gears. Because aiming a gun is an analog process, these computers did just as good a job as modern digital computers, but they were less reliable. Their vacuum tubes were prone to burning out. The gunner needed only to keep his gunsight aimed at the target and the computer would track the target's motion using a gyroscope mounted on top of the sight. The computer would then calculate a firing solution to properly lead the target so that every shell would hit unerringly.

INTERPHONE — An interphone was similar to an intercom, but instead of broadcasting over loudspeakers, it was heard only in the crew's headsets so as not to disturb those who where sleeping. The interphone was activated by pressing a button on the pilot's control wheel, or elsewhere near a crewman's duty station. There were two channels—one for the aircrew and the other for groundcrew. A crewman could disconnect his headset from the interphone by pulling its plug from the interphone jack.

IRAN — The country American bombers were supposed to go after a nuclear war. Iran had hundreds of square miles of salt flats where bombers could safely land. Drums of aviation gas and engine oil were buried in the desert so pilots could refuel their planes—though the idea of pumping 33,000 gallons aboard a B-36, with nothing but a hand pump, seemed ridiculous to most aircraft commanders. The democratically elected government of Mossaddeq was overthrown in 1953 by a CIA sponsored coup to install Reza Pahlavi as Shah. Later, American military aid built up the Iranian air force until it was the fourth largest in the world—to protect American bombers landing there from retaliation. The Shah was overthrown by the Ayatollah Khomeini in 1979 after detente with the Soviet Union made the landing sites irrelevant.

JAMMERS — These were radio transmitters that broadcasted noise on the same frequency as Soviet radar. The interference would render their radar useless. More sophisticated versions used a traveling wave tube amplifier to rebroadcast an incoming radar signal out of phase to make an aircraft's radar blip disappear from the screen.

KC-97 — The Boeing KC-97 Stratotanker was a cargo version of the B-50 powered by four of the same 3500 horsepower engines used on the RB-36. It had a boom on its tail for in-air refueling. Later models were also equipped with two jet engines under the wing tips to better keep up with the B-52. Forcing the big jets to fly slowly during refueling limited the amount of fuel that could be transferred.

LITHIUM DEUTERRIDE BOMB — A type of hydrogen bomb that uses lithium as fuel. When bombarded by a neutron from a fission reaction, lithium 7 expels two neutrons and changes to lithium 6. It is then capable of being fused into helium and heavier elements to release even more energy. Deuterium fusion is necessary to get a Lithium fusion reaction started, so Lithium is chemically bonded with deuterium to create a light weight, stable solid that can be packed into bombs.

LORAN — LOng RAnge Navigation or LORAN was a system of determining an aircraft's position electronically by comparing the time delays between the arrivals of three or more radio signals transmitted by several different radio stations at the same time. Position was determined by measuring the distance between the peaks of two saw-tooth waves on a small oscilloscope screen and comparing it to hyperbolic curves printed on a special map or chart.

MiG-15 — The Mikoyan-Gurevich MiG-15 was a swept wing, single engine interceptor armed only with cannon. It was the best fighter of the Korean War. It decimated B-29 bomber formations, though its slow firing cannon were less than ideal for shooting down fighters.

MiG-17 — The Mikoyan-Gurevich MiG-17 was a single engine interceptor armed only with cannon. It was an improvement over the earlier MiG 15 used during the Korean War because it had a larger engine to climb to altitude more quickly.

MiG-19 — The Mikoyan-Gurevich MiG-19 was a twin engine, single seat supersonic interceptor armed only with cannon. Russia's first supersonic interceptor, it was an improvement over the earlier MiG-17 because it could reach the altitude at which the RB-36 flew. It was this airplane which ended heavy reconnaissance missions over the Soviet Union.

MIKE SHOT — The world's first hydrogen bomb exploded November 1st, 1952. It vaporized an island, leaving behind a mile wide crater two hundred feet deep. It was a two stage device consisting of a Nagasaki style Mark 5 atomic bomb mounted on top of a cryogenic vacuum flask filled with liquid deuterium. It was the first device to use radiation implosion to compress the deuterium, fusing it into helium and heavier elements. Surrounding the flask, was a uranium casing that would shrink when exposed to gamma rays from the primary explosion and compress the contents of the flask. The outer casing had a plastic lining to reflect the proper wavelength of gamma rays to implode the uranium casing. In the middle of the deuterium flask was a smaller tritium flask to help ignite the deuterium.

MORS AB ALTO — Latin for Death from Above

My-4 BISON — The Myasishchyev was the Soviet Union's largest jet bomber. It could deliver a 11,000 lb. bomb a distance of 5,035 miles—enough to reach the United States, but not enough to return. Crews were expected to bail out and become prisoners of war after dropping their bombs.

NB-36 — The Convair Crusader was the only aircraft ever to carry an operating nuclear reactor. The reactor did not power the aircraft, but it proved that atomic jet engines would work. It was converted from one of the B-36's damaged in the Labor Day Tornado of '52 and fitted with a thickly shielded cockpit to protect the crew from radiation.

NIGHT WITCHES — Female Soviet W.W.II bomber pilots. Russian women also flew fighters. The top female ace of W.W.II had eight confirmed kills.

NUCLEAR FISSION — The process of splitting large, unstable atoms such as Uranium 235 or Plutonium 238 into smaller atoms to release tremendous amounts of energy.

NUCLEAR FUSION — The process of assembling small unstable atoms such as deuterium or lithium 6 into larger atoms to release tremendous amounts of energy.

OPERATION BOOT STRAP — A series of tests completed in 1957 using concrete filled ballistic casings, identical in appearance and weight to hydrogen bombs, to determine if thermonuclear weapons could destroy deep underground bunkers. Soviet officials were not thought to care very much about their nation's people, but even the most evil of people care about their own families, so an effort was made to try to destroy bunkers as much as a mile underground, where the families of Communist officials were thought to take refuge in the event of war. While a hydrogen bomb only produces a crater one or two hundred feet deep, it fractures the rock underneath so that a second bomb can penetrate the earth much more deeply. To accomplish this, the second bomb must approach its target straight down, so a technique of releasing bombs at the beginning of an aerobatic loop maneuver was devised to launch the bomb straight up from a low flying B-47. The bomber would complete a loop as the bomb continued upward and fly away to escape the blast as the bomb came back down. Many bombers would be assigned the same target so that, eventually, a pit would be blasted a mile wide and a mile deep. Operation bootstrap was terminated when stress cracks were found in B-47 wing spars, though by this time, enough data had been obtained to program bombing-navigation computers to automatically perform the maneuver without requiring the pilots to practice it.

OPERATION CASTLE — A series of tests of large lithium deuteride bombs which were completed in 1954

OPERATION RED WING — A series of tests of smaller hydrogen bombs that were completed in 1956.

RADAR CAMERA — If a radar scope or "plan position indicator" was fitted with a hood that fit snugly to the eyes, it was known as a radar camera.

RADIATION IMPLOSION — This is the opposite of refrigeration.

In a refrigerator, gas such as freon is compressed until it emits thermal radiation as heat. The gas can then be decompressed inside the refrigerator to absorb heat, thus making the things inside cold.

In a hydrogen bomb, uranium is irradiated by gamma rays from a nuclear explosion until it shrinks. Because it is very heavy, uranium does not expand very much when heated. Instead, it reflects rather than absorbs gamma rays. Before it can re-emit the gamma rays, however, its electrons, which in a normal metal flow in a straight line between the atoms as electricity, get wound up like springs, vibrating at the same frequency as the incoming radiation. As the incoming radiation is re-emitted, these springs shorten, pulling the uranium atoms toward each other with an immense tractive force, causing any object made of this heavy metal to shrink in size. A flask made of uranium will compress the deuterium inside until nuclear fusion takes place, vaporizing the flask.

RAVEN — A Ferret electronic intelligence radio operator. Also called "Crows," they compared themselves to birds that rested on telephone wires who supposedly could listen in on telephone conversations through their feet.

RB-36 — The Consolidated Vultee RB-36 was the largest reconnaissance aircraft ever built. It had six 3500 horsepower engines and four 4700 pound thrust jets. It was equipped with 17 cameras, more than any other aircraft in history, as well as flash bombs for night photography.

The on board film developing lab held five wide angle multi-cameras for stereographic mapping, three vertical cameras with up to 48" focal length for close-ups of objects on the ground, and two movable lateral cameras attached to the walls which could be aimed at distant targets. Under the floor of the lab, there was one fixed lateral camera pointing down and forward, and three very wide angle trimetrigon cameras for pinpointing locations using known landmarks on the horizon. In the forward cabin, there were two radar scope cameras and a hand held bombsight camera. One RB-36 carried the Boston Camera, the largest camera ever built, which had a twenty foot focal length folded into a compact eight foot wide unit by two inch-thick optically flat mirrors. Improvements in film technology which allowed finer film grains rendered the Boston Camera obsolete.

Before the advent of the hydrogen bomb, the RB-36's mission was to detect enemy forces so they could later be targeted by bombers. One in every three B-36's built was an RB-36. Film developed on board would be parachuted to command and control centers located in Turkey or Iran. The photos could then be used to direct the bombers. This mission became less important when hydrogen bombs became so powerful that direct hits were no longer necessary.

When the MiG-19 was introduced, heavy reconnaissance missions over the Soviet Union were considered too dangerous. Most RB-36's were converted to bombers carrying one 15 megaton hydrogen bomb each—enough to decimate small countries. Only a few aircraft, such as RB-36 tail number 51-13730 in the Castle Air Museum near Atwater California were not converted.

Most RB-36's were equipped with the "Ferret" electronic intelligence gathering system. Because they were vulnerable to advanced Soviet fighters, RB-36's would exploit their incredible range and endurance by flying along the Soviet border until a gap in the radar net was detected, then fly through the gap to drop their bombs. The RB-36 in the Castle Air Museum does not have a Ferret system. It may have been used for armed photographic reconnaissance over third world countries not possessing a radar air defense system. RB-36's mapped the entire world in the 1950's, overflying unknown regions of Africa and South America.

RB-47E — The photographic reconnaissance version of the B-47 with cameras in the nose and bomb bay. It could also carry flash bombs in lieu of cameras in the bomb bay. It did not have an on board film developing lab like the RB-36, so its films had to be developed on the ground. Like most B-47's, they were equipped with tail-guns to defend themselves from Soviet fighters.

RB-47H — The electronic reconnaissance version of the B-47. It had three additional crew members in a pressurized compartment located in its swollen bomb bay to operate the "Ferret" system. The Ferret antennas were located in the nose cone and in a special long radome under the tail. They carried no cameras and were normally unarmed, but could be fitted with two tail guns.

RF-84K — The Republic RF-84K Thunderflash was a special reconnaissance version of the F-84 Thunderjet. It had a retractable hook built into its nose to engage the trapeze of a GRB-36 FICON flying aircraft carrier. The horizontal stabilizer was bent sharply downward so as to fit into a special groove in the mother ship's belly. Two lifting shackles were provided behind the cockpit so it could be hoisted into the bomb bay after attaching itself to the trapeze. It usually carried cameras instead of guns, but in unusual circumstances, it could be armed with a nuclear weapon.

RGA — Radar Guided Artillery. These were Soviet copies of the German 88mm Flak which were fitted with gyroscopes and aimed by a radar antenna fitted to a gun-laying system computer. The guns could shoot accurately up to 25,000 feet and often beyond. A magnetic proximity fuse exploded the shells when close to their target.

ROTC — Reserve Officer Training Corps

SELSYN MOTORS — Small electric motors attached to a gyroscope mount to detect changes in an aircraft's attitude.

SCANNER — An assistant gunner on Featherweight III aircraft. Because the Tail Radar Gun-laying System Gunner could not see the target he was aiming at, others had to scan the target with binoculars before firing, to be certain that the target was not friendly. Scanners also watched the engines, flaps, and landing gear for malfunctions.

STALL — When the air flowing on the upper surface of an airplane wing becomes turbulent and no longer flows smoothly, causing a loss of lift. An aircraft in a stall must dive to increase speed, or it will fall out of the sky.

TAIL RADAR GUN LAYING SYSTEM — The Tail Radar Gunlaying System Gunner was provided with one or two radar screens on which approaching aircraft would be seen as blips. Using a joystick under his console, he would manually aim an antenna at a blip he selected before pressing the fire button. The antenna would then automatically track the blip and the computer would detect the motions of a gyroscope mounted on the antenna to calculate a firing solution. If the Tail Radar Gunlaying System was equipped with two antennas such as on the General Electric APG-41, the gunner could continue to observe the other blips as the guns fired.

TDY — Tour of Duty

TRIMETRIGON CAMERAS — Three very wide angle cameras which were mounted under the floor of the RB-36 photo lab to pinpoint the location of the ship when photos were taken. Two of the cameras were aimed at the horizon, one on each side, with a third aimed at the ground. The distance between objects on the ground and known landmarks on the horizon could then be calculated.

TRITIUM — An extremely rare form of hydrogen with two neutrons in its nucleus as well as a proton. Ordinary hydrogen has only a single proton.

Tu-95 BEAR — The Tupolev Tu-95 was the Soviet Union's Largest and most successful bomber. It had four 14,795 hp. turboprops driving eight blade counter-rotating propellers and could deliver a 11,000 lb. bomb a distance of 9,290 miles — enough to reach any city in the United States before landing in Cuba.

TX-14 ALARM CLOCK — This was the first deployable hydrogen bomb to enter military service. It had a "layer cake" of uranium and lithium deuteride around its primary plutonium core to increase the number of neutrons that would be produced in the initial blast. It had unrefined lithium deuteride in its secondary fusion stage which would convert to lithium 6 and tritium during the primary explosion. It was 18 feet long, 5 feet in diameter, and weighed 29,850 pounds. It was not the first layer cake design, however. The Soviets exploded a layer cake bomb without a second stage in 1953.

TX-15 SHRIMP — The first hydrogen bomb small enough to be carried by aircraft smaller than the B-36. It was 11 feet long, 3 feet in diameter, and weighed 7,500 pounds with an expected yield of 2-3 megatons.

TX-16 JUGHEAD — This was a weaponized version of the Mike device, a cryogenic bomb developed in case the Bravo device was a failure. It had a vacuum flask containing liquid deuterium, but no tritium or lithium. It was 26 feet long, 5 feet in diameter, and weighed 43,000 pounds. It was never tested.

TX-17 RUNT — With an expected yield of 10-15 megatons, this lithium-deuteride bomb was the most powerful weapon ever developed by man. Designed as the main weapon of the B-36 and RB-36, it was 25 feet long, 5 feet in diameter, and weighed 41,400 pounds. It was equipped with a ribbon type drogue parachute to slow its descent and allow the bomber time to escape its earth shaking blast.

TX-21 — A medium size, high yield H-bomb designed for the B-52

U-2 — The Lockheed U-2 was a single seat, single engine jet with a huge wing for Ultra-high-altitude flight. It replaced the RB-36 and RB-47 for most photographic reconnaissance duty over Russia in the second half of 1956.

V-2 — The World's first ballistic missile, it was designed by the Nazis to terrorize London, but was mechanically similar to smaller rockets invented by the American rocket pioneer, Robert Goddard.

VO-VIDEO OBSERVER — Also called the Bombardier-Navigator.

In the 1950's, before videotape was invented, the word "video" meant radar. The earliest video tape recorders were reel-to-reel audio tape recorders modified to record radar signals and replay them on a radar-bombing simulator. Only later, after videotapes were used to record television programs, did the term "video" come to mean any type of visual recording and not just radar.

With the advent of city-killing hydrogen bombs, it was felt that better targeting accuracy could be obtained by removing the human being from the bombing process. Computers were programmed to arm and drop thermonuclear bombs automatically, without any human input which would require a moral or ethical decision on the part of a human bombardier. The Video Observer needed only to turn the system on and position a dot of light on the radar screen with the joystick on his desk as he approached the target. A Lucite plate containing a radar image of the target was positioned over the screen to help him position the light beam on the radar image. knobs were provided to offset the dot from the actual target if the target did not show up on radar. The Video Observer thus needed only to observe to see that the computer was functioning properly rather than make a moral or ethical decision whether to press the release button on top of his joystick when the time came to incinerate millions of people.

YO-YO — An aggressive vertical combat maneuver.

WASP's — Women Auxilliary Service Pilots. During W.W.II, These American women ferried aircraft from factories to seaports where the aircraft could be shipped overseas. These women were not allowed to fly in combat, but they were eventually recognized as W.W.II veterans.

WEAPON SHACKLE — The release mechanism to drop a bomb. It was locked during flight to prevent an accidental salvo, except during takeoffs and landings when jettisoning the bomb might be necessary.

WO-WEATHER OBSERVER — It was the WO's job to estimate pressure and humidity over the target by observing cloud formations. This data was entered into bombing navigation and firing solution computers to obtain better accuracy for bombs and guns.

X-6 — This was to be an improved NB-36 with an additional four atomic jet engines suspended under the bomb bay in addition to the B-36's normal 10 engines. With 14 engines, it would have set a world's record for the number of engines to power an aircraft if it had been built. The world record for the greatest number of engines to power an aircraft is held by the Dornier Do-X flying boat which was the largest plane in the world in 1921. It had 12 engines.

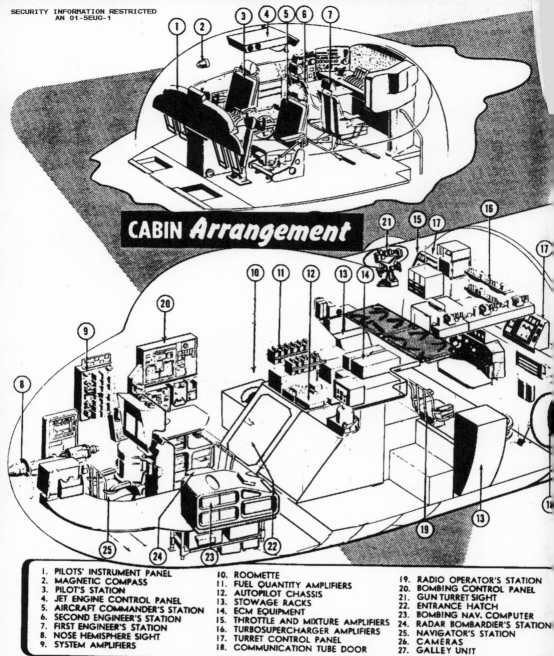

CABIN *Arrangement*

1. PILOTS' INSTRUMENT PANEL
2. MAGNETIC COMPASS
3. PILOT'S STATION
4. JET ENGINE CONTROL PANEL
5. AIRCRAFT COMMANDER'S STATION
6. SECOND ENGINEER'S STATION
7. FIRST ENGINEER'S STATION
8. NOSE HEMISPHERE SIGHT
9. SYSTEM AMPLIFIERS
10. ROOMETTE
11. FUEL QUANTITY AMPLIFIERS
12. AUTOPILOT CHASSIS
13. STOWAGE RACKS
14. ECM EQUIPMENT
15. THROTTLE AND MIXTURE AMPLIFIERS
16. TURBOSUPERCHARGER AMPLIFIERS
17. TURRET CONTROL PANEL
18. COMMUNICATION TUBE DOOR
19. RADIO OPERATOR'S STATION
20. BOMBING CONTROL PANEL
21. GUN TURRET SIGHT
22. ENTRANCE HATCH
23. BOMBING NAV. COMPUTER
24. RADAR BOMBARDIER'S STATION
25. NAVIGATOR'S STATION
26. CAMERAS
27. GALLEY UNIT

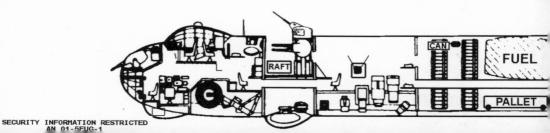